# The Lodgers

## Eithne Shortall

CORVUS

First published in Great Britain in 2023 by Atlantic Books,
an imprint of Atlantic Books Ltd.

10 9 8 7 6 5 4 3 2

A CIP catalogue record for this book is available from the British Library.

Hardback ISBN: 978 1 83895 189 4
Trade Paperback ISBN: 978 1 83895 190 0
EBook ISBN: 978 1 83895 191 7

Printed and bound by CPI (UK) Ltd, Croydon CR0 4YY

Corvus
An imprint of Atlantic Books Ltd
Ormond House
26–27 Boswell Street
London
WC1N 3JZ

www.atlantic-books.co.uk

# The Lodgers

# Also by Eithne Shortall

*For my friend Dawn, who deserves a book*

## Blackpool, England

**M**uriel Fairway could have put it in the regular post.

She could have entrusted the Royal Mail and whatever its Irish counterpart was called with getting the item to Bea Pearson safely. But she hasn't trusted the postal service since her twelfth birthday when her grandmother put a five-pound note into a card and personally handed it to her village postman. When it arrived through Muriel's door three days later, the envelope had been torn at the top and there was no longer any money inside.

Fifty years on and Muriel still doesn't put anything of value into a post box. She has a granddaughter of her own now and for her birthday she transfers money to her son's bank account and posts a card to little Sadie (she just about trusts them with empty cards) to say her father now has fifty pounds belonging to her.

(Fifty pounds for a child's birthday! How's that for inflation?)

So Muriel has taken the parcel to Delivery Dash. She wasn't going to take any chances, not with an item of such importance.

She has wrapped it securely, written the name in clear, bold letters – BEA PEARSON – and the address: Hope House, Nevin Way, Howth, County Dublin, Ireland. She has included a hundred-euro tip for the courier who gets it to where it needs to go in Dublin. She wouldn't usually leave such a large tip, but

1

it's Bea's money and Muriel is just following the young woman's instructions.

Delivery Dash are reliable. The package will be in Dublin by Monday. Bea might not be there yet – Muriel isn't sure when exactly she's leaving Blackpool – but she'll be home soon. The surprise party 'of the century' is in a few weeks – and who'd want to miss that?

It's crazy how much Muriel knows about Bea. Before last Sunday, she'd never clapped eyes on her. One minute Muriel was walking her dog alone on Blackpool beach, the next she was finding out all about this Irish woman and her family. It's funny how someone can come into your life like that, unexpectedly and all at once.

She knows about Bea's brother Senan; about her deceased father Bernard; and about her mother Tessa, whose birthday is fast approaching. It's an important one, a 'roundie' as Muriel's husband calls the birthdays that mark the start of a new decade. And there's going to be a celebration.

But perhaps the most intriguing detail about Bea is her home on the edge of Howth hill. *Hope House*. What a beautiful name. Muriel has never been to Dublin, but she has been given a clear picture of this place; rose bushes and oak trees that lend privacy to the vast property, cast-iron gates, and of course the breathtaking, unobstructed view of the expansive, glistening Irish Sea. It is the same sea that laps the coast of Blackpool, but Muriel believes it is even more beautiful on the other side.

Muriel loves family celebrations. After all those months of not being able to see each other, never mind celebrate anything (unless you were the prime minister, of course; then different rules applied), she is delighted when anyone gets to hug and dance and fete their loved ones. All the better if those joyous hugs are a bolt out of the blue.

Muriel signs the docket and hands it over to the Delivery Dash receptionist. Oh how she hopes this little package will be the cherry on the cake of the young woman's homecoming.

It's not her biggest hope though.

Her biggest hope is that Bea's family can forgive her – and that Tessa's surprise party goes off without any drama.

# TESSA

· · · · · · · · · ·

## THE SAME DAY
## Howth, Ireland

I'm not sure how it happened, but there's an estate agent standing in my hallway unspooling a measuring tape while I hold the other end.

He has already done a walkthrough of the 'property' (aka my beloved home of forty-two years), jotting down the number of rooms (twelve; seventeen if you include the second-floor and basement scullery, which have been shut off for forty-one of those forty-two years) and condition of everything from the floorboards (original; oak; excellent) to the fireplaces (original; cast iron; not in tip-top form, but all functioning). He says he could 'flip' the house in a fortnight and that it would 'do the three'.

My son Senan and grandson Otis, who are currently yielding a second measuring tape in the opposite direction, gasp at this.

'What does that mean? Do the three?' I ask, as the estate agent tugs the tape, and by extension me, towards the centre of the hall.

'It means I can get you three million.'

'For this house?' I exclaim, almost letting go of my end.

'At least.' He peers down at the tape and writes the number in his gold-edged ledger. 'What have you chaps got for the width?'

Otis squints at the implement in his hand. 'Fifteen foot.'

'But it doesn't even have central heating! Who's paying three million to have to put on their long johns every time they need the loo in winter?'

The man shrugs. 'Everything's a USP.'

'A what?' Another tug, and I just about get my stick moving in time. We're measuring the depth of the fireplace now.

'A unique selling point,' he says, snapping the implement into its holder. I let out an involuntary yelp as it flies from my fingers.

'Frozen pipes are a unique selling point?'

'We are operating in a seller's market, Mrs Doherty. There's nothing that can't be reframed as character.'

'It's true, Gran,' says Otis. 'My geography teacher is renting a shed in Raheny for €2,000 a month. It doesn't have central heating either – just the family's tumble dryer, which produces a bit of heat if you open it straight after a cycle.'

'People are renting out garden sheds? As homes?' I am aware of the desperate state of the housing market – I have attended several rallies demanding adequate housing for all – but it seems there are always new depths to plumb.

'There's a market for cosier, more affordable properties, and it's a nice side earner for the owner. We have a few on our books,' says the agent. 'I actually noticed the little building you have out the back.'

'What little...' I frown. 'The *fuel store*?'

He raises an eyebrow. 'Or is it a bijou studio?'

'It's definitely a fuel store.'

Another shrug. 'Like I say, potential is in the eye of the seller.'

I park this scurrilousness momentarily. 'But *three million?*' I repeat. 'That's...who has that kind of money? There's been a leak in the attic for nearly a year now, and the plaster at the back is crumbling. If this house is worth three million, how can *I* afford to live in it?'

'The joy of inherited properties,' the agent retorts, putting his various notepads and tapes into a monogrammed briefcase. 'Look, Mrs Doherty, my advice would be not to look a gift horse in the mouth. Accept your good fortune, sit back and think of what you're going to do with all that money. You could buy one of those nice new apartments down by the harbour – no stairs, no draughts, bridge tables in the foyer – and you'd still have more than two million left.'

The man reaches into his breast pocket and produces two business cards.

I take one, but only so I know who I'm reporting when I contact the Residential Tenancies Board.

'Would you be taking the furniture with you?' he asks, rubbing a hand along the carved wood of a sideboard that once belonged to my late husband Bernard's parents, and probably grandparents before that. 'I could get you another hundred K for the contents.'

'I won't be taking any furniture because I won't be going anywhere.'

Senan sighs loudly, but I ignore it. A valuation was all I agreed to, after persistent badgering. The idea that I'd leave this house is ridiculous.

'Mrs Doherty,' says the estate agent, flashing me his flashiest smile. 'We see this a lot. People get attached to homes and they don't want to leave, no matter how impractical they might now be for them. And this is a particularly lovely home. I understand. Who wouldn't want to live here? All these rooms, all this space. But just think about how happy you'll be making some young family. You'll be giving them a place to live; you'll be making all their dreams come true.'

I know what he's doing. He's trying to guilt me into a sale by appealing to my sense of civic duty, even though he's only interested in the sweet two per cent commission that would go with selling a house for three million. (*Three! Million!*) This man is part of the problem, but he's relying on me wanting to be part of the solution.

More annoying than being manipulated is that it's almost working. The state of housing in this country is a disgrace. I don't have a lot of money – despite what this recent valuation might suggest – but I have a standing order donation to the Simon Community, and I raised housing with every candidate who called to my door ahead of the last elections. I even think there's something to the suggestion that older people consider downsizing.

But not me and not this house. What was Senan thinking, having the man come here?

'Goodbye now,' I say, thrusting my stick forward as I move towards the man. It's an aluminium pole, like a crutch but with a curved neck at the top and, at the bottom, it spreads into four feet, each with a rubber soul for grip. It is an offensive pain in my backside, but it will be gone soon enough.

Senan, who can probably sense I'm about to clout the chap, takes the other business card and sees the estate agent to the door.

'If you really were keen to stay on, I could look at making it part of the contract for any potential buyers. Maybe retain the fuel store,' the agent calls after him. He slides on a pair of ludicrous wraparound cycling sunglasses as he heads down the steps, over the gravel and towards his car. 'Give me a call, Mrs Doherty. It would be an honour to make you a very wealthy woman.'

When the door is closed again, and we hear the tyres rolling out of the driveway, Senan turns and smiles. 'Three million, Mam? Can you believe it?'

'I'm not selling. No way, no how.' I hobble over to the sideboard and start sorting through my handbag.

'Mam, you're not even considering it.'

'You're right,' I agree. 'I said you could have the house valued, but I never said I'd sell. And I certainly wouldn't let that man do it. I couldn't live with myself if I knew someone as morally bankrupt as that was making money from my house. Whatever about forcing people to live in garden sheds, did you hear what he said about bridge? He comes into my house, uninvited—'

'I invited him, after you okayed it.'

'Uninvited,' I continue, 'and then he insults me?'

'How did he insult you?'

'By assuming I play bridge.'

'You do play bridge!'

'I play bridge *ironically*, Senan, as you well know. But that's not the point. *He* doesn't know that. He thought, "Oh, she has a stick, she must be old, she must need to go and live in some clandestine old folks home and spend the rest of her decrepit life playing bridge". Well I'm not old, Senan. I'm in my sixties. Just like Demi Moore.'

'Excuse me?'

'You heard me.'

Senan sighs.

'It's a fact that this house is big and difficult to get around,' he says in a tone that suggests I'm the one trying *his* patience.

'Do you think that snake oil salesman would be telling Hollywood legend Demi Moore to sell her house, which is probably bigger and therefore more difficult to get around than mine? Would he suggest she go play bridge until death comes for her? No, he would not.'

Senan throws out his arms. 'I give up.'

'And Demi Moore wears glasses,' I continue. 'Meanwhile, I only really need mine for watching TV. She hasn't made a decent film in twenty years and I'm still doing some of my best work, even if I'm not paid for it. I go on marches. I have an active social life. Up until that stupid fall, I played tennis more days than not. I still teach twice a week. And speaking of, I have a class in half an hour, so I need to get going.'

'Gran is the same age as Demi Moore?'

'Yes, Otis. Yes, I am.'

'No, she's not! No you're not, Mam. You're sixty-nine. You're almost seventy. I don't know as much about *Hollywood legend Demi Moore* as you suddenly do, but I imagine she's sixty. Sixty-one, tops.'

I sniff at this. I've no interest in semantics. But Otis grins at me. He introduced me to the magic of IMDB last month and knows I've been addicted ever since.

'That doesn't make you the same age, and it also has nothing to do with anything,' says Senan, who it seems is not as done as

9

he said he was. 'This is what your grandmother does, Otis. She distracts, she flummoxes. She's a champion arguer. She did it for decades; arguing for housing, more resources – and her clients were lucky to have her because she's very good at it, but this is different. Mam, you're not a social worker any more. And I'm not going to let you talk rings around me.'

'I've no idea what you're talking about, darling,' I say, rooting about in my bag for my keys. 'Otis, would you be a pet, and get me the box of supplies I left in the library? They're on the desk.'

My grandson gives me a salute and heads off.

'Mam. Please. Don't make me feel like some awful son who's trying to turf you out of your home. I would never have suggested it if it wasn't for your fall.'

'My fall,' I guffaw. What did I do in my former life to be cursed with such dramatic children?

'But *now*,' he soldiers on, 'this house is completely unsuitable for you to be living in alone. The lack of central heating is only for starters. But on that, you're not able to carry in wood and briquettes any more and you weren't going to be able to do it indefinitely anyway. The dining room is damp. There are stairs everywhere. The kitchen is miles from the sitting room which is miles from the bedroom. There's no toilet downstairs.'

'Wasn't it good enough for you and Bea to grow up in?'

'That was years ago. It's just you here now and needs change.'

'I might be the only one living here, but this house doesn't just belong to me. It's yours and your sister's too,' I contend. 'And you're talking about selling it without even consulting her?'

'I'm not making this about her,' he says flatly, and my heart sinks. Is it my fault he's still so angry at his only sibling?

'All right then. What about your father? Hmm? This is the building where he took his last breaths, where I cared for him, where I raised a family with him. How could you sell all that history? If you truly believe there's a suitable price for memories, then I failed in raising you.'

'Memories don't live in buildings; they live in our heads. We take them with us wherever we go,' he says, parroting what sounds suspiciously like something his wife Audrey would say.

'You used to make slides on all those stairs. Do you remember?'

'A six-year-old sliding down the stairs is a lot different from a seventy-year-old having to climb them a dozen times a day.'

'I'm sixty-nine!'

'For another six weeks!' Senan sighs again. 'We're going around in circles here. I know you're not old, Mam, but with the stick, you need help. What if you fall again?'

'Firstly, the stick is temporary. It'll be gone soon. Secondly, I tripped over some shoes on the landing. Next time I need to go to the toilet during the night I will turn on the light. Lesson learned. It won't happen again.'

'You nearly died!'

'Oh come on. I didn't even really break anything. A little fracture to my hip, that's it.'

'You were lying there for hours. If Audrey hadn't found you, you would have died of hypothermia.'

I roll my eyes, probably a tad too forcefully, but I never know how to react when he brings this up.

Senan thinks the reason relations between myself and his wife have been worse than usual is because Audrey found me sprawled across the landing wearing nothing but a pair of ancient grey underpants. And I, who am as comfortable with my body now as I was when I protested naked outside Dublin city's fur shop several decades ago, want him to go on thinking that that's all it is.

'I'm just repeating what the doctor said,' says Senan.

I put my handbag down on the chair that once sat beside his father's sickbed – and indeed deathbed – and look my son squarely in the eyes. 'I can't leave this house. So you need to stop suggesting it.'

I expect him to shrink under my gaze, but he just looks sad. He feels sorry for me, his mother. He sees me as a lonely woman clinging to a house of memories. It's splashed all over his face, and I can barely take it.

Otis reappears in the hall with a box of coloured paper, card, scissors, crêpe paper and string.

'Perfect, love, thank you,' I say, turning my back on my son to face my grandson. 'You can carry it out to the car for me in a minute.'

But Senan isn't finished. 'What about a carer?'

We've been through this already. It's worse than selling the house. Well, maybe not worse; but definitely more insulting. 'A carer. Jesus Christ,' I mutter. 'I'm sixty-nine. Not ninety-nine. I'm probably still young enough to get a job as a carer.'

'I know you're more comfortable helping people than being helped, but—'

'You think I need someone to give me a sponge bath and wipe my derrière?'

'You need someone to help around the house. To bring in firewood and clean a bit, to carry the boxes that are too heavy or awkward for you now.' He looks meaningfully at the class supplies in my grandson's arms.

'You could rent out a room?' suggests Otis.

I laugh. 'A housemate?'

'I dunno. You could think of them as a tenant – a lodger or whatever.'

I ruffle my grandson's hair, though the reach up does cause a twinge in my side. I'm five foot ten but he's even taller. And so skinny. He turned sixteen over the summer and took a serious stretch. I don't mention it because I think I offended my daughter-in-law last time, but, honestly, where's the harm in adding a few more potatoes to his dinner plate?

'I'm a tad old to be bumping into a stranger outside the bathroom, don't you think?' I say.

I throw my arm around my son, then. He really does look worried. 'I'm fine, I promise. I can do most things myself. And for the odd jobs, don't I have you and Otis and your lovely wife just down the road?'

'But we're not always at home.'

'You usually are,' I say, gently, not wanting to directly point out that I have a more active social life than my son these days. 'You didn't go away once this summer.'

He gives me a look like he's going to disagree somehow, but then shakes it from his head. 'Me and Audrey work,' he says instead. 'Otis has school, and now that we're into the new school year, I'm going to be putting in long hours there too.'

I consider mentioning that he can always get here when it suits him – like taking himself and Otis out of school early when he knew the Bijou Henchman was coming – but I bite my tongue.

Senan is principal of the local community school and he's a good man, just like his father. Bea, I'm afraid, takes after me; wilful and passionate and not interested in ever being wrong. I'm very proud of the work my son does and how he's done in his career. I should tell him that more. I make a mental note to do so, soon, after my class. But right now it really is approaching 4.30 p.m. 'I need to get going. Otis, will you take the box out?'

I make for the door, my grandson walking ahead of me, my son behind.

'I can't help thinking what would have happened if Audrey hadn't called that morning,' says Senan. The man is relentless. 'She nearly didn't, you know. She was going to visit her sister, only her sister had a vomiting bug so she knocked into you instead. I just...' He shakes his head.

He's always been empathetic, even when the concern is unnecessary. I'm his mother. I should be the one worrying.

And, actually, he is pale.

'Are you getting enough sleep, darling?'

Now that we're out in the afternoon sun, I can see clearly that he is not. No denying the dark crescents under those eyes. I will pick up camomile tea for him on the way home.

'What would have happened if Audrey hadn't called? Who would have found you? What state would you have been in?'

I squeeze his hand and give him a kiss on the cheek. I feel confident then that his wife didn't tell him everything about that morning. 'But you always do call. So it's fine.'

Senan sighs. He appears to be out of arguments, finally. But just in case, I move quickly. I point my keys at the old Skoda so Otis can open the back seat and slide in my teaching supplies. Then I position myself on the top step. I'm a dab hand at descending these with the stick now. I pause at the halfway point and look straight ahead, out over the sea. An instant sense of calm descends. It really is a glorious day – excellent weather for doing some good.

'Anything else, Gran?' asks Otis.

'That's it. I'll see you in the morning. We're low on wood, so you might chop a bit then if you have time?'

'Mam, Otis can't—'

But Otis throws his dad a look. Quite right. This is between my grandson and me. He calls most days before school, and I never have him late. Besides, tomorrow is Saturday.

'No problem, Gran,' he says, opening the driver's door for me. 'See you in the morning.'

I kiss him on the cheek. 'Thank you, my love. I'll rustle up some pancakes in return.'

Someone needs to put fat on his bones.

•••••••••

The North Dublin Community Project is a programme of free classes, workshops, counselling groups and training opportunities available to anyone, from anywhere, who needs them. It's a ten-minute drive from my house when there's no traffic, which today there isn't. I pull up in front of the former parish hall and grab the box of supplies from the back of the car.

Senan is wrong; I can carry my own materials. It just takes a little longer.

I've been coming here for almost ten years. I started out as an attendee, but I've always gotten more out of helping than being helped. My son was right about that bit. This term I'm signed up to teach two of my most popular courses. On Tuesday mornings, it's Beginners' Gardening. And today, as with every Friday: Radical Activism.

'Sorry I'm late,' I call, dropping the box onto the laminate table at the top of the room. Some years – usually after a general election or an increase in local parking fees – Radical Activism is in such demand that we have to use the main hall. This year I only have five sign-ups, so we're in one of the smaller spaces off to the side.

'I've been writing letters, Mrs Doherty,' barks Malachy who, as always, is seated at the desk right in front of mine.

Malachy is a large man; tall and stocky with limited neck and a tightly shaved head that turns myriad shades of red whenever he gets worked up – which is all the time. He is a dedicated student and the only one still wearing the battered name tag I gave out on the first day of class.

Malachy was directed to the Project via a scheme for the long-term unemployed. He wanted to upskill, but when the labour market continued to elude him, he decided to throw himself fully into the community centre. When he's not attending one of the thirteen courses in which he is currently enrolled (a Project record) he volunteers on the reception desk.

Now he is riffling through a stack of folded paper in front of him. 'I haven't posted any of these yet because I wanted to see what you think,' he says, in his usual intense and clipped speaking manner. It's like he's only allowed so many breaths per day, and he's rationing them. 'I took on board what you said about not including threats of physical violence. You're right;

it distracts from the issue. I kept them short and to the point. I think they're good now, Mrs Doherty. I think they're fucking excellent, to be entirely honest with you.'

'You big lick!' calls Reggie, who is sitting on top of one of the tables at the back, still in his school uniform. Reggie is the youngest participant. He gets out of school one period early so he can make it to the Project on time.

He likes to remind everyone that this sanctioned truancy is the only reason he's here.

He's actually here because his parents thought it would be good to channel his disillusionment into something more constructive and less incriminating than spraying 'Reggie woz 'ere' on every wall within a two-mile radius of their home. Especially when he's the only 'Reggie' for at least a ten-mile radius.

Malachy is too absorbed to register the teenager's taunts. 'I know you're not keen on cursing, Mrs Doherty,' he says, shaking out one of the folded pages, 'but you're always saying how important it is to channel our passion – and I think these letters show my passion. I wrote the same letter to every local politician and I stuck to my point, just like you said. I'll read you one.' He nods furiously to himself.

'Let me just get set up first, Malachy, and I'll...' But he's already off.

'Dear Mr Foley. My name is Malachy Foster and I am a resident of your electoral constituency...'

He looks up. This is the starting template I provided last week. I give a firm two-handed thumbs up.

'I am writing to you today in relation to the removal of the

17

public bin at the junction of Seafield Terrace and Sutton Drive...'
Another glance up.

I nod encouragingly.

'I personally believe this decision to be a fucking disgrace.'

'Ah. I'm not sure...'

'It is also my personal opinion that you had better put that bin back. Or else. Yours sincerely, Malachy Foster, 11 Seafield Terrace.'

My friend Maura, who has a few vigilante tendencies herself, breaks into a round of applause. Reggie, meanwhile, has fallen off his table in a fit of laughter. 'A fucking disgrace!' he howls.

Again, the jeers wash over Malachy, who is staring at me with such intensity that his left eye starts to twitch.

The other two attendees have just arrived. Susan is a forty-something mother of four young boys who only joined us last week and has yet to reveal much else about herself, and Trevor is a widowed retiree on the hunt for romance. He had his sights on Maura, but although he's a decent man he's also an awful know-it-all, and Maura had no interest in being mansplained to in the bedroom. 'I'll just about put up with it at the garage,' she reasoned. 'But what expertise I lack under the bonnet, I make up for under the sheets.'

'What do you think, Mrs Doherty?' asks Malachy now. 'Whack a stamp on it, yeah?'

'Mmm.' I pick up the letter from his desk. 'It might be a tad... Yes, I think so...' I pretend to have to reread the five sentences, but actually I'm wondering if the reason we discourage schoolchildren from writing in red pen is because it makes everything read that bit more sinister. 'A tad aggressive still, I think.'

'Where's the aggression? Where?' asks Malachy, sounding aggressive.

He can't help it, the poor lad. He's a lovely man, actually very gentle – he attends my gardening class too where he has proven to be something of a flower whisperer – it's just how his passion manifests. I've encouraged him to grow out the skinhead and to keep his sleeves rolled down over the meat cleaver tattoo, but it's the innate aggression that's keeping him from getting a job. He was so close with the hardware shop last month, but then he told them he'd fucking kill someone to work there – which is just Malachy for 'I'm excited for this opportunity' – and, well, there was no second-round interview after that.

'We can't threaten people, Malachy.'

'More's the pity,' says Maura.

'There's no threat,' retorts Malachy, his head pinking. 'I took out the whole bit about setting a rottweiler on him – like you advised. Dano doesn't have many going at the minute anyway.' Malachy's friend Dano runs a dog obedience school, though I'm not sure how good he is, since he's always offering canine brutes to his pals for the purposes of intimidation. 'The dog was the threat. And that's all gone.'

'Yes, but you left in the "Or else".'

Malachy's pink head progresses to fuchsia. 'Could mean anything.'

'That's true,' agrees Maura. 'Mr Foley doesn't know about Malachy's friend's rottweiler. It could mean, "Put back the bin, or else I'll be disappointed".'

'Yeah,' says Malachy, clicking his fingers in Maura's direction.

'Maybe I'm saying put back the bin or else I'll write you another strongly worded letter.'

'Well, that might work—'

'Ya scaldy sleeveen.'

Susan flinches. She's the nervy type and if you don't know Malachy well enough to know he's a lovable puppy under it all, his way with words can have too much bite.

'Okay. Let's come back to this,' I say. 'But it's definitely an improvement, Malachy. The lack of nooses in the margins alone makes it so much better.'

Malachy pulls the chair in, sitting straighter, delighted with himself.

Maura leans forward and gives him a pat on the back.

'Last week we made a start on letter-writing. Today we're going to discuss the power of a good banner and of collective protest.'

'Nothing like a march to make you feel alive,' chimes in Trevor, a veteran demonstrator. He may originally have signed up to this class to pursue Maura, but he has come to enjoy the ample opportunities to detail his protesting knowledge.

'I've never been to a protest,' says Susan with reverent awe. 'Have you gone to many?'

'Don't get the old man started,' groans Reggie, who likes to wind up Trevor almost as much as Malachy.

'Hundreds.'

Reggie throws his head back before flopping it onto his desk with a thud.

'I won't go through them all,' says Trevor, pointedly. 'But I'm a founding member of Grandparents for Trans Rights, so we go on a fair few outings. We actually store the banners in my greenhouse. I'd been to hundreds of protests before that too. I find them good for the soul.'

'Agreed,' I say. 'Protesting is about the personal as much as the collective. That's what a lot of people don't understand. If you're angry, like really hopelessly angry, there's a short window before the fire in your belly turns to a dead weight that you're forced to carry around like some stodgy cake you can't digest for the rest of your life. But if you can get that anger out in time and channel it into something productive, it might just be the thing that saves you. The aim is not to become bitter; to take your anger and turn it into a force for good.' I beam at the group. 'We might go on one this year, if we can find a cause we all feel strongly about.'

Susan looks both excited and scared by the prospect.

'I'm not much of a marcher myself,' says Maura, who is only in this class to chat to me. 'I prefer direct action. But we went on one as part of the course last year, and you should have seen Tessa. Some young one handed her a megaphone while she sorted out her placards and next thing you know, Tessa is leading the troops.'

'That was a lovely demonstration,' I agree. 'Reminded me of the old days, only without having to chain myself to anything.'

'You used to chain yourself to stuff?' says Reggie, incredulously. 'Like what?'

'Oh, whatever was going. Railings usually, but sometimes lamp posts, other protestors, an officer of the law once or twice.'

'An officer of the... As in, a *garda*?'

'Yes, Reggie,' I say, enjoying the shock on the teenager's face.

The way he's looking at me now: that's the person I am – not some old woman hobbling about on a stick. 'Sometimes you have to disrupt to get people's attention.' Malachy's eyes light up at this so I row back. 'But that's a last resort. First, we ask for things politely. We make posters and we get walking. Now,' I say, pulling coloured card from my box of supplies. 'Let's make those posters!'

Everyone gets to work. Trevor constructs a banner to add to his trans rights collection, while Malachy spends forty minutes doing elaborate mind map brainstorming before settling on 'We Want Bins'. Reggie threatens to make a 'Remove All Bins' poster but switches to 'Graffiti is Art' when Malachy's head goes so red it looks like he might pass out. Susan can't think of anything, so she offers to do a second trans rights one, which suits Trevor because now he has someone to whom he can give instructions. Maura opts to make lots of mini signs to leave on the cars of the people who keep parking on the double yellow lines outside her house.

'Move your car or get keyed,' I read, picking up one.

'Malachy's suggestion,' says Maura, cheerfully. 'Good, isn't it?' When she's finished turning the tail of the 'y' into a zig-zagged scrape, she puts down her magic marker. 'How goes Operation Downsize? Senan sold the house from under you yet?'

I sigh. It really is depressing that at just sixty-nine he thinks I can no longer live in my own home. 'He is worried about me,' I say, 'which would be irritating if it wasn't so well-intentioned. You'd swear I'd ended up in a full-body plaster cast the way he goes on.'

Maura picks up the marker again and starts slowly drawing a cartoon car in the corner of one of her signs.

'What?'

'Nothing,' she says, bending her head closer to the card.

'Maura Gilbert. Since when do you hold your tongue?'

She puts down the marker. 'I know it's only your hip that is the problem...'

'Exactly. One little hip.'

'... but it does mean you can't live independently.'

'I *do* live independently!'

'You live on your own. But you couldn't live without Senan and Audrey and Otis calling in every day to fetch fuel and help with the cleaning and carry certain things.'

'None of that takes them more than a few minutes, and I more than pay it back by cooking for them or giving Otis lifts.'

'I'm just saying your life is different now, and so is theirs.'

'How is their life different?'

'They have to call in every day.'

'They always called in.'

She raises an eyebrow. 'Every day?'

'*Most* days.'

'And what if they're not around? What happened when they were in France this summer?'

'Well now, that's where you're wrong,' I say, triumphantly. 'They didn't go this year. So it wasn't an issue.'

'I thought they went to France every August.'

'Yes, but not this year. Something about Audrey's work. She had a lot on.'

'So this was the first year they stayed at home? And it was also the first time you couldn't be left alone?' The raised eyebrow is joined by a tilted chin. 'What a coincidence.'

Before I can argue, Reggie is beside me, slipping his poster onto the desk between myself and Maura. 'There,' he mumbles. 'Can I go now?'

'Reggie!' I exclaim, taking in the skilful lettering. He's drawn the word 'Graffiti' like a mural. 'This is exquisite. Look at that detail – the brickwork, the depth. It's a work of art. Your talents were wasted on your neighbours' walls.'

'It's whatever,' says the teenager. He gives the poster another side glance. 'I'll probably just throw it in the bin.'

'I'd bring it home if I were you. It's really excellent, Reggie.'

Malachy is out of his seat and peering over my shoulder. 'That's dead good that is,' he says, forcefully. 'You've got skills, mate. Meanwhile, I tried drawing a bin and it ended up looking like a post box.' He glances back at his own poster, and I surreptitiously wipe his spittle from Reggie's. 'That's just going to be confusing.'

'Turn it into something else,' says Reggie.

'Like what?'

'A ball of paper? A crumbled-up election leaflet or something, being thrown into a bin.'

'That's a deadly idea, but I couldn't do that.'

Reggie sighs. 'Come on,' he says, dragging his poster from our table and heading for Malachy's. 'I'll do it for you.'

'I've never met an artist before,' says Malachy, slapping him on the back.

Reggie stumbles, then shrugs him off, but there's no denying the blush.

'You know Otis made the basketball team this year?' says Maura when they're gone.

I laugh. 'No he didn't.' My grandson has been obsessed with basketball since he was too small to hold one. He tries out every year but never makes it past the reserves. Between the recent growth spurt and a summer spent flinging the ball into the net at the side of my house, I had thought his time might finally have come. But if it had, I'd be first on his list of people to tell. Otis is my only grandchild and we've always been close.

'He did. Jason told me.' Jason is Maura's grandson. He's in the same year as Otis, and Reggie, and he's a star of the basketball team. 'One of the guys broke his arm jumping out of a tree, and Otis got called up.'

'You must have it wrong. I'm telling you; Otis would have mentioned if he'd finally made the team.'

Maura gives me a look that says she's so sure of her position, she doesn't need to argue any more. I grit my teeth.

'Reggie!' I call.

The teenager looks up from where he's hunched over Malachy's poster.

'Is Otis on the basketball team this year?'

'Otis Pearson? How do you know Otis Pearson?'

One of the many upsides of having kept my own name is that Reggie has never made the link between myself and Otis or, more importantly, Senan. I want to give the teenager a safe space – I don't want him to think I'll be reporting back to the principal.

'He's a friend of my grandson's,' retorts Maura. 'Now answer the question.'

'No,' says the teenager, returning to his drawing. 'Otis is not on the team.'

I smile triumphantly at my friend, but before I can say 'I told you so', Reggie interrupts.

'Like, he was offered a place. After Shane George downed a naggin of vodka and became convinced he was an eagle, there was a spot. But Otis turned it down.'

'That doesn't make sense,' I say, mainly to myself. My summer was soundtracked by the basketball walloping the side of my kitchen wall.

'Said he couldn't commit to training in the mornings,' says Reggie. 'I don't blame him. Going to school an hour early just to bounce a ball around? And on Saturday mornings too? Nah, you're all right, Fellow Tall Nerds, I think I'll stay in bed.'

Maura turns back to me with a look that says, 'Now do you believe me?', but my own expression must be as awful as I suddenly feel, because it softens.

'He didn't tell them he helps you in the mornings,' she says, quietly. 'He just said he had other commitments.'

But this only makes me feel worse.

How could I have missed the sacrifices my family was making? How could I not have questioned Senan and Audrey skipping their annual trip to France? How did I not realise I was monopolising my sweet grandson's time?

'Oh dear,' I say, remembering the exchange before I left the house this afternoon.

Senan was trying to tell me not to ask for Otis's help tomorrow morning. I didn't even register it.

I've always been so stubborn, so instantly sure of my own position. I am a crusader in the best and worst sense. When I was working, I put my clients' needs before those of my family.

I promised myself I wouldn't let them down again.

'You're right,' I say. 'I've become a burden on my family.'

'I never said that!' exclaims Maura.

'Well, it's true. I have. That bloody fall. This stupid stick!' I grab the thing by its curved neck, as if to throttle it. 'But I won't be a burden any longer.'

'What are you going to do?'

'I'm going to live by my words. I'm going to take my anger and turn it into a force for good.'

Across the room, Reggie is giving his poster a furtive look of admiration, before rolling the thing up and quickly stuffing it into his bag. Malachy is proudly brandishing his sign – the bin now reimagined as a leaflet and a more experimental bin opening drawn at the bottom – while Trevor and Susan 'ooh' and 'ah' encouragingly.

If I can do my best for these people, then I can do my best for my son.

'I'm going to take in a lodger,' I declare, recalling what else Otis said this afternoon. I lift the stick and bring it down with as much force as four rubber soles can exude on a cheap linoleum floor.

'Like, have a stranger live with you? In your house?' says Maura.

'Yes.' I swallow down my qualms. It's the least bad option. At least this way, there's the potential to help someone. My house is huge – too huge, I've always said. I was never comfortable with its illusion of wealth, even if we could barely afford to maintain it most of the time. I can look at this as my chance to give purpose to its magnitude.

'You sound like you mean it.'

'I do,' I reply, literally banging home my point.

'See?' she says, pointing to my stick. 'It is good for some things.'

# CHLOE
· · · · · · · · · · ·

'Chloe?'

'Yes, hi. I'm here.'

'Hello? Chloe?'

'Yemi! Hi,' I shout, louder this time, turning my head towards the passenger side dashboard, where my phone is wedged between a washbag and several balls of colourful wool. 'Can you hear me?'

'Just about. Where are you?'

'I'm in the car. I'm driving. I have you on loudspeaker.'

'So you're okay, then?' she asks.

*In eighty metres, turn left.*

I indicate and move to the next lane, which is riskier than it sounds because the farside mirror is obscured by the duvet and pillows that occupy the passenger seat. The back seat is filled with a large haversack, several boxes of books and a couple of plastic bags stuffed with clothes and more bright wool. A lamp, a wash basket, a tangle of cords and several pairs of shoes partially block the rear window, but there is just enough space to see out. I'm fairly sure there's nothing coming.

'Chloe? Are you still there? Are you okay?'

'Yes, I'm still here. And I'm fine, I'm just navigating a tricky...' I make it into the lane without being rear-ended. 'Phew. Okay. You have my attention. What's up?'

*Turn left.*

'Shoot!' I nearly miss the turn, but just about spot it in time.
'Where *are* you?'

'I'm on a job,' I reply. 'Just picked up a package for delivery.'

'So you're okay then? Everything is okay?'

'Yes, everything is okay. Why do you keep asking?' Was I supposed to take that turn too? Since my mobile doesn't have GPS, Delivery Dash provide me with a Satnav. It's a relic from their storeroom – possibly the original Satnav prototype – and it is often several instructions behind.

'Your mam phoned me,' says Yemi.

'*What?*'

I'm in the middle of changing gears and the car almost cuts out. I go to pick up speed again but there's a ball of wool rolling around at the pedals.

'Yemi, I'm so sorry,' I say, reaching down and flinging the orange fabric into the back. 'I can't believe she did that. I'm mortified. How did she get your number?'

'She said you gave it to her when you came on my hen.'

It's easy to remember because Yemi's hen party is the only night I spent away from home in the past two years. I only went because Mrs Sweetman from next door insisted upon it. She said she'd check in on Mam regularly.

'Oh god, Yemi,' I say, head turned towards the phone. 'I really am sorry. I never thought she'd ring you.'

'Don't be silly. It's fine. As long as you're fine. Are you? Fine? She said you're not answering her calls.'

'I haven't had a chance,' I lie. There are already eighteen missed calls and a dozen texts that I can't bring myself to open.

'Did you guys have a fight?'

'No.'

'Because you never fight with your mam.'

'Yes, well, it's hard to fight with someone with stage three cancer.'

'Especially if you're you,' agrees Yemi.

I am not known for my combative nature, it's true, but I am also not the total pushover Yemi believes me to be. Just last week I returned fruit to the supermarket after opening the punnet to find two plums covered in mould.

'She said she woke up from a nap looking for you but all she found was a note.'

My stomach twists. I bite down the guilt.

'Which really doesn't sound like you,' adds Yemi.

*At the next roundabout, take the second exit.*

'What happened?'

Maybe we should have fought. Would that have made leaving easier?

'I don't really want to talk about it,' I reply eventually. 'Not yet. I just need to get through this job. I'm sorry, Yemi. I know you're trying to help.'

'Well, if you want to talk, I'm here. And if you don't want to talk, I'm also here.'

I'm so lucky to have Yemi. Truly. It's not easy being friends with a carer. I say no to things far more often than yes, and I frequently cancel plans at the last minute. Even if I do make it out, I rarely have anything interesting to say. My only news is related to the state of my mother's health. And that's never good.

'Chloe? Are you crying?'

'No.'

'Oh my god, you *are* crying. Where are you? I'll come and meet you right now.'

Yemi thinks I'm not a crier because she never sees me do it. But actually, I am. I cried so much as a baby that my dad left. He couldn't take any more wailing, which is why my tears give Mam PTSD. They remind her of being abandoned. So by nature, I'm a crier. But by nurture, I'm stoic. I've learned to keep my blubbing for when I'm entirely alone. Not when I'm about to make a delivery, in the middle of the day, on the phone to Yemi.

But then all the rules are out the window today. I've been swinging between crying and giving myself 'first day of the rest of my life' pep-talks since 9.30 a.m.

'I'm fine,' I insist. 'You just had a baby. You are not going anywhere.' I shake my head and force a smile until the happiness makes its way into my voice. 'I'm *fine.*'

I catch my reflection in the rear-view mirror and the car jerks again. Blotchy face, manic grin, mascara splodged under my eyes, hair in desperate need of a wash, and car full of all my earthly possessions. Thank Christ my phone isn't capable of video calls. I look like the Joker – if the Joker was suddenly homeless and a secret knitting enthusiast.

'Your mam phoned me because she didn't know where you were. You didn't mention it in the note.'

My 'note' was all of five words long. So no, a forwarding address didn't make the cut.

'She'd no idea who else to phone. She thinks you moved out, Chloe. I told her that wasn't the case, that you probably just needed to blow off some steam or whatever and you'd be back. I mean, you wouldn't move out. You wouldn't just leave her. Right?'

*Take the second exit.*

'Why am I asking? Of course you wouldn't. But it might be worth phoning to let her know. Or I can phone if you don't want to speak to her just yet. I know she can be difficult, but, well, you know...'

As I veer off the roundabout, something topples from the backseat onto the floor and makes a loud clatter.

'What was that?'

I glance in the mirror, careful to avoid the horror that is my face. 'Record player. I hope it's okay.'

'You have your record player in the car?'

'I have everything in the car.'

'Shit, Chloe, seriously? You really did move out?'

'It's a break,' I say. 'I'm just taking a break.'

'What...' begins Yemi, before trying and failing again: 'Why...'

I sympathise. If someone had told me this yesterday, I'd be equally lost for words.

'Where are you going to go?' she manages eventually.

Every change, wanted or not, is an opportunity. I read that recently. Given that I've just made the biggest change of my life without an iota of forward planning, I have got to believe that this will be one hell of an opportunity. 'I'll figure it out,' I say, readopting the manic grin. *Fake it till you make it.*

'Well, you can stay here. Peter and I would love to have you. And Akin.'

'Oh, Akin! I didn't even ask how little Akin was doing! Did the public health nurse call? Was everything okay?'

'Yep, all good. He's great. Looks more like his dad every day. But forget about the baby – he has somewhere to live. Come and stay with us. Please.'

'Thank you, Yemi, but I am not about to arrive in on top of you three weeks after you've given birth.' I glance at the Satnav. I must be nearly here now.

*Turn right.*

'Where are you going to go?' She doesn't say it because she is a good friend, but she knows what my mother knows: If I'm not at home, and I'm not with Yemi, I don't have anywhere else to go.

'I'll be fine. More than fine. This is a good thing,' I say, telling her what I told myself this morning, as I drove around the same roundabout so many times that I started to feel seasick, tears streaming down my face, a mixed CD from over two years ago – the only CD I own – blaring Adele through my tinny car speakers. 'I'm actually excited about the possibilities,' I add. 'This is going to be good for me. Great, even. Probably. Definitely!'

'You have no idea, do you?'

'Wow.' I slow the car further, as I gawk out the window. 'These houses...'

'Don't change the subject, Chloe.'

But I'm not. Nevin Way is a quiet off-road; bumpy tarmac, grass growing in clumps at the verge of an uneven narrow footpath, a few streetlamps and not much else. You might miss the houses altogether if not for the ornate plaques informing you that what dwells beyond these gates is not storage units or farmlands, but decadent homes. Homes so posh they don't have numbers, only names. Some of the houses are obscured by shrubbery and tree-lined avenues, but the ones I can make out are all huge, unique, and breathtaking. This delivery comes with a pre-paid €100 tip. That sort of money is unheard of in the courier business, but it makes sense now. To the people who live here, it was like giving someone bus fare.

'Chloe! Hello? I'm asking what your plan is.'

'Hi, yes, sorry. It'll be okay, Yemi. I have a plan.'

'Which is?'

I take a deep breath and prepare to tell her what came to me so clearly that morning it could only be described as a vision. I was off the roundabout – having finally found the strength to decide on an exit – and pulled over in a hard shoulder, still sobbing, still lamenting my sorry excuse for a life. When suddenly it hit me; the last time I was truly happy. The greatest loss of my life. Which was also the greatest love of my life.

Another deep breath, then: 'I'm going to get Paul back.'

When she says nothing for several seconds, I congratulate myself on the dramatic delivery. Only it turns out the silence is one of confusion. 'Who?' she finally responds.

'Paul! Paul Murtagh! The love of my life?'

'Oh, *Paul*,' she says. 'Paul, yes. I remember Paul.'

How could anyone forget? Paul was so gentle and handsome and smart. He had the cutest way of straightening his glasses when he got nervous or authoritative. And he loved me. My god, how he loved me.

'I thought I had to let him go, but I was wrong. I made the wrong choice. And I'm going to get him back,' I say, rotating my shoulders like I'm already preparing for the battle.

*In 200 metres your destination will be on the left.*

'If you're happy, I'm happy, Chloe. But I meant where are you going to live?'

'Oh. I don't know about that bit yet.' I squint, the still-strong September sun at my back as I read the names on the plaques. *Hallow House, Binn Eadair Beag, The Orchard* all dotted along the street at generous intervals. No sign of *Hope House* yet. 'I'll probably just rent somewhere.'

Static comes through the phone and I reach over to adjust it before recognising the sound as laughter.

'Yes, because it's that easy. It took Peter and me weeks to find this place, and we can just about afford it – on two full-time salaries! I'm not being funny but, like, I know what those courier shifts pay. Do you know what rent costs? Have you ever paid to live somewhere?'

She knows I haven't. Paul and I were supposed to rent a flat, we'd paid the deposit, but then Mam came home with a Hodgkin's Lymphoma diagnosis and all talk of how many cushions a bed needed and whether eggs should be kept in a press or the fridge was forgotten.

'I read the news,' I reply defensively. 'And I got a big tip for this job. And now that I don't have the same responsibilities at home, I can take on more deliveries. If worst comes to worst, I can stay in a hotel for a few nights.'

'A hotel? In Dublin? That tip would want to be astronomical.'

'Well, a hostel then.'

'A *hostel*? Chloe, are you trying to give me a heart attack? Just come stay with us, okay? You're not ready for the big bad world.'

'I'm not a child, Yemi. I'm the same age as you.' You'd be surprised how often I have to remind her of this.

'I know. But your experience of the world is more...'

'Yes?' But at the same time that I ask this, I turn my head to the right and give a genuine, wind-knocked-from-my-sails wheeze.

'Oh, now. Oh, wow,' I mutter.

Yemi is still searching for a tactful way to tell me that the most interesting thing about my life is how boring it is, but my attention is right here. Out this window. Focused on this view.

This is why all the homes are located on the left-hand side. If you were to build on the right, you would be blocking *this*; the most magnificent sea view I have ever seen in real life. Or in any virtual form for that matter.

*You have arrived at your destination. Your destination is on the left.*

The clouds part and the sun shines straight down onto a patch of the Irish Sea, like some sort of celestial beam calling souls up to Heaven.

*Your destination is on the left.*

'Your experience is more limited. That's all,' says Yemi eventually. 'I worry about you, out there by yourself...'

'Wow,' I whisper again, barely listening. The unspeakable upset of this morning fades, falling from my shoulders and gliding straight out into the vast body of water. My problems seem so insignificant when faced with the unending expanse of the calm, glistening sea. I am humbled by the water, I am calmed by it, I am—

'Oh no.'

I am off the road.

'Oh no, no, no.'

I have come to the end of Nevin Way and unwittingly mounted a low kerb and I am now on a modest green, wheels rolling over soft grass and I am travelling slowly but with increasing speed towards a hedgerow. There is a gap in the shrubbery and all I can see through it is blue. At first I take this to be sky but, as the distance between me and it continues to narrow, I recognise it as sea.

*At the next opportunity, rejoin the road.*

'No, no, no, no, no!'

'I'm sorry if I offended you, Chloe, I'm just trying to say…'

*At the next opportunity…*

I slam on the brake and push my body back in the seat. Nothing appears to change but then, after another awful few seconds, the car slows. It comes to a stop.

I close my eyes and pull up the handbrake.

*Phew.*

I swivel around and, over the laundry basket, see the last house on the road peeking out from behind a wall of trees and a thick flowering bush – Hope House, presumably. Closer to the car, at the edge of the green, there's a sign. I can read it from here. It says: 'Stay off the grass.'

'Yemi, sorry, I have to go. Don't worry. I will be fine.'

'Okay, just one last thing.'

'Yes?'

I reach down onto the passenger side floor and scoop up the package. It is light, well-wrapped, has a UK origin stamp, and is addressed to one 'Bea Pearson'. Maybe Mrs Pearson doesn't know she's getting a package. Maybe the tip was paid on the other side, and she will add a generous 'thank you' of her own. (It could also be a Mr Pearson. Paul's granddad was Beaufort. Something like that could come with a 'Bea' nickname.)

'What about your mam?'

'What about her?' I say, cringing at how defensive I sound.

'Is she going to be okay without you? If the cancer has spread this time, she's going to need to start treatment ASAP. I know that's tough on you, and I know the past two years have been beyond tough, but you can't just—'

'Jesus!' My two hands, and thus the package, fly to my chest, as a silhouette appears at the passenger window.

'What is going on over there?' comes Yemi's voice down the line, as a man knocks on the window.

'Yemi, I've got to go,' I say, reaching over and taking the phone off loudspeaker. 'There's a strange man looking for me to get out of my car.'

'Wait. What? Chloe! What man?'

He takes a step back and, holding one hand above his eyes, bends down and peers in the window. Then he knocks again.

'One of those men who can't quite grow a beard but insists on trying anyway,' I say, giving him an exaggerated thumbs up. 'Please don't worry about any of it. I'll speak to you later. Love to Peter and little Akin.'

'Yes, I see the sign!' I shout when I've hung up and positioned the phone on top of my duvet. 'Thank you!'

That would be the downside of living on such an exclusive road; highly involved residents. I understand the desire to stop people parking on the grass – I also wouldn't want anything obstructing this view – but I've been here less than a minute.

If he got over to me this quickly, he must have seen that this wasn't where I wanted the car to end up either.

He is gesturing behind him and saying something I can't make out. So I give him a cheery smile and another enthusiastic thumbs up. 'No parking, got it!'

But he just looks at me like I'm some sort of simpleton who can't understand basic instructions. He's still talking and now he's pointing down. He wants me to open the window.

My car is extremely old. You have to roll the windows manually, and there's currently a duvet in the way. Not that I'd be inclined to do it anyway. He's pretty worked up. It's just a bit of grass.

I still don't know what he's saying. Something about sinks? It's starting to stress me out.

'All right, all right,' I mutter.

I open the door and climb out. But not before reaching under my seat and pulling out the crowbar I carry to help open the larger crate deliveries. He's an irate stranger. Whatever Yemi thinks, I'm not totally clueless.

He is older than me, but not by much, and while his beard would best be described as 'rust-coloured', the hair on his head is dark brown.

'Hi, yes, I saw the sign, I'm just—'

'You're sinking,' he says, raising his straight eyebrows, which are darker again. 'Your car is sinking.'

The casual tone is at such odds with his words that it's difficult to process. 'Excuse me?'

He thrusts down and I realise it's not the window he was pointing to, it's the wheels, which are rapidly disappearing into the soft grass below.

'Oh! Oh, no! Oh, no, no, no, no, no!'

'We can roll it back onto the path,' he says. 'Take off the handbrake, and we'll push it.'

But we've switched roles, only I'm far more worked up than he ever was. I'm too busy shaking my head and muttering 'No' to do anything useful.

With just three steps, he's beside me, a large hand against each arm as he moves me aside and reaches into my car to release the handbrake.

'Come on now,' he says, rolling up his shirt sleeves as he moves around to the front of the car. 'Push!'

He has both palms flat against the bonnet, veins straining against freckled skin as his forearms tremor and he pushes one knee forward. He's at least half a foot taller than me, broad and soft. He doesn't look like he works out but he still looks strong, and he must be because the car nudges forward. Only then it stops. It won't go any further.

He switches legs, a grimace spreading across his face.

I place the crowbar on the bonnet and my hands beside his, then I lean in with all my weight. I feel the sun on my calves and I watch the colour leave his fingers and the veins push out further. There's another slight budge but then nothing as my own feet start to sink into what, it turns out, is not grass so much as mud with a green veil. How can the ground be so soft? It hasn't rained in days. 'It's too heavy!' I wail. 'I'm carrying too much stuff!'

'It's not that. This is a former marsh,' he says, teeth gritted with the effort as we continue to push.

'What?' I despair. 'How is anyone supposed to know that?!'

41

'And that gap in the bushes leads down to the cliff walk and, yeah, the cliff. Another few metres and you'd have been done for.'

'Oh god!' I stare back in horror at how close I came to mortal doom.

'Keep pushing.'

I return my attention and force back to the car – although I think we both know my contribution is negligible. I'm not strong. Which is unfair, because I'm not willowy either. If the universe is going to give you chunky arms, it should at least put some force into them.

'Do you want to try the steering wheel? See if it gives the wheels more room to manoeuvre?'

I glance around to see if there might be other options. I've never been good at decision making. I try to think of what my mother would do, but there is absolutely zero chance of her ending up in this predicament, so I come up blank.

He stops pushing and abandons his position.

'Wait! Don't give up! You can't just let it sink!' I shout. 'This car contains everything I own and it is currently my best option for accommodation tonight and every other night for the rest of my life!'

He doesn't say anything, but he stops at the driver's door again, leans in and starts pulling at the steering wheel. At my feet, the wheels move from side to side, spraying more mud up onto my calves.

Three even strides and he is back at the bonnet. He resumes pushing. I turn my side towards the grill, as if that's where I've been keeping my secret bodybuilder strength all along.

The car begins to move, and this time it doesn't stop.

'Oh – oh! Oh, oh, oh, oh, oh!'

We push it bit by bit over the green and back onto the road. When all four wheels are on tarmac, he reaches into the car and pulls on the handbrake.

'Thank you!' I gasp, hands on hips as I catch my breath.

He nods. He's not panting like me, but his breathing is deep.

I was unfair about the beard. It's the lighter hue. The way the sun caught it through the car window made it seem patchy. He's handsome, in a very Irish way; fair-skinned but with a hint of red, a generous smattering of freckles across his arms and face, and blue eyes – although these are a deeper blue than you'd expect. He's no Paul, whose hair is uniform sandy-brown and who has been adorably clean-shaven since the day we met, but he's not without merits.

'I owe you one, seriously,' I gush. 'You basically just saved my life.'

He nods again.

'I didn't intend to park there, I just got distracted by the view, but if it's a former ...'

'There used to be,' he says, flicking a dried piece of muck from his charcoal-grey slacks. There's no point in me even starting down that road. He has a light smattering, mainly around the cuffs, but my legs are destroyed with the stuff. It's how I'm made; I just attract mess.

'Right, yes, and I'm not saying it's your fault that the sign's gone – it's not the residents' responsibility – but the council or whoever it is that's in charge of that stuff really should keep the sign up, to make sure visitors are aware.'

'There is still the "keep off the grass" one,' he reasons.

'Yeah, but you could easily miss that.'

He glances towards the sign, which is about twenty metres away and perfectly readable. When he brings his eyes back, I can feel him assessing me.

His forehead creases and something approaching wonder crosses his face. I give him a bashful smile.

'Did you say you're living in your car?'

'No,' I retort, smile vanishing.

'When you thought I was leaving it to sink. You said it was your best option for accommodation tonight.'

'Figure of speech.'

'Huh,' he says slowly. 'Don't know that one.'

His eyes flick a millimetre upwards and I remember that since I last saw my reflection, I have added sweat, mud, and beetroot cheeks to the mix.

That is not wonder on his face – it is bewilderment.

'I'm here for Hope House,' I say, before there can be any further questions about my living situation.

'You don't say,' he deadpans.

Was he waiting on the delivery? Was that why he was out here monitoring my parking?

I reach back into the car for the package. I knock my phone from the top of the duvet onto the floor and leave it there. Any break from my mother's calls is welcome. When I re-emerge, he's already heading for the house. I shove the package into the waistband of my denim shorts and try to put some order on my hair as I scurry over to catch up with him at the footpath. I realise too late that I'm still carrying the crowbar.

He stops outside what is indeed Hope House – there's a chip missing from the top of the plaque, but the name is fully intact.

He scratches at the hollow of his left cheek and watches me. He makes no attempt to open the gate.

Does he want me to hand the package over here? Maybe he's Bea Pearson's husband. (I don't think he's Bea; he's both too hip and not hip enough to pull off Beaufort.) I'm not likely to get a tip standing on the pavement though. Nobody carries cash any more. You need to get them at the door. Were I to make a career pivot into burglary (and if Yemi's right about the cost of accommodation, never say never), I'd know exactly where to go for the cash stack: the drawers of the hall table.

I look at him expectantly, but he just mirrors the expression. It's unnerving. Do his irises have more pigment than everyone else's?

Mam says beautiful people deserve our pity; their worth is wrapped up in their looks and no matter what they do, those are only going in one direction. That's why I'm lucky to be plain; at least my looks are falling from a lower height.

Then he pulls his mobile from his pocket and starts scrolling.

'Do you... Don't you live here?'

'Me? No,' he says, still flicking. 'Not yet anyway.'

'So you're not Mr Pearson,' I mutter.

He looks up and frowns, yet somehow manages to look amused. I shake my head.

'But you knew about the marsh?'

'I've seen the sign,' he says. 'It was there until last week.'

'And you knew I was here for Hope House?'

'The car full of all your stuff sort of gave it away,' he says, clicking his phone closed and pushing it deep into his trouser pocket. 'Some might see turning up to an initial room viewing with your bags already packed as presumptuous, but I admire the self-belief. It's ballsy.'

I haven't a clue what he's talking about.

'But,' he says, rolling down his sleeves and redoing the buttons, 'I'm still going to have to trump you in there. I'm very good at interviews and this house is perfect for me. It's not personal.'

'Right...'

I do my best to catch up.

There's a room viewing happening today and he's going for it.

A room viewing – as in, there's a room available to rent.

Here. In Hope House.

I peer back up through the gates and shrubbery and catch a glimpse of dark brickwork, a projecting stone porch and one large white timber window. Red-dappled ivy drapes it all.

'What did they say the rent was again?' I ask, doing my best to sound casual.

He gives me a look and glances back at my car.

How is *that* a suspicious question?

Is this one of those things where rich people consider it uncouth to discuss money?

'Where did you see the advert for the room?' he asks.

There's a beat. Damn it. 'The internet,' I reply. *Vague. Safe.*

'Huh.'

It's the piercing colour, I think. He's probably as deep as a paddling pool, but the sharp blue gives weight to every glance.

I do my best not to blink.

'I saw it at the community centre,' he says, still watching me. 'I thought the rent was the most noteworthy thing about it.'

Oh god, it's extortionate. Of course it is. Look at this place. Look at this man's *shoes*. They're a little muddy sure, but their expensiveness shines through. This is a different world, one for wealthy people. I don't live in this world; I just deliver to it.

There's a crunching from beyond the cast-iron gates and a tall boy of fifteen or sixteen approaches. He lifts the clasp – which wasn't locked, just shut – and pulls the gate inward. There's a clearer view of the house and I feel my jaw drop.

'I'm Otis,' says the teenager, who is dressed in runners and basketball shorts. He's thin and tall and has an unusually pleasant demeanour. I'm twenty-four and I still cross the road when I see teenage boys coming. They're an intimidating cohort.

He puts his hand out and I shake it.

I rub at the area under my eyes and try using my foot to knock some mud from my leg but just end up spreading it around. It's the crowbar, though, that takes the bulk of his attention.

'You're here for the viewing?' he asks as I swing that arm behind me.

'Yes,' replies the man, who also takes Otis's hand. His handshake is much better than mine. More casual, confident; he's definitely had practice. 'I'm Conn Horgan.'

'Chloe Darvin,' I add hastily.

'We did think we'd have a few more applicants...' Otis peers around. But Nevin Way is otherwise deserted.

'Same,' says Conn. 'You're renting the place out, but for free. I did read that right?'

My jaw comes undone again.

A room, in this house... *free of charge*?

'Not the whole place. My grandmother will still be here.'

'Mrs Doherty?'

'Tessa Doherty, right,' says Otis. 'How did you know?'

'A chap at the community centre told me,' replies Conn. 'Malachy, maybe? That's where I saw the notice.'

'That's the only place we put it. Gran's very attached to the community centre and she wanted the right people to see it.'

'And the free of charge bit?' I venture, clearing my throat. Attempts to keep my voice relaxed have given it a shrill edge.

'Gran wouldn't feel right taking money for it.'

I nod, like this is a totally reasonable attitude for a landlord to have.

'So the community centre is the only place you put the advert, ay?' says Conn, turning his head slowly towards me. 'You didn't put it online at all?'

I narrow my eyes.

Otis sighs. 'I wanted to, but she wasn't having it,' he says. 'And when Gran says no... Wait until you meet her. You'll see.' He glances between us, picking up on the friction.

'We did mention that we're not looking for couples...' he says carefully.

I don't think I truly knew what a 'chortle' sounded like until just now. 'Oh, we're not together,' says Conn, who is having a great time entirely. 'Definitely not.'

I throw him a dirty look, but he's too busy stroking his chin like some bargain basement philosopher.

'Didn't put the advert on the internet. How unusual...'

'And it's permanent,' I interject. 'The room? It's available for a while?'

'Three months initially. I think we said that on the notice too...'

'You did,' confirms Conn. 'Anyone who saw the advert would have seen that the room was available for a three-month period to start.'

I do some rapid moral, economic and rest-of-my-life maths. I could explain that there's been some confusion and I am actually here to make a delivery. But what good would that do anyone? If Tessa Doherty is the only person living here, then they've got the wrong address and the package will be returned to the depot anyway. It happens all the time, especially when there's no house number or Eircode. So nobody will get their post and I'll still be homeless. I could also say I didn't see the notice but am interested in the room, but the community centre connection appears to be important.

'Your granny's definitely the only person living here?' I ask. 'There isn't another woman... sometimes...? Or your granddad...' Perhaps Beaufort was popular with a particular generation. You never know.

'My granddad's been dead for twelve years.'

'And his name was...'

'Bernard.' Otis frowns, looking down. 'Why?'

My left hand has swung back out. I push the crowbar behind me again.

'Ignore me, sorry. I'm getting confused.'

'So much confusion,' murmurs Conn.

'And it's just one room?' I clarify.

But Otis's attention is elsewhere, so Conn happily steps in. 'Yes, Chloe, just one room available. That titbit was on the notice too.' The light dances across his irises.

'Does that car belong to one of you?' asks Otis, who has moved a couple of steps closer to the vehicle but is now thinking better of it. He says 'car' like it comes with its own question mark.

I squint at the mud-soaked eyesore.

'It's hers,' supplies Conn. 'It got stuck on the marsh.'

'I didn't know it was a marsh.'

'All these signs, just passing you by...'

I can see Otis trying to decipher the contents of my car and since I can't think of a satisfactory explanation, I just swallow my pride and say nothing.

'Will we go up to the house and meet Gran?' he says eventually. He is mostly addressing her. I get the impression he's scared of me.

This could be the first time anyone has ever been scared of me.

It is not as thrilling as you might imagine.

'That'd be great,' replies my newly minted rival. 'It'd be lovely to meet her.'

Conn's tone – relaxed, friendly, *nice* – is unbearable. He doesn't care about meeting this woman, he just wants to live rent-free in her palatial home. My pathetic predicament is mere entertainment to him. The way he told me he was getting the room, like it's a foregone conclusion.

I can't let an elderly woman end up living with someone so smug. That would be far more amoral of me than reneging on the courier code of conduct.

What were the odds of me being sent here today of all days? And then there was that celestial beam out on the water... It has got to be a sign.

'Chloe?'

'Hmm?'

I cover the package with my hands and push it around my waistband until it's at the back of my shorts. Neither of them clock it. It was probably the least bizarre part of my 'look'. The parcel is less secure at my back, but I hold it there with my free hand.

If Conn wants to battle for this room, I'll give him all the fight I have.

'Yes, wonderful,' I say, untucking my t-shirt so it covers the package. 'Lead the way!'

# TESSA

· · · · · · · · · ·

'Oh, hold up! Here they come now – the first contestants!' Maura turns from my kitchen window, face gleeful. 'Come on, Tessa. Stand up and take a peek.'

'I'm fine where I am, thank you,' I say, stirring my tea, even though the sugar has long dissolved.

Maura helped Otis and me to draw up the advertisement for the room. Otis was there for his graphic design knowledge and general computer skills, and Maura just invited herself along. Her main contribution – that we should mention the need for the lodger to be 'in good physical condition' – was ignored. Neither were much help with the wording, to be honest. Otis's suggestions all made me sound like I had one foot in the grave, and you'd swear Maura was writing the job spec for a brothel.

Then Maura insisted that in return for her not very helpful help I should let her sit in on the viewing. I am already regretting it. She has been pushing for a scoring system and for the interviews to have a 'talent portion' since she got here.

'Oh my lord, would you look at your one,' she says, face so close to the glass she keeps having to wipe away the condensation. 'Nobody's getting through to the next round in that state.'

'For the last time, Maura, this is not the *X-Factor* and you are not Louis Walsh.'

'I was being nice taking Louis,' she says, indignantly. 'Everyone knows Simon is the most fun.' Maura wipes at the window again. 'Just come and look at this girl. She looks like she's been wading through cow pats. And is she carrying... Is that *a crowbar*?'

*Clang, clang, clang* goes the spoon in my cup.

I have largely come round to the idea of a lodger in the days since we drew up the ad and hung it on the Project noticeboard. This is real, no-nonsense help in the face of a crisis. I will be meeting a fundamental need – housing – for someone who requires it. I have taken my anger with the wider societal situation – and yes, my personal situation – and turned it into a force for good.

Still, something is insisting that my hands remain busy.

I'm not usually a woman for sweeteners either, but I was a tad dizzy this morning so I'm giving the blood sugars a boost.

'I'll see the applicants when Otis brings them in,' I say, forcing myself to relinquish the spoon.

Maura wanted me to charge a nominal rent 'to stave off the loo-lahs and hobos', but that would detract from the gesture. We did however limit the advert to the hall, and left it up for a short period, so hopefully there won't be too many people to turn away.

'Tessa, if this is going to happen, if you're going to have a stranger living with you, you might as well have some fun with it. Isn't that right, Senan?'

My son, sat at the far end of the kitchen table drawing up a tenancy agreement, gives an ambiguous murmur.

'Which brings me to another great idea I had...' Maura bends down with a low groan and rummages in the bag at her feet, just about taking her eyes off the window long enough to produce three oversized table tennis bats.

'Ping pong tournament?' I hazard. 'Best of three sets gets to avoid homelessness?'

'They're scoring paddles! Jesus, Tessa, do you watch *any* television? We mark each contestant – sorry, *applicant* – out of ten and write the score on these. See? You just use chalk. Otis can tot them up, and maybe fashion a leader board from some of your teaching supplies. Senan, you can be Sharon Osbourne.'

'I'm honoured,' he says, still not looking up. 'But I don't think my cheekbones are up to the job.'

Maura swivels, pointing a paddle in my direction. 'Simon?'

'Definitely not. No rating people out of ten, no making applicants stand up to answer questions, and no asking them if they have a song prepared.'

'Not just a song,' she protests. 'A dance, or a monologue, a poem... You like a nice poem.'

'I am not making people sing for their bed.'

'You might need a tiebreaker,' Maura argues. 'I can only imagine how many have turned up. The queue probably winds the whole way down onto the cliff walk.'

I swig a large mouthful of sweet tea and remind myself that any unease with taking someone into the family home is illogical. Bea has no affection for this building, Senan is delighted about the decision, and Bernard would have been proud. This was the kind of thing he loved me for.

I am doing this to help. What qualms could compete with that?

Maura goes back to her position at the window. 'Although why Otis only has two contestants with him, I don't know,' she says. 'We'll be here all day if he's going to drip feed them.'

'Two?' echoes Senan, finally looking up from his papers. 'This isn't actually a day off for me. It's an in-service and as the principal I'm not in much service if I don't make it into the school at all.'

'And I've to drop things down to the Project,' I say. I promised the life-drawing teacher I'd share some art supplies.

'Maybe he's starting the whittling down process for us,' muses Maura. 'I mean, your one does look like someone you'd be drawn to, Tessa. A definite veneer of desperation.'

'I am not drawn to desperation. I'm just looking for someone I can help. That's all.'

'A real air of stray dog,' continues Maura, ignoring me completely. 'Stray, unwashed, rabid dog...'

Senan goes over to join her at the window. 'Oh, right. I see. Is she wearing face paints?'

'That or she's been bawling.'

'Can we stop casting aspersions on people until we meet them, please?'

But neither of them is listening.

'Might she be going for the sympathy vote?' considers Senan.

'Clever tactic,' says Maura. 'You can be sure Soft Touch Simon over there will give it to her.'

I sigh loudly and knock back the last of the tea.

'Hold up!' says Maura, scurrying away from the window. 'They're coming in.'

The sound of the front door being unlocked. Maura gives a low squeal in the seat beside me. We turn our attention to the kitchen door. But when it opens, it's only Otis.

'Nice to see you all too,' he deadpans. 'They're in the hall. Will I bring them in?'

'Why have you only got two, Otis?' asks Senan, his voice low. 'We haven't time for that.'

'They were the only ones out there.'

'Two people? Only two people turned up for the viewing?'

My grandson nods.

'That makes no sense,' I say. 'Malachy promised he would give the poster prime position on the noticeboard. Everyone who goes into the centre passes the noticeboard.'

Maura sighs. 'Definitely won't be needing the paddles, so.'

'The guy who did turn up said the noticeboard was covered in planning permission applications. All the other notices were hidden underneath. I guess nobody saw it?' says Otis.

'Planning permission?' I ask. 'Permission to do what?'

Otis shrugs. 'And not that this should sway you, Gran, but the woman already has all her stuff in her car.'

Maura gives a low whistle. 'That girl has a deck full of desperate cards and she's going all in.'

'Well come on so,' says Senan. 'Bring them in. And think of it this way, Mam. Now you only have one person to reject.'

When my grandson returns, he is followed by a tall, bright-eyed man dressed smart-casual in trousers and a shirt and a young woman who – and I say this as someone who literally burnt her bra for a woman's right not to be judged on her appearance – looks like she's been dragged through a bush backwards. Her face is puffy and there are black smudges under her eyes. Her clothes – a long-sleeved white t-shirt and denim shorts – are splattered with mud. Her legs are caked in it. She has one hand pressed to her back and the other is indeed holding a crowbar.

I push myself up, but my legs are a little weak so I have to hold onto the table with my left hand as I extend my right. An annoying first impression. 'I'm Tessa. Welcome to my home,' I say, somehow resisting the urge to add 'And I'm still in my sixties – same as Demi Moore!'

'Conn Horgan. Thank you for the opportunity,' says the man, with a handshake so assured he must work in finance or law or one of those professions where deals are regularly closed by encircling someone else's fingers with your own.

His shirt is lovely, made with thick grey linen. Definitely expensive. He has an easy smile, a sense of comfort despite being in a stranger's home and the sort of manners that only come from being well-reared. This is not someone who needs my help.

The young woman, however, is a different story.

'Hi, hello, hi, Chloe Darvin, me not you, obviously,' she hums, looking down at her own body as if perplexed by the lack of an available hand. 'Sorry, didn't mean to bring this in,' she says, placing the crowbar on the kitchen table. 'Can I leave that... do you...? Sorry...' She switches the hand at her back and eventually takes mine. Her palms are damp. She is nervous, unsure of herself, and her efforts to mask it with enthusiasm have the opposite effect. She flashes me the loveliest, most unguarded smile and I can't help but return it. Still. She might be too much, even for me.

'Well, do sit, both of you,' I say, pushing the plate of biscuits across the table. 'Would you like some tea? Maura – could you stick on the kettle?'

'Just making some notes here, Tessa. First impressions are very important. How tall would you say you are?'

'Six two,' answers Conn. He smiles. I smile back. He seems grateful to be here, excited even, but I am already writing him off. Surely he could afford to rent somewhere in the city.

'Six two,' mutters Maura, jotting it down. 'Tall is good. Tall is useful...'

'I'll get the tea,' says Senan.

'And you – how would you describe your physical condition?' Maura jabs her pen in Chloe's direction. 'Middling? You appear to have a bad back anyway.'

'Oh, no. No, no,' says the girl, who seems only to realise now that she is still holding a hand behind her. 'My back is fine – it's great. It's just, you know, my shorts, they're a little loose.'

Maura jots something down. 'Rickety *and* boastful,' she mutters.

I give her a kick under the table and smile at these two strangers. 'Why don't I tell you a little about myself, and the house?'

'Sorry, can I just, before we start. I just want to apologise for my appearance. I don't usually look like this,' says Chloe, looking at us all with her big, beseeching eyes. 'My normal state is a lot more put together.'

'We didn't notice anything,' says Senan, who has always been a kind man and a terrible liar.

'I had a bad day, and there was some car trouble...'

'They had to push her out of the marsh,' provides Otis.

'I didn't know it was a marsh.'

'There's a sign. It says "marsh".' That's Maura, notebook out again. 'Can you read?'

'Yes, I can read, but there wasn't any sign...'

'To be fair, it is a *former* marsh,' says Otis, 'and the marsh sign is gone.'

He's right. The Kearneys are trying to sell Binn Eadair Beag and they thought the sign would put people off. Joseph Kearney removed it last week. Although the 'Keep off the Grass' one is still there. So Maura's question is valid. Not that literacy is a requirement for getting the room.

'I'm just saying I don't usually look so...'

'Dishevelled?' offers Otis.

'Disturbed?' says Maura at the same time.

'Right,' says Chloe. 'And if I'd realised that I was coming here for this, I would have been more presentable.'

'Did you not realise you were coming here for this?' I ask kindly, wondering if the bad day included a blow to the head, and lamenting the fact that I am going to be rejecting two applicants and starting the whole process over again.

Everyone is turned towards Chloe. Senan and Otis look concerned, Maura sceptical and Conn like he's more invested in her answer than anyone else.

She looks around, open-mouthed. Conn takes a large bite of a chocolate digestive. He does seem oddly at ease here, though not entitled. Chloe, meanwhile, doesn't appear to know whether she's coming or going.

I push the biscuit plate a little further in her direction. The poor creature.

'Do you want to tell them about the situation, Mam? What the tenancy will involve?' suggests Senan, approaching the table. 'Tea?'

The two applicants turn to take the mugs and I make a face at my son, letting him know this is a waste of time.

They busy themselves pouring in milk and Senan tilts his head at me.

I give an inaudible sigh.

They've come all this way. I suppose I can give them a few more minutes.

'My name is Tessa Doherty,' I say, Chloe already nodding eagerly as she wipes Jammie Dodger from her bottom lip. 'I was a social worker for forty-three years and I've lived in this house almost as long. It belonged to my late husband's family. We inherited it. It's not perfect – we don't have central heating and it's difficult to keep clean – but the views are unbeatable. On a clear day, you can see all the way to England from the top floor. We're on the cliff walk, technically, but the main path veers back up to the car park before it gets to us so we miss the hordes. Although you will find a few stragglers wandering about in summer.

'I have two children. That's my son, Senan. And one grandson, Otis, who you've met. I've been on my own here since my daughter left and there's all this space. So why not take in someone who needs the room? Senan's old bedroom is just up there gathering dust.'

Senan clears his throat.

I turn to him. 'What? It is. I don't have time to dust everywhere.'

'I mean,' he says softly, 'maybe tell them what they would have to do?'

'Oh.' I make an unconcerned 'pffff' sound. 'Mainly this is a philanthropic endeavour. Housing is a national disgrace and every politician should be obliged to open up their spare rooms, free of charge. But if we were waiting for anyone to lead by example in this country, we'd be waiting for eternity, as I learned a long time ago, so.' I turn my palms skywards and spread out my arms.

Senan coughs louder.

'And I suppose I could do with the odd bit of help,' I add reluctantly. 'Nothing much, just if the lodger wanted to provide some sort of payment. Because I won't be taking money. Where would the good deed be in that?'

'Mam had a fall a few months ago—'

I cut Senan off before he gets carried away with the dramatics. 'A minor slip. Nothing broken. My son tends to worry. I'll be done with this stick soon.'

'But still there are things she could do with some help on.'

'Like getting the jam down from the high shelf,' I say, dismissing my son with a wave of my hand. 'And opening the jar.'

Senan gives me a wary look. 'And bringing in wood and briquettes from the store out the back, clearing out the ashes, maybe giving the stairs a hoover every now and again.'

He makes it sound like I'm looking for Cinderella. *I'm* the one making dreams come true!

'Tall equals helpful. Dodgy back not so much.' That's Maura.

'I'm good at that,' says Conn gamely. 'Opening jars, I mean.' His smile shows off a gap in his front teeth. It's unexpectedly goofy and makes him seem less put together. In a good way. He's definitely likeable, even if he's more used to liberating caviar than jam.

'I'm good at cleaning,' says Chloe, quickly. 'Hoovering, dusting, whatever you need. And I know all about helping with mobility issues. I've read everything there is to read on it. I used to be a professional carer – well, not really professional, but full-time, for my mam. Days, nights, around the clock.' Her cheeks flush. 'I'm a good cook too. Cooking and cleaning; I can do them both. My mam actually was a professional cleaner and I used to go on jobs with her as a kid. So I've been doing it forever.'

'Even with that back?'

'I don't have a bad back,' she says, removing the hand from behind and waving it at Maura. 'See? You won't find a better help around the house than me, honestly. I have so much experience.' She turns towards Conn. Both hands are visible, but her movements remain awkward; she looks like she's performing a balancing act. 'I doubt your other applicants will be able to say that.'

'I can't say I spent my childhood working as a cleaner, no,' he agrees, amicably.

'Sorry to hear about your mother,' I say. 'I hope she's okay now?'

Chloe stuffs another Jammie Dodger in her mouth. 'Mmm.' She makes an apologetic gesture for the full mouth, and then eventually, after much chewing: 'She'll be fine.'

'Glad to hear it. Although I'm not sick, and I don't need a carer. I really don't need someone to do all that much for me. I live a full, busy life and I do all my own cooking. I'm only sixty-nine.'

'It's more about having someone here,' supplies Senan. 'In case of another fall, or whatever. We're down in the village – myself, Otis and my wife Audrey – and we call in a lot, but...'

'They can't be here all the time, of course,' I finish. 'It's about providing a room for someone in need and also peace of mind for my son. They're the main things.'

'Oh well, I can be here,' says Chloe. 'No problem. I work as a courier, deliveries, you know, but it's shift work and I pick my own hours so I can be here whenever you like.'

'I'm very available too,' chimes in Conn.

'Yes. What do you do?' I ask. 'Finance? Law?'

'Both, actually.'

I give myself a mental pat on the back. The day I lose my intuition about people is the day I can no longer trust anything.

'Or I used to,' he adds. 'I was an in-house lawyer for a finance company based in Dubai. I did that for two years but quit when I came home in June.'

'And you don't have a job now?'

'I'm between.'

'Where do you live, so?' asks Maura.

'I'm staying with my parents at the moment, in Dun Laoghaire,' he says. 'Hence I don't need much money to get by. I do a bit of freelance work, but it's always from home. I can literally be here all day.' He smiles. 'The only deliveries I have to make are done by email.'

Chloe glowers, but then sees me see her and instantly blushes.

'And nights? Not to pry into your social lives, but do you go out much?'

The young woman laughs. 'Oh sorry,' she says to Senan. 'You're serious, of course you are. Em, no. I have precisely one friend. Finally, that's a good thing. Ha-ha. So yeah no, I definitely don't go out much. I can be here in the evenings, and at night. And whenever you need, really. I'm incredibly available.'

She looks from Senan to me and smiles hopefully. There's a soft thud in my chest as my heart lurches towards her.

'I suppose there isn't much time for friends when you're caring for someone full-time.'

She nods.

'That's a lot of responsibility,' I say.

She holds my gaze and her frantic edges calm, if only for a moment.

'Why did you come back from Dubai?' asks Maura, pointing a pen across the table. 'The heat, was it? I'd say it was the heat. Freckly ginger skin like yours? You might as well put yourself on a skewer.'

Conn smiles. Then he says: 'My brother died.'

'Oh, Jesus, I'm sorry,' says Maura. 'And there's me talking about being burnt alive.' She pauses and I swear I can see her thinking better of it but going ahead anyway. 'Was he sick?'

Senan tuts from down the table.

'He killed himself.'

There's a collective intake of breath. The simplicity of the sentence lands like a smack.

'I'm really sorry,' I manage.

I'm not sure why I'm so taken aback. Do I think self-assured people don't experience tragedy? I know well that they do.

Maura puts the top on her pen. Her own little mark of respect.

Even Chloe, who has bristled at much of what Conn has said, looks both horrified and like she might burst into tears. 'I'm sorry too,' she half-whispers.

Conn nods his acknowledgement. 'So that's why I came home,' he says. 'I just wanted to be where he had last been.'

He shifts in his seat.

I give him a small, reassuring smile. I know exactly what he means. It's why I can't sell this house.

'Otis, can you pick up my stick? Actually, never mind, I can get it.'

'Where are you going?' asks Senan, as I reach down under the table. My poor son, burdened with a mother of action. He thinks I'm about to abscond.

But the situation has taken a one-eighty. A familiar sensation courses through me. There are two people here who need help and I am in a unique position to give it. After all, what is the point of there being air in your lungs and blood in your veins if you're not going to do some good?

'A tour, my darling,' I say, tapping the stick against the floor. 'We can't expect someone to take the room without showing them around.'

# CHLOE

· · · · · · · · · · ·

They've told us to go ahead into the hall.

They're obviously taking a minute to talk about us, which is fine. Well, it's not really fine. It's one thing looking like the only survivor at the end of a particularly brutal horror film, I don't need everyone sitting around *agreeing* that that's what I look like.

I would wager it is not going well for me. I talk too much. It's because silence makes my heart race and my stomach churn, but all those extra words rarely have any substance. And I'm not used to people, especially new people, so I'm expunging even more pointless words.

I do not possess natural charm. Or a dead brother. Not that I'm wishing for a dead sibling. What an awful thing. It's just that it is clearer cut than a sick parent. How sick? What kind of sick? Shouldn't you be looking after her sick? Whereas dead is just dead. There are no degrees of that.

At least this brief, unsupervised window gives me a chance to dispose of the package. Finally I can stop holding myself like I should be the one with the walking stick.

I go on ahead of Conn, back the way we came, casting around for a suitable surface. Where the long hallway meets the vast, dark foyer, there's a full-length antique mirror. Jesus, but it's even worse than I thought. All I'm missing is an axe.

*Don't get distracted, Chloe, do not get distracted.*

The hall table. Perfect.

There's a pile of stationery at one end – notebooks, envelopes, pens, highlighters – so I leave the package slightly apart from that, slipping it out from the waistband of my shorts. They can be the ones to realise it's been sent to the wrong house and return it to the depot.

I feel a little bad about pocketing the €100 tip, but I did get the parcel to where I was instructed to bring it, so I have done my job. Better than usual, you could argue; I brought it *inside* the house.

Footsteps behind me.

Conn.

I adopt my friendliest, least antagonistic face and turn to greet him.

Combat isn't working for me. His arrogance is impenetrable. So, new plan: I'm going to appeal to his humanity.

There must be a bit of it in there.

'Conn! Hello.'

'Hello, Chloe,' he says pleasantly, as if he can already tell what I'm up to.

'I know you want this room,' I say. 'I get that.'

'That's good.'

'But you see, me, I don't just want it, I need it. You saw my car.'

'I did,' he says. 'The one you're not living in.'

'Right.'

He nods.

'Well, I'm not living in it *yet*,' I correct myself, 'But if I don't get this room, I'm going to be low on options. You're watching a girl at the last-chance saloon here.'

'Oh dear.'

'Yeah,' I say emphatically. 'So, like, I really need it.'

He scratches that same hollow below his cheekbone.

'The room,' I clarify. 'I really need the room.'

'Huh.'

That's it. *Huh*. Nothing else.

My skin itches with irritation.

'By the sounds of it,' I continue, tone still amiable, 'you have a lovely place with your parents. Dun Laoghaire; that's a nice part of Dublin.'

'One of the nicest,' he agrees.

'And very far from here.'

'The complete opposite side of the city.'

'And since you can work from anywhere, you really don't need to be here,' I reason, 'so far from home and your family, especially after what you've all been through.'

Two lines appear across his forehead.

'I have to be around here. I've no choice. North Dublin is my courier beat.'

He bites his lip, a further crease appearing between his eyebrows as he considers what I'm saying.

I feared the brother reference was too much. But maybe it was just enough.

'Do you have friends in Howth?'

He shakes his head.

'Know anybody here at all?'

'Not a living soul.'

'Well there you go then,' I say, raising an arm and letting it flap down against my side. 'You'd be lonely, just you and Tessa,

68

rattling around in this house. You're used to going out, meeting people, wheeler dealing.'

'Wheeler. Dealing,' he echoes slowly, as if mulling over the meaning of the phrase.

He leans back against the hall table, where I've just left the parcel, and slowly folds his arms, legs meeting at the ankles. His limbs are long, his movements confident.

Despite it being significantly cooler in the foyer than outdoors, Conn appears equally comfortable. I ignore the goosebumps forming on my own legs.

'You know what I mean, you work in finance, you're' – I gesture from his expensive leather shoes up to his short, but still subtly styled, hair – 'you're a people person. You go places – cool, exclusive places, probably – you talk to cool, exclusive people.'

His nose twitches. He's back to looking very amused. 'Cool, exclusive people like you?' he says. 'Because you were the first person I spoke to today. The first person I spoke to in a couple of days, actually, if you don't count my parents.'

I don't know if he's making fun of me or playing mind games or what.

'No, not like me,' I say. 'I'm more suited to somewhere like here, with someone like Tessa. That's more my scene.'

'That sounds like a fun scene. And, actually, rather exclusive.'

'There's got to be somewhere more suitable for you. I know this place is free, but—'

'Yes?'

'Well,' I say, waving my hand the length of his body again, 'you can survive without free, clearly.'

'Clearly.'

I'm flustered, embarrassed. I'm not sure which is more irritating; him agreeing with everything I say or repeating it. Or maybe it's the general sense of having a jolly good time at my expense.

'I just mean, you worked in financial law, and you could do so again. That's a well-paid sector.'

He nods. 'Extremely well paid.'

'And like I said, Dun Laoghaire, it's a nice area. Forget working as a cleaner, your parents probably *had* a cleaner when you were a child.'

'Still do.'

Never mind. There's no contest. The agreeability is definitely more infuriating.

I'm stating facts, but I'm also pointing out his privilege. Shouldn't he be more embarrassed by his good fortune? We're Irish for god's sake, not American.

'I'd say it's a nice house.' I just about manage to get the words out.

'It's lovely,' he says. 'They're lovely people too. A bit sad these days, as you can imagine, but still lovely.'

'So you could just keep staying there then.'

'I could... And you could keep staying with your mam.'

'That's different.'

'Because she's sick?'

I think about the five-word note I left on her bedside locker as she slept. I clench my teeth. 'It's complicated.'

Something shifts in his eyes. Pity, remorse; I can't tell.

'So you want me to... just give you the room?'

A sigh of relief.

Finally. He's listening.

'Yes,' I say, breathlessly. 'That would be brilliant.'

'No problem.'

Another elated exhale. 'Thank you.'

'Will I draw up a legal document, signing it over to you, or...?'

'Well, that bit is probably for Tessa to...' I clamp my mouth shut. 'You're being sarcastic.'

'I am,' he concurs.

How can someone so agreeable be so bloody unhelpful?

I take back what I said about him being handsome. There isn't a single attractive thing about this man. Where most people have myriad personality traits, he has only smugness.

He looks even more delighted with himself now, as he scrunches up his face and pretends to think about something.

'What?' I ask flatly.

'I'm just...' He turns his eyes upwards as if searching his brain. I instantly regret asking what he was thinking. If only I could stand a modicum of silence. I've played right into his hand. 'What was it you said when I rescued your car from the marsh?'

Now it's my turn to play dumb.

'Ah yes,' he says, looking at me squarely. 'You owe me.'

'I meant a small favour, not my home!'

I inhale deeply. Time to put my pride to one side. 'If I don't get this room, I will be sleeping in my car tonight. There's no "probably" about it. I'm not low on options; I'm out of them. I have absolutely nowhere else to go. All right? That's how desperate I am.'

'So you need a room?'

'That's what I'm saying!'

'Yes, but I need *this* room,' he says, sharp eyes even more intense. 'I need to be in this house.'

'Why do you need to be in this house?' I all but shout, looking down the corridor to make sure the others haven't emerged yet. *How much is there to say?* 'You just agreed that you don't need to be here – or anywhere, in particular. And you don't need free.'

'I never agreed with that bit. You just said it.'

'I know you have money,' I exclaim. 'Your shoes and your teeth are too shiny for you not to have money!'

'I don't work,' he contends.

'But you could! This is Dublin, we're not short on financial sectors to work in.'

He doesn't say anything, just looks at me.

'So you could just go and get another job.'

This man had a lucrative career in soul-destruction or whatever, and he just stopped working because, what, he didn't feel like it any more? Meanwhile, I am a few hours away from sleeping in my front seat, crowbar in hand in case of carjackers.

'No,' he says, wistfully.

'No what?'

'No I can't just go and get another job.'

'Why not?'

He pushes his hands deep into his pockets. 'Like you say: It's complicated.' And that's it. He feels no obligation to say any more.

Down the hallway, the kitchen door opens and footsteps emerge. I resist the urge to kick his shins. And how did I end up covered in ten times more mud? I glare instead. Yemi says even my glare is apologetic; but she hasn't seen this one.

'Let me take that bag for you, Maura,' I say, stepping forward as they approach. 'See? No problem with my back. Are we going upstairs? I can help you with the steps, Tessa.'

'I can manage, dear. But thank you.'

'No problem,' I say, throwing Maura's bag over my shoulder and looking at Conn triumphantly.

He widens his eyes into patronising delight.

'Have I said how beautiful your home is?' I gush, attention back on Tessa. 'And the name. Hope House. It's perfect.'

'I thought it was sickly sweet at first,' says Tessa, 'but it grew on me. It's actually named after the man who built this place, rather than the emotion. It's not as unique as you'd think either – there's one in Skerries, and another in Arklow. We get their post all the time.'

I glance at the package on the hall, feeling instantly better about the whole thing. They've been here before; they'll know what to do.

'So, this is the entrance hall,' says Tessa, sweeping her free hand behind her. The front door is taller than a standard one and probably twice the width. It's made of heavy, dark wood and is flanked by two tall but narrow windows built into recesses. 'The hallway you've just been down leads to the kitchen and the pantry. Off to the left here we have the sitting room, then this is the dining room – though we never eat in there, the table is too big – and straight ahead is the library.'

She pushes open the doors to all three rooms so we can glance in. They are all large and sparsely furnished, mainly with wooden pieces, though the sitting room has two very comfortable-looking couches. There are small sections of paint, mainly in the far top corners, starting to peel and they each contain a wood-burning stove, though the sitting room has the only one currently in use. It's also the only space without a glimpse of the sea. There's a single French window at the rear of the room that looks out onto a small coppice of what looks like oak.

The library is amazing; wall to wall books, an actual bookcase-attached ladder to reach the top shelves, and two larger French windows along the external wall that fill the space with light. Through the windows, which actually operate as doors, you can see almost nothing but water. There are two mismatched armchairs with faded floral upholstery, a dark hardback chair and small matching desk, and a few worn rugs layered over each other on the floor.

'I'm a big reader,' explains Tessa. 'My late husband referred to books as dust-catchers. Somehow, I loved him anyway. But that's why I decided to keep them all in one place, so he could stop doing exaggerated coughs every time he spotted more than two together.'

'I love to read,' I gush. My solitariness is really coming into its own today. 'I read anything and everything. I just finished the latest Chelsea Mangan. Do you know those books?'

'Oh, I love Chelsea Mangan,' exclaims Tessa, suddenly excited. 'My daughter and I used to devour those books. I've rediscovered them recently. *A Country Life* is still my favourite.'

'Mine too!'

'She's a great writer,' says Conn who must, for the first time, be feeling like I could be a threat.

'Who's that?' I ask, barely able to contain myself.

'Chelsea Mangan.'

I'm positively beaming now, but I let Tessa set him straight.

'Chelsea Mangan is the protagonist,' she says, kindly. 'They're written by Robin Leech.'

There are few things you can rely on like the self-assuredness of a privileged white man. He will not be deterred. 'That's who I meant,' he says. 'She's a great writer.'

Tessa nods, clearly willing to let this one go. My face is aching from the smile.

'Let's go upstairs, will we?' she says, leading us back into the hallway where, I suddenly notice, a grand staircase to my left. The bottom of the steps are in darkness, but there's a large, panelled window ahead on the return.

Tessa puts one hand on the rail and keeps the other on her stick.

Maura and Senan follow her.

Then it's Conn. Then me.

'Robin Leech,' I whisper, skipping two steps so I can fall in beside him, 'is a he.'

The main staircase is two flights and the window occupies the entire breadth of the return. On the first full storey, we emerge onto a long narrow corridor. There's a small window at one end, mainly looking out onto the trees that separate Hope House from its neighbour, and a door at the other, with several more doors dotted on the opposing walls between.

Tessa walks us down to the window end. She opens the furthest door. 'The bathroom...' It leads to another long but narrow space, with a toilet at the far end and a bath, shower and sink against the walls. It's old fashioned, but in good condition.

'This is the door to the next storey, but it's closed off. Then these are bedrooms,' she says, turning and making her way through us. She walks the length of the landing, gesturing. 'Or they can be. I don't see the need to keep beds in all of them. There are more rooms up on the second floor, but that's been shut off since I moved in. Same with the scullery in the basement. We didn't need the space and it's too hard to keep clean.'

'Again, just to say, I'd be very happy to help with the cleaning.'

'Okay, Chloe. Thank you.'

Tessa leads us up to the other end of the corridor where her bedroom is located. On either side of it is a door. 'This is my daughter's room,' she gestures to the left, 'and this was Senan's. He has finally cleared out the last of his junk so that someone else can have it.'

'I found magazines in there that were older than Otis,' he says.

Tessa pushes open the door on the right. The room is as sparsely furnished as all the others, with a large oak bed, a matching desk and chair, and nothing else of significance. There's a thick, deep purple throw at the end of the bed, which matches the curtains. The space is vast and there's a huge bay window with a built-in box seat on the opposite wall. Beyond it is an uninterrupted view of the sparkling sea. It's the same sight you see on the drive up here, but the extra elevation makes the expansiveness even more startling.

'Wow,' I gasp.

I glance at Conn. For once, we are on the same page.

'It's perfect,' he whispers.

His reverence surprises me. Surely Dubai was full of amazing views. Why is he so set on this house?

'So that's it really,' says Tessa, pulling the door closed again. My heart quickens, a sense of sudden panic. If I want everything to be okay, this has to be it; I need to be sleeping in that room tonight. I can feel it in my bones. 'If anyone has any questions?' she asks.

I consider falling to my knees and begging for the room (dignity was never part of my candidacy) but Maura gets in first. She produces her notebook and flicks through the pages. 'Re general availability, I don't think Conn confirmed his nocturnal schedule. Do you have much of a night life?'

'As in going out to clubs and parties? No. Not since I got back from Dubai.'

'So you'd be here?' Senan verifies.

There's a pause, and I feel a sudden surge of hope that all is not lost.

'I do go out sometimes, at night,' he admits. 'Not clubbing or anything. Just... out.'

'Late?'

'Fairly late.'

Maura goes to ask for more details, but Senan shuts her down with a look. I guess they can't pry into Conn's privacy.

'I would be open to friends or partners staying over occasionally, but I would want it run by me in advance,' says Tessa.

'It's not a girlfriend,' says Conn, quickly. Even though it definitely is.

Why doesn't he just move in with her? And leave this place to me.

'I'm always here at night,' I interject. 'You can count on that. I have absolutely nowhere else to be.'

Conn can definitely feel the balance shifting in my favour too because he suddenly has a question.

'Chloe,' he says, unexpectedly. 'Where did you see the notice for the room?'

I narrow my eyes. I know exactly what he's doing. But this sneaky little toerag didn't count on my excellent memory. Mam says it's because I haven't destroyed all my brain cells with mindless scrolling. 'The community centre, of course,' I say sweetly. 'Where else? That was the only place Tessa put it. Weren't you listening when she said that earlier?'

'On the big noticeboard, the one outside the centre, beside the entrance?'

'Yes.'

Tessa frowns slightly and looks to Maura, who is distracted by something else, and I realise too late what he is doing.

'I mean, it was a noticeboard, I can't quite remember where...'

'I have a question,' says Maura, shifting her body ninety degrees so Senan is no longer in her line of sight. 'For Conn. Why won't you be here at nights? If it's not a girlfriend, is it a boyfriend?'

'That's an excellent question,' I say, turning towards him too.

He glances around the group.

'You don't have to answer that,' says Senan, warily.

Conn shakes his head good-naturedly. He looks perfectly relaxed, but I know he's not. I just know it.

'It's no problem,' he says. 'No boyfriends or girlfriends.'

Then he spreads his hands out. 'I go owl watching.'

'Owl watching?'

I've heard of the one per cent enjoying yachting, polo, even a spot of hunting, but owl watching is a new one.

'Is that a euphemism or...?' asks Maura.

'Nope. It's just watching owls.'

He smiles at me. 'It's a lot of fun.'

'Can I just say,' I counter before the balance can shift again. Who knows if these people are buying his dreadful cover story, or how they feel about nocturnal birds. 'I really, really want this room.'

'Me too,' interrupts Conn.

My jaw clenches. 'And I may not know this road as well as Conn knows it, but I love the area and—'

'You know this road?' asks Tessa.

'No,' replies Conn, confused.

'You do.'

He shakes his head.

'You said, outside, about the marsh and the sign? That it was there until last week?'

He's still looking at me blankly.

'You said this was the perfect house!'

'Maybe you're still confused?' he says. 'I know it's been a tricky day for you.' The smug arse has the audacity to look concerned.

I glance around at the rest of the group for support, but they all look mildly worried for my sanity too.

I shut my mouth and feel the breeze as the pendulum slips from my grasp and lands where the balance of favour always lands: on the side of people like Conn Horgan.

# TESSA

. . . . . . . . . .

Senan closes the door. It's just him and me in the kitchen. Otis and Maura have stayed out in the entrance hall with Chloe and Conn so that it looks less like we're squirrelled away talking about them for the second time.

'I know neither of them are ideal,' says Senan, launching into a spiel as soon as the latch clicks into place. 'He's into owls and she's, well, you know, kooky – but it's only short term, and otherwise we have to start the whole thing—'

I put him out of his misery. 'I'll take them both.'

'What?'

'I will take them both.'

He opens his mouth, then closes it again. 'Really?'

'Yes, really.'

'And when you say take them both...'

'Into my home. I will take them both into this house and give them each a room, Chloe and Conn. I'll have two lodgers.'

He considers this for a moment. 'What's the catch?'

'No catch,' I say.

'I thought...'

'You thought I was going to find a way to talk my way out of the whole thing.'

'It is what you usually do,' he says, only a little contritely. 'And you're very good at it.'

'True. But this time there's no need to get out of it. I can see how beneficial the situation could be.'

His face lights up. 'Mam, yes, I... This is such good news. It really will be beneficial to have two people in the house with you, especially when their schedules sit so well together. He'll be here in the day, she'll be here at night. It's perfect. Oh, I'm really so happy about this now, I can't tell you. Thank you, Mam.'

I smile and nod and don't correct him, even though he has taken me up all wrong. My poor, anxious boy.

I wasn't talking about me benefiting from the situation, I meant I could see how beneficial it would be to *them*: Chloe and Conn.

Chloe has an admirable spunkiness, but it's built on people-pleasing and nervous energy. If a life in social work has taught me anything, it is that people need certainty to thrive. Stability is the greatest gift we can give our children; financial certainty is a godsend to us all; family in whatever form it might take – friends, relatives, a home, once there's something that's always there – allows you to live a more confident life. I'll need to get to the bottom of her specifics, but Chloe is crying out for certainty.

Conn appears more together but the loss he is dealing with is monumental; the cruelty, the sorrow, the guilt. Missing someone pulls you back to where they were; but if you're not careful, the guilt will keep you there. I can help with that. I can make a difference with him.

'One of them can have your old room, and the other can go in the first guest room. Leave Bea's as it is. There's too much of her stuff to sort through.' Whoever said girls were the tidier sex never met my daughter. 'The guest room has the same view anyway.'

'All right,' says Senan, who would probably throw his kidney into the bargain at this point. 'No problem.'

Then, because he clearly thinks I could change my mind at any minute: 'Will we call them in and deliver the good news?'

We run the proposal by them. Senan explains that Conn will generally try to be at the house during the day and Chloe at night. I interrupt to make it clear that nobody needs to be here *all* the time; popping in and out is enough. And of course there will be crossover.

'I actually have one thing on Tuesday mornings that I need to go to. If that's okay?' says Conn.

'Yes, of course, you really don't need to clear that. I'll be at Beginners' Gardening anyway, but even without that, it's fine. It's not a strict timetable. Just think of it as your home,' I say, so they all understand. Particularly Senan.

Conn is delighted from the get-go. Chloe, whilst outwardly grateful, takes a few minutes to come around.

'Both of us?' she clarifies. 'Me and him?'

Conn beams. 'You and me, roomie,' he says, and something clicks at the side of her jaw.

'Senan will run through the details with you, but let's have dinner together tonight,' I say, heading to the worktop where I've left my handbag. 'Give me a chance to get to know you both better – to hear your stories, to learn how you tick.' My tone is jovial (though of course I'm deadly serious) but it's hard to say which of them looks the most uncomfortable. This only intrigues me more. 'I have a lasagne that just needs to be heated up,' I add. 'We'll eat at seven. If I'm not back in time, Conn, you can stick it in the oven, yes?'

He nods. 'That's great, thank you, Tessa.'

'Yes, thank you,' says Chloe, coming around. 'This is... thank you.'

A warmth fizzles inside me as I flick through the debris of my bag for my keys. Senan says I'm uncomfortable with emotions, but I just don't like to dwell on things.

Up and at them – onto the next; that's my approach.

'And no hanky-panky,' says Maura. 'Tessa doesn't need a couple in the house, making her feel like she's the third wheel, trying to get squatters' rights and stealing the place from under her.'

'Maura, please.'

'That will absolutely not be a problem,' says Chloe.

Conn grins at this. 'Definitely not,' he concurs.

Then I remember. 'Conn, did you tell Otis the board at the hall was covered in planning permission notices?'

'That's right. Something to do with making the building taller. Maybe adding a floor? I'm not sure. I was looking underneath for a taxi number, which is how I saw your notice. I didn't read them properly.'

'Do you know anything about this?' I ask Maura.

My friend sticks out her bottom lip. 'Haven't been there since Friday. I'm sure it's nothing. What could it be?'

'Well I'm going down to check it out. I promised I'd drop in some supplies for tomorrow's life-drawing class anyway.'

'Are they still going ahead? I thought they couldn't find a model.'

'They couldn't. So Malachy is stepping in.'

'Ah for feck sake!' says Maura. 'Again?'

'He's a good subject. The longer the session goes on, the more he concentrates on holding the pose. Apparently, it's a real challenge for the students to capture that skin shade.'

Maura shudders.

'Could you pack up the things on the hall sideboard for me, Senan?'

'I just need to print out another contract for Chloe...'

'I can do it,' says Conn. 'If I'm going to be useful, I might as well start now.'

I grimace. But this is the deal. I help them, and they can help me. I give a sharp nod.

'It's everything on the hall table? I'll just put it in a bag?'

'You can take that,' I say, nodding to the box by the window. 'And yes, everything that's out there. Don't forget any of it. You can leave it by the car. Mine is the one with the Ukrainian flag bumper sticker.'

Conn and the box disappear through the door.

'I suppose I'll go to the hall with you,' sighs Maura, shoving the unused score paddles back into her bag. 'I've a couple of things to do there myself. Deregister from the life-drawing course, for a start.'

* * * * * * * *

Monday afternoons at the Project are busy. There's Rumba for Retirees, which is one of our most popular and dangerous classes (it has been responsible for two heart attacks, but also three second marriages, so the odds are still in favour of keeping it going); Pottery for Beginners, which Malachy attends despite having to go straight into Mindful Meditation afterwards to deal with the stress; and Darts and Crafts. The latter was the result of bad timetabling and the need to find a shared space for beer-bellied men who speak little and move less and capable women who are chatting and stitching from the second they arrive. The only thing the crafters love more than a gossip is a project, which is probably why Darts and Crafts has produced as many romantic matches as Rumba.

When we pull up at the hall, there are three men standing out front smoking.

'Afternoon, gentlemen. Looking well, Jimbo,' I say as myself and Maura push open the glass door. I don't know all the darters' names, but there's always at least one called Jimbo.

Two of the men tip their index fingers to their foreheads and grunt in acknowledgement.

Inside, the foyer is empty. I can hear calls of 'Rotate your hips! Rotate your hips!' from the main hall and peer through the small window to see couples shuffling across the floor. 'Follow Trevor's lead,' the teacher says, and I see that Trevor from Radical Activism is in the middle of the floor, demonstrating some sort of shimmy to two couples. He has excellent rhythm. I'm about to beckon Maura over, but she calls to me first.

'This is the planning notice.' She drops the box of supplies for the life-drawing class at her feet and unpins an A4 page from the noticeboard. 'They're going to knock the place down.'

I turn from the window so quickly that I almost trip over my stick. I take the paper from Maura and read it, then I scan all the other pages on the noticeboard. The thing is plastered in them. No wonder nobody saw my advert.

'They can't...' I mutter, reading through as much as I can. 'The money-grubbing...'

'Box step! Box step!' comes the instructor's voice from the main hall.

There are change of use notices and others seeking planning permission to alter the structure. A lot of the pages are duplicates. I've protested the demolition of a fair few historical buildings in my time and understand the basics of the planning system. The property owners – in this case a small consortium of businessmen who rent the premises to the local council for community use – are legally required to give notice that they intend to seek permission from the planning authorities to make these changes. They need to make sure this notice is visible; hence the board being wallpapered in them. The actual effect is one of overwhelm. I doubt if anyone took the time to sort through these.

'What exactly are they planning to do?' says Maura. 'The community project has been running for twenty years and the hall has been here longer than that. Why would they want to change it?'

'Money,' I say, pulling three more pages from the noticeboard. 'This' – I wave two sheets at her – 'says that they are planning to knock down the hall entirely. They say there are fire and safety issues, among other things. Which is absolute nonsense since we fundraised to upgrade the building just three years ago. And these pages' – I shake the others – 'are a notice looking to build a six-storey hotel in its place.'

Maura stares at me open-mouthed. Then she takes the pages. 'But they can't do that, can they? They've rented it out to the council. They can't just take it off them.'

'It was a twenty-year lease,' I say, my mind already racing through the logistics. 'It ends… next month, I think? Maybe even this month. Technically, they can do what they want with it then. And there seems to be no end to the appetite for hotels in Dublin. I can only imagine it's a damn sight more profitable than renting a modest hall to the council to hold free classes in.'

*Forward step and swing your hips!*

'But they can't just knock down the centre. Hundreds of people use it every day. Where else will we go? I might be deregistering myself from sketching Malachy's nether regions, but I'm still doing three classes here every week – and you're teaching two of them. Where will I go? Where will you go? Oh my god,' she looks at me, alarm descending. 'Where will *Malachy* go?'

*Rotate! Forward and rotate!*

'There has to be a health and safety argument for keeping the Project open at the very least,' says Maura. 'Without this place to contain him, Malachy will be out roaming the streets, aggressively handing in CVs to anywhere with an open door and chaining himself to bins.'

As if on cue, the side door that leads down the corridor to the smaller rooms opens and Malachy appears. His hands are covered in clay and his head is somewhere between crimson and tart.

He's steamrolling towards the exit, a man on a mission, when he spots us, and marches this way instead.

'Three years I've been doing Beginners' Pottery. Three years! And I still can't make a bowl that doesn't look like a shiteing plate! I'm following the instructions. The teacher says I mustn't

87

be but I am I am I fucking am!' He stops sharply and takes three very stressed breaths. 'I told her I needed a smoke or I was going to put my own head on the wheel and spin it. Couldn't end up much worse. I'm going to bum one. Is Jimbo out front?'

'Not to send your blood pressure completely through the roof, but have you seen this?' says Maura, pushing the pages towards him.

He glances at them for a couple of seconds, then looks away. 'You know I'm not good at that sort of reading. Mr Bentley put those up on Saturday. He said it wasn't anything important, just some official requirement he had to look after. I'm sorry it covered your notice, Mrs Doherty. I did my best to keep it visible, but he was very insistent.'

'It says they're going to raze the hall, Malachy.'

'They're *wha*'?!' he roars.

The planning notice takes the brunt of his spittle.

I give him a brief summary of the notices and a couple of minutes to get all the expletives and general threats to the physical safety of Mr Bentley and his 'fat cat cronies' out of his system.

'We're not going to burn out anyone's car,' I say, when he starts to run out of steam. 'Nor are we going to dismember anyone.' I hold up a finger. 'Not even their pets.'

'Tessa's right,' says Maura, deflated. 'It's their hall, legally. The greedy feckers. They can do what they want with it. No point getting ourselves in trouble when there's nothing we can do.'

'I never said that,' I counter. 'Of course there's something we can do. Activism 101: There's nothing as strong as people power. This hall may not have double-glazed windows, and the doors might groan like every spirit that ever returned to earth is haunting them, but this place is run on people power. You could generate the national grid with it.'

'So what are we going to do?'

'We're going to fight back. We're going to do everything we can to stop this from happening. These are notices of an intention to apply for planning permission. It hasn't been granted yet. This thing is far from over. First step is to hold an emergency Radical Activism meeting ASAP.'

'I've got nowhere to be,' says Maura.

Malachy nods his agreement. 'It's best for me and the pottery wheel to give each other some space anyway.'

'Let's get Trevor too. He's in there, dancing up a storm.'

I slip a copy of each of the notices into my blazer pocket and lead the troops into the hall.

'Trevor!' I call from the sideline. He's dancing with a woman now and quicksteps her over to us.

'Tessa, hello,' he says, still swaying the woman from side to side. 'Maura, you look divine as always. Malachy, you... nice to see you.'

Malachy wipes a line of sweat from his forehead.

'What can I do for you chaps? That's it, Gloria, swing the hips. Swing them!'

The woman frowns, sweat forming on her hairline too. Trevor, meanwhile, doesn't miss a breath.

'We're holding an emergency Radical Activism meeting.'

'I can't leave now, Tessa, I'm helping Senora O'Reilly give today's class. The rest of the students don't quite have my Latino rhythm, to say the least.'

His dance partner's brow furrows further. It's unclear if her protruding veins are down to physical exertion or Trevor.

'Come on, Gloria,' he enthuses. 'You're not dead yet. Feel. The. Beat!' He throws his head back and swings it in a semi-circle. He looks possessed.

'It's an emergency, Trevor,' I say, wondering now why I'm bothering to involve his Latino rhythm at all. 'It's to do with the hall. There's a plan to knock the place down, and we need to come up with a counter-attack. Immediately.'

'All right,' he says. 'If it's an emergency.' He signals to Annie O'Reilly that he's stepping out. 'We're nearly done anyway. Gloria, I want you to keep moving, keep grooving, and, for the love of all that is Latin, swing your hips!'

'I'm doing my best with what the surgeons gave me,' she snaps.

'Should we call Susan too?' asks Malachy.

'Good thinking,' I say. 'I'll see if I have a phone number...'

Trevor extricates himself and Gloria continues to hold the pose, moving from side to side.

He conducts the woman as he follows us out of the hall. 'Swing. Your. Hips!'

'For the last time, Trevor Shaughnessy, these are not my hips!'

'I think I'm on to a winner there,' he says, catching up and falling into step with me.

'How do you mean?'

'Gloria. Couldn't you feel the energy?' Trevor pushes the door open and I glance back at the woman still shuffling awkwardly around the hall with her invisible dance partner and a glower that could start a fire. 'The woman is stone mad about me.'

# CHLOE

· · · · · · · · · · ·

**T**he three of us are in the bathroom and Senan is explaining how the immersion works. 'The pipes make quite a bit of noise when they're getting going, but you're both sleeping at the other end of the house, so it shouldn't be an issue,' he says, rooting through the hot press until he finds the right-sized sheets. 'Just one more pillowcase...'

I don't mention that I already have a full set of bedding in my car. No need to draw more attention to the fact that I turned up fully ready to move in.

'Thunder Cats or My Little Pony?' he asks, holding up the two faded items. 'My sister and I had very gender-normative interests.'

'Thunder Cats,' I say, hastily.

But Conn gamely takes the My Little Pony case from Senan. 'I always had a soft spot for Sundance.'

The linen is deposited to the bedrooms (I'm in Senan's old room) and we head downstairs where we're given spare keys and a demonstration of how the stoves work. Then Senan takes us out back to see where they keep the fuel.

'It's okay at the moment,' he says, standing in the dilapidated shed, shovelling coal into a large plastic tub that once contained paint. 'It's only the living room fire that's kept going all year round. But come next month, maybe even the end of this one, it'll require several trips out here every day to get enough coal, briquettes and wood to keep the place warm.'

To show my commitment to helping, I take the bucket from Senan and insist on carrying it into the house after him.

Conn and I both go to exit the tiny shed at the same time. He is carrying a few blocks of wood in the crook of one arm.

'After you.'

'No, no. You go first,' I reply, not budging from the curved doorway where we're both forced to stand sideways, facing the other.

There's barely enough space between us for the bucket, and there's not enough space for him to stand up straight.

'I insist,' he says, rotating his right shoulder away from the arch at his back.

I shake my head, bringing my second hand to the handle.

He looks down at the container. 'That's going to get heavy pretty soon.'

'Not as heavy as your conscience,' I say, resisting the urge to put down the coal.

'Excuse me?'

'Pretending you didn't say this was the perfect house for you, denying that you're familiar with the street. What are you up to exactly? Are you casing the place?'

He laughs. I feel the warmth of his breath on my crown. 'Says the woman who no more saw the advert for the room than took a shower today. You were the one who turned up carrying a crowbar.'

I glare at him – or more – I glare at his chin. It's the best I can do without tilting my head the whole way back.

He runs his free hand through his hair until it lands at the back of his neck. It's supposed to show how relaxed he is, how he could stay here all day, but I see the effort to stretch out his hunched shoulders.

'You really should go in,' I say, gesturing towards Senan, who is standing across the yard at the steps that lead up to the side of the main house. What used to be the door to the shed is now rotting on the grass outside so I have a clear view. 'Your back will be as destroyed as your trousers in a minute.'

'You must be getting us confused. I managed to keep my clothes clean.'

I allow the bucket to swing forward slightly.

'No you didn't.'

It's dark and squashed in here and I can't get a sharp enough angle to see his face properly, but I feel the grimace.

'Soot doesn't make any difference to the state of your legs, I suppose.'

'Nope,' I say, pleasantly. 'Manky and proud.'

Turns out he was on to something. Agreeing with someone who's trying to get a rise out of you *is* very enjoyable.

He doesn't move. Neither do I.

My shoulder sockets feel the strain.

I suck in my cheeks to mask the effort and readjust my stance.

'Let me carry that,' says Conn, quieter, more reluctant, like he actually means it.

I tilt my face up as far as I can.

He has one deep vertical line above his right eyebrow but the rest of his skin is remarkably smooth, almost cherubic. It betrays the sharpness of his cheekbones and gaze.

'It's a bit late for chivalry now,' I say, inches from his face. 'You were trying to make me homeless an hour ago.' The bucket is heaving at my arms but I try to keep my breathing level.

He blinks. Brown lashes sweeping the slight depressions below, eyes still vibrant despite the lack of light.

'I'm not being chivalrous,' he says, steadily. His Adam's apple rises, then falls. He doesn't do anything in a hurry and it's making me even more scattered. 'I just don't want my trousers completely destroyed.'

'Are you two coming?' calls Senan, from about thirty metres away.

I hold out for as long as I can, maintaining eye contact, resisting the urge to swallow, but I start to feel light-headed. The longer nobody speaks, the more I feel like I'm letting someone down, like Senan is standing at that door getting increasingly irritated.

I keep looking up, neck straining, legs weak. But then, maybe because of the prolonged silence, or maybe because Conn's stare never lets up, I break.

I swing the bucket around, taking a decent last swipe at the dark-grey material that covers his legs, and head for the main house.

Somehow, I resist the urge to look back.

The last thing Senan does before heading to the school is get us to sign tenancy agreements. They're straightforward; highlighting the lack of rent, that both parties can terminate the contract with two weeks' notice, that the initial tenancy period is for three months but may be extended.

'Mam is adamant she'll be back to her former physical condition by then, but I'm keeping a more open mind,' he says.

'I thought it wasn't a bad fall,' I venture.

'That's Tessa's narrative, and she's an impossible woman to disagree with. She'd have you accepting that black was white. When she wants something, she's like a dog with a bone. You'll find out soon enough.' He takes the pen from Conn and hands it to me. 'I hope neither of you have any great secrets because my mother will get those out of you too, she always does.'

I glance at Conn, who looks suitably perturbed.

*If you won't tell me what you're up to with this house, then just wait until Tessa finds out.*

'She's young enough though,' says my new nemesis, steering the conversation back.

'Don't I know it,' replies Senan. '*In my sixties* is emblazoned on my brain. Although she'd have you believing she was an ingénue. She'll be seventy next month. We're throwing her a surprise party, even though she hates surprises and her birthday and last time we tried to throw her one it was a disaster. There's every chance she'll walk in here, see all her loved ones, turn on her heels and march right back out before we have a chance to yell "surprise". But I am nothing if not a glutton for punishment.'

'Sounds like fun,' I enthuse. 'I've never been to a surprise party.' I've been to very few parties full stop.

'We won't say anything,' adds Conn.

'No,' I agree. 'Will your sister be at it? It'd be nice to meet her.'

Senan takes the signed form from me and places it on top of the other. 'I'm afraid that won't be happening,' he says.

'Oh, that's a pity.'

I glance at Conn, who gives his head a short shake. There's a shift in the atmosphere, but I feel it too late.

Of course it'd be me who'd open a can of worms.

'Does she live far away?' I add hopefully.

'Not exactly,' says Senan. 'My sister is dead.'

I open my mouth, but the words stall. 'I'm... I'm sorry...'

'Not that we have a body. But that's what happens when you jump in the sea, without a thought for everyone you're leaving behind.'

'I'm sorry.'

'Don't be,' he says, tapping the contracts against the table before shaking them into a large envelope.

I beseech Conn to say something, but he is no longer meeting my gaze.

'The way Tessa talked about her,' I begin. 'I just thought... She said she left home.'

'My sister walked out of this house one night and never came back,' says Senan. 'We got a presumption of death order last year. She threw herself off the cliffs. Myself and my mother used to agree about that, although recently Tessa's been talking like she's still here.'

'It must be so hard for you both.'

'I've come to terms with it,' he says. 'But I suppose she'll always be Tessa's baby. She was five years younger than me and she very much fulfilled the annoying younger sibling brief. She was smart and complicated and difficult. And then she was missing. And now that's all she is: missing, presumed dead.'

He speaks like he's merely imparting information, but there's an edge.

'That's terrible,' I say, desperately, worthlessly. 'You must still be reeling. It's so recent. It's... I'm really sorry.'

Senan looks at me.

'Recent? Oh no,' he says. 'We got the death cert last year, but my sister has been missing for ten years.'

# TESSA

● ● ● ● ● ● ● ● ● ●

I'm driving down the Dublin Road looking for somewhere to pull in so I can phone my new lodgers and suddenly I am thinking about Bea.

She'd like Chloe and Conn – or she'd be interested in them, at least. She'd probably have shown Chloe straight to the shower and shut the door after her. And she'd fancy Conn – he's a less-dishevelled version of her type. I imagine it's how her taste would have evolved.

For a long time, I didn't think about Bea. I thought about the cause, the fight for answers, but not the person. Not about the brilliant, fierce daughter I grew inside me, fed from my body, and adored whether she felt that adoration or not. First time I held Bea I swear she frowned. She was hard on people from the off, not least herself.

For a long time, thinking about her was too painful and pain is not an emotion I dwell on. There is nothing useful in pain.

But then three months ago that changed. The mind goes to unexpected places when you're lying on your landing floor, waiting to be discovered.

I don't believe in ghosts. And I hope with all my heart that there is no afterlife. The idea that Bernard might have been looking down on us, seeing how I favoured work over our children, is too much to bear.

He was always better with Bea than I was and she worshipped him. Daddy's little girl. A patriarchal construct, but true nonetheless. He was more patient, more accepting, and they got on better than me and her ever did. But that doesn't mean I don't love her as much as her father did, or more even. I understand her in a way he couldn't and on those rare occasions when she needed me, nobody else would do. From the time he could talk, Senan called me 'Mam', but with Bea it was either 'Mammy' or 'Tessa'. I'm her best friend or her mortal enemy. There's no in-between.

I knew she was depressed. I just didn't believe she was *that* depressed. I was working with some of the country's most vulnerable people on a daily basis – people entirely forgotten by the state and society – and despite all my professional knowledge of how mental illness works, I still couldn't help thinking: 'What does my daughter have to be depressed about?'

She was twenty-six; she didn't need monitoring, and if I was in the house we just fought. My presence made things worse. In the final few months, just asking how she was made her incandescent with rage. She'd always been dramatic and, to my shame, I thought she was spoilt. So I was absent. There were a lot of people elsewhere crying out for my help.

Sometimes Bea would roar that she was going to go to France or America or England and never come back. I never heard her say she was going to throw herself off the cliffs. But others did. Afterwards, I thought this was because she knew that, professionally, I'd be duty-bound to act if she made threats to her life. But in the past few months I've wondered if it was because she didn't kill herself. Maybe I was the only one to whom she'd actually told the truth.

So yes, I don't believe in an afterlife because I can't stand the idea of Bernard up there, watching me fail us both, flittering away our years of effort. But I also hope there's not an afterlife because the Bea I experienced when I was lying on the upstairs corridor felt like the future, not the past.

I don't want to believe it was a shadow of wjat had been before.

I want to believe it was a premonition.

It was more solid than a vision. I could see her, though I knew she wasn't really there.

And I was comforted. I was so comforted.

We talked for hours about memories and books and love and about her dad and brother and nephew. It was probably the best we'd got on since that day on the beach.

*She* was the one who reminded *me* about that photo.

When she first disappeared, I used to cling to the fact that the picture of her and me and Senan on Curracloe beach was missing too. Her dad took that photo and she adored it. It hung in her bedroom from the day we got it developed until the day she vanished. Why would she bother taking it if she was going to kill herself? Somehow, in the intervening years, I forgot about its significance. I also forgot that there had been no suicide note.

It was like she'd come back to remind me not to give up. I had to stop talking about her in the past tense; I had to keep the faith. So I made the shift to thinking about Bea in the present and suddenly everything was brighter, less painful.

She stayed right there with me until Audrey arrived and scared her away.

It's the most un-me experience I've ever had. Which is why I haven't told anyone (if I was looking to have it explained away, I could do that myself) and also why I put such stock in it.

The experience revitalised me. It filled me with determination and renewed hope.

Foolish, irrational, beautiful hope.

And now, would you look at that.

Another sign to never give up – in the form of a parking space on this notoriously busy road.

I pull in between a white van and blue mini and have produced my phone before it occurs to me that I don't have a phone number for either Conn or Chloe. I call the landline.

It takes me a moment to remember my own number. It's been years since I've phoned it. It's been years since anyone was there to pick up.

It feels strange to know there are other people in the house again, but it doesn't feel like a betrayal.

In fact, it doesn't feel bad at all.

It's actually sort of exciting.

# CHLOE

· · · · · · · · · · ·

'You have to see it, Yemi. It's incredible. I didn't know Dublin came with views like this.'

'And just one more time, so I'm clear,' comes the voice from my phone, which is lying on the bed. My bed. My new, *massive* bed. 'How much is the rent?'

I take a pile of books and stack them vertically on the floor by the bay window. 'Still the same as the last time you asked.'

'Nothing?'

'Nothing,' I confirm. 'Zero. Nada. Not a dime.' I remove a few books from the top of the teetering pile and start a new column. 'Would it be rude to buy some furniture, do you think? How does it usually work? I could do with shelves.'

'How it usually works is that you pay an eyewatering sum to a faceless landlord every month and don't have enough money left over for anything to put on shelves let alone the shelves themselves, and it doesn't matter anyway because you don't have the space for them. You're lucky if you have the space to unfold your wall bed without hitting the oven.'

The water is incredible, twinkling and dancing and looking as giddy with possibilities as I feel. And even though I can't swim, I am overcome by an urge to find the nearest path down to a beach and dive in. 'I've never had this much space, ever.'

'You've only ever lived in one place, Chloe.'

'Yes, and it was a lot more cramped than this.'

I keep thinking I've unpacked the last of the wool and then another ball appears – like this orange cashmere lurking at the bottom of my wash bag. I place it at the top of the mini wool mountain that sits inside the door. Having unloaded everything, I can confirm that I did not, in fact, pack any knitting needles. Just twelve balls of wool.

I left in a whirlwind. There wasn't exactly time to consider what was going in the bags.

So I am repurposing the wool as a contemporary art installation, to give the place colour.

'Okay. Photos. Now,' demands Yemi. 'At least then I'll have something to give the police. A "before" to go with their "after". What the crime scene looked like prior to Chloe's axed body lying in the middle of it.'

'Ha, ha,' I say, back kneeling at the window box, trying to put order on the books. 'And you know I can't send photos.'

'Right, yes. I forget you're the only person I know with a phone older than them. No wonder this pensioner wants you living with her. She's probably delighted to have found someone who knows less than her about the twenty-first century.'

'Tessa has a high-tech phone actually. And those wireless earphone things you have. I saw her putting them in her bag.'

'What's the place called again?'

'Hope House.'

'Hope... House... Found it.'

'Where?' I say, looking around me and then out the window.

'On the internet, Chloe. Heard of it? Your new landlady can fill you in.' The sound of clacking down the line. 'Just switching to street view...'

I can picture Yemi at her tiny kitchen table, laptop open, phone on speaker beside it and the new baby sleeping on her chest.

'Oh, wow. Wow. Chloe!'

'I know!' I shriek, clambering up from the ground and taking my own phone off speaker. 'Isn't it amazing?' I say, throwing myself back on the bed.

'It's massive... I mean, I can't see it all, but even what I can... Those rosebushes!'

'Can you see the sea?'

'Hang on...' Faint typing. 'Holy shit! It's phenomenal!'

'Majestic,' I say, twisting around so I'm lying on my front, facing the window. 'Any time I'm looking anywhere else, I feel like I'm being ungrateful.'

'Okay, if you're not chopped into a thousand pieces by the time I get around to it, I am definitely coming to visit.'

From under me, I pull out the notebook where I have written my goals for the week. I am excited for my new-found freedom, but I'm also unmoored without Mam and the daily structure of pills, cooking, medical appointments. I crave structure. Mam being sick was probably the first time I really had it. Before that, life was led by whims.

The second task on my list – get more work shifts – has already been ticked off. The Delivery Dash office manager has me down for a full day of drop-offs tomorrow and the two days after that.

To complete the first task, the most important one, I was going to go to the library. But between work and wanting to put in time here, I'm not sure I'll be able to get there.

'While you're doing your internet sleuthing,' I say, twisting the phone slightly, 'do you think you could look up something for me?'

'What is it?'

'Well more someone... Paul Murtagh?'

The clacking stops. 'You want me to Google stalk your ex?'

'If you don't mind.'

The clacking resumes. 'You'd think I'd know what he was up to,' says Yemi, 'but Peter hasn't heard from him since graduation.'

Peter and Paul shared a flat when we were all at university. Yemi and I became friends in first year; she and Peter began dating in second year; and Paul and Peter were housed together in third. That was when we started going out. By fourth year, Yemi and Peter were engaged, and Paul and I assumed that one day we'd go the same way.

'Surely you've looked him up since you broke up?'

'Not in a while,' I say. 'Last I knew, he was doing that journalism master's.'

I used to search him obsessively. Every time I went to the library, I'd sit down at the computer and immediately type in his name like I was entering a password. I forced myself to stop that first Christmas when Mam came home from the hospital with news that her initial chemotherapy had not been successful. I needed to stop thinking about Paul Murtagh. I was only taunting myself with an impossible fantasy.

'Okay, I've got him on Twitter,' says Yemi. 'I forgot we follow each other... or we used to anyway! The fecker must have unfollowed me. Competition entry retweets not good enough for you, no, Paul?'

'Yemi, what does it say?'

'Paul Murtagh. Award-nominated journalist. Mmm... He's working for the *Dublin Press*.'

I sit up straighter, delight erupting inside me. 'Is he really?'

'LinkedIn says he's been there a year. City affairs reporter.'

'Wow. He would only have just finished the master's when he got that. The *Dublin Press* was his dream.'

'Pretty impressive.'

'Yeah,' I say, faintly.

I'm happy for him, I know I am, but as quickly as it came on, the joy dissipates.

Getting that job would have been one of the best things that ever happened to Paul, and I knew nothing about it. My stomach churns with the thought of how much I've missed, how much of my life has passed me by.

'The *Dublin Press* offices are in the city centre, right?' I ask.

*Clack clack clack.* 'Yep. Just off the quays.'

That means they'll be on Delivery Dash's books, and media organisations get tons of packages.

I can't get back the lost time, but I can ensure we don't waste any more.

I take back the list and put a tick beside item one: Devise Plan to Win Back the Love of My Life.

Downstairs, a phone is ringing. It's a landline. Tessa's landline.

Conn is down there, heating up the lasagne. I saw him on my last run in from the car. He offered to help on my first trip – when I was carrying *a duvet* – but he said nothing when I was heaving boxes of books up the stairs. I did at least notice

106

that the package is gone – hopefully winging its way to Skerries or Arklow.

'Just looking through some of his articles... He writes a lot,' says Yemi, as the phone downstairs continues to ring. 'I've read some of these actually,' she adds, 'but I never clocked the name.'

I remember Paul's excitement when he got his first by-line in the college newspaper. I can still see him, strolling into the canteen, sliding the page onto the table in front of me as he throws his other arm around my shoulders.

I close my eyes against the ache.

Since I left my mother's house, there's been an onslaught of memories – all these things I haven't thought about for so long hitting me like a tsunami. Hence the tears in the car. Paul gave me that CD for our one-year anniversary. It was extra special because of how hard it was to find a blank CD or a laptop with a disc drive that would allow him to fill it with songs. Paul never made fun of me for not being ultra-modern. My car has a CD player, but I didn't own any CDs. Until that one. When we broke up, I hid it away in my bedroom. In my hasty packing this morning, I found it, right beside my teaching degree and Lonely Planet Europe guide, as if I'd stashed all my roads not taken together. But what made it most special of all was the tracklist he'd written out on the back. A word highlighted in each line.

I Need a Forest Fire
When Will We Know
Now or Never
Love Yourself
If Anyone Cares

Set Fire to the Rain
Lost Your Way
Like That
I Can't Go On
Love Me Like You Do
See You Again

That was how Paul told me, for the first time, that he loved me.

I have to trust that he won't have forgotten about me.

How has Conn not answered the phone yet? The house isn't *that* big. He could have made it from the kitchen to the entrance hall by now.

'Oh shit,' mumbles Yemi.

'What?' I demand, sitting up straighter. 'He didn't write a piece about the wench who broke his heart, did he?'

'No, it's Akin,' she mutters. 'He just dropped off the boob and the milk sprayed all over my laptop.'

'How is little Akin?' I ask, ignoring the incessant ringing.

'Great,' she says. 'He never stops feeding. I haven't known a male so into my breasts since my first boyfriend.'

'Cute,' I say, grinning. 'But also kind of gross. Though you do have excellent breasts.'

*Ring ring.*

'Says the woman with the knockout figure.'

Yemi is one of the beautiful people my mam feels sorry for, only she's also beautiful on the inside so she insists on bigging me up – the compliment's verity is irrelevant.

'I'll come see you guys soon.'

*Ring ring.* 'See how Akin is...' *Ring ring.* 'See how he's...' *Ring ring.* 'See how he's doing.' *Ring ring.* RING RING. RING RING. 'Flipping hell! How hard is it to answer a phone?!'

'What?'

'The landline, downstairs, it's just ringing and ringing and he's not picking it up. How long does it take to put a lasagne in the oven? He probably doesn't know how to answer a phone. He's probably down there looking around, wondering where his PA has got to.'

'Who's he? The other lodger? Sean?'

'Conn,' I correct her. 'It's not that hard, Conn! You just put your hand on the receiver and... Okay. It's stopped. Finally.'

'What's his story anyway? Is he our age? Is he... normal?'

'He's a few years older probably. He was some sort of lawyer-banker who worked in Dubai until June. These days he doesn't work because he doesn't want to and I guess he doesn't have to now that he has a free place to live.'

'Interesting.'

'He goes out a lot at night, apparently. Wouldn't tell us where. I assumed it was a girlfriend, but he spun some story about going owl watching, which instantly makes me think he's up to something dodgy. Maybe *that's* how he's getting money...'

'What's owl watching? Oh wait, is that the kinky thing with the—'

'No, no, stop,' I say, thrusting my hand out into the air. 'He means literally watching owls. But who's ever heard of that? So then, where does he go? Whatever it is, it has him too busy to find time for paid labour.'

Yemi is about to say something, but I cut in. 'And he's not just smug, he's sort of *faux cool*, like nothing really bothers him. He thinks he's handsome. That's very obvious. He thinks *a lot* of himself. I honestly think he could be a psychopath.'

'So what you're saying is when the gardai come to me with the "after" crime scene photos, I should suggest Conn as the chief suspect rather than your landlady?'

'I'm just annoyed on Tessa's behalf. She's trying to do something nice by letting people live here for free, and he's taking advantage. Anyway,' I say, with a deep breath, 'it doesn't matter because one entitled co-habitant is a small price to pay for free accommodation and a chance at an independent life.'

'Speaking of... your mam's still calling me.'

I wince. 'I'm sorry,' I say. 'I'll text her.'

She's still calling me too. There were an additional nine calls by the time I got back out to my car and there's been two call waiting beeps since I started talking to Yemi.

'Don't apologise. Just tell me what to say. I'm not being all "As a mother" about it but like, now that I am a mother, I feel for her. She's really worried about you. She's sick, Chloe, and she doesn't understand why you left.'

The guilt, the guilt. In the nights when I would lie awake worrying about all the things that were trying to kill my mother, I often thought it would be the guilt that got me. Will I never be free of it?

'Did she get her latest results?' Yemi asks gently. 'Was it bad news?'

I make a sound somewhere between a groan and a whimper.

'Maybe if you talked to her doctor, there'd be some positive—'

'I did talk to her doctor,' I say, cutting her off. I don't want to talk about this and I don't want to hear her talk about it either.

'When? Recently?'

'First thing this morning.'

How was it only this morning that I sat in front of Doctor Conlon and listened as she burst the bubble of my very existence with her kind, practical, devastating words? I went straight from her surgery to the house where I packed all my belongings, except my knitting needles, and left.

'Was it bad news?' she asks though she already knows the answer.

'Yes. It was bad news. Now can we stop talking about it, please?'

'You could organise for external help, from the state. I always thought you should do that anyway, you took on too much, but you can't just leave her, surely.'

'I've got to go,' I say. 'I'm late for dinner. The three of us are eating together, presuming Conn had enough brain capacity left to figure out how to turn on an oven after mastering the landline.'

'Check that lasagne is cooked through before eating.'

'I will,' I say, hauling myself up from the bed. 'Talk to you later.'

# TESSA

• • • • • • • • • •

**I**'m sure one of them will answer – what with all their talk of being at home a lot, and the fact that we are supposed to be having dinner in three minutes – but nobody does. I need to let them know I won't make it back in time after all. I let it ring so long that eventually it hangs up on me.

Well, I tried. And whilst I don't make a habit of breaking engagements, some things are more important.

I indicate back out onto the main road and double-check the address and directions that Malachy has jotted down in lettering so large as to almost be insulting.

The Radical Activism EGM was surprisingly productive. Susan came along, but only for twenty minutes because it was her wedding anniversary and their sons were cooking them dinner; she had to get home before they burnt down the kitchen. Trevor observed that she was the only member with a significant other and asked if she might have any tips. (Reggie could be attached, but he's sixteen, so it hardly counts. He wasn't there. We didn't think he'd welcome the interruption to his leisure time.)

Anyway, she couldn't stay long but she does have a brother who used to work at An Bord Pleanála. So she gave him a call to check how the whole thing works. He gave us a few pointers – namely that the decision will likely be made in the next eight weeks, and that we have about four more to lodge any objections. He also said a lot of these disputes are settled before they ever cross the planning authority's desk and that the first step should be to talk to the hall owners.

Malachy was disappointed by this – he was pushing for an immediate chaining of ourselves to the building, or maybe even starting a small fire in the vicinity of Charles Bentley's home. He had his address in the reception files. I suggested we use it, instead, to go and talk to the man.

Trevor thought he should be the one to go, but everyone else voted for me. There was some talk of Malachy coming along, but it was agreed, not least by Malachy, that this might lead to a more confrontational meeting than was desired. So, instead, he wrote out the address in text so big it could be the first line on an eye test chart and stuck it on my dashboard.

We agreed on the three main points I should make. Firstly, that the benefit of the hall to the local community is truly priceless and that it creates enormous goodwill towards its owners. Secondly, that those who use the hall could contribute more to the day-to-day running of the place through fundraising and perhaps some membership fees if this would entice them to leave it as is. And, thirdly, that planning permission laws near the seafront were very strict and we would be sure to fight them on every detail.

Ideally, things would go well and we'd be able to stop after point one or, at a push, point two.

I pull up outside Charles Bentley's house and leap from the car. (Well, 'leap' might be an exaggeration, but whatever the movement is I make it too quickly and blood rushes to my head.) I am making my way up the driveway before I have really taken it in. It is a mansion. Now, I know people in massive houses shouldn't throw stones, but I doubt if this place has a leak in the attic or several rooms shut off or if it relies on solid fuel for warmth.

It's my least favourite type of house; an extremely new one made to look extremely old. Neo-classical pillars flank the entrance, there's a Merc and – oh my, yes – a *Bentley* in the driveway. And the *pièce de résistance*? There are turrets. Four honest-to-god turrets. Who, with the exception of Rapunzel, has any call for a turret?

I press the buzzer and an orchestra of bells and glockenspiels starts playing Beethoven's Fifth Symphony from inside. I am gawking in the side window when the front door opens and I see that, yes, that thing in the centre of the foyer is indeed a replica of the *Venus de Milo*.

A pleasant, smiling woman appears in the doorway.

'You must be Mrs Bentley. Or maybe not Mrs Bentley. I kept my own name so should know better than to make that assumption about other women. I'm Tessa Doherty. I was looking to speak to Charles Bentley? If he's home?'

From behind her, a voice barks. 'Natalia! Who left the clothes in the fountain? I told—'

'Mr Bentley,' the woman in the doorway says. 'There is a lady to see you.'

He approaches the door. 'Thank you, Natalia,' he says, several octaves lower. 'You can go back to what you were doing.' He waits for her to leave, then moves into the centre of the door frame. 'Charles Bentley. What can I do for you?'

He's not exactly rude, but he's not welcoming either.

The woman, who I now realise is the housekeeper, scurries

off. I have plenty of friends with cleaners – Senan and Audrey have one – but I don't know anyone with a *housekeeper*. I did think her blue smock dress was a little unusual; now I realise it was a uniform.

'Charles, how do you do? My name is Tessa Doherty and I am, among other things, a teacher at the North Dublin Community Project at your hall.'

'The Lusk hall?'

'No, the Howth one.'

'Ah yes. Nice to meet someone whose gotten use out of the place.'

'Oh, I certainly have,' I enthuse. 'Hundreds, thousands of us have. And I am here today on behalf of those people. We have read your planning notices and wanted to see if, human to human, we could appeal to you not to go through with the sale of the building.'

'Well, we don't plan to sell the building...'

'I'm appealing to you not to knock it down and not to build an unnecessary hotel in its place.'

He raises his unruly eyebrows and does the softest throat clearing.

'A committee of us from the hall have been discussing it and we wanted to make you aware of the huge benefit the facility has been to the local community. If you were interested in stopping by, we'd be delighted to show you some of the classes, projects and support groups that we run.'

'I am aware of what is being held there, thank you.'

'Then you'll know that as a community centre, in its current form, the hall is truly priceless.'

115

He is squinting slightly now.

'What you may not know is just how much goodwill the existence of the hall creates towards its three, clearly generous owners. That's the sort of positive publicity that money can't buy.'

'Ah, ha. And can you name the other two owners? Towards whom this abundance of goodwill is directed?'

'Well...' But there's no point racking my brains. The information is not there. 'Not currently. But were you to make it known, maybe even put your names up in the hall, I am certain your social generosity would have a knock-on benefit to your other business interests.'

His expression is one of pity. 'The kind of people we do business with are not the sort that would ever find themselves in that hall and so would not know of our *social generosity*.'

'You could leverage it for wider exposure,' I counter.

His face is blank now. 'People die of exposure,' he says. 'And you say the hall in its current form is priceless. It is not. It is worth a paltry €60,000 a year in rent. That's not a percentage of what we could get from running a hotel on the grounds.'

'You are evidently a very wealthy man,' I say, signalling to his garish home and the scared housekeeper within. 'It can't all be about the money.'

He howls at this. 'Very good, very good,' he says, chest shaking gently. 'You're serious? Of course it's all about the money. It's *only* about the money.'

I centre myself and try to remember the main talking points. This is not going as we had hoped.

'The members of the Project would be willing to contribute

more towards the running costs of the hall. We could possibly cover all the running costs – utilities, caretaker, etcetera. It would take some fundraising, but we are confident we could do it.'

'Look, Tess—'

'Tessa.'

'Tessa. I appreciate what you are trying to do, and I am glad you've enjoyed the hall for so many years. But why don't you just take this as a sign, permission to step down and put your feet up. There's no point getting all het up about this, it's not good for the heart, and it's pointless anyway, because we will be knocking down the hall, and we will be building a state-of-the-art hotel. Did you read the planning notice? It'll have a pool, with public opening hours. They'll be limited, but I am sure there'll be an OAP discount.'

He glances at my stick and it takes all my self-control not to clatter him with the thing.

'I didn't want to get adversarial, but you're not leaving me with much choice,' I say, shifting my weight so the stick is behind me. 'The members of the community project feel extremely strongly about that hall and your plans for it. We are getting expert advice from the planning authorities and we fully intend, if necessary, to fight you at every step of the process.'

I purse my lips and stand as straight as I can. I am letting him know I mean business. And it seems to be working because the man's face is twitching, like he wants to say something, but he can't find the words.

Except no. That's not it. He was suppressing a laugh, and now it is out.

'That's it?' he splutters. 'You've talked to someone in An Bord Pleanála? Oh no, I'm shaking in my boots. Tess, do you know—'

'Tessa.'

'Do you know,' he continues, 'how many lawyers we have working on these applications? Do you have a single lawyer, between you? No?'

I'm caught off guard. My face clearly gives away my hand because his lips have curled and his expression has returned to pity.

'Thank you for calling, Tessa. I look forward to reading your planning objection. It is possible to submit one without legal help, but it's tricky, so you should probably get working on it now. And, in the meantime, you can enjoy using *my* hall free of charge,' he says, smiling generously.

'I'm using the hall that the local council pays for. That makes it everybody's hall!'

'Not any more,' he says. 'The lease was up last week. So, currently, you are there thanks to my good grace.'

'Well, no longer!' I retort. 'I don't need your hall!'

'Then what are you doing here?'

'I mean... I'm not saying...'

'Goodbye now,' he says. 'And the very best of luck to you.'

The door shuts.

I can hear him barking for Natalia as I turn and clip my way down the steps and through the driveway. At the entrance gates I look back at the house and feel frustrated, angry and, worst of all, deflated.

I don't have a lawyer. I've hired legal professionals for specific purposes – transferring the house from Bernard's parents to us, dealing with Bernard's will. I doubt if anyone else at the community project has a lawyer – expect maybe whoever got them out on parole.

I make my way to the car, still raging about the corrupt legal system and how the cards are stacked so the house keeps on winning. This is why we protest. This is why we must keep protesting.

Who are these people who *have lawyers*? Are the legal professionals just lounging around their homes waiting to be called up? How often must you be suing people to *have a lawyer*?

It's utterly corrupt, utterly unfair, utterly ridiculous.

I am in the car and have the engine running when suddenly it hits me.

Me.

It's me!

I turn off the engine and hit the horn twice in delight.

I am now one of those people who has a lawyer lounging around their home.

And, right at this minute, I imagine he's helping himself to a slice of my homemade lasagne.

# CHLOE
· · · · · · · · · · ·

**I am halfway** down the stairs when I stop, overcome by a sudden sense that I have forgotten something; the morning tablets, the afternoon tablets, the evening tablets, forgotten to check that Mam has done her physio or how much water is left in her bottle or if she needs the bathroom, forgotten to make the breakfast, the lunch, the dinner. But none of those things apply. Not any more.

I stare at my phone. Trying to figure out what I can possibly say that won't invite further conversation. There's a sloshing in my stomach – hunger mixed with the familiar guilt and worry and fear – but I ignore it. I lock the phone and continue down the stairs, slower, my feet curling down onto the worn, carpeted steps. It's so strange to be out on my own. I'm trying to appreciate it. I can do anything, go anywhere, be anyone.

If I think about it briefly, it's exciting; focus on it for too long, and I'm overwhelmed. Who am I without Mam? If she's not there to confirm it, how can I be sure I exist?

Standing in the hallway, just beyond the kitchen door, I take out my phone again.

Please stop calling. Don't call Yemi either. I'll be in touch soon.

I stare at the words. I don't recognise the distant, callous daughter who would write them. I have never spoken to my mother like that, ever.

The kitchen door opens and, with a deep breath, I look up and I press Send.

Conn has an oven glove on each hand and a tea towel thrown over his shoulder. His cheeks are flushed and there's a look of shock on his face. He's just sort of staring. Not the usual stare; more dazed.

'What?' I demand, slipping my phone away.

Is he that unused to cooking for himself? Is he shellshocked?

He shakes his head, swallows, and seems to come around. 'You managed a shower,' he says.

My hand instantly goes to my still-damp hair and I brush it through with my fingers. Senan was right about the pipes. For the whole shower, it was like there was a percussion section playing in surround sound. Not that it bothered me. I was happy to wash away what has felt like the longest day of my life.

'And you look like a man who's spent the day cooking a multiple-course gourmet meal as opposed to reheating a lasagne,' I say, stepping past him to where the smell of cologne gives way to one of burning.

I push up both windows, then stare down at the charred dish sitting on top of the green range. 'RIP dinner,' I mutter.

'You're both late,' he says, defensively.

'I'm ten minutes late. Ten minutes wouldn't have saved that.' I grab an oven glove from his hand and a fork from the draining board and begin scraping off the top layer. 'Maybe we can salvage the middle of it...'

'It was the Aga,' he says. 'There are no degrees on the thing. There are no markings at all. I even checked the back. Are you supposed to instinctively know when something is ready? Does the spirit of an ancestor descend and say "gruel is done"? It's like cooking in a caldron over a fire.'

He's flustered. In fact, I would classify this as babbling. Have I found his Achilles heel? Is it cooking?

I've successfully removed the top layer and am now banging at the middle with the spoon. It's still frozen. 'Do you actually not know how to cook?'

He laughs. 'I *know* how to cook.'

'Ah ha, and when was the last time you did it?'

He thinks about this, for too long.

'I see.'

'Nobody is allowed use my mother's kitchen except my mother. And before that, I was in Dubai, where I had a cook.'

'As in, a live-in cook?'

'A housekeeper. She did everything.'

'Seriously?'

'Everyone at our company lived in the same compound and each house came with a housekeeper, a gardener, and a live-in nanny if you had kids.'

I am, and I think this is the correct word, aghast.

'The housekeepers were all Indian women, bussed in together every morning from the same impoverished part of the city that none of us Westerners ever visited.'

'That's disgusting.'

'Yes, it is,' he says. 'I never asked what she was paid. Probably because I knew it was a pittance. I didn't even realise how amoral the whole thing was until my brother pointed it out to me. Another reason I left.'

Part of me wants to hammer the point home, to let him know

that he is confirming all my ideas about rich people, but his self-awareness stops me. I don't know what to do with that.

'This is for the bin anyway,' I say, grabbing the second oven glove from him and emptying the dish into what I hope is the compost.

'I guess Tessa isn't going to make it?'

I glance out the nearest open window. 'I guess not. Who was on the phone?'

He looks at me cluelessly.

'The house phone? A few minutes ago? Who was calling?'

'Oh I didn't answer that.'

'Excuse me?'

'I wouldn't answer the house phone in my own home,' he says.

'Are you being serious? I honestly can't tell.'

'The only people who call landlines are telemarketers, wrong numbers and Nigerian princes.'

'And older people,' I say. 'It could have been Tessa saying she was going to be late – or maybe she got into some sort of trouble.'

'Oh,' he says, after a couple of seconds.

'Yeah,' I reply.

I slide the casserole dish into the sink and turn to observe the kitchen. The dynamic has shifted since I came downstairs, as if I caught him on uneven footing. 'You wash that and I'll find something else for us to eat. You can wash up, right?'

He smiles at this. 'Washing up, my mother does allow.' He turns on the tap. 'Jesus – is that the pipes? It sounds like a caged animal trying to escape.'

In the fridge, I find a tomato, lettuce and a few eggs. I pour some water into a saucepan and wait for it to boil. I've never used an Aga either, but it's hardly rocket science. While searching the presses, I spot a dishwasher in the corner. I open my mouth to say something, but quickly shut it.

He's currently reading the back of a packet of scouring pads.

There's half a sliced pan in the bread box.

'Is there a toaster?'

He knocks on a ground-level cupboard with his foot. 'Saw it while looking for Aga instructions.'

I think it's supposed to be a joke.

'I was thinking we could do some extra jobs around the place,' he says. 'The fuel shed could do with painting for one – and a new door.'

'I don't know how to *make* doors.'

'I do,' he says.

'Is it that you pay someone else to do it?'

He laughs.

I keep thinking I'm being rude, and he keeps enjoying it.

'My dad was a woodwork teacher. He taught us a few things. So I could do that, and you could paint.'

'I haven't painted anything in years,' I reply because I'm incapable of just admitting it's a good idea.

'It'll come back to you. It's like riding a bike.'

'Well I can't ride a bike so that doesn't bode well.'

He turns from the sink. 'You can't ride a bike?'

I gawk back at him. 'No,' I say. 'I can't.'

While the eggs are boiling and the bread toasting, I slice up the vegetables. He's still cleaning the same dish. I close both windows and lob some cutlery down on the table.

'You don't like me much, do you?' he says, sounding more

amused than hurt, which only adds to my irritation. I know people talk about not caring about the opinions of others, but I didn't think anyone ever really achieved it.

'I don't know you,' I say, blushing slightly as I start hunting for plates.

'Well that's true. But first impressions are unavoidable. I've been trying to change mine, but I guess I'm not doing a very good job.'

I close the cupboard. 'I just think you don't need this room. I think you're taking advantage of Tessa's generosity.'

'Why don't I need it?'

'Because you have money,' I say, looking him straight in the eye. 'You're clearly privileged.'

Under any other circumstances if someone accused me of not liking them, I would die a death from the mortification. Then I would ensure I was reincarnated just so I could dedicate my second life to apologising to them and insisting it wasn't true. But not Conn. I am the polar opposite of my deferential self with this man. If I knew having a nemesis evaporated all shame, I'd have looked into it long ago.

'In some ways I am,' he agrees. 'But there are different kinds of need. Not everything is material.'

'You told me this was the perfect house for you but when Tessa asked, you acted like I was making it up. How do you know this house? And why are you pretending you don't?' I'm still opening and closing cupboards, but I'm paying little attention to what's inside. 'Your mysterious nocturnal activities and your secret Tuesday morning escapades...'

Finally, I register two plates.

'And I know you don't go owl watching,' I blurt, because apparently I can't stop until I get a reaction.

He fills two water glasses and brings them to the table. I run the eggs under the same tap.

'Okay.'

'Okay, you admit you don't go owl watching?'

'No, okay you don't believe me. That's your decision to make and I accept it.'

I stare at him as he takes a seat at the table. He looks up pleasantly and smiles.

So, what? He really *does* go owl watching? None of the others called it out. Is it actually a hobby of the one per cent? This is a pretty posh house; maybe Tessa has done a spot of owl watching herself.

'I liked you more when you were flustered,' I mutter, dividing the meal between two plates.

'Thank you,' he says, taking one of them.

I crack my eggs on my plate and build a little shell mountain beside the sugar bowl.

'You don't like me either,' I say. I mean it to sound accusatory, but it comes out defensive. Why can't *I* be one of those people who doesn't care what anyone else thinks?

'Sure I do,' he says, peeling his own eggs and adding to my mountain. 'I think you're very funny. And I like you more because you don't like me. Clearly a woman of taste.'

It's the smile in his voice I don't understand. Is he slagging me or is he being serious? Either way, I don't need his observations.

'You're so...'

But his sentence goes nowhere.

I put down my forkful of egg. 'Go on. Say it.'

Okay so, I don't *need* his observations, but that doesn't mean I'm not interested. I'm only human.

He looks at me straight on, face deadly serious, and he says: 'You're so alive.'

The words hang between us until I manage to swallow them down. It says more about my mental state than what he has actually said that I feel the sudden desire to cry. Of course I'm alive. We are all of us alive.

'Best thing you can say about me is that there's blood running through my veins,' I shoot back, taking up my fork and shovelling on a new pile of egg. 'You're a big fan, clearly.'

I lift the fork but somehow miss my mouth and stab myself in the lip instead.

I'm thrown now and stupidly emotional and all I can do is give my plate undue attention.

When I do eventually look up, Conn has taken all the elements of his tea and turned them into a sandwich. Is that a male thing? Paul used to do the same.

*Paul.*

Even the thought of him is enough to set me right again.

'The views here really are amazing,' I say.

Conn glances up from his sandwich, which is so stuffed with filling it is more just a pile of food in his hand. 'You know you don't have to talk to me, right?'

'Actually, I do,' I say, stabbing another bit of egg. 'I'm a people-pleaser and I am incapable of silences.'

'Well now that you mention it...'

'You noticed?'

He's nodding. Then he's grinning. Reluctantly, I do the same.

'And where does that come from, do you think? Not to come over all Doctor Phil...'

'Who's Doctor Phil?'

'The TV guy,' he says. 'You know, bald, American, gets people on to air their family's dirty laundry? No? Really? He's like a mix between Oprah and Jerry Springer.'

'I know Oprah...'

He puts down his sandwich. 'You've never heard of Doctor Phil or Jerry Springer?'

I shake my head. 'I wasn't allowed to watch a lot of TV.'

'They're still on, constant repeats.'

I meant I wasn't allowed at any age, even last week, but I realise how strange that sounds so I don't say anything.

'My mam was very strict.'

'Mine too, I guess.'

I shake my head. 'I had colic as a baby and she was convinced I was going to die of cot death. Then when that didn't kill me, she became convinced everything else would. Like cycling a bike.' *And learning to swim and flying and going in cars without her...* 'She was trying to keep me safe. But not allowing me to do anything sort of reduced the ways she could teach me right from wrong. All she had left to take away was her company. So sometimes she had to opt for silence. If I was late home from school, a day of silence. If I snuck out to go to the cinema with a friend...'

He raises his right eyebrow and I redirect my attention to my plate. That was a truly terrible month. I had constant diarrhoea with the worry – and all for what? I don't even remember what the stupid film was called.

'Longer,' I mumble.

'And TV? Your mam thought that would kill you too?'

'No, that was in the same category as social media and the internet generally. It would rot my brain.'

'I did notice the brick phone.'

'I'm actually quite happy not to have a smart phone,' I say, parroting what I said throughout college. I think it's true though. 'Maybe I'd like a laptop,' I allow, 'but I use the computers at the library when I need to.'

'You don't have a laptop? Who doesn't have a laptop?'

I give him a look.

'Yeah, those privileged vibes I'm giving off are a real mystery to me,' he says, and I can't help but laugh.

What is this? Are we... are we getting on? Maybe we can achieve cordial relations. Good. I don't want anything to ruin my set up at Hope House.

'But seriously, you don't know what you're missing,' he adds. 'Maybe...'

Silence descends and I know it's one of those comfortable ones people talk about, but old habits die hard. 'It's terrible about Tessa's daughter, isn't it?'

He gives a curt nod as he moves his fork across the empty plate.

'I can't imagine what that must feel like, especially to have it happen so close to your home,' I say, as he pushes his chair back with a screech and collects the plates and crockery.

'Except they don't know it did happen there, or happen at all.'

'No, but...' We both heard what Senan said.

I push a couple of stray crumbs together. 'Poor Tessa.'

'I don't think we should talk about it.'

I'm taken aback by his tone. 'Sorry,' I say instinctively.

'Talking about it is...'

'It's desperately sad,' I allow, twisting in my chair as he pauses in front of the sink, plates in both hands.

'It's voyeuristic,' he says, turning towards me. 'It's crude.'

I draw my head back as if I've been smacked.

'I wasn't being *voyeuristic*,' I say. 'I wasn't looking to discuss the details. I was just expressing my sadness that something like that happened to someone so decent.'

But he doesn't respond. He just turns on the faucet and starts making heavy work of the sponge.

My whole face is on fire.

'Fine,' I mutter, pushing back my own chair and making for the door.

I give one pointed look to the dishwasher and say nothing.

It seems we're back to where we started.

# MURIEL

· · · · · · · · · · ·

**M**uriel Fairway is searching the internet for a pattern for her granddaughter's Christmas jumper (she is determined to get a head start this year – avoid the annual December knitathon) when her notifications ping.

One new email.

It's an automatic one from Delivery Dash, confirming that her parcel has been delivered.

This is why she rates the company. Impeccable service, even after they've got your money.

Delivered to intended address.

Signed for by recipient.

Muriel beams. She can picture Bea, not long home, maybe still unpacking and being called to the door. Confusion, initially, as to why she's getting a registered delivery from the UK. Then wonderful relief when she opens it. Muriel imagines her mother, Tessa, comes up behind her to see who's at the door and Bea spinning around to show what has just been delivered.

Muriel knows her imagining of the event couldn't possibly be accurate, if only because in her mind's eye Bea and Tessa are too close in age. All she has to go on for Tessa's appearance is the old photograph that Bea carries with her – the one of her and her mother and brother on a windswept beach in the early 1990s.

She has no idea how Tessa has aged, but she knows she was beautiful then, and very like her daughter now.

When she saw Bea's cherished photo – the one she, quote, 'keeps with her always' – Muriel felt a smidge of regret that she had never had a daughter. No way either of her sons carry a picture of her on their person.

Girls are just different, aren't they? Even when they've grown into women. And Bea is a sentimental sort.

Still, Muriel consoles herself, at least she has little Sadie.

She closes out of her email account and resumes the search for the perfect festive design.

She's thinking pink this year.

There hasn't been enough pink in her life.

# TESSA

· · · · · · · · · · ·

I had barely finished asking Conn for help with the planning permission objections when he said yes. I had expected to have to cajole him or to at least find myself defending my position; asking for professional help the day after he moved in made it look like there was always going to be a price for living here – and this really wasn't a tit for tat situation.

But the young man instantly pulled out his phone and started typing in the information as I relayed what details I had.

'Planning law isn't my area of expertise but I can brush up,' he said. 'When would you need this by?'

'We have our next Radical Activism meeting on Friday. I know that's only a few days away—'

'Friday is perfect,' he said, wiping milk from his chin and typing the timeline in too. It was Tuesday afternoon when we were having this conversation. I was eating lunch and he, who had the eyes and hair of a man not long awake, was having a large bowl of Honey Loops. 'I'll look into it and I'll have something to present to you all on Friday.'

'Are you sure?'

'More than sure.'

'We couldn't pay you...'

'All the better,' he insisted, pushing himself up from the table.

'Really?'

'A social enterprise that helps everyone and makes no profit? This is what I came home to Ireland for,' he said, rinsing his bowl and placing it on the draining board. 'Thank you,' he added. Then he gathered up his phone and headed for the door in a cloud of enthusiasm.

A couple of times during the week I tried to clarify what exactly he was thanking me for, but he'd always jump in with some specific question about the hall.

It was a rather unsuccessful first week, in terms of gathering information on Conn.

All I've learned is that his parents are retired teachers and that he was at Trinity at the same time that Bea was doing her PhD there. I didn't get to ask him much about that either. I'd love to find out if he knew her at all, if their paths ever crossed. I so rarely get to talk about my daughter.

Anyway, however surprising his enthusiasm, it was genuine because here we are on a rainy Friday at 4.30 p.m.; Conn sitting at one end of my long dining room table, myself and the additional five Radical Activists crowded around the other.

Reggie is the last to arrive and he can't decide if he should focus his attention on how massive my house is or how awkward it was to get to. Currently, he's staring up at the chandelier that has hung there since the days of Bernard's grandparents. I'd get rid of the things only they work so well, and throwing out perfectly good chandeliers would be more bourgeois than keeping them.

'If I knew you were this rich, I'd have asked you to send your chauffeur to collect me,' says the teenager.

'I don't have a chauffeur, Reggie, and I am not rich.'

'Y'okay,' he replies, neck still craned.

If there was an alternative to having the five of them to my home, I'd have taken it, but since my encounter with Charles Bentley I have vowed not to hold another class at the hall until it is out of corporate hands.

'Apologies, Conn,' I say, focusing my attention across the table. 'We're all here now, we've made all the introductions, so please do begin.'

Reggie throws his school bag to the floor, takes a seat and yawns. Malachy jumps his own chair in another inch towards the table (any closer and he's going to start squashing internal organs) and Maura winks at my lodger. I choose to believe it is a wink of encouragement.

'No problem,' says Conn, readjusting his own chair. He has actually told me a bit about his work and how he used to consult on deals worth hundreds of millions, including once advising the king of a small African nation on the ramifications of selling off the national grid. Yet somehow, he looks nervous.

His gaze keeps travelling to Malachy who, if you don't know Malachy, does look like he might pass out from the concentration.

I give him a nod of reassurance.

He nods back. 'Okay, hello, my name is Conn Horgan. I'm a solicitor specialising in banking and financial services.'

Reggie drops his head and snores loudly. Trevor, who is sitting to his right, elbows him.

'Ow!'

'Carry on, Conn,' calls Trevor, as Reggie massages his ribs.

Conn's eyes flicker again to Malachy, who is gripping his notebook so tightly his fingertips look bruised.

'Planning laws are not my speciality,' he says, pulling his

gaze back to the group, 'but I've been doing a bit of reading and I think I'm up to speed. Now I could run through the various sections of the Planning and Development Regulations 2001 to 2023 that apply to your particular situation—'

'We're good for that, thanks, pal. Ow!'

This time it's Maura who quietens Reggie with a gentle clatter to the back of the neck.

'When did you all get so violent?' he grumbles, slouching down in his chair. 'Must have been when you were off holding your special top-secret meeting without me.'

'Now, Reggie,' I say, patiently. 'You're always saying you're only here because it gets you out of school.'

'Yeah,' he says, defiantly. 'I am.'

'Well, it was an evening. We didn't think you'd want to come in your free time.'

Reggie folds his arms and slumps down further. 'Still would have been nice to be asked...'

'Apologies, Conn,' I say. 'Please continue.'

'So, I could go through all that... or I could just outline the options for what to do next, and my advice on that.'

There are a few nods and a general murmur of agreement.

'Right, well, first thing we should do is lodge two objections; one for the change of use application and one for the request to build a significantly higher structure where the hall currently stands,' he says, stifling a yawn. 'Excuse me.'

'See? Your man's even boring himself.'

Every day since the lodgers moved in, I've noticed that Conn gets up late or goes for a nap during the day. He must really be committed to this owl watching business.

'Lodging an objection costs twenty euro each time you do it,' he continues. 'We have another three weeks to get them in, but the sooner the better, I think. So you'll need to decide the grounds for objecting.'

'Charles Bentley is as thick as mince?' suggests Malachy. 'And a bare-faced liar.'

'Subjective grievances aren't really grounds for complaints...'

'It's not subjective. It's a fact. Took him four goes to get into the hall. It says "Push" on the fecking door. Can't parallel park to save his life either.'

'I met him at the centre a few years ago,' says Trevor. 'Introduced myself three times, still he called me Terence.'

'See?' says Malachy. 'He's an ignorant fucker as well as a dozy one.'

'Those aren't the sort of considerations—'

'Oh,' says Maura, hand in the air. 'He wears those shirts where the chest is pin-striped but the collar is a block colour.'

'Those shirts are awful,' concurs Susan.

'The worst,' agrees Maura. 'They should be grounds for objection. Crimes against the eyes. Or they could be proof that he doesn't have the mental stability to be making big planning decisions.'

'I'm not sure...'

'Maura might be onto something there,' says Trevor, wagging his finger thoughtfully. 'If we could prove that Mr Bentley is unfit somehow...'

Maura shrugs. 'If that's what he'd put on his own back, god knows what he'd put on our green space.'

The group returns its attention to Conn, who appears to be fighting a grin. He scratches the side of his jaw.

'Those are all interesting points,' he allows, doing a decent job of sounding like he means it.

It's traits like that that tell you his parents are good people. Handsome too, I'd imagine.

'But planning considerations are more about if the proposed building goes against the objectives of the local development plan, which in this case it might,' he continues. 'There are also local considerations – namely the removal of a vital residential facility and the effect the development will have on building density in the area, parking provisions and increased traffic. And then of course there's the public health and environmental implications. I think these are all aspects you could focus on in your objection. It might also be more beneficial if everyone puts in individual objections, as opposed to a collective one.'

'All six of us?' I clarify.

'Yes, and anyone else who has an issue with the plans. You say there are hundreds of people using the hall, right? It would be great if you could get them to put in individual observations.'

'Are we allowed back in the hall, Mrs Doherty?'

'Of course you are, Malachy,' I say. 'This is a personal protest I'm making.'

'Because I don't want to be a scab.'

'You wouldn't be.'

'I'd rather cut all my limbs off and your limbs, Mrs Doherty, and eat them raw than cross a picket line.'

'Good thing there's no picket line, so.'

'I'd rather eat my own face.'

'I know, Malachy. It's okay.'

'The local residents aren't happy either,' says Susan. 'My neighbours are furious. They don't want a hotel right outside their front door. Nobody in the area wants the additional traffic.'

'Great,' enthuses Conn. 'Get them to object, too. The more the merrier.'

'We should get a few local politicians on side. Right?' I ask.

'Officially, they don't make the decisions, but it definitely wouldn't hurt. The more attention you can get this, the harder it will be for the plan to be approved.'

'Local press?' suggests Susan.

'National press, even,' I say, a familiar tingle of excitement running through me. 'There's a lot of public displeasure with the proliferation of hotels in Dublin lately.'

There's a knock on the dining room door and my other lodger appears.

'Chloe, come in!' I say, waving an arm at her. 'You can lodge an objection, too.'

The young woman shuffles into the room. She's twenty-four – twenty-five next February. She's also an only child, grew up without a father and really does read a lot. She refuses to speak about her mother, which is annoying because most of her life seems to revolve around her. We had dinner and watched a film together on Wednesday evening – which was when I did most of my data mining.

I was convinced I didn't want people cooking for me, but she was making a curry and insisted there was more than enough for two, and I have to say it was delicious. Since Bea left, I never really bother cooking unless Senan or a friend is coming around. But it was lovely to have a proper homemade dinner. Chloe even went up to the bathroom to turn on and later off the immersion for me. I'll fight Senan tooth and nail on this house – but he's right when he says the layout is impractical. It was definitely built to be run by young, sprightly servants.

'I'm just finished deliveries,' says Chloe, dutifully following my hand as it flaps in the direction of an empty seat halfway up the dining table. She turns the chair to face us, though the ferocity suggests its more about having her back to Conn.

'Oh!' she says with a start. 'Is this about the community centre?'

I filled her in on the saga at dinner. She nodded furiously and said 'you're so right, you're so right' when I was talking about the importance of the centre. Then she shook her head and switched to 'awful man, awful man' as I relayed my run in with Charles. I wanted to both shake her and take her into a hug, but instead I told her it wasn't necessary to keep agreeing with me; I knew she was listening.

Although I might have hurt her feelings, because she checked several times during the film that I wasn't annoyed at her.

We have a plan to watch *Four Weddings and a Funeral* tonight.

'What can I do?' she says, animated now. 'I want to help.'

'We're forming a plan of action,' I say, not wanting to lose momentum. 'And I'm thinking we should have a fun day.'

This gets a strong murmur of excitement from the group.

If Charles Bentley isn't interested in seeing what we do at the hall, then fine; we'll show everyone else instead.

'Malachy, could I have a few pages and a loan of your pen if you don't mind?'

'I've got a whole pack of them here, Mrs Doherty,' says my top student, pushing the chair back with such force that there's a collective tensing of shoulders as the legs screech against the ancient oak floorboards. He reaches down into his bag and thrusts a Biro at me.

'We have a full timetable of varied classes and support groups all week long. What if we put on a sort of showcase.'

'You mean a talent show?!' yelps Maura, nearly tripping over the leg of her own chair in excitement.

'No. No competition, just a chance to show all the great things that the hall does.'

'Like an open day?'

'Yes, Susan,' I say, wagging the pen excitedly. 'An open day. Exactly! The choir could do a few songs. We'd have a performance from the Irish dancers and one from Tai Chi and Decaf Tea.'

'Tai Chi and Decaf Tea?' queries Conn.

'It's a relaxation group for people with dodgy tickers,' I explain, jotting it all down as I think of it. 'They could help with refreshments too. Meals on Wheels could sort a buffet. My gardening class could talk people through the herbs we're currently growing. And how's Am-dram doing? They could perform a segment of this year's production. I assume it's not the *Diary of Anne Frank* again...'

'No. *Angela's Ashes* this year,' says Malachy.

'Really? Well, I'm sure they have something uplifting in their repertoire.'

'Rumba for Retirees could do a dance marathon,' suggests Trevor. 'If nothing else it'll kill off the deadweight holding us back.'

'The crafters could do a knitting marathon,' says Maura.

'Excellent, excellent. Anyone else? Keep the ideas coming!'

I love when it stops feeling like you're driving a campaign, when it gathers enough steam to be off on its own. A runaway train – that's always the aim.

Malachy shoves his arm above his head. 'I'd be happy to provide the subject for an open-to-all life-drawing class.'

'Let's just remember, we're trying to draw people to the centre, not scare them away,' says Maura. 'How about a first-aid demonstration?'

'Yes, all right...'

'Some beginners meditation?'

'Pilates?'

'Pottery?'

'Line-dancing?'

'I'd actually be available to do two life-drawing sessions.'

The ideas come thick and fast and, within a few minutes, I have the outline for a spectacular showcase. I'm buzzing with energy and so is everyone else. Even the lodgers are getting caught up in it; Chloe volunteers to help with refreshments and Conn says he could contribute an artwork to a raffle.

It is agreed that Conn and I will draw up the main objections – one for the change of use, and one for the request to build a huge new premises – and send them around, with everyone submitting variations on those. We will print off some objection forms to distribute at the centre and, of course, to bring to the open day, which is planned for Saturday two weeks. It's only when I go to put it into my calendar that I realised what the date is: Bea's anniversary. But I don't say anything.

Maura is the only Radical Activist who knows about my daughter.

Maura and Malachy will get in touch with all the teachers and class leaders, while Susan and Trevor are going to approach local politicians. Trevor claims to be on first-name terms with almost all the councillors. 'It's because of my Grandparents for Trans Rights group,' he explains. 'They all want to be on the right side of history.'

'What about the press?' I ask. 'Anybody got media contacts? Conn?'

He seems my best chance in this group, but he shakes his head. 'I have a friend at *Cork Online*, but that's no good to us,' he says.

'I know someone,' says Chloe, excitedly. 'He works at the *Dublin Press*.'

'The *Dublin Press*?' I say, impressed and surprised. Didn't she say she had one friend?

'He works on the news desk. Writes about everything. He had a great piece last year on a campaign to save some old buildings in Temple Bar.'

'He sounds perfect! Do you think he'd cover it? Are you good friends?'

'We used to be. We used to go out, actually.'

At the top of the table, Conn turns. He looks as taken aback as me. Who knew Chloe would be the one with media connections?

'And you're okay getting back in touch?' I ask.

She nods eagerly. 'I'm planning to see him soon actually.'

'Excellent!' I exclaim. I can practically hear the tooting of the runaway train, hurtling all the way to liberation station! 'Really excellent. This will be a superb display of people power; a joyful celebration of what we do, rather than an angry protest.'

'I quite like an angry protest,' muses Maura.

'Me too,' agrees Malachy. 'Maybe we could do an angry protest, as well?'

'Let's try the peaceful route first, shall we?'

'I suppose...'

'And if that doesn't work, we'll chain ourselves to Mr Bentley's front gates and maybe set a few of his bins on fire.'

This cheers Malachy right up. 'Deal!'

'All right, everyone,' I say, leaning my stick against the table and clapping my hands. 'Let's go forth and save! This! Hall!'

# CHLOE

• • • • • • • • • • •

'I have his package here somewhere...' I say, rummaging in the Delivery Dash satchel that contains the electronic signing pad, my purse, a half-eaten apple and absolutely nothing else.

The security guard watches me with a jaded sense of inevitability. He appears to know as well as I do that I will not be producing a second parcel from this bag.

Nearly a week I've been waiting for a *Dublin Press* delivery to come up. Due to the constant traffic and dearth of free parking, city centre deliveries are reserved for bike couriers. But I phoned the depot last Tuesday and asked to be put on the next drop. I wish I could say that Penny, the office manager, likes me but it's more that she feels sorry for me; I'm forever having to pass on jobs because Mam isn't feeling well or I need to bring her to an appointment. So after about five warnings that journalists don't tip, she agreed to put me down for the next *Dublin Press* delivery.

And now, finally, here I am. On the fourth floor of a seven-storey building with a dozen cupcakes addressed to a Ms Aimee Wenders, features editor. (I don't open customers' mail, by the way. I know they're cupcakes because the top of the box is see-through.) I told the security guard I had two packages: one for Aimee, and one for Paul Murtagh. He said he'd take them but I spun him a yarn about needing the recipient's signature. With a heavy sigh, he reached for the phone and called down to the features desk.

'Aimee is on her way,' he says, dropping the receiver back onto its holder.

'And Paul?'

He blinks, boredom descending into full scepticism. 'I'm going to need to see that package first.'

After another pointless rummage in which I get apple flesh caught in the band of my watch, I remove my empty hand and rub it on my shorts. 'I must have left that one in the car.'

'Ya-ha,' says the guard, his attention already drifting back to his desk, where a newspaper lies open on the showbiz pages.

'Hi, were you looking for me?' I turn to see a smiling woman in cropped black trousers and a cropped striped top coming towards me, her block heels clopping. 'I'm Aimee Wenders.'

'Oh yes, hi,' I say, reaching back to the reception desk to grab the cupcakes. The security guard sighs, but this time it's not at me. An elderly man has just come through the entrance. He's wearing an ill-fitted *Pirates of the Caribbean* t-shirt and carrying a placard. He looks straight ahead, eyes twitching slightly, then thrusts the sign over his head. It says: 'Armageddon is near. The Lord will smite the MSM.'

The security guard slumps off his stool and plods over to the man. 'All right, Mr Fitzsimons,' he says, not kindly. 'What have we done to upset Him today?'

'Do you want one?' asks Aimee, pulling open the cupcake box as if there's nothing remarkable about the scene unfolding beyond us. 'We never get through them all.'

She proffers the box, and I shake my head.

'No, thank you. What's MSM?'

'Mainstream media,' she replies, removing a bun topped with

white icing and placing it on the reception desk. She's probably the same age as me, but the self-assuredness makes her seem older.

'I'll leave one for Graham anyway,' she says. 'A reward for dealing with Mr Fitzsimons. He's boycotted our paper so many times I'm amazed he has any idea what's in it.'

'Actually,' I say, suddenly. 'I have another package for Paul Murtagh. Is he here?'

'Mmhmm,' she replies, swallowing the bit of cupcake she has broken off for herself. 'He sits opposite me. Want me to drop it down?'

'Eh, no.' I glance behind to ensure the security guard is still occupied. 'I need him to sign for it himself.' I give her a tight smile. 'Sorry.'

'No worries. I'll send him up.'

When she's gone, I watch the security guard patiently nod as Mr Fitzsimons talks passionately and at great speed. I can't make out everything he's saying but there are a few mentions of Elon Musk and something about China not really existing. He is just launching into the details of a 'government-sanctioned' something or other when there's a light tap on my shoulder.

'Oh!' I exclaim, jumping slightly before spinning around. I forgot I was waiting on somebody. 'Oh!' I say again. Because I forgot who I was waiting on, too.

He looks the same.

I cannot believe that I am looking at him and that he is still him.

Realisation dawns and his mouth opens slightly. A dimple appears to the right of his lips.

Still Paul. My Paul.

There's this alarming sensation behind my ribcage and for one awful moment I fear I will burst into tears.

My chest tightens and I put my hand to my heart to steady it. Something courses through my body – cortisol? I feel the fight or flight impulse, absolutely, but there's a third instinct presenting itself: fling. I reach behind me for the reception desk, tethering myself to its edge before my body makes the unauthorised decision to fling itself at Paul. It's like the past two years never happened and this body is supposed to be on top of that one.

I am startled by my own desires, but also bizarrely I am thinking of Conn. He was wrong in what he said last week in the kitchen. He acts like he has me sussed, but he does not.

It is only *now* that I am alive.

'Chloe,' says Paul, his light-brown hair still floppy, his pale-blue eyes still framed by thin-rimmed glasses. They might even be the same glasses. He puts a hand to his head, his cheeks flushed, and smiles broadly. 'Wow. I wasn't expecting this.'

'Hello, Paul,' I say, the grin on my own face threatening to spread up to my temples. 'Long time no see.'

How can it be that he's the same? That he was here, like this, all that time? It's not that I expect people to change, but I suppose it made it easier to handle, to think that my Paul stopped existing at some point two summers ago, that he shed the skin that had been mine alone to touch. It made it easier to be without him. The idea that he was here all along, just like I left him, only I wasn't with him...

I bring my hand to my eyes and keep smiling. The tears don't spill, they just pool in my waterline. It's a lot. I came here on purpose, but I still find myself taken by surprise.

'You all right?' he asks. He dips his head and his smile expands to make room for concern.

'Fine,' I say, shaking my head. 'I have these eyes well trained. I didn't even cry during *Little Women*, remember?' I cringe slightly. The night we watched *Little Women* was the first night we had sex. I didn't mean to bring up sleeping together, not before I'd even asked how he was.

Although, by the look on his face, he's struggling to remember the film. My pride is a little wounded, but I don't jog his memory – overt references to sex definitely count as post-niceties conversation.

'So how are you?' I say, brightly, all emotions back under control. 'Working as a journalist, here, obviously.'

He looks around him, nodding. 'Yeah. Did the journalism master's after we... after the teaching degree. Got a placement here, and yeah, they've kept me on. So far, anyway.' He smiles, eyes twinkling. People say that all the time, that eyes twinkle, but Paul's really do. It's not unlike the view from my new bedroom – the urge to dive in is pretty similar, too. 'And what about you? You're a courier now?'

'Yeah,' I say, shrugging, embarrassed, annoyed at being embarrassed. 'It's just, you know, money.' *And time.* Taking care of Mam made any full-time, career-orientated job impossible.

'Right,' he says, nodding emphatically. 'Actually, did you have something for me, or... Aimee said there was a package out here.'

'Oh, yeah. Em, no. Sorry, no, I don't... I was doing a delivery here anyway and I thought I'd say hi but your security is pretty strict so I just said I had something...' I cringe. 'Is that weird?'

'No, not at all,' he says, smiling. 'It's innovative – the sort of creativity a journalist can appreciate.'

'Okay, good. Phew.'

We're both just standing here now, nodding.

Nodding and smiling.

Nodding and smiling and standing.

'Okay, well, I should—' I begin, not wanting to leave but feeling like I'm supposed to.

But at the same time, he says, 'Do you want to grab a coffee?'

'Oh. Yeah, sure, that'd be—'

'Oh no, if you need to—'

'I don't.'

'You sure? I know you're working.'

'Well you're working too,' I point out.

'True. But I can always say I'm meeting a source on a story.'

'Innovative, I see.'

'But only if you have time?'

'I have time,' I say, smiling.

Paul pats his pockets, before half producing his phone and pushing it back in. 'Great, let's go.'

'Afternoon, Mr Fitzsimons,' he says, as we pass the man with the placard who, with the reluctant agreement of the security guard, is dumping a small pile of miraculous medals into the glass bowl, which up to that point was home to a few wrapped mints.

Paul holds the door open for me and Mr Fitzsimons bounds out ahead of us and down the stairwell.

'The day is coming! The Lord is coming! Your end is coming!'

'Good to know,' shouts Paul, hitting the call button for the elevator. Then to me: 'Pity he can never tell me when the 39A is coming.'

There's a small café across the road and we sit in the window. It's the only free table but it also allows me to keep an eye on my car, which is parked in a loading bay outside. It stresses me out to be parked illegally, but not enough to cut the interaction short. I keep thinking Paul is going to have to leave, and then he doesn't.

We've been here half an hour and I wish I could slow time, soak it all up. I try to file away the information, so I can dissect it later. I have zero desire to talk about my life so I mainly ask Paul about his job and the master's degree and how it feels to be living his dream. A pathetic part of me wants him to correct me, to say his dream is actually to be with me. He doesn't, of course. Instead he tells me about the two journalism awards he's already been nominated for.

'It's weird, isn't it? Not a lot of people from our year became teachers in the end,' he says, skirting the rim of his cup with his index finger.

'Yemi did.' I see him struggling to remember. 'Yemi of Yemi and Peter,' I add, though I'd be surprised if he knows another Yemi full stop.

'Yemi! Yes. God, of course. I haven't seen her in years either. How is she? Good?'

'She's great. She just had a baby actually. A boy called Akin, named after her dad. He's so cute, like unbelievable cute. Seriously, you'd have to see him. She's teaching in Donabate when she's not on maternity leave. Her and Peter are renting an apartment out there. He's working in Portmarnock, but yeah, not as a teacher.'

'They're still together? Ah, that's great.'

'They're married. It was a small ceremony, during lockdown.'

He smiles. 'Were you maid of honour?'

'I was. My speech made everyone cry. Well, there was only six of us there but you know, still.'

'I bet it did,' he says, and the way he looks at me makes my body sing. 'That's amazing. They're two great people. You know when you think of someone and you just smile? Peter...' He shakes his head, grinning. 'I had some great nights out with that lad.'

I beam, delighted with his delight. We had been a tight foursome for a while – Yemi and I talking about how we'd all be each other's best men and maids of honour. Things change, I guess. But that doesn't mean they can't change back.

'Do you see anyone else from college?'

'Not really,' I say.

'Nah, me neither. Just Philly, Ger and Simon mainly, and I play football with Ryan and Seamus on Thursdays. I guess I see Fiona a bit, she's a reporter with the Court Service now, did you know that?'

I shake my head.

'Oh, and Ciara and Una, they live around the corner from me so we go for a drink sometimes, but yeah that's it. You? Yemi and...'

'Just Yemi.'

'Yeah,' he says. 'Life gets busy, doesn't it? It's hard to stay in touch with everyone.'

'Mm...'

'Oh god, Chloe,' he says, palm flat on the table. 'Your mam! I never asked about your mam. How is she?'

I watch him carefully. There's no sign of animosity or resentment. He really does seem to care.

'Yes, thanks for asking, but she's...' I shake my head.

'I heard the chemotherapy wasn't successful initially. But then they tried something else? I can't remember who told me that now. Ciara, maybe? I think she's still in touch with Yemi...'

I watch his hands shift across the laminate tabletop. His fingers are thin, like the rest of him, with sparse light hair up to the knuckles. I used to bite those fingers during sex. It was a bit of an affectation, I guess, I was never really so overcome by passion as to turn cannibal, but I liked the feeling of them between my teeth; the sense that I had snared them and they were mine for ever.

*Fuck you*, I think, bringing my own knuckles up to my teeth now, and letting my anger restrict itself to them.

The sudden sense of having had something stolen from me...

'Chloe?'

His face holds an expression of concern I've seen many times before.

'I hope I haven't upset you.'

I shake my head.

*Fuck you, Mam.*

*Fuck you, fuck you, fuck you.*

'I went to email you so many times after I heard about the chemo,' he says. 'But I wasn't sure you'd want to hear it. I felt awful about everything I said about your mam when we broke up. I was a selfish arsehole. I really was sorry to hear she was getting worse.'

I shake my head again, a tight smile hiding locked teeth which are just about keeping all the emotions in my body.

153

'Are you still at home?'

I take a mouthful of tea, grateful for the slight change in direction. 'Just moved out actually.'

'Oh, wow,' he says, genuinely taken aback. 'That's... Wow. That's great.'

A niggle of irritation. Just because I didn't move out with him, doesn't mean I was going to live with my mother forever. We're still in our mid-twenties; loads of people live at home in their mid-twenties.

'I'm in a shared house in Howth now. It's gorgeous. It's right up on the cliff and it has the most beautiful sea views.'

'God, that sounds great.'

'It is,' I say emphatically.

'I'm sure. I love Howth. In fact that's where—'

'It's a mansion, technically,' I add. 'And there's just three of us living in it.'

He catches my gaze, eyebrows arched. 'That really does sound great.'

I smile back, bashful. All irritation gone now. 'Thanks.'

'I should go, unfortunately. I have a news conference in five and I still don't have any decent story ideas to present,' he says picking up the discarded sachets of sugar and sticking them in his empty cup.

'Right, yeah, me too. Not the conference, but yeah, work.'

He takes a half-step before throwing the rubbish into the bin.

I get to my feet. I guess we're really going.

'We should meet again,' I say, too urgently. 'I mean, when I'm in town, or if you find yourself out in Howth...'

'Absolutely, let's not leave it as long.'

'Great.' I try to load the word with meaning, to make it clear I really do want to see him again, that it's not just a social nicety, but his eyes are on his phone.

'Sorry, I'm down in the courts tomorrow and the schedule just came through...' He sighs and shoves it into his pocket. 'I'll find you online. I don't think we're friends anywhere, are we?'

'I don't have social media. Remember?'

'Oh yeah,' he says, smiling, recalling. He always enjoyed how I managed to live semi 'off grid'. 'Well, I'll email you,' he says, 'if I'm ever in Howth.'

I can feel him slipping away, leaving the conversation and me, already back on the fourth floor, at his news conference, preparing for whatever court case he's covering, maybe enjoying one of Aimee's over-iced cupcakes.

And then I remember.

There are *two* reasons I'm here.

'I actually do have a news story for you.'

'Really?' He stops on the pavement, just as he's about to cross the road.

'Yeah, I totally forgot. It's part of why I wanted to see you.'

'Okay,' he says, turning, hands in the pockets of his combat trousers. He was never very interested in clothes. 'What is it?'

'Well, there's this big hall in Howth. They run the North Dublin Community Project out of it. It's a sort of community initiative with loads of classes and support groups, all for free.'

'I've heard of it,' he says. 'I interviewed a woman who went to a bereavement group there.'

'Okay, great. Well, not great for her, that she's bereaved but—'

'Chloe.'

'Sorry,' I say, as he grins. 'Well yeah anyway, it's very popular. Hundreds of people use it every week and it's a really valued local resource. The woman I live with is involved and it does sound like a properly amazing place. But now the owners, these businessmen, are planning to bulldoze the whole thing and build a massive hotel in its place.'

'Just what Dublin needs.'

'Exactly. The locals are annoyed and all the people who use the hall are too. They're devastated actually. But they're not giving up without a fight. There's a big drive to save the place. They're getting all the people who use the hall to send in planning objections, the local residents too. They've started putting up posters – I'm helping on a flyer drop this evening – and they're planning a huge open day to show everyone all the great things that the hall provides. They've already got a few councillors signed up to attend and at least one TD was very interested in coming along too. I mean, it's sort of a local story, but—'

'No, Chloe, that's a great story. And a TD getting involved really helps; any member of parliament elevates it. Besides, all news is local, and everyone in Dublin is sick of stuff being knocked down to build hotels. I wrote this piece last year about a landmark building in Temple Bar being knocked—'

'I know, I read it.'

'Oh, okay,' he says, visibly pleased. 'Well yeah, the response to that was amazing; all these letters and other media picked up on it. There's an appetite for these stories. And they can really effect change. Without my Temple Bar article, that building would be rubble. And now another hotel? We're knocking down our heritage. What are these legions of tourists going to visit when they come to Dublin? All the other hotels?'

He's really warming to it now, hands out of his pockets and gesticulating, face animated as a stain of colour appears on his perpetually pale cheeks. 'I can really see this doing well online. It's the sort of campaign people will share – they'll quote tweet it and post to Facebook groups... and an open day will be perfect for pics. So no, yeah, it's a great story, Chloe, really great. It's going to kill at my news conference.'

'Great,' I say. 'Well, like, I can help you with it, in whatever you need. My... my housemate is actually running the campaign to save the place, so I can put you in touch with her if you like?'

'That'd be brilliant. Good on her. Dublin would be totally destroyed if it wasn't for the young campaigners holding the authorities to account.'

I nod vigorously, not seeing the need to correct him. I don't want him to feel sorry for me because I've swapped living with my mother for living with someone even older. 'Young' is a subjective term anyway.

'When's the open day?'

'Saturday week.'

'Twelve days... We can do a piece in advance of it, maybe even a couple if it gets any traction, and then something bigger around the open day. It could spawn a long read; a wider piece on the destruction of Dublin, with this one community centre as the case study – a symbol for all the other good being threatened by constant development. Sorry,' he says, hands back in pockets. 'I get like this sometimes. My editor assures me I'll be jaded and cynical in no time.'

'No chance,' I assure him. 'You were always passionate. I loved that about you.'

Love! Love! Did I just say love?!

*Jesus Christ, Chloe, do not mention love!*

But he doesn't recoil. He doesn't even blink at it. He's still smiling, still excited, still grateful. 'Can I give you my number?' he says.

'I have it.'

'Oh right, yeah, well can I get yours?'

'You have it.' I pause. 'Don't you?'

'I mean, I did, obviously. But after we broke up...' He is cringing now. 'I didn't take it well, as you may remember. I guess I was trying to start afresh.' He rolls his eyes. 'Stupidly dramatic, I know.'

'No,' I rush to correct him. 'No, no, that's fine. I'll text you, okay, and then you'll have mine.' I take my phone from my pocket, write 'Your fly is open' and press Send. 'I'm sorry, you know, about how it all happened, the break-up. I didn't mean to hurt you. If I could—'

'Jesus, no, Chloe. I'm the one who should be sorry,' he says, pulling out his phone at the beep. 'Your mam was seriously ill and I was acting like everyone was out to get me. I should—' He bursts out laughing. 'Is it really—?'

'No,' I say, as he stretches the material that covers his crotch. 'Just had to write something. And it's always amusing to make someone check.'

'True, true.' He glances back at his phone. 'Shit! I really have to go now. I'll talk to you later and thanks again.'

'So I was a good source after all?' I shout after him. He's already halfway across the road.

'Too good!' he calls back. 'I've never been late for conference before! My editor puts latecomers on the dead-end stories – I'll probably spend the afternoon investigating Mr Fitzsimons' prophecies!'

'Oh no, I'm sorry!'

'Don't be,' he hollers from the other side of the street, his gloriously geeky face beaming. 'It was definitely worth it!'

# TESSA

· · · · · · · · · · ·

It's been three days since the Radical Activists met at the house and my dining table has been lost entirely to the campaign. Conn is sitting to my left, clacking away on his computer, and I'm searching through the sprawl of letters, legal documents, stationery, posters and books to try and find the map that I had in my hand no more than thirty seconds ago.

We're hitting the streets this evening and I need to work out how much ground we can cover and what areas can deliver most bang for our buck in terms of canvassing.

We'll be delivering flyers hot off the presses – literally. A courier dropped them off twenty minutes ago and they were still warm. Trevor's printer did us a deal and he put a rush on the order. (Don't ask me why Trevor has a printer. He could well be one of those people who 'has a lawyer' too.)

I pull out what I think is the map, but it's actually a floor plan of the hall.

*Where the feck did I put the thing?*

I've always been good at holding multiple strands in my mind – it's a skill social work required – but my capacity is being tested. Senan has promised to drop in a whiteboard, which should at least streamline things.

'How's it going?' I ask, peering over Conn's shoulder. He's wearing a lovely thick jumper – more of a geansaí, really – and it's very smart. He dresses well, for a young man. Block colours and good-quality material, and all his trousers seem long enough for him.

He's putting the final touches to the template for the planning application objections before we send it out to the not unsubstantial list of email addresses we have already gathered. Maura and Malachy wasted no time contacting the various group facilitators who use the hall. Every single one of them was shocked to hear of the plans and entirely behind our efforts to stop them. They in turn trickled the word down to their participants. Trevor has even got a few councillors willing to speak to the press about their opposition to the proposals. So now, we just need the press to agree to write about it.

'Any word on how it's going with Chloe?' I can't quite make out the clock on his laptop, but it's got to be after 4 p.m. She said she was seeing her journalist friend in the afternoon.

Conn gives a half-laugh. 'I don't think she'll be contacting me,' he says, verifying something on his screen against the planning application notice beside him.

I have noticed relations between my lodgers aren't the easiest. Conn left the toilet seat up on Saturday morning and you'd swear he'd slashed the tyres on Chloe's car.

At first I thought it might be a flirtatious friction, but Chloe talked at such length last night about her ex who works at the *Dublin Press* that I missed about a third of *My Best Friend's Wedding*. So I'm not sure she has the headspace to be keen on someone else. Conn seems to quite like her though and isn't perturbed that it's not returned. It's a curious thing, but he doesn't really do a lot with his time and yet I get the constant impression that he has bigger things to deal with.

I shift a few paper mounds around the table until I find my mobile under a large packet of markers. No new notifications. She said she'd be back in time to go canvassing; I guess we'll know then.

Conn yawns.

'Late night?' I ask, pretending to study the hall floor plan.

I heard him heading out last night, shortly after midnight, and I'm desperate to know where he was going. Otis looked into owl watching and his findings were that 'it's not a thing'. So then what exactly is he up to between the hours of, from what I can deduce, midnight and 4 a.m? Every time I ask Conn about his life, he changes the subject. If I'm going to find things out, I'm going to have to do it by stealth.

'Mm,' he mutters. 'Didn't get much sleep.'

'Owl watching?'

'Right, yes.'

'What's the most common owl in Ireland?'

'Sorry?' he asks.

'You must know that. The most common owl?'

'Did I tell you I'm going to make a new door for the fuel shed?'

'You did, yes. Is it the long-eared owl? Is that right?'

'Mm,' he says, typing loudly.

'What sort of indigenous owls do they have in Dubai? I wouldn't know much about those.' I'm staring at the graph so hard now that the lines are starting to move.

'I didn't do much owl watching in Dubai?'

I glance up. 'Oh? Why is that?'

'Wasn't a lot of time for hobbies.'

'All work, work, work, was it?'

'Work hard, play hard – that was the ethic,' he mutters, hitting the return key. 'There was a club called Foxy that we used to frequent; that was about as close as it came to wildlife.'

'And you didn't enjoy that? The lifestyle?'

He looks up from the screen, catches my eye and blinks.

'This is ready,' he says, pushing the computer over. 'If you want to take a look.'

*Damn it.* Should have kept studying that floor plan.

He points to the screen. 'There are two variable sections, where each complainant can identify their specific grounds for complaint, and then the personal details section.'

'Ah ha,' I say, reading it through. 'This all looks good,' It really does, very professional.

'I can tweak it a bit if you think it should be less formal.'

I shake my head as I read to the end.

'It's brilliant,' I say. 'Perfect.'

He looks unduly delighted.

'I know this is small fry compared to your usual work, but it means the world to us.'

'My usual work is making rich people richer; this stuff actually matters.'

I'm about to probe into this tiniest of disclosures when I hear the front door.

'Chloe,' I say, hopefully.

But when the dining room door opens several seconds later, it's my daughter-in-law Audrey behind it.

'Hello, Tessa, how are you?' she says warmly. 'I feel like I haven't seen you in forever.'

'I've been busy, actually,' I reply. 'There's a whole business with the hall...'

'Otis told me. I was sorry to hear.' She pushes up her sleeves to reveal a clatter of thin gold bands and silver charm bracelets. 'I've been offering up powerful intentions on behalf of the Project.'

'No need for the planning objections so,' I mutter. Conn glances at me but Audrey doesn't hear – probably drowned out by her jewellery.

*Glinda.* That was Bea's private nickname for her sister-in-law because she reminded her of the Good Witch of the North from *the Wizard of Oz.* The two women got on for the most part, though there were arguments; mostly about homeopathy. Well, Bea argued with Audrey. I doubt if my daughter-in-law has ever had a heated exchange with anyone. Bea and Senan were close too, until the years before she disappeared. Bea doted on Otis, but she also felt excluded by Senan's new family, and my son refused to indulge this. He had little patience for her episodes.

'You must be Conn, it's truly lovely to meet you.'

She crosses the room and takes his hand. The man beams. Whilst I find all Audrey's talk about energies hard to take, it's undeniable that she has a magnetic quality. People just take to her.

I took to her fine too, contrary to what Senan might think. Her hippier qualities mightn't be my style, and I find her wishy-washy positivity a bit hard to take – you can't just crystal your way to a more just society – but I do think my daughter-in-law is a good person. She's a great wife to Senan and an even better mother to Otis (even if she could stand to feed him a little more). It's the daughter-in-law role I find tricky – because the 'in-law' bit isn't always obvious. People have mistaken Audrey for my daughter. I know I've hurt her feelings with how strenuously I correct them.

There's a photo in Senan's hallway from the day he was made principal and it's like a stab to my chest every time I pass it. We were all at a celebratory dinner at the school and Otis took a picture of Senan, myself and Audrey standing outside his new office. There's something about that photo in particular that makes me think it should have been Bea standing there; it should have been myself, Senan and Bea snapped in a giddy joyful mood, just like that photo on Curracloe beach.

Sometimes it feels like Audrey has replaced Bea. As sweet and kind and good as she is, I can't help resenting Audrey for the void she has filled – or, more accurately, for how she has made it look like there's no void there at all.

'I love your hair, Tessa. The cut is so sophisticated, so impressive; so you,' she says, raising a hand as if to cut a blunt bob across her own long, dishwater-blonde hair. 'It really has been ages. I've barely seen you since...'

Ah yes. And that's the other thing. However relations were between myself and Audrey before my fall, they were infinitely more complicated after she found me raving on the carpet about the daughter who'd been missing for a decade but who I was insisting had just that moment vanished. She has tried to talk to me about it a couple of times since, but the thought is enough to make me take for the hills.

'I forgot you have a key,' I say, cutting her off.

Her smile doesn't budge, but there's a slight spasm and I instantly regret saying it. I can hear Senan already: *Where would you be if she hadn't had a key three months ago?*

'I have a whiteboard for you, Tessa,' she says. 'Senan asked me to drop it in.'

'I thought he was bringing it himself.'

Audrey smiles anew at Conn, who is watching the awkward exchange. 'He had to stay late. But I collected it. Shall I bring it in?'

'Yes, all right,' I say, trying and failing to drop the defensiveness from my voice. 'Do you need a hand?'

'No, no, it's just here...' She disappears back out the doorway and reappears a few moments later with a large white screen. 'There are extendable legs at the back,' she says, waddling awkwardly over to us as Conn jumps up to assist.

'Thank you,' she says with a relieved sigh. (I did ask if she needed help.) 'Or you can attach it to a wall,' she adds, brushing down her long skirt.

I go around the back and pull down the legs.

'I can set it up for you?'

'No, no,' I say. 'We've got it, thank you.' Conn has let go and the thing is standing unaided. 'You can go on. I'm sure you've got lots to do...'

When I come out from behind the board, she's still standing there, smiling.

'Thank you, Audrey,' I say again.

She looks from me to Conn and I can tell there's something she'd like to say, but I'd really rather she didn't. Conn's eyes are batting between us.

'Is there anything else I can do for you, Tessa?' she asks.

'No, no. I'm knee deep in Project stuff, so...'

She nods, but it takes her a couple more seconds to get going.

'All right, well, maybe we'll get a chance to chat next time.'

'Sure,' I reply, grabbing my stick and walking her to the dining room door. Of course what I'm thinking is: *Not if I can bloody help it.*

'Okay then, talk later. Bye, Conn. See you again soon too, I hope.'

'Yes, it was nice to meet you, Audrey,' he says.

Then she exits the room and his eyes rest on me.

'Mother-in-law–daughter-in-law relationships are notoriously difficult,' I say defensively.

'I didn't say anything.'

I start divvying leaflets into cloth bags to be brought on the drop later and Conn forwards the finished objection templates to the campaign email address. Trevor and Susan have agreed to man it. Now they just have to forward them to all the hall users who have expressed support. Hopefully after tonight's canvass, we'll have plenty more locals looking to submit their own objections.

'So,' I say, stacking the bags on top of each other. 'Are your parents into owls then?'

An involuntary laugh escapes from Conn.

'What?'

'You really are a dog with a bone!'

'I'm just trying to get to know you,' I say, innocently.

'All right, go on,' he says, shaking his head. He pushes back his laptop and raises his straight, slightly unkempt eyebrows at me. 'What do you want to know? Only don't ask me any more about owls. Okay? We both know I'm not going owl watching.'

The admission catches me off guard, but I admire it. 'Fair

enough,' I say, turning my chair slightly. 'Tell me why you came home. Your brother died. Was that the whole reason? Because the other day you said something about good causes like this being what you came back for.'

'It's both,' he says. 'My brother and doing some good. They're sort of the same thing.'

'Go on.'

'Fergal, my brother, was an excellent person. I was never as good as him but after I got my flashy job, I was worse. I won't go into the details because I know you wouldn't have liked the person I was either.'

'Fair enough.' I don't need the details; I believe it.

'I had too much money and not enough family. I should have come home six months earlier but... This is the best I can do. I wanted to be where he had been, to maybe stand where he stood or look at something he saw. I'll never know any of that for sure, but just the possibility makes me feel better. And then, sort of as part of that, I came home to make amends.' He cringes. 'That sounds trite.'

'It doesn't.'

He pulls the computer back to him and I think he's done, but then he says: 'Fergal was the kind of person the world is worse off for not having in it. I came home to make up for him no longer being here. Jesus, even that sounds arrogant.'

'What did he do, your brother?'

'He was an artist; immensely talented but self-critical. Never critical of anyone else though. A wealth of empathy, which was maybe part of the problem. You'd have liked him. Everybody did. He saw the good in people.'

'Sounds like Audrey.'

He considers this. 'Yeah. They have a similar vibe.'

'So you want to honour his memory?'

'More like I'm trying to make up for my mistakes.'

'Do you blame yourself for your brother's death?'

He winces, but he doesn't turn away.

'I know Senan told you about my daughter,' I say. 'It's fine. I used to not like talking about her, but now I do. Bea. Short for Beatrice. When she disappeared, I was consumed by guilt. I knew it was all my fault.'

'Everyone always thinks it's their fault, and then the twist in the story is that it's not actually. But it's different with me,' he says. 'I really could have stopped it.'

'From Dubai?'

'It's complex.'

'Mm. Well, I wasn't going to say that I had some epiphany and realised it wasn't my fault after all. No. I still believe it's my fault. It is my fault. I was her mother and I knew things weren't okay with her. What time has allowed, though, is acceptance of that. I'm constantly trying to make amends for it too. That's why I took in you and Chloe, in a way. Since my fall, I have been an imposition on my son – and I couldn't let that continue.'

He's looking at his computer screen now, but his eyes aren't moving. A few seconds pass before he says: 'Do you think she's dead?'

The way he says it discombobulates me. Nobody ever asks me that.

'I used to,' I say, carefully. 'For years, I did. I started to forget what she looked like without the aid of photographs and

I imagined that her body was somewhere decomposing at the same rate as my memories. But then, out of nowhere, I saw her again. Three months ago. On the landing upstairs.'

Why am I talking about this? I haven't admitted it to anyone. But I trust him and it feels safe.

'It wasn't actually her, I should say. It was an illusion, a dream, a delirium probably, but something about it felt like a sign. Like, she was on her way back to me.'

He's looking at me now. There's no visible incredulity at least.

'It was when I fell and did in my hip. I was probably so bored of lying there looking up at the same y-shaped crack in the ceiling that my brain just conjured her up for something to do. But, still. It felt very real to me.'

'How did she look?'

The sides of my mouth curl up, which is strange, because there are suddenly tears vying for the same ground. 'Beautiful,' I say as I swallow away the pang. 'She didn't look like she did in the photos. I mean she did, but she had changed. Her hair was shorter, her freckles a little lighter, a couple more lines on her face. And she was talking to me. It wasn't anything decipherable, nothing that could be contained within words, but I knew exactly what she was saying and she was soothing me, making me laugh, making me remember her. The way she was before she was only allowed to be someone who disappeared. And then...' I sigh.

'And then...?'

'And then my daughter-in-law arrived.'

'Ah. So that's why you're so strange with her.'

I groan at the memory. 'Audrey must have thought I'd completely lost it. Lying there in my underwear, sobbing and saying Bea's name over and over. If it had been anyone else that found me... Honestly, I think I'd have taken Otis over her.'

'I don't know, Tessa. If I saw my granny lying on the floor in the nip, I reckon it would top my brother killing himself as the worst thing to ever happen to me.'

'True,' I say, grateful for the chance to smile. 'But Audrey's just so sweet and concerned. She kept telling me Bea was gone and that she was Audrey, my daughter-in-law, as if I don't bloody well know that.'

But this is not what I wanted to say. I need to make Conn feel less alone, not myself.

'The point I was making is that I understand,' I say. 'I understand wanting to be where they were – Bea is why I'm still in this house – and I understand wanting to make up for their absence. And even if it is your fault, which I doubt, but even if it is, you do have to forgive yourself, just a little, if you're going to be of any use to the rest of the world.'

I take in his large frame, his manly arms, his beard, his shoulders. He's so grown, so impressively capable, such an *adult*, and yet I see the boy in him so clearly.

I'm not a hugger, but it takes a lot not to envelop him.

*Brrr-ong.*

The doorbell chimes, or rather it creaks. Like a lot of this house, it's been on the cusp of giving up for years.

Conn is already on his feet. I pull myself up onto my stick.

'It's probably Audrey,' I say, shuffling after him. I shouldn't have made a thing of her having a key. I'll say sorry; insist she go back to letting herself in.

171

Conn is pulling the front door open just as I make it into the entrance hall. I know straight away that it's not Audrey. It's a woman's voice, but frailer, older.

Where Audrey's tone is serene, this woman sounds apologetic.

'Hello,' she says, as I approach Conn from the side and he shifts over, pushing the door wide. 'Sorry to disturb you.'

I am often embarrassed by the outward grandeur of my home – the way delivery people gawk up at the place makes me want to engage them in idle chitchat until I can find a way to casually mention that I couldn't afford it either – but the slightness of the woman on my front porch takes it to another level; like I'm guarding the entrance to Versailles.

Her loose clothes cannot hide the thinness of her body, just as her headscarf cannot hide the absence of hair. Now that I see her, I doubt if she's much older than fifty. The quiver in her voice is the result of illness, not age.

'I didn't mean to just show up like this, but I was getting so worried. I didn't know what else to do...'

'Tessa,' says Conn, giving me a look. 'This is—'

But the woman, taking a half-step forward then back, interrupts. 'Sorry, I just feel a bit...' She sways slightly.

'Would you like to take a seat? Or can I get you some water? Something to eat? Or...'

But the woman is steady again. She shakes her head. 'I get flushes, sometimes. I'm fine now. Sorry.'

'This is Laura Darvin,' says Conn, stressing the name as if it should mean something to me. Then, when I clearly don't register what he's telling me: 'Chloe's mother.'

'Oh,' I say, looking from Conn to the woman, who is now observing us with glazed eyes. 'Oh. Right.'

I'm not sure what to say. I knew Chloe's mother wasn't well, but didn't she say she was on the mend? Or did I assume that?

This woman doesn't just look sick; she looks terminal.

'Ms Darvin, would you like to— Oh! Conn!'

But it's too late. She is mid-fall by the time I glance back, and although Conn lunges forward with his arms outstretched, he just misses her.

Her lithe body makes a muted thud, but there's nothing soft about the way she lands; side first, no fat to cushion her, straight down onto the grey concrete slabs.

# CHLOE

· · · · · · · · · · ·

The whole drive back to Hope House, I cling to that image. Paul glowing from across the street, so indisputably happy to have seen me, to have spent time with me. It's like a blanket wrapped around me as I sit in city centre traffic watching bikes zip past my car before accidentally ending up on O'Connell Street and nearly colliding with a bus. I zoom the rest of the way home, passing St Pat's College, where we first met, and many other sites of our great romance.

It's not so much that meeting me was worth getting into trouble with his boss for – although that is great, too – it's how easily and willingly he declared it; literally shouting it out on the street for all to hear.

I have to phone Yemi, ASAP. I need to run through it all with her, get her take on everything.

But first, I need to deliver the good news to Tessa.

And shoot! The flyer drop! I completely forgot about the flyer drop. I hope I'm not late; I hope they're still here. I don't think they were leaving until six.

Tessa's car is in the driveway, but that doesn't mean anything. The plan was for Malachy, one of the Radical Activists, to source a mini-van and drive us all in it.

I put my key in the lock and push the heavy wooden door. 'Hello? Anyone home?'

Tessa and Conn appear from the dining room; her wearing

a thin neck scarf and a long, light tan jacket, him in a charcoal wool jumper and carrying two boxes, one on top of the other.

'Sorry I'm late,' I gush. 'I was coming from town and I'm not used to the route and then the traffic was terrible. Have I made you late? Were you waiting on me?'

'You're fine, Chloe, dear,' says Tessa, her calm tone making me sound even more harried. 'We're still waiting for Malachy to collect us. He had some issues with the mini-van, but they should be here any minute. Why don't you sit, catch your breath. We have something to tell you, anyway. We had a visitor today—'

'Oh no, me first. Sorry. I don't mean to be rude. I just, I have some great news. You're going to be a very happy woman when you hear this.' I draw a breath, looking at them both expectantly.

Conn slumps the boxes onto the armchair. He does not look interested in what I'm about to say, never mind excited.

Tessa, at least, gives me a smile. 'All right, go on,' she says.

Conn Killjoy Horgan frowns at her, but Tessa just turns the palm of her right hand towards the ceiling. 'Make me a very happy woman.'

'Paul, my... friend, the journalist, he's interested – like really interested. He's going to write an article about the campaign. Probably several articles. For the *Dublin Press*, like.' I look to Tessa, waiting for her usual upbeat fervour to kick in. 'That's good news, isn't it?' God help me, I even throw a glance in Conn's direction. But they're just giving each other looks that I can't decipher.

What's going on? Is this about me? Has Conn been giving out about me? I feel a wave of nausea hit.

'I thought that was what you wanted...'

'It is,' assures Tessa. 'That's great. I'm delighted. It's just...'

Why does she keep looking to him? And why do I, who has long been accustomed to being left out of everything, suddenly feel horrendously excluded by a seventy-year-old woman and a man I can't stand?

'Your mam was here,' says Conn, finally.

'Earlier,' adds Tessa. 'She... Well, I'm afraid she collapsed.'

I understand that I am supposed to speak. That the next line in this exchange should come from me, but I cannot do it.

'Chloe?'

'She was okay,' says Tessa. 'We brought her in. She didn't want to come in, but of course we insisted. She didn't seem to think it was a big deal. She said it happens all the time.'

Is that... Is my head... Yes. I have managed a nod.

'Conn drove her home in her car. We couldn't let her drive herself.'

And now a blink. Buzzing head.

It's all over. Tessa is going to ask me to leave.

'And she was fine, wasn't she, Conn? You saw her to the door?'

Conn was in my mother's car. Conn was outside my house.

Full movement has returned to my head and I position it towards Conn. Tessa at least is regarding me with concern, like I might find some of these details upsetting, but not Conn. His brow is furrowed and he's watching me so intently, my skin starts to itch. Does he think I'll suddenly shed my skin and reveal the heartless witch he clearly believes me to be?

My mother came here, fainted, and got driven home.

How did she know where I was?

I want to ask them this, but I'm still struggling with words.

176

And then suddenly, the mechanics of my vocal cords are working again: 'Did she tell you she has cancer?'

'Yes,' says Tessa. 'I'm really sorry. I know you said she was sick, but since you had moved out, were moving in here, I had assumed...'

Another shared glance from them and another nod from me, as the gnawing dread in my stomach competes with a fire of fury blazing through my skull. They think I've abandoned my mother.

How dare she come here and try to ruin this for me.

How dare she spread her poison into yet another corner of my life.

I can feel Conn's eyes boring into me, judging me.

'She said...' Tessa begins. I swear if they look at each other again, my heart is going to break right here in this poorly lit foyer. 'She said you just left her, the day you came here.'

'I wrote her a note.'

'She mentioned. Six words.' *Five. It was five words.* 'I don't know what it was about, but... She misses you and she was so worried. Your friend let her know where you were. She was very apologetic about turning up out of the blue.'

Yemi. I close my eyes. The new mam guilt got to Yemi.

'I'm very happy to have you here, Chloe, but I don't want to be the cause of a rift between a mother and daughter. I know those relationships can be difficult, but take it from me, they're irreplaceable.'

Oh god. It's actually true. Yemi says I catastrophise when it comes to what other people are thinking about me. But this time they really do think I'm a monster. Tessa's about to throw me out. Where will I go? What will I do?

'I think you should call her, at least.'

This is it. I have two choices. I can let it fall apart, give up on this first stab at an independent life and go back to how it ever was with my mother. Or, I can tell them the truth.

Why is that so hard to do?

What am I protecting her for? When she has only ever used me to protect herself?

'She's lying.'

I open my eyes and they're both still there, not moving, not speaking, not – in one silver lining – looking at each other.

'You didn't abandon her?'

I shake my head. 'She's not lying about that,' I say. 'About being sick.'

That's what I wrote on my five-word note to her: I know you're not sick.

Another glance.

'Chloe,' says Tessa, cautious now. 'We saw her. We... She has no hair. She's definitely sick.'

'She's not. It's an act. I thought she was sick too.'

And another one.

'I believed it for two years,' I go on, 'but then I was in the bathroom brushing my teeth one night and I knocked over a tube of her pills. I bent down to pick them up, panicking that I'd lose some and she'd miss a dose, and I got this smell of mint. I thought it was the toothpaste at first but then I realised. It was the pills. Maybe I knew on some level because I put one in my mouth and bit. They weren't pills at all. They were mints.'

No glances now. All eyes on me.

'I went to see her doctor the next morning, the day I came here. He didn't know anything about cancer, no record of any of the appointments I had dropped her to his surgery for, no record of her being a patient at St James where I have been taking her for months, no record of chemotherapy or trials or prescriptions or any of it. The only record he had was of her last visit to him, nearly two years previous, when she turned up insisting there was something wrong with her – something that would require constant care.'

Conn shifts and I can't bring myself to look at him. Pity, scepticism, an expression that suggests I'm crazy – I don't want to see any of it.

Tessa, however, is right in front of me. She's horrified. 'Why would she do that?' she says.

There's a sound behind me and I jump.

*Brrrong.*

I forget the doorbell doesn't sound like a doorbell.

From the porch beyond, there's the faint sound of bickering.

'She's definitely not sick?' says Tessa.

'It's pretty clear she's sick,' I say flatly, 'but she doesn't have cancer.'

*Brrrong.*

'Hurry up, Mrs Doherty! If the hives don't kill Trevor, Maura will!'

'For the last godforsaken time, get your scaly skin away from me!'

'I better get that,' I say.

*Brrrong. Brrrong. Brrrrong.*

I've never been so grateful to hear a bell ring.

# TESSA
· · · · · · · · · ·

**I**'ve never been so enraged to hear a bell ring.

You spend all afternoon trying to extract the most basic information from one lodger and then the other turns up and completely blindsides you by revealing more than you could ever have thought to ask.

Chloe's mother is pretending to be sick...

There is nothing wrong with the woman who collapsed on my doorstep less than two hours ago...

How can that be? Could Chloe be lying? But no, I don't think so. Nothing else about her aligns with the idea that she would leave a sick mother to fend for herself. Everything about Chloe suggests a young woman who has never felt secure.

But who does that – and to their own daughter? What effect must such a breach of trust have on a person? What sort of mother did Chloe grow up with? The girl is practically begging me to open a case file on her. I have so many questions, so much more I need to know.

And now I'll have to wait to find out, thanks to the Project's most enthusiastic student and his ability to bulldoze into any situation.

'What's the emergency that has you knocking down my door, Malachy?'

'Sorry, Mrs Doherty,' he says, his freshly shaved dome glistening with sweat. 'Things were getting a little testy in the mini-van.'

'For the last time, that is not a mini-van!' snaps Trevor, who has one hand down the back of his polo shirt and the other up the left sleeve.

Malachy turns on the older man, as if there's one fuse left and it is about to blow. 'And for the last time, yes it fucking is! It's a van. And it's mini. WHATTHEFUCKELSEWOULDYOU CALLIT?'

'Watch it!' yelps Maura standing on the porch between the two men. 'Between him flaking skin all over me and you spitting, I'll never be clean again!'

I look past the three of them to the vehicle pulled in behind Chloe's Toyota.

It's a white commercial van that has seen better days. There's a driver and passenger seat at the front and a sliding side door that provides access into the back. Where a mini-van would have windows and rear seats, this vehicle has a massive cartoon drawing of an angry pitbull biting a man's leg and the words 'Misunderstood Mutts' written large above his head. In smaller writing at the bottom it says 'Phone Dano for obedience training' and then there's a mobile number that I'm pretty sure has one digit too many.

'I thought you were getting the loan of a people carrier?'

Malachy whips his head back to me, the muscles beside his left eye jigging a reel. 'A mini-van,' he half-whispers. 'I said I'd source a mini-van. That –' he thrusts his arm behind him '– is a mini-van.'

'No it's not, it's just a van!' Trevor has swapped his arms around, so his left hand is up his right sleeve and his right hand is down the back of his shirt. 'It's a van used to transport dogs. Dogs, which I am allergic to.'

'You keep threatening to break out in hives, Trevor, but so far, I have yet to see a single one. Unless they're invisible hives. Are they, Trevor? Are they invisible hives that you get from sitting beside invisible dogs?'

'Are you calling me a liar?' demands the older man, arms dropping as he squares up to Malachy, who is at least a foot taller and probably the same again wider. To be fair to Trevor, he throws a good shape.

'Spare me,' mutters Maura, who descends the steps, sits on the second last one, and produces a vape.

Chloe is still standing in the threshold. She's watching the madness unfold, though I'm not sure how much she's taking in. The information looks to have been as shocking for her to reveal as it was for me to hear.

'It's not quite what I was expecting,' I begin, but Malachy's whole face is red now and the twitch has spread down to include the side of his mouth. It looks more like he might cry than scream. 'But if there's space for us all...'

'There is. Dano took out the cages. There are benches in the back; plenty of seats for people.'

'They're beds for dogs, not seats for people!'

'Trevor,' I caution.

'That's where all the dog hair is,' he whines, but quietly at least.

'Okay, let's go, so,' I say, as Chloe steps out ahead of me, and Conn grabs the two boxes of flyer-stuffed bags from the armchair.

'He's coming too?' Chloe asks as Conn descends the steps and I pull the door after us.

'Conn is as committed to saving the hall as any of the Radical Activists,' I say, annoyed to be talking about such mundane things when all I want to do is pry into her home life. Not the sort of thing one can do in company, alas. 'I want the planning office flooded with objections by the end of this week, so it's all hands on deck.'

We walk down the steps and across the gravel to the van. 'We'll work in pairs. Every Howth resident should receive a leaflet. If we work well, we can get the whole place covered tonight.'

Malachy steps forward and pulls open the sliding door at the side of the van.

It takes a few moments for my eyes to adjust to the cavernous space, but, when they do, I can see that Trevor has a point.

There are three large dog beds taking up all of the floor space and a deep bench running along the far wall. Susan and Reggie are sitting in the middle of it.

'Hello,' says Susan, with a small wave.

Reggie, to her right, doesn't look up from his phone. 'There's no signal in this yoke. What are the walls made of? Titanium?'

'You know, I'm just doing my best, trying to help the cause, and I'm sorry but I am starting to feel like I'm not very appreciated.'

I put an arm around Malachy's damp shoulders and pat him gently.

'I'm feeling under a lot of stress here, Mrs Doherty. I'm trying to summon up the mindfulness, but it is not working.'

'The van is great, honestly,' I say. 'Plenty of space.'

'Atch-shoo!' Trevor has freed one arm from his shirt and is wiping it across his nose. 'I'm sorry, Maura, but I cannot sit in the back this time. I cannot! Atch-shoo! It will kill me.'

'Well if you sit in the passenger seat, I'll probably kill you, so...'

'I know you're joking, Malachy, but has anyone ever told you that you come across a tad aggressive?'

'Who says I'm joking?'

'Shouldn't Tessa sit in the front?' says Conn.

Several pairs of eyes travel to my stick.

'It's fine, I don't mind. You can have the front seat, Trevor,' I say, pushing the stick in ahead of me and clambering up with a hand from Reggie. Conn and Chloe follow me in. 'Come on, Maura. Climb up.'

My friend takes a last puff of her vape and allows Conn to pull her in. She just about squeezes in beside him as Malachy slides the door shut.

Reggie and Susan immediately turn on their phone torches (not their first rodeo, clearly). The engine starts and Trevor makes a loud hacking noise from the front.

'I feel like I'm being trafficked,' mutters Maura.

The van staggers forward twice before taking off at an alarming speed, sending us all skyward as it flies over the small dip just inside my front gate. It seems Malachy drives in the same manner that he conducts the rest of his life.

I turn to the teenager beside me as we lurch out onto the road. Or at least I'm fairly sure we're out on the road. I can't see a thing. 'I'm surprised to see you here on a lovely sunny evening, Reginald.'

'Yeah, well,' he mumbles, still scrolling through his phone. 'I wasn't going to have youse all leaving me out again, was I? And I did do the tag for the leaflet. Had to make sure you weren't messing up my art.'

I pull a flyer from one of the boxes and present it to him. It gives a summary of what's happening with the hall and details of where to send objections, either by post or email. We've included our campaign email address if people want to get more information. It's a way for Trevor and Susan to send interested parties a template of the planning objections without looking like we're out soliciting complaints.

Reggie did a fresh take on the North Dublin Community Project logo and we have positioned that at the top. 'It's really good,' I say, as his finger traces the outline of the graphic. He's drawn the acronym so that it forms the shape of the hall.

'I should have made the "N" darker.'

'I think it's perfect.'

'It's whatever.'

I pat his hand. 'And I'm very glad you're here.'

'So what's the plan, Tessa?' asks Susan, from the other side of Reggie. We're turning a corner now, and she grabs the teenager's t-shirt to stop herself being flung off the bench.

'The plan is to get a leaflet to every household in the town and the area surrounding the hall.'

'Might be worth doing some guerrilla marketing,' says Reggie.

'What's that?' shouts Malachy from the front seat, where Trevor is still sneezing furiously.

'We did it in Business Studies. It's like spraying slogans on the ground and stuff. I have a few cannons in my bag. I could lash up some signs.'

'Cannons?' queries Susan, grabbing Reggie's sleeve again as her phone flies from her hand. I'm used to bad driving – my Bernard was atrocious – but she looks a little pale.

'Spray cans, like.' Reggie leans over and unzips his backpack. 'Paint.'

'No. Absolutely not. No graffiti,' I say. 'Defacing buildings is not how we're going to win public support.'

'It's not defacing. It's enhancing.'

'No. No graffiti. All right?' I take a breath. 'We'll work in twos. Malachy will drop us off at different points. If we put in a couple of hours, three tops, we should get everywhere covered.'

'I might not be able to stay that long,' says Susan. 'My boys are at after-school activities, but they'll be home in an hour wailing with hunger.'

'Can they not fix themselves something?'

'It's half an hour making them something or three hours cleaning up the mess if they do it. And I'm just too tired for that.'

I'm starting to get an idea of what brought – or, more like, drove – Susan to the Project. 'Well then, you can do the area nearest the hall, so you don't have far to get home. We'll drop you there first. All right, Malachy?'

'Roger that, Mrs Doherty.'

'I'll go with Susan,' says Trevor. 'Atch-shoo! Anything to get me out of this van.'

'No arguments here,' calls Malachy.

'And I'll go with Chloe,' I say, determined to get answers to my rapidly multiplying questions. 'We'll take the housing estates just beyond that. Malachy and Maura can keep the van and go out the Howth Road – those houses are spread further apart. And then Conn and Reggie can take the village. All the residential streets.'

'Which are the residential streets?' asks Conn, who hasn't said much since he got back from dropping Laura Darvin home. He hasn't taken his eyes off Chloe since we got in the van.

'Reggie can show you,' I say, forgetting that Conn is new to Howth. 'From Cairns Street over to Regency Place really.'

The teenager looks at me blankly.

'You *live* on Regency Place, Reggie.'

'Yeah, but I don't know what any of the others are called. Who remembers street names?'

'*Everyone.* How do you find your way around?'

'Eh, technology?' he retorts, waving his phone at me. 'It exists so you don't have to waste your time remembering stuff.'

I try to restrict the amount of despairing of the youth I do, but sometimes they really push you.

'Maybe we should be with people who know the area?' Conn suggests.

'I know Howth,' interrupts Chloe. 'I've been doing deliveries here for years. I could go with Reggie, and you could have Conn.'

'Oh, well no, I thought we'd—' I begin.

'Yeah,' enthuses Reggie. 'How do you feel about graffiti?' he asks Chloe.

'I like it when it's good.'

'I'm very good.'

'No graffiti, Reggie!'

'Understood, Mrs Doherty,' he says solemnly, before leaning over me to wink at Chloe.

'Forget it,' I say. 'I'll take Reggie and keep an eye on him...' Beside me, the teenager sighs loudly and slumps down on the bench. 'And, Chloe, you and Conn can cover the town.'

Chloe is horror-stricken.

'That's okay, me and Reggie will find our way,' says Conn, getting in before her. 'We can ask people for directions if we need to.'

'Or I can keep an eye on Reggie,' says Chloe. 'I won't let him spray anything.'

'I'm not a baby, you know,' asserts the teenager. Then quieter: 'You'd need more than one eye to catch Rapid Cannon Reggie.'

'No, that's it,' I say, as the van comes to a halt with such velocity that Susan would be lying in the dog beds only Conn got his arm out in time to catch her. 'I'm taking Reggie, and you two are teaming up.'

Chloe goes to say something but stops herself. Conn finally pulls his gaze away from her.

The sliding door opens and Trevor appears.

'Ah! Fresh, uncompromised, non-toxic air!' he declares, inhaling deeply.

'First pair out,' I say, as Susan hobbles off the bench.

'I'll never take the joy of this sweet nectar caressing my nostrils for granted again.'

'God speed, Susan,' I call, as the door slams shut once more.

# CHLOE

· · · · · · · · · · · ·

**We're only** on our second street and I don't know how I'm supposed to finish this road, never mind drop leaflets to another twenty-something of them.

We've started with the terraced streets where Conn suggested I do every first house and he do every second. I would have preferred to take a full side of the road each – thus not having to constantly walk past him or, more irritatingly, have him walk past me – but mainly I want to avoid any sort of conversation, so I just agreed.

At least the constant movement means the silence isn't so visceral.

Still, I can feel his eyes on me; when I'm opening the gates, closing them, pushing the letterboxes wide, stuffing the leaflets in.

Again now, as he walks up one short, tiled path and I stride down the adjacent one, arm out for the gate though I'm still a couple of feet from it.

Let me put another house between me and his judgemental gaze ASAP.

The thought of Conn in my mother's car. It's at least a twenty-minute drive between Hope House and home, plenty of time for her to woo him with her medical knowledge. How much research must she have done to maintain the charade for so long? Though a debilitating illness did fit with her pre-existing lifestyle of keeping to herself and not leaving the house unless strictly necessary. The woman is very convincing – it can't just be naivety that had me believing her.

*No*, I think as I reach for another gate, *it was love too.*

I'm not looking as I turn out onto the footpath, too busy facing the reality of being lied to by the person who should love me most. I turn for the next gate and my foot catches on a crack in the pavement.

'Woah!' says Conn, appearing from nowhere to break my fall.

'You good?' he says as he rights me, a large steady hand on each of my arms. His torso eclipses my view of the street beyond.

For a moment I do actually feel faint. But then, I'm fine again. I shake him off.

'I know you don't believe me,' I say, moving my fistful of leaflets into my left hand and pulling my cardigan straight.

Conn is carrying the tote bag with the bulk of the flyers on his shoulder. He readjusts it and looks at me with those intense, inscrutable eyes.

I really wish he'd blink more.

'You believe my mam. You think she's sick. You think I'm the liar and that I'm just looking to get out of caring for her. God!' I say, teeth clenched. The stress is pouring in from every part of my body. 'From the moment I met you, you've thought you're so much better than me!'

I rotate my shoulders and shake myself slightly, but it's no use. The only way to relieve myself of this wretched feeling is to be gone from here.

When he speaks, the words come slowly. 'When I was in your house...'

My head snaps up. 'You were in my house? You were *inside* my *house?*' I squeeze my eyes shut. 'It just gets better and better.'

Conn was looking around our tiny two-bed stuffed with old newspapers and knick-knacks and reams of junk that my mother refuses to throw out. Dear god. Without me there to clean it, I can only imagine the state the place is in.

'When I was in your house,' he begins again, 'I saw an electric razor and a bucket with hair clippings stuck to the side of it in the sitting room.'

I close my eyes again. Could I give tripping over that pavement another go? Maybe this time I could bang my head and pass out.

'I asked your mother what chemo drugs she was on. My mam had cancer, years ago. She's fine now, but I still remember how upset she was when her hair started to fall out, and I wondered if your mam was on the same medication.'

I eye him cautiously. 'What did she say?'

'Nothing. She didn't say anything. She grabbed the bucket off the carpet and stomped out of the room. I stood there for another minute or two, thinking she'd come back. But she didn't. I went into the kitchen to say that I was off and goodbye and make sure she was okay. She didn't say anything to that either. She just banged around some stuff at the bin and the sink. It was like I wasn't there, and I couldn't understand it. That's not normal behaviour. The whole taxi ride home I felt like I'd done something terrible, and then I remembered what you said about how she used silence as punishment.'

'I never put it like that,' I object.

He looks at me expectantly.

Realisation dawns. That's *exactly* what she was doing.

'And I thought about how on the car ride over, she asked all these questions about what you were doing. She wanted to know if you'd had any friends over, if you were watching TV, if you were spending time on the internet. I thought it was her way of finding out how you were, but she never actually asked that. It was more about monitoring.'

A familiar panic is rising. I ignore the impulse to ask what he told her. That would make it all sound worse again. I scratch at my arm. 'That's just how she is,' I say. 'She's protective.'

His brow furrows. 'When I mentioned that you and Tessa had watched a film one evening, she was determined to find out what it was.'

'*Four Weddings and a Funeral*.' We've actually watched three films this past week, but that was the one Conn walked in during.

'Well I didn't know that, but does it really matter? She would not let it go,' he says.

'She likes to be involved.' If he thinks that's bad, he should have seen her when I was going out with Paul. She wanted to know every single thing we did together. And if she didn't believe me, she'd go through my stuff looking for evidence that I was lying to her.

Conn looks at me like I'm an idiot. 'Chloe, that's not how parents are supposed to behave.'

'All right. I get it,' I say. 'It's nothing to do with you. I don't know why I'm making you so angry.' I open the next gate, walk up to the letterbox, and stuff in a leaflet.

'I'm not angry at you,' he says, too loudly. A woman pushing a buggy past gives Conn a second look. He steps in towards the house. 'I'm not angry at you,' he says, quieter, walking after me as I go on to the next house. 'I'm angry *for* you. I'm angry at her. I don't know what kind of situation you grew up in but in your house today, with the curtains drawn and all the stuff everywhere, I got an idea.'

'When I was there, I opened the curtains.'

'I'm not judging you; I promise I'm not. I just... When you said she was lying about having cancer, I believed you, instantly. That's what I'm saying. It made sense. And maybe she is a different kind of sick, but it's still inexcusable. It's not okay. And I want you to know that.'

An older couple pass us now, and we move in again, just about making space for them.

Conn gestures to a bench on a small green a little further up the road. 'Let's sit, okay?'

I nod and turn to lead the way.

I brush some leaves from the wood and take a seat, shifting over so Conn can fit too. He places the bag of leaflets on the far side of him.

'Why are you being nice to me?' I ask, not even trying to hide my wariness.

He smiles. 'I like you, remember? Even if it's not reciprocated.'

'You like me because I'm, what was it you said, breathing?'

'Alive.'

I do actually remember. It was such a weird thing to say, but I've been thinking about it ever since.

'Or do you like me because I'm voyeuristic and crude?'

He baulks.

I widen my eyes.

He rubs at his cheek. 'I didn't mean you were voyeuristic and crude.'

'That's exactly how it sounded.'

'It's the topic, talking about Tessa's misery. I find that voyeuristic.'

'I was just acknowledging an awful thing we had both heard about that afternoon.'

'I know,' he says, throwing his head back so the newly illuminated streetlight catches the hardness of his jaw and the red in his beard. 'It's complicated,' he manages, eventually.

I clear my throat. If he wants forgiveness, he has to explain.

'My brother killed himself, you know that,' he says, placing both hands on his thighs.

I nod. 'And I'm sorry.'

'It's something I think about all the time. I'd say it takes up ninety-five per cent of my head space. I dream about it. I daydream about it. I'm thinking about it when I don't even realise I'm thinking about anything. But I don't talk about it. And the thought that other people would be talking about it, gossiping about it...'

I want to butt in, to insist that I wasn't gossiping but I hold my tongue.

'... people that didn't even know him...' He makes a low droning noise. 'It makes me feel insane.'

'I can get that.'

'And I don't want to be that person for Tessa and her daughter. I know you weren't being disrespectful, but I would feel disrespectful, talking about it. It's me, it's just about me.'

He turns now and looks at me, checking if this is okay.

It is.

'Okay,' I say.

'Okay,' he says.

We return to facing forwards. He crosses his long legs at the ankles and I pull my cardigan tighter. He's wearing different shoes today, suede loafers, but they're as expensive-looking as all the rest.

'So what do you think about when you think about your brother? Is it him alive or him dying?'

Conn looks at me. 'You really are bad at silences, aren't you?'

'And yet I love the library.'

'Unexpected.'

I shrug. 'It's the one place where everyone is supposed to be silent. No chance someone's giving you the cold shoulder, or everyone else in the building actually hates you. They're not talking because they're not allowed to. Rules,' I say, with a satisfied sigh. 'Blissful.'

'At first, you seem like you make no sense. But keep going, and you start to make a lot of sense.'

I smile. 'Plus, I love books.'

'Ah yes. Especially the Chelsea Mangan series.'

'You remembered.'

'I looked it up. I downloaded the first one onto my Kindle.'

I turn. '*You* have a Kindle?'

'It's my mam's,' he says, defensively. 'She has two. She insisted I take it.'

'And? Are you enjoying it?'

'Haven't gotten past the first chapter,' he says. 'I used to be a great reader, but not lately.'

'Too busy thinking about your brother?'

He faces me now, too.

'Don't think I didn't notice what you just did there; changing the subject,' I say.

He turns back, allowing his body to relax into the bench, his legs sliding out further.

A group of teenagers pass us; three on bikes, two on scooters and one on crutches.

'In the best moments, I think of him alive,' says Conn. 'He was like you in that he was very alive.'

'And unlike you.'

'Exactly.'

I was being sarcastic, but Conn is not.

'Was he mentally unwell?'

'He had bipolar disorder. He was medicated, but he didn't like taking it. He was convinced it was interfering with his creativity. Fergal was a painter. A few months before he killed himself, he had a gallery pull out of a solo show and he believed it was because the work he had created for the exhibition was crap. He blamed the medication.'

One lad on a bike grabs the injured one's crutch and cycles off. The rest of group howl.

'Most of the time though, I think of the few minutes before,' says Conn, inspecting his hands, rubbing at a callous on the knuckle of his middle finger. 'He phoned me, just before he did it.' He delivers that bit with dull vigour.

I wait.

'I didn't answer.'

'You can't blame yourself for missing a call.'

He shakes his head. 'I didn't miss it,' he says, voice still matter of fact. 'I screened it. I knew he wasn't well. I'd talked to Mam the day before and she'd filled me in, and I just didn't have the time to deal with it. I thought if I picked up, I'd be on the phone all day. It was six in the morning and I'd been out the night before and I just... couldn't be bothered.' He squints. Then he drops his hand. 'So mostly, I think about that.'

I want to tell him that it's not his fault. I want to say that he doesn't need to feel guilty for the actions of his brother. That it's a travesty, but if his brother was that unwell it's very unlikely Conn could have done anything to change the course of events.

But I don't say any of these things because either he knows them already or he's not able to hear it. Sometimes we need distance to see clearly.

Ever since I left Mam's house, memories are flooding my brain; they're coming out of nowhere and a lot of them are being recast. It's like I'm viewing them through a wider lens.

I was heading to bed last night after *My Best Friend's Wedding* and Tessa pulled herself up to give me a hug. I know it's normal behaviour, but it felt as strange as if she'd stuck her finger in my ear.

I remembered a time when I was about fourteen and this man had broken up with Mam. She was devastated. She refused to eat or get dressed or go to work. So I cooked and phoned in sick for her. She was too sad to be left alone so I stayed home from school. What I mainly remember is sitting on her bed, Mam's head in my lap as I stroked her hair. I had, up until this week, considered that a nice memory, a sign of our mother–daughter bond. But there was something in Tessa's hug that made me see it anew. I know Mam was sad, but shouldn't she have made me go to school? Shouldn't she have pulled herself together, for me?

I have been trying to think of a single time she told me she loved me without it being part of a guilt trip and I can't.

But maybe that's all she was capable of. Love is not a quantifiable unit and I do not have to match what I give to what I receive. Mam needs vats of the stuff just to get out of bed in the morning. I have survived a lifetime on scraps, and I'm fine. We're all made differently. It's nobody's fault.

I don't want to share the warped memories. I don't want to be disloyal. So instead I tell him about the Emmas.

'My mam's not all bad.'

He looks at me, surprised by the shift in topic but grateful, I think. 'I'm sure she's not,' he says.

'When I was in primary school, there were two girls in my class, both called Emma, and they were picking on me for not having a dad. One day I came home in floods of tears and I told Mam what they'd said, but I begged her not to go to their parents. I was convinced that would make it worse. What do you think she did?'

'Went to their parents?'

'You see that's it, she didn't. She agreed not to and she kept her word. Instead, she walked me into the yard the next morning, just before the bell, and she went up to the two Emmas and she bent down, and she said something to them. I have no idea what she said but whatever it was it worked, because for the remaining two and a half years of primary school, those girls didn't say a word to me. Not about my lack of a dad and not about anything else. I couldn't believe it. Mam never did stuff like that. She didn't really like to talk to other people. She did it for me.'

Conn shifts on the bench, pulling the bag up onto his lap. It's getting dark. We should get back to leafletting.

'Even if she wasn't always the Mam I wanted her to be, she's all I've had for my entire life.' *Except for when I had Paul,* I add silently. I think about him turning back to me with joy on his face as he crossed the road this afternoon, and I'm inching away from Conn before I even realise I'm doing it. 'She's been through a lot. My dad left her and she fell out with her family. So she only had me, and she thought I was going to abandon her when I moved in with Paul.'

'Journalist Paul?'

'Yeah,' I say cautiously. It sounds a bit sarcastic when he puts it like that, but there's nothing on his face to suggest he's making fun. 'And I think Paul sort of knew, or he suspected something anyway. He never said he didn't believe her, but he would make a point of saying what a coincidence it was that something always broke in the house or she was unwell or there was some sort of emergency when I was supposed to be staying at his. She could tell that I was really into him, that I loved him.'

Conn glances over and I feel myself blush. 'I think that's why she made it up. She didn't want me to leave.'

'That's no excuse.'

'I know. But if I don't forgive her, then what? I don't have her in my life? She really is all I have. Without Mam, I don't have anyone. I don't have any family.'

'Had.'

'Sorry?'

'Your mam is all you had, but she's not all you have,' he says. 'We can be born into families or we can build them. Being in your life at the start isn't an entitlement to be in it forever. You decide who gets to be in your family, not a birth cert.'

'Were you listening on the first day when I made the pathetic admission of only having one friend?'

'You only need one friend. The whole time I was in Dubai, I didn't have a single true friend.'

'Really? You seem like someone who'd have friends.'

'I played golf with my boss but at the same time I was sleeping with his wife.'

'*What?*'

'I know,' he says. 'I was an awful person. Feel free to judge me.'

I can't stop staring at him. 'How does something like that even happen?'

'My point is, you have one true friend. You're doing well. And you have other people who care about you. Like Tessa.'

I nod. I think Tessa does care about me, though god knows why. I can tell she likes watching TV with me, even if I talk too much, and that makes me happy.

'So yeah, you have your friend and you have Tessa and you have...'

'Paul,' I say, nodding again as I finish the sentence. Then, when he doesn't say anything: 'Right?'

'Yes, right. Journalist Paul.'

There was definitely an edge of sarcasm that time.

'What I'm saying is that whoever the people are, you can build your own family. Getting to be on your team should be an honour, not an entitlement.'

How is this the same man I've been sparring with since I moved in?

'What?' he says, as I continue to ponder whether lobotomies are still a thing.

'Nothing,' I reply. 'Just wondering how you got to be so wise. Did you catch it off the owls?'

He bursts out laughing and I grin. It's a good laugh; goofy, very unsophisticated.

'Just been to plenty of therapy, that's all.' He raises an eyebrow at me. 'That's where I go on Tuesday mornings.'

'Ah.'

'And just so you know,' he adds. 'I do work. Not a lot, for reasons I can't really get into, but I work.'

'If you say so.'

'This morning I legalled a document for a tech company that's just setting up in Ireland. It took me two hours. Do you know how much they paid me?'

I shake my head.

'Six hundred euro.'

'It would take me a full week to make that!'

He stands from the bench and swings the tote bag up over his shoulder. Either the straps are too short or his arms are too big, but it's comically ill-fitted. It's kind of adorable, actually.

'The world is a fucked-up place with fucked-up priorities and all the wrong people are paid the big bucks,' he says.

'I know that's true.'

'So now' – he holds out a hand for me to take – 'let's go deliver some leaflets and try to right one injustice in this money-obsessed hellscape that is life.'

# TESSA

· · · · · · · · · · ·

'The thing about guerrilla marketing is that it's thinking outside the box. It's finding alternative ways to get your voice across. You can appreciate that, Mrs Doherty. That's the kind of stuff you're always going on about.'

I hold out my hand and Reggie takes another wad of leaflets without slowing his pace.

'Yeah, you could go the official route and write a letter of complaint to your local politician,' he says, turning into the next driveway and making for the door, '*or* you could make your way to the seat of power and chain yourself to the goddamn rails. You know what I'm talking about, Mrs Doherty, you know.'

Reggie hops over a short wall, into the next garden, fires that leaflet into its letterbox and is back out on the road before I've budged.

'We're not doing any graffiti, Reggie. Not a tag on a laneway wall, not a stencil on the kerb, and not a slogan on the windscreen of a car that you have a "feeling" is abandoned.' I should have recorded myself a dozen repetitions ago. At least that way, I could just press Play.

'Are you familiar with Gucci?'

I sigh. 'Why do I feel like this is a trick question?'

'Gucci,' he says, returning for a few more leaflets, 'is one of many high-end brands that uses graffiti as a means of advertising. It did this sick series of murals. High art...' He holds one finger aloft as if he's making a particularly pertinent point, '... to draw attention to high fashion.' He fires the flyers through the next pair of steel slats with muttered 'pew-pew' sounds.

'Can we change the subject please?'

Reggie shrugs, coming to a stop in front of me. 'Which way now?'

I point out to the main road, where there's a relatively large estate on the other side.

'Here, give us that,' says the teenager, removing the canvas bag from my shoulder and slowing his natural pace as we make our way along the footpath.

Despite what he might like people to think, Reggie is a caring boy. He has insisted on carrying everything this evening and has done the vast majority of legwork. If anyone passes us, he shoves a flyer in their hand and talks passionately about how deadly the hall is 'for getting off school, but like, for *learning* and stuff too'.

He puts an arm out as we cross the road and I take it without acknowledgement.

'When this stick is gone, I think I'll do a half-marathon,' I say. I had considered a full one, but even Demi Moore would draw the line at that.

'When's that going to be?'

'Imminently,' I say. 'Doctor's appointment on Thursday. She'll take it from me then.'

'Could I have it?'

'My stick?'

'Yeah.'

'For what?'

He shrugs. 'It's a good stick. You can always use a good stick.'

We enter the larger estate and do what we've been doing thus far; Reggie takes a bunch of flyers from me and weaves in and out of gardens, while I walk a little further up the path and position myself at the point where I think he will need to reload. If there's a low wall, I'll sit on it; my legs are weaker in the evenings.

'Have you ever played team sports, Reggie?' I ask, as he zips up and down. 'You're so nimble.'

'Nerd sports,' he says. 'Couldn't be playing nerd sports. It would do nothing for my cred.'

'Which ones are nerd sports?'

'All sports are nerd sports,' he calls, zooming into the next garden. It's dark but several of the gardens have sensor lights. He's blazing a trail. 'It's the effort,' he reasons, zip-zip-zipping along. 'There's something very nerdy about trying.'

He does a couple more houses, then takes another stack from me.

'I did athletics for a while at weekends. But if you tell anyone that I will deny it and heavily suggest that you are at the later stages of going senile.'

'Understood,' I reply. 'Why did you stop?'

'A: Because it's a massive nerd sport for massive nerd alerts. Like, I was winning *medals* for the *high jump*.' He stops right in front of me and raises both eyebrows as if to say, 'Need I go on?'

'And B?'

'My step-mam was very into it. She was a runner when she was at school. She wanted me to relive her youth or whatever.'

I hand over another stack. 'Maybe it was an attempt to bond with you?'

'Yeah... I'd rather she would just leave it out, to be absolutely honest. Y'know when someone's trying too hard to be nice and make everything okay, and you're just like, maybe don't?'

A picture of my daughter-in-law and her unwavering smile pop into my head. I don't want to make her awkward, but I'm also not responsible for reassuring her that all is rosy. The simplest option would be for her to forget she found me that morning and stop trying to talk about it.

'Yes, I'm familiar with that sensation,' I tell Reggie.

'She's always asking how my day was or if I need help with homework. I think she feels bad cause Dad's at work a lot, but that's cool with me. I was always on my own in the house and I liked it. Now I'm not allowed to be on my own.'

'We all need a bit of space.'

'That's what I like about the Project. I only go because I get off school.' He shoots me a look.

'Absolutely,' I agree, not pointing out that it's nearly eight on a Monday evening and nobody is making him be here.

'But, you know, I like the space too. You're working together, but like, you're also on your own. It's space, but it's not lonely.' I can see him considering this. 'I dunno. Like, it's... It's all right, is what I'm saying.'

I smile. 'It's community.'

'Yeah,' he says, shoulder jerking slightly. 'And like, if the hall goes, will you still do Radical Activism at your house? Doesn't matter to me,' he adds, hastily, 'but for saddos like Trevor and Malachy. They're going to need somewhere to go.'

'I don't think I could,' I say, 'there's a lot of stuff around insurance and that...'

Reggie considers this. 'Right, well, we just can't let anyone knock it down so. Those tossers can't win,' he says, coming to a house with a mailbox and slam-dunking the leaflet in. 'Someone's got to think of the saddos.'

'Agreed,' I say, as he quickens his pace again. 'Not on the saddos bit, but, otherwise, yes.' I must have a word with Senan when I get home. See if there might be some way of the school enticing Reggie back onto the track. The boy is brimming with potential, even if he's determined to obscure it.

We wind our way through the roads, covering more houses than I could have imagined, until we reach the final property in a very lengthy row, back at the entrance to the estate.

The occupant is heading out the front door with six dogs – each of them on a lead, none of them keen to hang about.

He takes the leaflet from Reggie.

'Youse must be Malo's mates,' he enthuses, scanning the thing. 'I gave Malo my van to help with the campaign. Fight the power!' He attempts to lift a fist, but the dogs are straining at their collars and they don't let his act of solidarity get above waist level.

'And you must be Dano,' I say, extending a hand, but encountering the same canine obstacle. 'I'm Tessa. This is Reggie.'

'Malo!' cries the teenager, shrieking with laughter.

The man swaps all the dogs to one hand. Clearly a professional. 'Dano Lawlor, Misunderstood Mutts,' he says, quickly shaking mine, before a particularly yappy Alsatian almost breaks free. 'If there's anything else I can do to help, just say. I offered Malo the use of any of these lads,' he nods towards the dogs, whose collective drool is making such a significant puddle that I take a half-step back, 'but he says he's gonna try not threatening anyone and see how he gets on...'

'We would welcome a couple of planning objections if you'd like to submit them?'

'No problemo.'

'Great. There's an email address on the leaflet there.'

'Is this your house?' butts in Reggie, who has managed to compose himself. 'Do you own it, like?'

'Yeah. Bought it three years ago.'

'So that's your wall?' Reggie angles his head towards the side of the building, the one that faces out onto the main road.

'Yeah...'

'Could I have a shot of it? Do a mural for the campaign, like.'

'Reggie,' I warn him.

'No graffiti. Won't use any paint at all, swear to God,' he says quickly, making some peculiar hand gesture. 'Scouts' honour.'

'Were you a scout?'

'Yeah. You?'

'126th brigade,' barks Dano, standing straighter, despite the pull on his equilibrium.

'28th,' retorts Reggie, before looking at me. 'Say that to anyone and—'

'Mum's the word.'

'Go on, so,' says Dano, the dogs inching him past us and down the path. 'Do what you like. We've had a few advertising companies look to put a billboard on it since we moved in. I'm a socialist though, so I'm not taking their blood money. But this is different.'

'Thanks,' says Reggie, suddenly excited. 'Thanks a lot.'

Dano nods, turning out of the garden path. 'Fight the power!' he shouts again.

And while they're likely just barks of delight to be moving, it sounds like several of the hounds agree.

# CHLOE

. . . . . . . . . . .

'D o you like your job?' asks Conn, as we come to the end of our final terraced street and start to make our way up the hill towards the two apartment blocks also on our route.

We got into a rhythm pretty quickly. Conn's every-second-house method actually works well and the chat made the time fly by.

'I like driving and I like the time on my own,' I say. 'Or do I even? Maybe I've just gotten used to it… It's totally fine, but it's not what I meant to do. I studied to be a primary school teacher.'

'But you didn't want to do it?'

'I had just graduated when Mam got sick, or I thought she did at least, and I didn't want to commit to a full-time job. Couriering allowed me to be at home with her when I needed.'

'What's stopping you from pursuing it now?'

'I haven't even considered it to be honest. It hasn't been very long since my world got blown open. I guess all these things are possible again… I have thought I'd like to be a librarian as well.'

'Ah yes. The rule-sanctioned silence.'

We pass a large detached house on the sloped road and Conn lifts his arm awkwardly so I can grab a leaflet from the bag. He still smells of entrenched cologne. How is that possible when he's been walking for hours in a thick jumper? I would not like anyone to get a whiff of me right now.

'What about you?' I ask when I'm jogging back down the driveway.

'Librarian? Nah. Too fond of the Kindle.'

'Har har. I mean, do you like your work?'

'God, no. Hate it. Always hated it. I just did well in school so I kept on that path. Then you qualify and you're paid well, and you get used to being paid well... It's a hard cycle to break – until your brother dies and you suddenly realise that what matters in the world is definitely not the pursuit of tax loopholes.'

'Right,' I say, falling into step beside him. I take three for every two of his. 'So what would you like to do?'

'I wanted to be a carpenter when I was a kid. I was good at making stuff and cause of Dad we had a workshop in the house. But then sort of... I was the smart one and Fergal was the creative one and never the twain shall meet.'

I look over at him just as he glances down. 'Honestly, I haven't thought about it,' he says. 'I've got a greater purpose than work right now and I'm giving my time to that.'

I frown at him. 'Owl watching?'

He looks equally confused.

'No offence, but you don't seem to give your time to much else.'

'I just... I just mean this campaign, saving the hall. That's all.'

'Ah,' I say, not entirely convinced.

'So your journalist is going to write about the hall?'

I let this blatant subject change slide. I'm happy to get to talk about Paul. Ideally, it'd be with Yemi. But I'll take what I've got.

'He's not *my* journalist. But yes, he is,' I say, reaching over and grabbing another handful of leaflets from the bag. The audacity of him smelling this good halfway up a hill. 'Paul thinks it could work as a campaign – something for the newspaper to get behind. He thinks he can write several articles about it, actually.'

'Slow news week.'

'Excuse me?'

'Nothing,' he says, sauntering up the driveway of another detached house. I wait at the entrance.

'So why did you break up?' he enquires as we set off again. 'You and Journalist Paul?'

'He wasn't a journalist when we went out,' I say, trying to determine if he's making fun of me, or Paul, or both of us. 'We met at college. He was studying teaching too.'

'A college romance.'

'I guess.'

A few more steps.

'We were going to move in together, into this flat in the city. Paul's sister owned it and she was giving it to us at a good price. Small but with a great view; you could see all the way out to the Dublin Mountains.'

'Sounds lovely.'

'It was.' I feel queasy now, a little off-balance. 'But then, like I said, with Mam, I felt I had to stay at home.'

He's watching me again and I shake off the sick feeling.

'But what happened with Journalist Paul?'

'Why do you keep calling him that?'

Conn shrugs. 'He's a journalist and his name is Paul, is it not?'

I throw him a look, but he keeps walking. Maybe he's one of those mainstream media sceptics, like Mr Fitzsimons with the placard. Maybe he finds the very idea of a journalist amusing.

'Everyone needs a nickname.'

'Okay.'

'You never had one? Nobody ever called you anything other than Chloe? Your whole life?'

'A nickname would require friends. I have one, remember?'

He grins at this, jogging up another, shorter driveway and pushes in a flyer. 'What about Journalist – sorry, Plain Old Paul. He never had a name for you? A creative type like him?'

'There is a woman at the depot who calls me Prairie,' I say, ignoring his last question. Paul called me 'Clo'. Obvious, maybe, but nobody else ever called me that. 'It's after this TV series, *Little Home on the Prairie*.'

'*Little House on the Prairie*.'

'You've heard of it?'

The sides of his mouth twitch. 'Yes. I've heard of *Little House on the Prairie*.'

I start explaining why Penny says she calls me that, but he cuts me off.

'I get it. Trust me,' he says. 'It suits you. My nickname at school was Scrooge.'

I laugh loudly and it takes him by surprise.

'What?' he asks, half-smiling, wanting to be in on the joke.

'No need to explain that one either,' I say.

'I think there actually is...'

I look at him squarely and in my best version of his voice say: 'I get it. Trust me.' I'm not devoid of all cultural references. I have read *A Christmas Carol*. I do exist in the world.

He shakes his head, still sort of smiling. 'Okay, whatever. Let's not get off topic here. What happened with Paul? Not being able to move in together right away hardly meant the relationship had to end.'

'No,' I say, as we take another driveway each. 'But it was sort of the beginning of the end. The relationship between Paul and my mam was always tricky. He thought she relied on me too much. He didn't think she had my best interests at heart. I should have listened to him. I should have...' I should have chosen *him*, not her. But I can't bring myself to say it. It's too much regret to acknowledge.

'We made plans to go travelling the following year instead. But then Mam got worse – or I thought she did, because I believed her – so I couldn't commit to that either. There was a lot of stuff I couldn't do. Paul thought I was throwing away life opportunities. I was always cancelling plans, with everyone, and I guess it was hurtful. I couldn't really stay over at his any more, and he didn't want to stay at mine. There was a big fight.'

'Between you and Paul?'

'Between Paul and my mam.'

'Even worse.'

'He accused her of exaggerating her symptoms. He said she was glad to have a reason to keep me chained to her.' I flinch at the memory. It was a Saturday night. We had been out for dinner and Mam phoned to say she couldn't get her temperature down. When we got back to her, it was normal. She said the painkillers had kicked in. 'And I sided with Mam because she is my mam and I didn't know... you know?'

He murmurs his comprehension. 'Regret is a fucker,' he says.

'Yeah.'

I missed Paul so much for the first few months that it was painful. The absence was an ulcer. I couldn't eat or sit or lie down without feeling it. But then I'd think about Mam and the worry trumped the loneliness. I didn't think I could exist without her. I could never have imagined a life like the past week to be possible.

'Oh god. I've been talking for ages, haven't I?'

'Ah. We only missed a few houses.'

'Shoot. Really?' I ground to a halt and look behind us.

'No great loss,' says Conn, gently guiding me forward. 'They didn't look like the type to protect community centres, anyway. More likely to flatten them.'

'Why? Because they're wealthy?'

'The biggest obsession of wealthy people is staying wealthy.'

'Takes one to know one, is it?'

'Sort of, I suppose.'

I instinctively go to apologise. I'm not usually glib. But he doesn't seem perturbed. He never does. 'You know I'm a people-pleaser?' I say.

'You mentioned this before, but I have to say I'm not seeing a lot of it – presuming you would classify me as people.'

'Well that's what I was going to say. I am a people-pleaser – but not with you.'

Conn hoots. 'I don't know what to make of that. But you sound very happy about it anyway.'

'I am. It's never happened before, especially because, objectively, you're the kind of person I would usually be intimidated by.'

'You'll have to elaborate on that.'

'You know, wealthy and seemingly smart and...' I gesture up and down his empirically better-than-decent body, but he just looks at me dumbly. 'Tall,' I say eventually.

'Right, right.'

'I think it's because you rile me up.'

'I've noticed.'

'Yes, you're sort of annoying and delighted with yourself.'

I hold up a hand to say I'm not finished. 'You act like you have me pegged, even though you do not, and now apparently you're not actually a total arse.'

'The compliments, they just keep coming...'

'Better than someone saying the best thing about you is that you're continuing to inhale oxygen and exhale carbon dioxide.'

'Alive is the best thing you can be,' he protests.

'Whatever the *reason*,' I continue. 'I don't feel the need to be deferential to you and I like that. I find it... invigorating.'

'All right,' he says. 'I'll accept that.'

'You don't have a choice,' I say, coming to a halt outside the apartment complex. 'This one first.'

Conn glances at the silver plaque beside the door. 'Ninety-two apartments.' He winces.

'This is the smaller one. We have that place to cover too,' I say, gesturing further up the street.

'Isn't Malachy supposed to collect us soon—'

'Better get going so.'

Conn places his hand on the door and pulls, but it doesn't budge. 'Huh.'

From my back pocket my phone beeps.

'That Malachy? Determined to pick us up?'

'You wish,' I retort, fishing out my phone.

'I really do.'

The message is from Paul.

Hi Clo. Thanks for surprising me earlier. It really turned my day around. I've been thinking about nothing else since. I was going to phone earlier but wasn't sure if that was too soon. Will call tomorrow – don't think I can play it cool any longer than that! Paul x

'So?'

I blink at Conn. 'Hmm?'

'Is it Malachy?'

'Oh. No.'

'No,' agrees Conn, studying me. 'It's Journalist Paul.'

'No,' I lie, cheeks burning. 'Why do you say that?'

Conn is already heading back to the apartment complex door. 'Because,' he calls after him, 'you looked up from your phone as if I'd just walked in on you having sex.' He rattles the handle once more. 'We're going to need the code to get in.'

*It really turned my day around.* I cannot believe he said that, unprompted, like it was nothing. The old Paul would tie himself in knots trying to tell me my dress was nice. I said I love you *five weeks* (and three days, because you never forget a burn like that) before he managed to say it back. And he didn't actually *say* it; he let the tracklist on the mixed CD do the talking for him. He was not a man to declare his feelings easily. But here he is, telling me how I *turned his day around*, and how he has to phone me tomorrow because he can't play it cool any longer than that.

I am suddenly convinced I am hallucinating.

I unlock my phone and open the message again.

But there it is. Just as I read it the first time. Only this go around, I take in the exclamation mark! The x! The fact that he called me Clo!

I used to literally dream about a time when I might once again hear him say Clo. Not that I *heard* it, but you know, as good as.

'I'm trying to carry out a tricky bit of trespassing here, Prairie. And you're still standing there, all hot and flustered by whatever sweet nothings Journalist Paul is sending you.'

I blow air into my face and hurry up the path after him. 'Stop calling him that,' I say, pointlessly doing the same thing of pulling on the handle and being met by resistance.

'You let me know a better nickname and I'll be happy to switch it up.'

Sometimes, when it was just the two of us, I used to call Paul 'Num-nums'. But you could put me in a torture camp, under pain of death, and I still wouldn't admit that to Conn. 'We need the code,' I say.

'I've already registered that fact.'

'Just buzz someone,' I suggest.

'Hello, you don't know us, but could you possibly let us in so we can slide some junk mail through your door?'

'It's not junk mail,' I protest.

'I know that, but these people don't...'

I regard the door. He has a point. We don't want hostility before we've even set out our stall. There are glass panels to either side of the entrance, but they don't open. There is a corridor window on the first floor though, and it's ajar.

'I could go in through there and let you in.'

'Go in through...' Conn follows my eye line. 'Okay, Spiderman.'

'I could! We could stand on that wall and then you could give me a leg up and I could grab hold of the trellis with—'

'No.'

'Why?'

'Because I like my neck, and your neck, intact. And because it absolutely wouldn't work.'

'It's not actually that high.'

'No,' he says, strolling back towards the door.

'Fine,' I grumble. 'I'll do it myself.'

I climb up onto the wall without much bother, but there's still a fair distance to go. A little further away, there's a streetlamp with a wider base. I could stand on that. I make my way down, reach over and manage to pull myself up, but there's only really space for one foot. The other one is still on the wall. It's a rather undignified lunge. If I got a foot up, I could probably get my other foot flat across the wall and sort of climb horizontally...

'Hi,' I say, to the woman who has appeared from nowhere on the path below. 'Nice evening.'

She's still ogling me as she walks away from the building and I smile at her as if we share some secret.

'Conn, if you could,' I begin. 'Conn?'

But he's no longer there.

The door is now swinging open.

That woman must have just left the building, and Conn's gone inside.

By the time I get inside too, he is already standing in the corridor, looking at the row of doors.

'I was expecting you to abseil down from the first floor, *Mission Impossible* style.'

I hold my head high. 'Shall we take a floor each?'

'Slight problem.' He jerks his head towards the apartments. 'The doors don't have letterboxes and the post boxes are in a mailroom off the foyer for which we need another code.'

I survey the corridor. 'All right.' My foot starts tapping. 'We'll just have to slide the leaflets under.'

'For ninety-two apartments? Across eight floors?'

'Well, what do you suggest?'

'We could put them on the noticeboard instead.'

I glance back towards the foyer and the modest corkboard that takes up max one metre of one wall. 'We can't do that! Tessa said to get every home!'

'We'll plaster the board in them. People won't be able to ignore it. If we push it under their door, they'll probably put it straight in the bin. Plus, it'll save our backs.'

'If it's too much effort for you, I'll do it myself,' I say, lunging for the bag but Conn is too quick.

He rotates his arm away, laughing. 'You still think I'm lazy.'

'No,' I say, trying for the bag again. 'I just have a particularly strong work ethic.'

'Sure,' he replies, taking the bag off his arm and holding it aloft.

'What is this? The school playground?'

'My idea is better,' he says.

'No it's not!'

I stretch up for them, but don't even get close. I give a little jump, but he bunches the straps in his hand so it's further out of reach.

'Give it to me!'

'No.'

'Give it to me!'

'No,' he says, laughing as I grab hold of his arm, both my hands wrapped around the dark-grey wool, and pull it down. 'Jesus, you're surprisingly strong.'

'I've been lifting my mother in and out of showers for months for absolutely no reason,' I say through gritted teeth, eyes only on the prize but nostril marginally distracted. He really does smell suspiciously good.

I have the arm down slightly, but I need to get it further...

'Hey!'

I've put my left foot on his right one and am leveraging my right foot against his left leg.

'Are you... Are you trying to scale me now?'

He wraps his free arm around my waist and lifts my whole body with negligible effort. He clearly wasn't trying very hard earlier. He tilts me slightly to the side, arms away from the bag still held aloft and deposits me back onto the cream tiles, right beside him, my chest pushed up against his side.

'I am not this building,' he says, voice lower, heavier. 'And you are not actually Spiderman.' I can hear him breathing. I don't think I've ever heard him breathe before. It's very deep, very focused... very attractive.

I should move away now, I've given up on grabbing for the bag, but I don't.

He should let go now, but he doesn't.

We just stand there, bodies pressed together, both breathing heavily.

I feel something on my right arm. It's the bag. He has brought his left arm down and his hand is on my arm, moving towards my side.

I am trying to steady my breath, but it only makes it louder. He pivots ever so slightly in towards me, the coarse knit that covers his chest grazing against my cheek. I don't think I've ever been this into a jumper. I feel a tingle course through me, a warmth.

I can't like Conn. He's my housemate in a house that I cannot risk losing. Not to mention he's smug and self-satisfied. I cannot be attracted to a man who chooses not to work. He spends his free time with owls, for god's sake!

And Paul. Smiling, walking backwards, crossing the road away from me.

I take a deep breath and an even deeper step backwards.

'Fine,' I say, surprising myself with the consistency of my tone. 'We'll wallpaper the foyer.'

The next twenty minutes pass largely in silence that I wish would break, but for different reasons than usual. I wait for Conn to hand me a wad of leaflets – I'm not getting near him again unless strictly necessary – and I start at the opposite end of the noticeboard. When we meet in the middle, he steps back and lets me finish it alone.

'Give any more thought to a laptop?' he asks when I'm nearly done and I exhale the breath I wasn't aware I was holding.

'I'll get one someday,' I say, back still to him.

'But not someday soon? Not paying rent has got to be saving you money.'

'Oh I've already started saving. But not for a laptop. There's tons of computers at the library. I'm saving for shelves.'

'Shelves.'

'Yes, shelves. I do need some knitting needles too, but they're affordable, even for me. The shelves are a bigger outlay – and more urgent. I have nowhere to put my books. I like to place a finished book on a shelf. You can't get that sort of satisfaction from a Kindle. They actually let me put back my own books at my local library.'

I compose my face into a look of cheeky confidence and finally turn to face him.

'And I don't want just any shelves.'

'Oh god, no,' he says, face barely moving.

We've moved on, but I'm sure neither of our heads are fully in this conversation.

'I want ones that are deep enough for books, and I mean *all* books. I don't want shelves that are taken by surprise by a coffee table book or an atlas and leave me with no choice but to store them on their sides underneath other awkwardly squashed in books. I'm looking for roomy, accessible-to-all shelves. Finished.'

I step back to admire my handiwork. Conn was right. Fifty leaflets stuck side by side really does have impact. And now we definitely have enough to do the 100-plus apartments up the street.

Conn nods his approval. 'Do you know where else you can store books and they always fit?'

'A Kindle?' I ask, turning to face him. We're side by side, but there's a safe distance between us.

'Well yes, but also: a laptop.'

I scrunch up my face. 'Who reads on a laptop? Gross.'

'I actually—'

'Conn Horgan. I thought that was your voice but I told myself no, the PTSD must be back.'

Conn turns a split second before me and when I do the same, I gasp. I can't help it. It just comes out. This woman is *stunning*.

She is clearly used to such reactions because she doesn't even acknowledge me. She just pulls her handbag up her arm – black and expensive, just like her coat – and continues to bore holes into Conn.

'Linda.'

'Well at least you remember my name.'

'I didn't know you lived here,' he says and I have to turn to look at him because I've never heard him sound so meek.

The woman gives a loud laugh, or, more accurately, she says the word 'ha' very loudly. 'How would you possibly know anything about me? That would require getting in touch.'

'I'm sorry—'

'I thought you were in Dubai. Not that you told me that. In fact, you were there before I knew anything about it at all. Your *brother* had to tell me.'

'I meant to—'

'You meant to what, Conn? You didn't even send me a text!'

'I'm sorry. I tried to get in contact with you when I got back but none of the messages delivered...'

'I block assholes. It's a policy that tends to work for me,' the woman snaps. 'Is this your girlfriend?'

'Hi,' I say, raising a hand as she finally looks at me. I feel my mousey hair wilting and cartoon stench lines starting to appear around me. 'I'm Chloe. Nice to meet you.'

'Are you with him long?' she demands. 'I doubt it. He's never with anyone long, are you, Conn? Well listen, Chloe, however long it's been, I'd consider it long enough and get out now. Don't pay attention to anything he's said to you, and I don't care how good he might be in bed—'

'Linda, stop!' he entreats. 'Are you insane? She's not my girlfriend.'

Linda looks at me again. As if I'm the one fabricating things.

'I'm not his girlfriend,' I clarify, my face starting to heat up. 'Although I don't think it's *insane* that a person might think that...'

But Conn isn't paying attention to me. He has eyes only for the tall, thin goddess with the perfect eyebrows and lips that even I, a boringly heterosexual troll of a woman, want to kiss. 'I'm sorry about what happened and how I handled things.'

She says 'ha' again though, clearly, she doesn't find any of this funny.

'I really am.' He takes a half-step towards her and she takes a full step backwards.

'Don't.'

'I want to apologise.'

She's shaking her head now, fist tight around her handbag straps as though he's already taken her heart and he might come back for her money. 'You'd have to work very hard to adequately apologise to me,' she says and she makes for the outer door. Before she goes though, there's a look, a hesitation, like she really would like to be able to forgive him and take him back.

Conn must have seen it too because he goes after her.

'Hey!' I call after him.

'I'll be back,' he says, pulling the tote from his arm and dumping it on the tiles.

'We have a whole bigger complex to do and Malachy is supposed to be here in fifteen minutes. I won't be able to do that by myself!'

'I'm sorry,' he shouts after himself. 'I have to.'

'Have to what? You have to help me deliver these!'

But he's already disappearing from sight, and earshot.

Unbelievable.

Just as I was starting to think he might not be the entitled egotist he appears to be, he goes and proves my initial assessment correct.

He literally just abandoned me in order to chase a hot woman down the road! Of course, not before declaring her insane for thinking he might deign to go out with someone as unremarkable as me.

Ten seconds to gather myself then I storm out of the building.

Once an asshole, always an asshole.

I look both ways for Conn, but there's no sign.

I throw the canvas bag over my shoulder, march up the road and do the other apartment block on my own. This one's front door is broken and the mailboxes are accessible, so it actually only takes a few minutes. Not that Conn would have known that. Then I text my location to the number Tessa gave me for Malachy.

Just before the Misunderstood Mutts mobile pulls up, I get a message from Conn.

Sorry. On my way back. Be there in one minute!

Malachy pulls in by the kerb, leans over and pushes open the passenger door so I can sit up front. 'Where's the posh lad?'

'He said to go on,' I reply, pulling the door shut behind me. 'He's making his own way home.'

# TESSA

· · · · · · · · · ·

There are very few people in this world or any other who intimidate me. But Doctor O'Shea's receptionist is one of them.

Julia treats all patients with deep suspicion. She's an elite armed patrol and same-day appointments are her Fort Knox. I could be phoning with my arm hanging off and she'd still ask if I was certain it was urgent – and she'd say it with such scepticism that I'd be looking at the limb wondering if I could in fact just sew it back on myself.

Suffice to say, I'm a big admirer of the woman.

'Tessa Doherty for Doctor O'Shea,' I say, approaching the glass hatch with a wad of paper in one hand and my stick in the other. It feels good to walk into a room knowing that when I leave it, I'll be doing so solely on my own two legs.

'Take a seat,' she says, without looking up.

But, somehow, she still *sees*.

'What are you doing?'

'Hmm?'

Her eyes dart from my face to my now-empty right hand.

'Oh. That. I was just leaving a few flyers in your flyer stand here...' I reach back and straighten the Save Our Hall leaflets. I've wedged them between *Indigestion or a Heart Attack?* and *Five Signs You Are Having a Stroke*. 'It's for an important local campaign to save the North Dublin Community Project over at the old parish hall—'

'That stand is for medical pamphlets only.'

'Actually, didn't you attend our life-drawing classes? I remember you doing a very credible pear...'

'Medical. Only.'

'We teach first aid,' I say, marvelling at how a face can be both blank and glaring. 'And we do meditation – which is just healthcare prevention, really. Plus, the mobile blood pressure clinic stops by Rumba for Retirees twice a year...'

She blinks, slowly. It's like two meat cleavers coming down. 'Tessa Doherty?'

Doctor O'Shea is at the door to the far side of the hatch.

'That was quick. Right, well, I'll just leave those there anyway and if anyone asks the best option is to contact the email address on the...'

Julia's face doesn't move, but there's a low growl and nowhere else it could be coming from. I smile, do a sort of bow, grab my stick and hurry after Doctor O'Shea.

'How are you, Tessa?' she asks when the door is closed and we are seated in her office.

'Excellent, thank you,' I reply, shirking off my jacket. 'Raring to go.'

'That's good to hear. And the family? I saw Otis at the supermarket recently. He is turning into a fine young man, isn't he?'

'He's on the basketball team this year,' I say, brimming with pride. 'Practising every morning. He was on the bench for the first few games, but he got called up yesterday.'

'Good for him. Team sports are very important at that age. Now...' She clicks on her computer before placing both hands on the desk, one atop the other. 'What can I do for you today?'

'I'm here about relinquishing this, obviously,' I say, lifting the stick slightly, 'but I wondered if I could also pick your medical brain on something.'

She raises her greying eyebrows.

'Do you know much about Munchausen's?'

'Munchausen's syndrome? Where someone pretends to be ill?'

'I have a young lodger at the moment who thought her mother had cancer. She found out recently that she's been faking the whole thing.'

At first, everything Chloe told me about her mother's bogus illness was followed by a caveat or story to show that she had a good side. I respected the loyalty, though the yo-yoing energy stressed me out.

Eventually, she started to talk without the frantic worry that she was doing something terrible. Last night, before we pressed Play on *Notting Hill* (we are making our way through Bea's old DVDs), she told me a little about her extended family; grandparents she barely remembers from childhood and an aunt that her mother fell out with when Chloe was a teenager. Laura didn't like her sister interfering; she thought she was trying to take Chloe from her. Chloe can't remember all the details but, on balance, she doesn't think that was true.

'I can't say I know an awful lot about it,' says Doctor O'Shea. 'It's a psychological disorder, a compulsion. It's difficult to diagnose and harder again to cure. Some believe recovery to be impossible; even if the patient stops one pretence, they are likely to take up another. Was this a pattern of behaviour for the mother?'

228

'I don't think so.'

'Was she driven by a desire to be a victim, to elicit sympathy generally?'

'I'm not sure she presented the charade to anyone else. She was trying to stop Chloe, my lodger, from leaving home. It sounds like there was a pattern of controlling behaviour rather than pretending to be sick.'

Doctor O'Shea removes her glasses. 'The main thing I know about Munchausen's is that it is a lot more common in movies than it is in real life. I've never seen a case of it myself. What you're describing sounds closer to malingering.'

'What's that?' I ask, as she glances at the clock to the left of her window. 'And then I'll shut up.'

'Malingering is feigning illness for a definable reason; to get out of work, say, or to receive a benefit. It could be someone pretending to have whiplash for an insurance claim or a drug addict faking illness to get access to medication. Or, I suppose, feigning a terminal illness to keep someone tethered to you. Malingering is not considered a psychiatric condition and the perpetrator will have a defined gain. With Munchausen's, the only real gain is attention. Though I couldn't make a diagnosis without seeing the person and knowing more.'

This makes sense, though it doesn't do much to help me help Chloe. If Chloe's mother is in a pattern of acting against her daughter's best interests, I'm not sure I can encourage a reconciliation.

I've been getting on brilliantly with both lodgers this week. Although relations between the two of them have gone from bad to worse. Conn arrived home about an hour after we picked Chloe up from leafleting on Monday, and Chloe immediately left the kitchen and went to bed. Naturally, I've sought answers. So far all I've gotten from Conn is that there was a misunderstanding. I heard him trying to apologise on Tuesday, and I heard her refusing to accept it.

Since then, he's mainly been out the back working on a new door for the fuel shed. When I left today, he was hammering away, surrounded by far more wood than I'd have thought necessary, as happy as a pig in the proverbial. We've had lunch together the past couple of days – when Chloe is off on her deliveries and it's safe for him to be indoors – which has been lovely. Otherwise though, he's a man of the wilderness. He's even growing the beard.

'Let's get back to you,' says Doctor O'Shea, with two clicks of her mouse. 'How are you getting on post-fall? It's been...' She glances at her computer screen. 'Three months?'

'Three months and three days. I did try to come on Monday, but Julia was not willing to grant a start of the week appointment.'

'How are you healing?'

'Fine,' I say, sitting a little straighter. 'I barely have any pain at all.'

'Barely?'

'An odd niggle.'

'Can you describe it?'

'Maybe a wobble every once in a blue moon, but really it's fine.'

'Balance can be a hard function to regain.'

'I can balance,' I clarify, lest she get the wrong idea. 'To be honest, the stick is doing more harm than good at this point. I'm relying on it when I shouldn't be.'

'Any dizziness when you stand? Blurred vision? Legs feeling weak?'

'I...' My mouth clamps shut. 'No. None of that.'

Doctor O'Shea looks at me, then types something into her computer.

'So, now, shall I just leave it here, or...?'

'What's that?' she says, still typing.

'The walking stick.'

'Why would you leave the stick here?'

I frown. 'That's why I'm here. It's been three months, like you said. I've served my recovery time and I'm ready to get back to normal.'

Now she looks confused. 'Tessa, I never said you could go without the stick after three months.'

'You did. You said three months was the healing time for the hip.'

'Three months is how long it takes for the hip to heal, usually, but then it can be another nine months until the legs reach their full strength. And even then, half, if not more, of people who fracture their hip never return to their previous mobility levels. Sometimes it's down to overall health or age or just the luck of the draw. I did go through all this with you.'

I shake my head. I'm certain she didn't put it as bluntly as that. An outside chance I'd have to keep it, maybe – a prospect I might be facing if I'd fallen at eighty-nine, not sixty-nine.

'You might recover your mobility – but it would be another six months before we could tell. You're at a decent level as it is.

You seem to be getting around fine with the walking aid.'

'I'm sixty-nine. I'm hardly going to have a walking stick for the rest of my life?'

'Tessa, I had a patient this morning who is recovering from a hip replacement she had during the summer. She's fifty-two.'

'Did she break her hip?'

'Yes.'

'Well, I only fractured mine.'

Her eyebrows are climbing again. 'What do you think a fracture is?'

'The doctors at the hospital only ever used the term fracture, they never said break. Same as you.'

'They're the same thing, Tessa. I'm sure you know that.'

Now that she says it, I do. But I honestly don't think I realised until now.

'So, I'm... you're not taking the stick?'

'I couldn't, not in good faith, and like I say you're getting around great with it.'

I'm not getting around great. I can carry next to nothing without risking another tumble and I currently have two strangers living with me because I'm too big a liability to live alone. That's not an assessment based in reality, but one my son has made based purely on the existence of this stick. Also, Doctor O'Shea might be embracing her greys but she's still in her forties and so has yet to experience the most devastating symptom of ageing. The menopause, wrinkles, poorer eyesight; all fine. It's the rapid onset of invisibility that caught me off guard. Nobody told me that people stop seeing you.

One day you're getting hit on at a reproductive rights rally and the next a man is bumping into you in the tinned foods aisle of the supermarket and carrying on without a backwards glance or word of apology or even a wobble and you're wondering if you're really there at all. The stick was like adding another two decades overnight. The stick might as well be an invisibility cloak.

But it takes me too long to articulate any of this and Doctor O'Shea is already back peering at her screen. 'I see the anniversary of your daughter's disappearance is coming up,' she says. 'How are you dealing with that?'

I glance from her to the computer and marvel at how the most defining event of my life is probably summed up there in two clipped sentences.

'Fine,' I say.

She regards me for another moment then pushes back her chair. 'Okay,' she says with renewed energy. 'Let's say we'll check back in in another six months, see where we're at. All right? In the meantime, you should have a scan coming up at the hospital?'

I nod, pulling myself up with the stick then admonishing myself for not doing it unaided. You see, this is what I mean! The thing is making me worse, not better.

Doctor O'Shea walks me out to the waiting room, telling me to pass on her best to Senan and Audrey.

'Will do,' I say with absolutely no intention of telling my son and his wife about this visit. I do not want to confirm their long-running pessimism about my recovery. The doctors might have to do everything by the book, but I know my own body. More importantly, I know my mind and its ability to persevere.

I pass the reception desk and glance at the leaflet stand. There is now a clear gap between the Heart Attack and Stroke pamphlets.

Bloody brilliant.

Julia clears her throat and I try to pick up my face; I don't even entertain a notion of rebuking her. She inclines her head towards the door.

*All right, all right. I'm leaving.* The woman is wasted in this line of work. She'd have made a great prison guard.

I'm out in the lobby when I glance down and see that the low table, which has housed the same two plastic pot plants for as long as I can remember, is now home to a wad of leaflets too.

It's actually a more prominent location than the flyer stand. They're impossible to miss.

I look back through the glass door and mouth 'thank you' to Julia. But she turns away instantly and barks something at a teenager on the far side of the waiting room who drops his phone in fright.

As I recall it now, she really did sketch a mean fruit bowl.

# CHLOE

· · · · · · · · · · ·

**W**e're about thirty minutes into *Romeo & Juliet* when Tessa removes her glasses and reaches for the remote. I put my hand to my mouth to make sure words aren't accidentally coming out, but no. For once, she's pressing Pause because she's the one who wants to say something, not me.

'Will I go out and tell him to come in?' she asks.

I look at her dumbly, as if I too have not been trying to drown out the constant banging since the film started.

'If nothing else, he'll be freezing. It's getting cold out there.'

Conn has been wearing a uniform of black tracksuit bottoms and a grey t-shirt since he started his woodwork odyssey three days ago. I've watched him from the large window on the return – I've mainly stood there willing him to wallop his hand – and can confirm that he has never added a jumper nor altered the t-shirt.

If he doesn't sever a finger, hopefully a bacterial infection will get him.

'I'm sure all that hammering is keeping him warm,' I say, reaching for my phone to illustrate how little concern I have for the well-being of Conn Horgan.

But Tessa isn't appeased. 'You don't want to call him in, do you?'

I haven't spoken to Conn since he abandoned me for his Amazonian ex on Monday evening. I can't think about him without burning with rage. I thought we were getting on, forming a real connection, and then he goes and deserts me to chase after a woman with legs up to her armpits. He was the first person I spoke to properly about Mam, I hadn't even told Yemi, and he discarded it like it meant nothing.

I've got his number now, though. He's the type of man who gets a kick out of making women like him just so he can toy with them. Not that I like him, or ever would. Whatever that was in the apartment complex hallway must have been a delayed response to what happened with Mam. I was clearly out of my mind. *I'm* the one who wouldn't be interested in him. Not the other way around.

He has attempted to speak to me twice; once in the kitchen when Tessa was there. So she knows things aren't great between us. He probably thought her presence would oblige me to speak but he was wrong.

He was on to something when he spoke about building your own family (even a broken clock is right twice a day) and I am more comfortable in this house than I could have thought possible. Tessa and I have had lots of lovely chats and are continuing to work our way through her rather against-type DVD collection. And then I was on the phone to Yemi for the whole afternoon yesterday. Akin was doing a marathon nap so she couldn't leave the apartment, but she could talk. I told her about Mam and she didn't force me to dwell on it. I probably spent more of the call giving out about Conn.

'I'm going to go and get him,' says Tessa, getting out of her armchair unaided. She got the all-clear to retire the stick yesterday. Which is great, for her. Obviously. 'It's getting dark now too.'

She crosses the room to the single French window and reaches up to undo the bolt.

She moves perfectly. You'd never know there was anything missing. In fact, she has an extra pep in her step.

A wave of dread passes through me.

I know it's awfully selfish and that I should be happy for Tessa's recovery, and I am happy for her too, but I can't help worrying what her new-found mobility means for my future. I'm not sure I ever felt this relaxed with Mam. The psoriasis on my scalp has calmed and the amount of times I feel the need to check that everything is okay during our movies is definitely reducing.

But when we came into the sitting room this evening, she carried both mugs of tea. That's my job. And she was flying around the place this afternoon when the Radical Activists were over for a class. Trevor said she moved 'like a gazelle', whatever that is. If she's back to normal then surely she doesn't need lodgers any longer?

'He has the door on the hinges since this morning. It looks perfect,' says Tessa, peering out into the quickly dying light. 'God knows what he's doing out there now.'

'A nice new shed door and two grateful lodgers,' I say in my most jocular voice. 'You could almost say everything is perfect, couldn't you? Perfect just as it is.'

Tessa undoes the other bolt and a small chip of wood falls from the door.

'No need to change a thing, I should think,' I continue, because my desire for security has always been greater than my pride, and a few weeks in this house isn't about to magic that away.

Tessa reaches for one of the white handles and pulls. 'I'm going out.'

'Don't! It's dark!' I exclaim, getting up. 'The grass will be damp and you might trip. Just call him.'

So that's what she does. She sticks her head out and shouts around the side of the house that it's late and he's surely done enough for the day and that if he doesn't come in soon, he'll do himself an injury.

'We can only hope,' I mutter as I reach for my phone again. I unlock it and immediately go to the most recent message from Paul.

Conn shouts that he just needs another half hour and then he'll head inside.

Tessa shouts that he could watch *Romeo & Juliet* with us.

Conn shouts that it's okay and he wouldn't like to intrude, but thanks for the offer.

The last text message was sent this afternoon, by me. I am under strict instructions from Yemi not to write another thing until he has responded. I keep typing out what I would send him and then deleting it. Occasionally I send it to Yemi to see if something casual: e.g. Just watching a movie with my housemate. How's your Friday night going? might be okay to send. But her response is always the same:

NO!!!!!!!

So I'm holding strong.

Yesterday he found out he was shortlisted for this year's journalism awards and he texted me straight away because I'd always been so supportive of his journalism dreams and he knew it would make me happy. I literally hugged that message to my chest going to bed last night.

I sent him a big congratulations in response but I realise now where I went wrong; I didn't add a question. If there's no question, why would he reply? He probably thinks I don't want him to reply.

Oh god. What if he thinks I'm not interested in him any more?

Tessa is back in her armchair now, remote in hand. 'Shall we?' she asks.

'Yes, just one sec,' I say, before hastily typing out a message and pressing Send.

I read back over it.

Up to much this weekend?

Nothing needy there. Yemi can't be too annoyed about that. Then I push the phone down the side of my armchair and nod to Tessa, who presses Play.

About twenty minutes pass, during which time I take in absolutely nothing of what's happening on screen. Then the noise from outside reaches new heights.

Glasses off, remote back in hand.

'He's drilling,' she says.

'He's very inconsiderate,' I agree.

She listens a little longer. 'I'm sure he'll be finished in a minute.'

About thirty seconds more of drilling, then it stops.

'Okay, let's—'

*Brrrrrrrrrrr!!!!!!!*

'He'll be exhausted,' she says, brows joining together. She sounds like a concerned mother, the sort I've read about in books.

'He's used to staying up all hours to watch birds, he'll be fine.'

She gives me a quizzical look.

'What?'

'He doesn't really go owl watching. You know that, don't you?'

My cheeks redden. 'Yes.' Then three seconds later: 'No. I didn't know that. Where does he go for half the night, then?'

'Haven't a clue,' she says. 'But there's no such thing as owl watching.'

I knew it wasn't a real thing – and he convinced me otherwise! So he's a compulsive liar as well as everything else. Doesn't Tessa find it creepy that he sneaks off every night and neither of us have a clue where he goes? He could be up to anything.

I turn my body fully so I'm facing the French window. It's pretty pointless. The shed is at the back of the house. Anyway, it's so dark now that all I see is my own reflection.

Is it a girlfriend after all? Or maybe a series of girlfriends? Leggy Linda one night, Booby Barbara the next. That way he wouldn't technically have been lying when he said he didn't have a girlfriend; maybe he has several.

How could I, even under the most extreme psychosis, have come anywhere near kissing that man?

He'll be fine if we get turfed out of here. He'll probably have multiple boudoirs where he can make himself at home.

I turn back to Tessa. 'You know if I ever do anything that annoys you, like drilling late at night—'

'Oh I don't find it annoying,' she says. 'I'm happy for how happy he is out there.'

'Still. If I do anything, if I don't leave something the way you like it left or if I forget to close doors – I know that used to really annoy Mam – anything at all, you'll tell me, won't you? I never want to be irritating to you. I'd hate that.'

She smiles. 'You're not irritating, Chloe, and you don't annoy me.'

She reaches for another of my Special Occasions White Chocolate Chip Cookies.

'These are delicious,' she says.

'They're really easy to make. I'll whip up another batch tomorrow. I can make them whenever you want, just ask. And if you prefer dark chips, or fruit, I can do that too.'

She takes another bite, then another.

'I really do love being here, Tessa,' I declare suddenly and far too passionately. 'I love it. I know it's only been a couple of weeks, but this feels like a home. You've been… You mightn't need us any more and that's totally fine and it's your house so if you want me gone, I'm gone, but I just want you to know that it would be a privilege to stay and I'd do whatever I could to help.'

'Chloe,' she says when she's swallowed. 'Is this about the stick?'

'I'm so happy you have your mobility back, I really, really am—'

'I committed to a minimum of three months and I will not be reneging on that,' she interjects. 'I love having you here too. I haven't watched a full movie in this house for ten years. I love that this feels like a home to you. It feels more like a home to me now too.'

I exhale slowly and sit on my hands to hide their shake.

A pressure pushes at my eyes.

'Can we press Play?' she asks, biscuit crumbs wiped away and remote back in hand. 'I still have to be convinced as to why any young woman would choose Leonardo DiCaprio over Paul Rudd.'

# TESSA

· · · · · · · · · · ·

I pour us a second round of tea and settle back into my favourite kitchen chair; the one that's slightly ricketier than the others and has a rogue paint stain on the back. I take one chocolate chip biscuit and snap it in half.

'Chloe made these,' I say. 'If you'd like one?'

Paul glances up from his notes. He's made quite a lot of them. 'No thanks. I don't have much of an appetite when I'm working,' he says, flicking back through the pages. I wondered if the story might be too local, but he's not concerned about that at all. He says the only problem will be trying to fit everything into one article – which is why he's already thinking of a series. 'Just to verify, you said it's a decade you've been volunteering at the hall?'

I increase my chewing speed. 'Ten years attending, nine years volunteering. The place has changed so much since then.'

'In what way?' he asks, pen poised.

'Well, at first, the community project was mainly a couple of support groups, but then it started offering classes, holding dances and bridge tournaments, putting on stage shows,' I explain. 'I was the first to take a group outside, for a gardening class. There's an entire acre at the back of the hall and it wasn't being utilised at all. We spent a weekend clearing away the overgrowth and it's been a vital asset to the Project ever since. The local primary school goes there on nature walks too; it's a treasure trove of conkers and pine cones.'

Paul's hand flies across the page. 'That's perfect, Mrs Doherty. Very heart-warming. You have real community spirit.'

I tilt my chin. 'You're just plamásing me now. I know what you media types are like.'

'Honestly, I'm not. I'm a straight shooter. They're lucky to have you. And they'll definitely be glad of you when this piece comes out.' He taps his pad with his pen. 'This is proper David versus Goliath stuff right here. It's going to be really something. I think it could go viral.'

I told Paul I only had half an hour for the interview and he's been here fifty minutes already. I don't actually have anywhere to be – I just like to have a get-out clause. Although I don't feel the need to use it on this occasion.

It's a novelty to have a professional really listen to you. It's almost making up for my meeting with Doctor O'Shea.

Paul takes pride in his work, which I respect, and he has excellent manners. He is a little odder looking than I expected. Not that looks matter a drop, but Chloe is such a pretty girl and she's so enamoured with him that, shallow as it is, I suppose I was expecting someone... less knobbly, maybe?

'Now, the last thing I need is some details on next weekend's open day,' he says. 'I'll do my best to sell it and let local readers know that they're welcome to go along.'

'Not just Howth residents. People come from all over to use the hall. Everyone is welcome,' I clarify.

'I'll make that clear.'

Trevor now has three councillors *and* a TD confirmed for Saturday. There are also promising noises coming from a minister of state's office. Susan says the campaign's email address has been inundated with correspondence since our leaflet drop. And Maura's sister, who works in the Main Street post office, reported a run on stamps last Tuesday morning that they rarely see outside of December. They were having to dip back into the Easter-themed booklets, last we heard. I posted my own objections Tuesday morning too.

I talk Paul through the dance marathon, the theatrical performances, the various talks and demonstrations, the raffle, and the Meals on Wheels buffet.

As I list everything, I feel more and more positive about the situation.

'So are the Irish dancers performing *with* Tai Chi and Decaf Tea or...?' asks Paul, the hand worn off him at this point.

'No, separately. Although,' I say, making my own note on the back of an envelope. 'That's not a bad idea.'

I am explaining how a local drag queen is rebranding herself for one day – under the moniker 'Saviour Hall' – to perform a set that she promises will be both 'protest' and 'glamour' when Conn arrives into the kitchen.

He has that dazed look he often wears when surfacing in the afternoons.

'Sorry, didn't know you had company,' he says, voice still husky. 'I'll come back later.'

'No, stay – have some lunch, or breakfast. This is Paul, Chloe's friend. He's writing an article for the *Dublin Press* about the campaign. He's going to help us save the community project.'

'I'm not on any one side,' says Paul in a tone that declares the very opposite, 'but there's certainly a public desire to see the destruction of community amenities stopped.'

'Right, yes. Professional impartiality,' I say with a wink. Although actually, the only journalists I've ever admired are the campaigning ones. The world is too messed up for impartiality – we need people fighting to save it. 'And this is Conn, our other housemate.'

'Oh, is it? Hello,' says Paul. 'Chloe never mentioned there was someone else living here.'

'And yet here I am,' comes Conn's response as he opens the fridge and produce a yoghurt.

'But then Chloe didn't tell me you were so—'

'Old?'

'No,' he says, though a smidge of colour rises over his prominent Adam's apple. 'Fascinating. I had no idea.'

He's definitely plamásing me now, but I don't mind. The ego likes to be stroked every now and again. Just to remember it's still there.

'The hot water's still on the blink,' I tell Conn as he polishes off the Yoplait. I distinctly remember it taking him longer to eat his daily yoghurt when he first moved in. Ever since he's entered his lumberjack phase, he seems to finish all meals in three massive mouthfuls. 'I phoned the plumber but he doesn't answer at the weekend. Hopefully he'll be out tomorrow.'

'Do you want me to take a look at the pipes in the meantime?'

'Are you involved in the community project too, Conn?' asks Paul, as the other man opens the bin with his foot and drops in the yoghurt carton. 'You can recycle those, you know. Just run them under the tap.'

Conn fixes him with a stare.

Paul smiles back.

'I wrote the definitive article on recycling a couple of months ago,' he adds.

Conn's foot is still on the bin pedal and his eyes on Paul.

'I can send it to you if you like.'

'Conn is helping us with the legal side,' I say. 'He's a recovering lawyer and all round very smart man. He knew nothing about planning law a couple of weeks ago, but now he's our resident expert. He also builds an excellent shed door, but that's probably less relevant.'

Paul picks up his pen. 'What's your surname?'

'I don't want to be in the piece,' says Conn.

'No surname,' Paul teases. 'Interesting.'

'I'm serious. Leave me out of it.'

Paul picks up his pen and makes a show of crossing out the last few sentences.

Conn's shoulders remain tense as the door opens.

Chloe sees me first and flashes that perilously unguarded smile that makes me want to go round to her mother's house and throttle the woman. But then her eyes fall on Paul and I realise I've only been getting half wattage.

'I didn't know you were coming today! I would have gotten someone to cover my deliveries,' she gushes, one hand instinctively going to smooth down her lovely wavy hair as the other adjusts the Delivery Dash satchel slung across her chest. She giggles, inexplicably.

Conn turns on the tap and she clocks that he's there too. This version of her face can only be described in weather phenomena; thunderstorms, crashing seas, blazing fires.

'Did I not say I'd be here today? I meant to.'

She waves Paul's words away. 'Doesn't matter, doesn't matter. You're here now, which is brilliant. You look well – really, really well.'

'You too. I like your, em, dress?'

'It's a playsuit, I think. But yes, thank you. I like it too. I like the way it has buttons, you know? I always think they're better than zips.'

There's an awkward silence and I fear for Chloe's dignity if she fills it, so I step in.

'Paul thinks this story could have legs.'

'I think it could be huge,' he corrects. 'I did this article last year about a protected structure in Temple Bar—'

'Oh my god, it was such a brilliant piece, Tessa, you have to read it.'

I smile at Chloe. I want to tell her to play it cool, but I fear that may not be in the girl's repertoire.

'I won a justice media award for it,' says Paul. 'And it was in our top five most-clicked stories of the year. This one has all the same elements. It's going to go viral, I can feel it. I got a thousand new Twitter followers off the back of the Temple Bar one. This could bring me up to a full 6,000.'

'Wow,' Chloe murmurs.

I purse my lips.

From what I recall, she knows even less about social media than I do.

'Have you been here long?' she asks, pulling out the chair adjacent to where Conn is standing. She yanks it with such force that he barely gets out of the way in time.

'It's...' He flicks his arm around so the crumpled sleeve rises to reveal the black strap hanging from his thin wrist. 'Jeez, it's been over an hour. Apologies, Tessa, I know you have somewhere to be.'

'It's fine. I changed those plans.'

'Well I'm done now anyway. I can head off and leave you to it.'

'I could show you the hall!' enthuses Chloe. 'Give you a feel for what everyone's fighting for?'

'That'd be great if it's not putting you out?'

'No no,' she says quickly. 'Not putting me out at all. In fact, someone there might have an old laptop for me that he said he'd drop into the hall. So I'd have to collect that at some stage anyway.'

'Is that Trevor?' I ask, as Conn looks over at us from the sink.

Chloe nods. 'Says he got it off his printer.'

'You're getting a laptop,' says Paul.

'My first,' she beams.

'That's a pity. I always thought you'd be the last woman standing against the rapid onslaught of technology,' says Paul. 'Chloe used to carry a real map of Dublin when we were in college. It was very cute. And I used to check the balance on her bank account because she hadn't a clue how online banking worked and she never knew how much money she had.' He smiles wistfully at her. 'You were a real outlier.'

'Oh I doubt I'll use it often, it's just for emails really,' she says hurriedly. 'I'm still fighting the good fight against the onslaught, still no smart phone.'

Paul's smile deepens.

She smiles back.

Beyond them Conn is giving Paul a look that makes me grateful I'm sitting a good foot away from the man.

'I just want to finish up with Tessa about the open day and then I'm ready to go.'

'Super, yes,' says Chloe, clambering back out of the chair. 'I'll go and put my work stuff away.'

'Chloe, can I just—' begins Conn, following her out the door.

'Won't be long,' she shouts, cutting him off. Conn pushes the door shut after them, but thankfully the latch doesn't catch.

I lean as far back in my chair as I can without upending the thing.

'I wasn't chasing after her,' I hear Conn mumble from the hallway. 'I needed to make amends—'

Chloe, louder, interrupts: 'You told me you were an awful person and I should have believed you. My fault.'

'Woah!'

'You all right?' asks Paul, as I just about stop myself from tipping backwards onto the floor. I've been doing fine without my stick, proving myself right and Doctor O'Shea wrong. But swinging on a chair is asking for trouble.

I bring my attention back to the thin man in front of me as footsteps disperse in the hallway. 'Did I mention the crocheted dart boards?' I ask.

He peers down. 'Have that.'

'Well then, I think you have it all.'

# CHLOE

Yes, I can see the view from my bedroom window and, yes, I am aware that the house is situated along a literal cliff walk, but I don't think I truly appreciated how high up Hope House is until now.

I undo another button on the polyester cardigan and fan it out.

How am I still only on the road that leads to the road that leads to Nevin Way? And how is it possible that I am *still* walking upwards? What happened to what goes up must come down? Clearly, I am the exception that proves that rule.

Paul assumed we'd take our own cars to the hall. But I came in with a counter-suggestion that we both travel in his and then I walk home. I did a lot of fast talking about how I'd been sitting behind a steering wheel all day and the opportunity for a lengthy walk would be welcome.

That wasn't true when I said it – I just wanted to breathe in the same sweet recycled air as him – and it definitely isn't true now that I'm dragging myself up the hill in a cardigan that is open as far as my sternum but still feels like it's choking me.

I put this on when I went to dump my work stuff in my room. Yemi says I look like a nun in it, and the material is not comfortable, but Paul always liked it. He was never one for fashion but he said this cardigan was very me. 'Now you're yourself,' he'd say with a sigh if we were heading out and I added it last minute. I never told him Mam bought it; they actually have more similar taste in clothes than he'd like to think.

His car is much as I remember it. The air freshener has changed – it used to be a Leeds United crest but now it's a pink flower – and there are a lot more newspapers on the floor in the back, but otherwise it's just as it was in the year we were going out – the best year of my life.

We talked about the campaign to save the hall on the drive over. He got plenty of material out of Tessa. He wasn't so keen on Conn.

'Not very friendly. A bit cagey. Refused to as much as tell me his name.'

'He wants to know all about other people's lives but won't tell you a thing about his own,' I confirmed. 'He disappears out in the middle of the night and nobody knows where he goes. He had this cover story about owl watching, but of course there's no such thing. Tessa's great, though.'

'She's the dream case study for a feature like this,' he agreed. 'Inspiring and articulate and sympathetic.'

I was chuffed with that. It's probably silly, but Tessa feels like a reflection of me now; a choice I made. I can stand over her in a way I could never stand over Mam. But that's a terrible thing to think. Maybe getting to choose your family isn't fair either because while Tessa would have people knocking down her door, I can't think of who would choose Mam if I didn't.

She hasn't made any effort to contact me since she turned up at Hope House and Conn drove her home and dared to ask questions. This sort of silent treatment chills my bones, but I've resisted the urge to phone her.

I did consider telling Paul the truth about Mam's illness, but then his phone pinged. A TV actress he interviewed recently had just posted a link to the piece and it was amassing 'hits'.

It's probably for the best. I desperately regret saying anything to Conn. Though he's so self-centred, he's probably already forgotten. And telling Tessa was okay – it was cathartic, actually – but it took it out of me. When I think about how Mam would feel if she'd heard me, the shame reaches down to my toes. Best not to burden Paul with something so fraught so soon.

I want him to think I'm a fun, independent woman – not a tragic descendant of a mentally unstable egomaniac.

Instead, I asked if he's changed his mind about social media.

'Twitter is a vital channel for journalists looking to disseminate information in the internet age,' he said, checking his phone again. We were at a tricky turn but I didn't say anything. He was always the better driver. 'So it's just part of the job, unfortunately. If I could get away without it... Oh, wow! Solomon Leary just followed me.'

'Oh wow,' I agreed, doing my best to sound like I know who that is.

'Don't worry. The same thing will happen when we run this story. I think it'll be bigger. People have had it with hotels. And getting rid of a *free* social amenity? It's perfect. Yeah,' he said, putting the phone away and nodding to himself. 'I'll be at 6,000 followers by the end of the week.'

'That's good?'

'It's great,' he said, pulling up in front of the hall and killing the engine. 'The more people reading me is the more people reading about this cause. And it's all thanks to you.'

He grinned widely and looked at me. Like, he really looked *at* me.

A warm sensation came over me, like slipping into a bath. He took my hand, just for a moment, but the way he held it – firm and purposeful – I can still feel the significance.

'Let's go and see the hall,' I said, before my uncontrollable lips started mouthing 'I love you! Take me back!'

Malachy was on reception. His chest puffed up when he heard Paul was a journalist (Paul's chest did something similar when he declared it) and he insisted on giving us the full tour. I was honoured to be by Paul's side, and even more honoured when Malachy said how fond they all were of me. I've never known people – as in more than one – to be fond of me. And as if it couldn't get better, then Paul said: 'Who wouldn't be, especially when she has such an eye for a story.'

It is a marvel that between the words and the polyester cardigan, I didn't faint then and there.

When I walked Paul to his car, he said it would be great to tag along on another canvass before the open day and I wholeheartedly agreed. 'I'd love to see you in action' were his literal words. I told him he could join us on our rounds on Thursday night. Malachy, who came out to make sure Paul had gotten everything, said he didn't know anything about Thursday canvassing and were we kicking him out over the whole people carrier/dog-van thing and a couple of trips Trevor made to A&E, because if we were he'd rather have it said to his face.

I assured him that wasn't the case at all and that plans were still in early stages (as in, I'd just made them up right that second) and he blew a sigh of relief and told me to sign him up for it and anything else to do with the campaign because he'd always regretted not being alive during the War of Independence but now he'd found a cause that he'd be just as happy to lay down his life for.

Paul laughed a little too hard at that, but apologised when he saw that Malachy's feelings were hurt. He grinned at me instead and I swear it was like no time had passed at all, and we were standing before his sister lying about how we had absolutely no intention of bringing an animal into her flat even though we had the Jack Russell Terrier with the bad leg picked from the pound website already.

Usually my heart aches at those memories, but this time it sang. Because I was back where I was supposed to be, back in safety, where the upheaval of life couldn't touch me. I don't find the world quite as scary as I did back then, but Paul feels just as safe.

If I thought it before, I am sure of it now.

Paul is the one.

By the time I get back to Hope House, it's early evening. I smell sausages in the kitchen, which means Conn is cooking, so I go straight to the library. Tessa is there, but she's snoozing in the armchair. I've caught her snoozing nearly every day since she got rid of the stick. She insists that's nothing to do with it. I don't know why she's ashamed. Lord Muck down the hall is in his thirties and he takes a lengthy nap daily. We've both heard the snores.

I head upstairs to the bathroom instead. I'm not fit for public consumption anyway, not until I have a shower. Even if it's a cold one.

I stop by my room to grab a fresh towel and instantly know something isn't right.

Someone's been in here.

I can feel it. I can *see* it, even if I can't pinpoint what is different just yet. I sniff the air. I can *smell* it.

I gasp.

'My books!'

The seven stacks that I'd carefully arranged by the window box seat are gone.

There must have been one hundred books there. And now there are none.

Who breaks into a house like this, targets *my* bedroom, and leaves only with books?

There's a man down the hallway with shoes worth more than my car, for god's sake!

I turn for the door, ready to run down and rouse Tessa, but I don't get any further than that 180 degree shift before something stops me. A big, wooden something.

Just inside the door, about a foot from my balls of wool installation, is the most beautiful bookcase.

I gasp again.

It is *beautiful*.

'No,' I whisper.

It's made from the same wood as the new fuel shed door – mahogany, I think – and though it is simple, it is more elegant than plain. It has five rows of deep shelves and a ribbed backboard. The wood's natural imperfections, its cracks and its knots, are coated in clear varnish. That's what the unfamiliar smell is. It must barely be dry.

Each shelf is adorned with a dozen or so of my beloved books and, here's the bit that halts the breath in my throat, not one of them is lying on its side. Not a single book – not even the massive atlas that Yemi got me when we graduated – is poking out.

The shelves are beautiful and simple and deep. And the books fit perfectly.

'Oh,' I say, making my way slowly towards them. 'Oh, now.'

My books have never fit anywhere. How did I not realise that until now? In Mam's house, they didn't belong. They were awkward and undesirable. It was their home but they were not welcome.

Look at them now. They're so handsome on those shelves.

Home should mean acceptance. It should mean love. My books deserved better than that. And so did I.

I deserved a home.

How did I accept that treatment as normal?

Nothing about it was normal.

The back of my throat throbs, nose preparing to go.

'I'm sorry,' I whisper, to my books and my road not taken and myself.

All my books are exactly where they should be.

And so am I.

Finally, I think as the tears push for release, finally I understand 'home'.

# TESSA

· · · · · · · · · · ·

I place the bowl of steaming new potatoes on the kitchen table and take a seat. Conn is fishing cutlery from the drawer beside the range. Chloe offered to put out glasses, but is now distracted by her phone. I think it's the same mobile my Bernard had before he died.

I'm not sure I've ever seen a body trill at the ping of a mobile phone before. It's Paul. It's been Paul since she entered the room.

'Another radio interview request,' she announces, looking up at me. Then she goes back to the archaic mobile, her finger moving rapidly across the buttons.

There really would be no harm in playing it a little cool.

'I'll get the glasses,' says Conn.

Chloe looks up, chastened. 'I'm getting important updates on support for the campaign.' She says it with indignation, but her cheeks are flush and she doesn't actually look at him as she's speaking. The avoidance is different now. She didn't put up a fight when I suggested the three of us eat together and she has stopped leaving rooms when he enters them. She doesn't seem furious with him any more; now she seems sort of awkward.

'Another live tally of his Twitter stats so,' remarks Conn as the cupboard door closes.

'There's *more* than that,' she retorts. 'And Twitter is a vital channel for journalists looking to disseminate information in the internet age.'

'A vital channel for promoting himself, more like,' Conn mutters as he comes up behind me with three tumblers. But Chloe, whose face is back in her phone, doesn't hear.

Conn doesn't trust Paul. He told me this after reading the article. He says his journalism is 'sensationalist', pointing to the description of the hall as 'iconic' and our campaign as 'a crusade' as proof. Though I suspect his dislike has nothing at all to do with Paul's writing.

The *Dublin Press* article was published today. They gave it a lot of space – all of page three – and ran four photographs alongside it. I wasn't delighted to be described as 'outraged pensioner Tessa Doherty' in my picture caption, but it was almost made up for by the inclusion of a deeply unflattering photo of Charles Bentley smoking a cigar. And there's no denying the effect of the piece.

Three more councillors have confirmed their attendance for the open day since this morning, and the deliberating minister of state RSVP'd 'yes' at lunchtime. Paul has already been on four local radio shows and two national ones. I'd have thought they'd invite on someone from the campaign, but I suppose it doesn't matter who's doing the talking once the issue is being discussed.

The best bit of all came this afternoon. Charles Bentley phoned me making legal threats. Conn had just surfaced for breakfast so I put the phone on loudspeaker and let my lawyer speak. It was beautiful. I could practically hear the man sweating.

We're close; I can feel it. T-minus four days until the open day. The hall's salvation is within grasp. We just have to keep up the momentum.

'What does Paul say?' I ask, patting the chair beside me for Conn to sit before the fish goes cold.

'Firstly, he—'

'Gives his Twitter stats.'

Chloe ignores this. Although the rapid pressing of what I assume is the phone's Down button suggests Conn's not wrong. 'He apologises for the picture caption, Tessa. He says it was written by the sub-editors and that he will have a word with them.'

'It's fine, really.'

'But he is sorry.'

I smile at her sincerity. 'I know, darling. Oh – salt!' I push myself up to get the shaker and catch myself on the edge of the table.

'You all right?'

'Yes, fine, just stood too quickly,' I say.

'I can't get over how good you are without the stick,' says Chloe as I return from the worktop, shaker in hand. 'Seriously! You'd never know you'd had one.'

I smile again. It really has been a boost to be going in and out of shops or even just pottering around the house without a third leg. I felt more like my old self this week than I have for months.

'Well, this is nice, isn't it?' I say, as Conn passes me the spud bowl.

Chloe beams, but when she catches Conn's eye, she's like a rabbit in the headlights. She turns her attention back to her plate.

'The salmon is delicious,' she mumbles, as her phone pings again.

'He's been asked to appear on *Main Stage* tomorrow night!' Then a pause. 'Is that a theatre thing?'

'It's a TV show. Probably the biggest current affairs programme in the country,' I explain, once again curious about the life Chloe led before she came here.

'And his editor says the next piece, the 'on the campaign trail' piece, will run the morning of the open day. He wants to give it the cover of the Review section. That'd be great for us, wouldn't it?'

'Yes, brilliant,' I say, swallowing my salmon. 'And thank you again for organising one last canvass, Chloe. It was a lovely idea – a real final push for the campaign.'

'For the campaign, yes absolutely, that's exactly what I thought.'

'I wish I could go, but Otis is starting for the first time on Thursday.' To be entirely honest, my instinct is still that I'd be of a lot more use knocking on doors than I will be warming the bleachers in the school hall. But this is the promise I made; family first, everything else second.

'We're just doing a couple of estates. I'm happy to have Paul shadow me.' She blushes, and I suddenly wonder if she's ever had sex. I picture Paul trying to woo her into bed – pushing his glasses up and down over the bump on his nose, somehow making it suggestive – and I have to work hard not to giggle.

Chloe shoves half a potato in her mouth and chews. 'Malachy is coming too. He was very insistent.'

'I can go,' Conn chimes in.

'What? No,' says Chloe, reigning in her horror several seconds too late. 'I mean, it's fine. We have it covered.'

'No, no. That's a great idea,' I enthuse. This is the perfect time to build on the slight thawing in relations of recent days. 'You two did a brilliant job with the leaflet drop. You got through more flyers than anyone else. Even Reggie and myself didn't distribute as many and that boy has envious levels of energy.'

'You have envious levels of energy,' says Chloe, chewing. 'Seriously. If I have your get-up-and-go when I'm nearly seventy, I'll be delighted.'

I narrow my eyes. 'How do you know I'm nearly seventy?'

'I don't know... You told me?'

I continue to study her.

'You must have told me.' She laughs nervously and I'm not sure if it's because I'm staring at her or because she's been caught out.

'No,' I say slowly. 'Senan told you, didn't he?'

'No.'

'He's organising a surprise party.'

'What? No.'

'He is.'

'He's not. Or if he is, I don't know anything about it. Do you, Conn, do you know anything about a surprise party?'

My other lodger shakes his head, fork still in mouth. His poker face is much better.

'Is it your birthday?' squeaks Chloe.

'I told Senan I didn't want a surprise party. I've made this abundantly clear on several occasions,' I say, grabbing my own phone from the centre of the table and dialling his number, before getting up from my chair.

'He honestly didn't say anything about a party,' insists Chloe as I make my way out of the room and into the hall. 'If there's a surprise party, which there's not, it'll be as much of a surprise to me as you.'

I close the door behind me.

'Senan Pearson, I do not want a surprise party. I told you I never want a birthday party again.'

'Afternoon to you too, Mam, nice to get your call.'

I pause on the stairs. 'Don't be glib, darling, it doesn't suit you. It was always more your sister's thing.'

Senan sighs. I can hear a bell ringing in the background. 'I don't know what you're talking about. There's no surprise party,' he says.

I stop again. I'm on the return now. I look out onto the grass at the back of my house, my fuel store with its lovely new mahogany door and the cobalt sea beyond. It's choppy today.

'Really?'

'Really. Why did you think there was?'

'I...' I shake my head. 'It doesn't matter. Well, good. Because I don't want one.'

'Understood.' Some faint typing now.

'How are you? Still at work by the sounds of it. How's Otis?'

'Fine, yes and fine. He's very excited for Thursday; says he's dribbling balls in his sleep.'

'That's good. I'm excited too.'

'Mam.'

'What? I am!'

'He tells me you're missing a canvass for it. Big sacrifice for Tessa Doherty.'

'Are you being glib again?'

'No.'

I don't think he is.

I'm opening the door to Bea's room before I realise where I'm going. The hinges creak. Her smell left this place long ago; or maybe it's just hidden, lying dormant under layers of must. I cross to the window and open the heavy shutters.

'It's the anniversary of your sister's disappearance on Saturday.'

'I know, Mam.'

'Well you never mentioned it.' I pause. 'You never mention her.'

'*You* never mentioned her until a few months ago when you suddenly started talking as though she'd just popped out for milk.'

I observe the walls, her old desk, and the corkboard above it. 'She took that photo with her; the one of you and me and her in Curracloe. Why would she take it if she was going to kill herself?'

'Are we seriously back to this?'

'And there was no suicide note. You know your sister. She liked to make a statement.'

'She wasn't herself. She was mentally unwell.'

There are a few more DVDs on her desk. I flick through them. Did she watch all of these? Did she like them? If she was here now, would it be her and me sitting down together to watch *Muriel's Wedding*?

I'd love to be able to tell him about seeing Bea again, about the chats we had on the landing and how interested she was in his life and his son. She was far nicer about Audrey than I ever am.

'And I knew my sister. Knew,' Senan continues. 'She isn't here to know any more.'

I suppose it's understandable he'd be angry with Bea. If she hadn't monopolised the attention before, she certainly did in the years after she disappeared. Or maybe it's me he feels let down by. That is more understandable again.

'Still going without the stick?'

'Yes, and still feeling great,' I say, sitting on Bea's stripped bed. 'Chloe just said you'd never know I'd had it, and that's exactly how I feel. Zero problems. All is as it was, so please stop worrying.'

'I know, I know. It's just if you got tired or dizzy... But if Doctor O'Shea gave it the green light, who am I to argue?'

'Plumber called this morning,' I say, not wanting to dwell on my white lie. 'The hot water is back up and running but he says the pipes need to be replaced – he's not joking this time. He's going to send an estimate out next week, but I'm looking at €30,000 anyway.'

'Jesus Christ.'

'I know.'

'What are you going to do?'

'Same thing I always do,' I say, as I lower myself back so I'm lying on the bare mattress staring at the same ceiling she stared at every night for more than twenty years. 'Take my anxious energy and channel it into a force for good. You know what else is this Saturday, right?'

'I've got the whole teaching staff coming. I can't make it a requirement but, you know, I may have told them how well community involvement looks when going for promotion.'

At one stage, when she was about twelve, Bea stuck those glow-in-the-dark stars on her ceiling. She spent ages copying exact constellations from Bernard's encyclopaedia. I don't know if she pulled them down in later years or if they fell, but only tufts of adhesive residue remain.

'Thank you, Son.'

Another bell. 'Are we okay?' he asks.

'We're great.'

'Are you okay?'

'I'm great.'

'Okay, well, I have to meet a parent so...'

'See you Thursday?'

'You will,' he says. 'It's weird to be seeing you less often.'

'But probably healthy,' I reply, stretching out on my daughter's bed.

'Bye, Mam.'

'Bye, Son.' And then, for just a minute, I close my eyes.

# CHLOE

· · · · · · · · · · ·

Of all the afternoons I need my deliveries to go smoothly, Thursday is top of the list. But instead I have a man refuse to sign for his package until *I* open it and confirm it's not anthrax, and a woman at the top of a seven-storey apartment block with a broken lift and a very clear idea of what Delivery Dash's 'from our door to yours' policy means. So I'm late getting back to Hope House.

When I do make it home, the Misunderstood Mutts wagon is parked in front of the house. I am more cheered than anyone really should be by the image of a pitbull biting a man's leg.

'Sorry, sorry,' I call to Paul and Malachy, who are chatting beside the van. I pull my ponytail tighter. Paul always liked the swish.

'It wasn't about one bin – it was about *no* bin,' Malachy is explaining as I approach. 'It was about my rights. It was about a *human* right.'

'To bins?'

'Now you're getting it. How'ya, Chloe,' says Malachy. Paul is too bamboozled to give me or my ponytail his attention.

'So just to clarify,' he says to Malachy. 'You sent *sixty-three* letters?'

'Yeah, but I sent them all to the same three people.'

'So they got twenty-one each?'

'If you say so, Carol Vorderman.'

'And did they reinstate the bin?'

'As of yesterday morning,' says Malachy. 'Now, to be honest, I can't say it was the letters that did it. I may have borrowed a few of Dano's growlier rottweilers.' He jerks his head towards the van. 'And I may have taken them for a midnight walk past the director of waste management's home, *if* you know what I'm saying,' he adds, lifting one patchy eyebrow.

'It's... you literally just said it,' says Paul, but Malachy has already turned to the van and is yanking the sliding door to the back section.

'We're all here now, so let's get going,' he calls as the hatch bangs open. 'All aboard the Radical Activism Express!'

Malachy opens the driver's door then and I see that Conn is already in the passenger seat. So he's still coming.

I haven't known what to say to Conn since I arrived home four nights ago to The Shelves. I believe I'm still allowed to be hurt over the incident with Linda at the apartment block, but I don't really feel it. Mainly, I feel confused. I know how much time he spent out there, working away, building that beautiful bookcase. And it really is beautiful. It might be the nicest thing anyone's ever given me, which of course makes me happy, but it also makes me sad about my life up until this point.

'You coming?'

Paul's angular head and long neck stick out from inside the van.

'Yep,' I say, taking his hand as I climb inside. Maybe it's weird that Conn built me a bookcase. It *feels* lovely, but when I imagine telling Paul about it, I don't picture him having the same response.

I hold his hand for a further six seconds inside the van – yes, I count them – before he realises.

'Oh, sorry,' he says, dropping my fingers and reaching into his bag for a pen and pad. 'You don't mind being named, do you?' His hand is already moving across the page.

'Nope,' I say, swooning. There's something romantic about seeing your beloved inscribing your name by hand. Maybe it's my imagination, but the letters look more ornate than usual.

He drops his voice. 'Your other housemate's still refusing to go on the record. If he doesn't want to be in the piece, then what's he doing here?'

'Beats me.'

'Malachy's good with it. Even gave me his confirmation name. Said I might need to "authenticate his details". Whatever that means. Is he all right, like mentally?' The van takes a speed bump by surprise, sending us both roof-wards. I grab Paul's arm to steady myself, and don't let go. 'He talked at me about bins for a good twenty minutes. Told me there was a career-making story in it for me if I was willing to go to some dark places in search of the truth.'

'Malachy's actually really lovely,' I assure him. 'He's been unemployed for a couple of years, so he spends a lot of time helping out around the hall. He's probably the only person who cares as much as Tessa does about saving the place.'

'She's really invested, isn't she?'

Another bump, another chance to touch him.

'It's a difficult time of year for her. I think she likes having this to focus on,' I say, feeling the static of his rayon sports top between my fingers.

'What doesn't she like about this time of year?'

'She had a daughter who disappeared, ten years ago. The open day actually falls on her anniversary,' I say, as the van sends us skyward again. This time Paul puts his arms out to steady me.

'That's terrible.'

'And she's so strong, you know? You'd think she'd have this tragic air about her, but she doesn't. She's always fighting for the next thing. She's all about other people. Malachy is sort of the same.'

'Do they have any idea what happened to her daughter?'

'Jumped off the cliffs, maybe? Nobody knows. Tessa's son is resigned to her being dead. They got a death cert last year.'

'What was her name?'

'Don't know. I don't feel I can ask— Woah!'

The van takes a corner and hits what I hope is a kerb, and we both come off the bench and land on the dog beds laid out in front.

I barely register the pain in my arm as it wallops the seat on the way down because I have landed, purely accidentally and not entirely gracefully, on Paul's lap.

'Sorry,' I say, rubbing my arm faintly, not budging.

'That's okay,' says Paul, repositioning his glasses as the van comes to a shrieking halt.

Neither of us look away.

Two, three seconds and we're still sitting like that, smiling awkwardly at each other.

This is it. It's going to happen.

It's not how I pictured our First Kiss 2.0 going, sitting on damp fur-ridden baskets in the back of a vehicle that is barely roadworthy, but then these aren't things you can control. And I'm ready. Chloe 2.0 is ready to be kissed.

And then Malachy roars from the front seat.

'I'll just see the blind woman across myself, so!' he yells out his now-open door. 'No, you keep walking! Wouldn't want you to be late!' he heckles, unclipping his seatbelt and jumping out of the cab. 'It's only a little thing called HUMAN DECENCY!'

Despite the fact that Malachy has now fled the vehicle, Conn's eye are on the rear-view mirror, staring back at us. I pull myself up onto the seat as Paul tries to get a better look at what's happening. 'Is everything okay out there?'

'Nothing worth getting your pen out over,' replies Conn, no longer looking in the mirror.

Paul shifts beside me. 'Oh, no, I didn't mean...'

'Ignore him,' I say, helping him up beside me.

The moment's gone, but at least it was there at all. He wanted to kiss me too. I could feel it.

We pull into the estate on the Howth-Sutton border (we did such a good job the first night that I had to stretch the town limits to find unleafleted territory) and spill from the van like the world's worst squat team. I try to shake the dog hairs from my trousers, but they've really pressed themselves in.

'What's the plan, chief?' asks Malachy.

'Oh. Yes. The plan. Okay,' I say, because I do actually have a plan. I chose the estate and got the leaflets printed; I just find these things hard to put into words on the spot.

'I can take this,' offers Paul, a reassuring hand on my upper arm.

I go to speak but, actually, this feels familiar. This is easier. He's better at public speaking than I am. We did a lot of projects together in college and they always went better when he presented.

I smile at him. He's already doing his adorable glasses rejig.

'We're looking for interesting conversations here; ordinary Joe Soaps on the doorstep with something to say or, better yet, *characters*. People who will give colour to my piece. I'm looking to get 2,000 words out of this. So you all do your thing, drop your leaflets, knock on a few doors, see if they want to discuss the hall or anything hall-adjacent, and I'll flit between. I'm embedded – this is on the ground, guerrilla reporting. So if you meet a character, call me over – but otherwise I'm not even here. Act like you're just out here campaigning for the hall.'

Malachy nods along rhythmically. I give a double thumbs up. I could never have delivered a speech like that. Conn, of course, looks less impressed.

'We *are* out here campaigning for the hall,' he says.

'That's the attitude,' replies Paul, pulling out his notebook. 'Now take that to the doors!'

Malachy grabs a bunch of leaflets from our box and hands some to Conn who is still glaring, specifically at Paul's hand on my arm. Is this an alpha male thing? Is he so used to the power of business that he can't have anyone else giving the orders?

'Do you want us to get the names of residents we speak to?' I ask.

'That would be useful, yes. But remember, if they're saying anything interesting...'

'Call you over.'

He smiles down at me. 'I could always rely on you,' he says and my knees actually quiver. 'Okay, let's go, and not too far apart, I need to keep a bird's eye view.'

I make my way to one side of the street and Malachy takes the opposite one. Work-shy Conn remains by the box. Paul trails after Malachy.

I thought he might start with me, but I suppose nobody better to sniff out characters than a character himself.

A few minutes in, I check behind me again. Paul and Malachy have disappeared and Conn is shooting the breeze with some man in a garden. He doesn't even have leaflets in his hand, never mind offering this guy one. I knock on my next door before turning around again, just in time to see Conn disappearing inside the man's house.

I go to seven more doors and have just one person answer – a woman whose only questions are about geography. 'This is Sutton,' she keeps saying. 'It's on the border,' I hiss, handing her a flyer. She must be the one Sutton resident who doesn't pretend to live in Howth.

I'm approaching my next house when Conn reappears.

I knock on the door, take a step back and curse my reddening cheeks. I resist the urge to ask who the older man across the road was. He probably wouldn't tell me anyway. The lad loves his secrets.

Conn takes the house next to mine. 'I thought Journalist Paul would be with you.' He doesn't even try knocking, he just slips the leaflet through the letterbox. 'What's he doing with Malachy?'

'He's reporting. You know, his job?'

'Everyone knows.'

I refuse to be riled. I wait patiently – and purposely – on the step, pretending not to notice the TV being switched off through the front room window.

Since Conn never waits to see if anyone is home, he's four houses ahead by the time I catch up again. 'We should probably slow down,' I say, glancing back. 'If someone colourful does answer, it might take Paul too long to get to us.'

'I'd say he's speedy enough. Does he always dress like that?'

'Like what?'

'Like the bottom half of him is joining the army and the top half is going for a run.'

'Why don't you like him?' I shoot, finally daring to look at him.

'I don't like how he talks to you.'

'And how's that?'

'Like you're the chair of his fan club.'

My face burns. 'No he doesn't.'

'Okay,' he says, moving on to the next door.

Just this once, I don't wait to see if A Character answers.

I hurry up the path next to his. 'He doesn't,' I repeat.

'Okay,' he repeats, delivering a leaflet and turning.

'Wait.'

He stops. 'Yes?'

'Thank you for the bookcase.'

He looks as surprised as me by the words. It's not what I meant to say next, but I'm glad it is out. Those shelves are already a lot more to me than somewhere to store books.

'So you did get it,' he says.

'I did.'

'And you like it?' He doesn't sound vulnerable exactly, but maybe vulnerable adjacent.

'Yes. I like it.'

'Good.' He regards me for a couple of seconds and I have to fight not to say anything but not for too long, because then he says: 'I'm sorry about what happened. I wasn't running after Linda to try and get her back. I needed to apologise to her, properly. As I think I've mentioned, I've a lot of people to say sorry to. Although I appear to just be adding to the list. I'm sorry that you had to do the last apartment block on your own, that wasn't fair.'

'It wasn't just that,' I say, blushing again. As if I'd be so annoyed just because I had to do a bit of work on my own. It sounds silly when he puts it like that. 'I thought there was... I thought we were getting on.'

'We were.'

'I told you about my mam.'

'And I told you about my brother.'

'Yeah, right, it was, you know, you were being a decent person. *We* were being decent people, to each other. I didn't think you were looking down on me.'

He frowns. 'That's because I wasn't.'

I purse my lips. 'Okay.'

'What?'

*Is he going to make me say it?*

'What?' he says again.

He is. He's going to make me spell it out. I cringe. 'Linda thought I was your girlfriend and you told her that was insane.'

His brow creases further. 'No I didn't.'

'Yes you did.'

He shakes his head.

'She asked if we were together long and you said, and I quote, "Are you insane? She's not my girlfriend." Not that the exact thing matters. I'm not looking to be your girlfriend, obviously—'

'Of course not. You've got Journalist Paul.'

'It was the idea that you would find it insane that someone might associate me with you. You think you're better than me. Admit it. It's probably not even your fault, not really. It's the world you grew up in; it told you that you were better than people like me.'

'And what are people like you?'

'Unremarkable people, poor people, plain people.'

He half-laughs. 'You're not plain, Prairie.'

'Look,' I say, trying and failing to find somewhere else to focus my gaze. 'Being wealthy doesn't automatically make you a bad person.'

'Good to know.'

I fold my arms. 'But it definitely increases the odds.'

He guffaws. 'Okay, well, firstly, as someone with actuarial training, I don't necessarily disagree with that probability. I went to a posh school, I have posh friends, I guess I am kind of posh. But I'm not a millionaire and I didn't grow up in some mansion. My parents were teachers. We had a cleaner yeah, but the house she was cleaning was fairly unremarkable. I'm not shunning work because I'm minted or lazy; I have other stuff on.'

'Like what?'

'Just stuff.'

'At night?'

'Yes, and it means I need some sleep during the day. So a proper job is tricky. Okay? Is that enough for you?'

'But what do you do every night? Where do you go? I know it's not owl watching. Is it drug dealing?'

'What, no!' he says, incredulously. 'You really are determined to think the worst of me. It's just stuff. Stuff that's more important than work. And to get back on track, I did not call Linda insane because she thought you and I were together. I called her insane because she started talking about my... about me...'

'About you being good in the sack?'

Finally! Someone's squirming and it's not me!

'Yes,' he says. 'I didn't want her to start going into details about my private life in public, in front of you. Jesus, can we...'

I hear someone jogging up behind us. The look on Conn's face tells me that it's Paul.

He drops his voice and speaks quickly. 'I wasn't saying the idea of us being together was insane,' he says. 'I don't think that would be insane. Not at all.'

'Hey!' I say, eyes switching away from Conn before I've taken in what he's said.

Now the words are sinking in and I'm confused and unsettled and don't feel at all like the breezy smile I've plastered on for Paul.

'How's it going?' I ask brightly.

'Great,' enthuses Paul. 'Malachy's just telling people all this mad personal stuff and how the hall saved him. He's a dream subject.'

'It's getting people interested in the hall?'

'Yeah, but more so it's perfect copy. He told one couple that he'd never had a girlfriend before meeting a woman at something called Darts and Crafts. He found love through the hall.'

'That's a nice story, I suppose...'

'But it didn't work out. She left him for a chap called Jimbo and he got pretty down over it, but then he did some other free class and that got him out of the depression hole. The man just loves that hall.'

'That's probably not stuff you should print.'

'I told Malachy it was all on the record.'

'I know, but he's a passionate person,' I say. 'He's more "do now, think later", you know?'

Paul puts an arm around my shoulders. 'You were always such a caring person, Clo.'

Touching me! In public!

Referring to me as Clo! In public!

Paul doesn't think I'm the chair of his fan club. I just appreciate him and he appreciates that. That's all.

'Why don't you come with me next, Paul?' says Conn, though it sounds more like a threat than an invitation.

Paul releases me. 'All right. Although if you're not going to let me use your name, it's sort of pointless...'

'We'll find things to talk about, don't worry.'

Tessa estimates that more than 40,000 people have used the services of the North Dublin Community Project – and what is the Project really except a bunch of people committing to helping other people? There's no financial chief, no profits to be made. It's not about that. It's about people. It feels so good to be part of this. Decency and goodness and humanity are on our side. With that sort of backing, how could we possibly fail?

I'm standing on a doorstep talking to a man who wants to swap my leaflet for one of his own (he runs a faith healer business from his shed out the back) when I hear raised voices. I peer up the street to see Conn and Paul squaring up to one another.

'Hey. Hey!'

The closer I get, the more I can see that Conn is doing the squaring, while Paul is trying his best to make an exit.

'What's going on?' I say, coming to a stop right in front of them.

Conn is on the kerb and Paul is backing out onto the road. I think they both started on the footpath.

Paul is looking at Conn like he's a madman and Conn is looking at Paul like he is also waiting on an answer to my question.

'Nothing,' says Paul, and suddenly Conn's face goes from irritated to enraged, but he doesn't offer any explanation of his own.

'Right, well,' I say, still looking from one to the other. Conn's eyes are on Paul, but Paul is at least looking at me. 'I'm going to do a few more houses up there, if you want to come and shadow me?'

'Please,' says Paul.

He links my arm and we start walking, him setting the pace.

'That guy is...' Paul begins when we're a safe distance away. He shakes his head and gives a sort of breathless hoot.

'He's not all bad.'

'No offence, Chloe, but you've never had great judgement when it comes to people.'

Mam. He's referring to Mam. He doesn't even know the truth and he's still not wrong.

'He's so nosy,' says Paul, looking back.

'I guess...'

'And he's so sure of himself. He thinks he knows more than the rest of us.'

That's more familiar.

'I had a woman offer to give €2,000 to the Save Our Hall campaign,' I say.

Paul turns. 'What? Chloe!'

I beam. 'I know! It's brilliant.'

'No, I mean you should have called me over. That's the exact colour I'm looking for.'

'Oh, sorry. I forgot.'

'Do you think we could go back to her? Which house was it? Maybe we could get her to repeat what she said. Did you ask her about posing for a pic? If we could get her to write the cheque and snap that...'

I look back and see Conn still standing where we left him, staring after us – or at least after me.

# TESSA

· · · · · · · · · · ·

I gulp in air and sit bolt upright in bed. I register the bang that woke me only after her name is passing through my lips.

It's involuntary, instinctive, magical.

'Bea.'

Is she here?

I hold my breath as my heart hammers against my chest.

But no. It's just me in the dark, the wind rattling the wooden frames beyond my shutters and the echo of the front door slammed shut by those same gusts.

Stormy weather is more extreme up here, looking out on the sea and the lands below.

It's Conn, I realise now, off on one of his nocturnal jaunts.

But surely that's not enough to shock me from sleep?

*Tick.*

My alarm clock flicks from 00.00 to 00.01.

*That's* why.

It's Saturday now.

Saturday.

Ten years exactly since Bea left.

A decade since the worst day. A decade since I completed the failure of the daughter I'd been failing for years.

There's a Mass card for Bernard on the bedside locker behind the clock. I miss him dearly at times like this. He's the only person, living or dead, who could possibly understand.

In the months after she disappeared, I spent my days getting angry, demanding answers, resources, investigations. But at night I walked the rooms of this house searching for signs that she would return. I looked for clues in the books in her room, the clothes in her wardrobe, even those DVDs on her desk. My whole existence ached with her absence. The cord that had tethered her to me since the womb was under strain. How far must she have wandered for the tugging to cause such pain? In the dead of night I tried to feel my way to the end of it, but I never got there.

And suddenly now, I can feel it again. A little pull from somewhere inside.

Is she still out there?

'Are you still out there?' I whisper.

What is it about today? Why is this happening now? Am I really still waiting for her to come home? Do I think the next bang of the front door could be my brilliant Bea?

My darling girl.

My only daughter.

My lost Beatrice.

# CHLOE

• • • • • • • • • • •

**I**'m out of bed and throwing on whatever is closest to hand – shorts, slipper socks, a jumper in desperate need of a wash – before I can talk myself out of it. It takes six seconds of groping blindly under the bed to locate a single sandal. There's no sign of its pair. 'Here, sandal, sandal,' I hiss, until my hand finally hits upon footwear. An ankle boot.

We're up to sixteen seconds now, and I have zero seconds to play with.

At least they're for alternative feet.

I pull them on and go flying over what I assume is the other ankle boot as I leg it towards my bedroom door. No time to change. He's probably at the end of the driveway now.

I was in the middle of an unusually steamy dream (me, Paul, a version of Dano's van, only water beds instead of dog ones) when the bang of the door shook me awake. I went through a quick succession of extreme emotions; arousal (dream still lingering), confusion (this bed doesn't *feel* very sploshy), embarrassment (was that *Mrs Sweetman* watching us from the corner of the van?), fury (a pox upon Conn and his noisy escapades), and finally: gratitude. I leaped from my bed.

This is my chance to find out where he goes.

I regret the shorts most of all as I leap downstairs, taking the steps in two, while the wind knocks against the large, panelled window on the return.

The uneven heel heights slow me as I clip-clop through the foyer and pull open the front door.

No sign of him. He's gone from the grounds already.

The wind tries to take the door from me, but I hang on until it's gently shut.

At least I know he's on foot, and the road – and footpath – only go one way from Hope House. I hurry across the gravel and out the front gates. I look left to the cliff and threatening, choppy seas. The moon is full and low and it gives a navy hue to the deep waters below. Then I turn right and make my way along the footpath, determined to find out once and for all what it is that Conn Horgan is hiding.

# MURIEL

· · · · · · · · · · ·

**M**uriel Fairway is wide awake.

She went to sleep at 11 p.m. and, one hour later, she is lying on her back trying to figure out the dream she just had.

She was playing on a beach with her dog, her granddaughter, and her son. Her granddaughter went into the water for a swim and she meant to go with her but she got distracted by something the dog was doing. When she looked back, the girl was gone. She ran into the waves searching for her. She thrashed about, panic rising as she screamed her name. It was only when she woke that she realised she wasn't shouting for Sadie at all.

She was calling the wrong name. She was shouting for Bea.

Bea Pearson. The Irish woman from Blackpool beach a few weeks ago.

She hasn't thought about Bea since she got that confirmation email saying the package had been delivered. She might never clap eyes on the woman again. But now here she is, literally losing sleep over her.

The dream was because of Bea's cherished old photograph; the one of her and her brother and mother relaxing on the sand. Muriel has figured out that much.

But why has that picture lodged so deeply into her subconscious? Why is she dreaming about the woman?

Why is she unable to return to sleep? And why is it happening now?

Muriel feels like she's missing a detail – but she can't for the life of her figure out what.

# TESSA

· · · · · · · · · · ·

Chloe is staring down at the newspaper but her eyes have stopped moving so I know she's finished reading. She's buying time. Trying to formulate a response.

The girl is a lot of things, but aloof is not one of them. You can read her like a book. And since she reached the end of the first paragraph, her face has been that of someone trying to swallow turned milk.

'Bereaved and Battling: A Monumental Day' reads the headline of the full two-page spread with a blown-up picture of yours truly from the shoot they did last week front and centre. Then there's a much smaller photograph of the hall in the bottom-right corner.

'It's not so bad,' says Chloe brightly, when she finally drags her eyes up to meet mine.

I tilt my head, and her face falls instantly.

'Okay it's awful, I'm so sorry, Tessa, it's all my fault. I told him about your daughter in confidence, it was off the record. I mean I guess I didn't say that it was off the record, but I thought it was pretty clear. I never for a second thought he'd include it, you have to believe me. I really am so sorry...'

When Malachy phoned at 7.30 this morning, I was still dozing. Conn's noisy midnight exit and my own dark moments of the soul had disrupted my sleep. It took a good two minutes of him rambling for me to figure out what he was talking about.

'I didn't realise,' he was saying, 'none of us realised. I'd have insisted we hold the open day next week, or the week after. Even tomorrow. It wouldn't have made much of a difference. We didn't have to have it on the *anniversary*. I didn't know you had one, let alone that she went missing. I'm so sorry if I ever said anything insensitive, which knowing me, I absolutely bloody did. That's Malachy; he'd put my foot in a glove if it was going, as my mother always says. And, Lord knows, the woman is never wrong.'

'Stop talking about your mother!' came a muffled voice beyond him, which finally focused my mind.

'None of us knew, except Maura, of course. But she forgot the date. She's being quite tough on herself.'

'No I'm not!' said the muffled voice.

'Is that— Is Maura there?' And then, a second later, as my stomach dropped: 'Are you talking about Bea?' I never told Malachy, or much of anyone else at the Project, about my daughter.

'Is that her name? The article didn't say... Hey!'

A scuffing sound as the receiver was manhandled and Maura appeared on the line. 'I knew it was this month but I didn't remember the exact day, I'm sorry, Tessa dear. You should have said.'

'What is – why is everyone suddenly talking about Bea? And why are you chumming about with Malachy Foster at seven on a Saturday morning. You didn't...? Maura!'

'What? No! I'm not that hard up! He came right over here as soon as he saw the newspaper. Well, not right here, he stopped by Trevor and Susan's houses on the way. Susan's husband was not impressed.'

It was 7.36, according to my alarm clock. But the increasing daylight was not offering much illumination. 'What newspaper?'

'The *Dublin Press*. The article Chloe's friend wrote.'

My stomach was a dead weight then. 'But that's about the campaign, about canvassing.'

'It is,' Maura agreed. 'But it's about you and your family too.'

Thirty minutes later and I was sitting outside Centra, mouth open in horror as I forced myself to read on.

> Ms Doherty's daughter disappeared into thin air exactly ten years ago today...
>
> ... perhaps Save Our Hall is a distraction, or perhaps it's a bid to find a situation in which she possesses an element of control...
>
> ... The exact circumstances of the disappearance have never been established, but family members believe the young woman took her own life and a presumption of death order has been issued by the courts...

Chloe is still apologising when the kitchen door opens again and Conn appears. This is the earliest I've seen him surface. He's pulled himself from bed for the open day. He looks exhausted. I heard him leave last night, but I've no idea what time he got home.

Chloe instantly stops talking and he looks from her to me. She looks tired too. Did nobody in this house get a decent night's sleep?

'What is it?' asks Conn.

'Nothing,' squeaks Chloe as his eyes fall to the newspaper on the table.

'Is that the piece about the canvass…' he says, walking over and rotating the pages so they're facing him.

Chloe opens her mouth, but snaps it shut again as Conn pulls out a chair and throws himself into it, his eyes scanning the newsprint rapidly.

'I'll kill him,' he says, before he could have gotten much further than the third paragraph.

He keeps reading.

Another thirty seconds and his eyes bulge as he looks directly at me.

He's clearly reached my favourite bit – about how, without this campaign, friends worried if I'd make it through the darker months.

'I will hunt him down and I will snap his scrawny giraffe neck in two.'

'We won't have to do much hunting,' I say. 'He'll be at the open day today; composing the third piece in his *series*.'

'It's not all bad,' insists Chloe, her face pleading for agreement. 'There is a lot in there about the canvassing, and the open day.'

'That's what the whole article was supposed to be about,' I say, pushing myself up from the table. I'm not the best on my feet this morning. It's the tiredness, and the shock of the article – I swear it took five years off me. I'll be all right when I get to the hall though; the adrenaline will see me through.

'Is this the bit you're referring to?' says Conn, still furious as he traces his finger down the fifth stanza.'"Ms Doherty's motley crew of Radical Activists were out knocking on doors on Thursday night. They were a good representation of people in need of the community project's help, and the response from the public was overwhelmingly positive."'

'Yes, that's it!' affirms Chloe.

'Hang on, not done. "The group included Ms Doherty's two significantly younger housemates; an unemployed lawyer who wished not to be named, and courier Chloe Darvin. They were joined by Malachy Foster, a middle-aged man who has been almost as unlucky in love as he has been in securing employment."'

Chloe whimpers. It's no good. No amount of sunny disposition can put a positive spin on this.

'Malachy was quite hurt by that description,' I say. 'He thought himself and Paul had gotten on like a house on fire.'

'I sound like a criminal who's been disbarred,' says Conn.

'We all sound like criminals. As well as the mourning mother, I'm the lecherous landlady peering through the keyholes of my sexy younger tenants.'

'I don't think that's how it comes across—'

'But the stuff about you, and your daughter, how did he know?' asks Conn.

Chloe whimpers again, louder this time as she puts her face in her hands. 'I'm so, so sorry, Tessa. I don't know what happened. I'm sure there's an explanation.'

'Are you really defending him?' says Conn.

'Paul would never do anything intentionally hurtful—'

'Do you need me to read out some more of this? It is completely exploitative!'

'He's just doing his job,' Chloe shoots back. 'You don't like him and so you're delighted to find a reason to get the boot in.'

'You think I'm delighted by this? Aside from portraying me as a layabout, he's taken this awful thing that happened to Tessa, that has nothing to do with the campaign, and he's exploiting it for paper sales and clicks and bloody Twitter followers!'

'Okay, enough,' I say, before there is yet another full-scale falling out between them. 'Chloe, I know it's not your fault. This is all on Paul, so please stop apologising. And, Conn, I appreciate the support, but losing the head isn't going to help anyone. What's done is done. Now we need to get down to the hall, okay? This is a big day for us and I need everyone at their best.'

I take their silence as agreement.

'Conn, you can come in my car. We'll bring the retractable tables. And, Chloe, you take the chairs, okay?'

'I'll load up now,' says Conn, and he leaves the room and a bereft Chloe.

'Everyone's going to hate him now, aren't they?' she says.

'Chloe, listen to me,' I say, a little crossly as I walk back to her, my leg still stiff. 'If you like Paul, it doesn't matter what anyone else thinks. You need to trust your own instincts. It's part of standing on your own two feet. How people feel about him has nothing to do with how they feel about you. All right? Okay?'

I tilt the girl's face up to me and she nods dolefully.

'You need to stop thinking about yourself as an extension of other people. You're your own person. Remember that.'

· · · · · · · · ·

'How mad are you?' asks Conn when we're out on the main road. 'Because the article wasn't about me and I'm fairly mad.'

I check my mirrors. 'It's the thought of all the well-meaning people who will feel obliged to express their shock and sympathy for something that happened a decade ago. Once it comes up in conversation, it's impossible to get people to talk about anything else,' I say, taking a left turn. 'I was on this dating site for a while, but I quit before I went on a single date. All the men had the same stock online chitchat questions. Where are you from? What do you do? How many children have you got?'

'Any brothers or sisters?' Conn chimes in.

'Of course. You understand.' I glance over at him. He's wearing a grey knit scarf and a thick mustard beanie, turned up. His beard is at proper wilderness proportions now. It suits him. He looks... himself.

'I would love to talk about Bea, if I was allowed to do it without the whole thing being shrouded in this awful dreary sadness. Apparently, nothing she did before she went missing is as important as the fact that she went missing. Now that she's "a missing person", it's not respectful to tell you that she used to sit on her big brother's back and insist he neigh like a horse as she rode him from room to room, giving me and her father the queen's wave as she passed.'

Conn gives a short snort.

'I could say: "My daughter had a black belt in karate, three Nobel prizes and she found the cure for cancer". And they'd still look at me with deep pity and say, 'Yes, but isn't she also dead?' We all die. It's the least remarkable thing about us, yet for Bea, it's the point everyone fixates on.'

I stop at the lights and turn on my indicator. I glance over again but Conn is looking out his window, watching a young woman try and fail to unlock her bicycle. The lights change and I hit the accelerator.

'What about your parents? How are they coping?'

'Mam's going to a counsellor, I think. Dad just stays longer in bed. None of us talk about it. It's kind of like you said, when you have that hanging over your family, nothing else seems worth saying. So we just don't really talk at all.'

'I was very against support groups until I went to one,' I say. 'A woman I worked with at the time literally came to the house, put me in her car and drove me down to the North Dublin Community Project. They had three groups at that time. Alcoholics Anonymous was one, the Bereavement Circle was another.'

'What was the third?'

'Rumba,' I say. 'Oh yes. The rumba will outlive us all.' I pull out onto the next road. 'I didn't utter a word during that first bereavement meeting, I just sat there annoyed that I'd been made to come. It wasn't my style, going somewhere for help. I spent my days offering help. I knew all the advice. I was as surprised as anyone when I drove myself back the following week, and the week after, and the week after. It gave me one lifebuoy in each relentlessly bleak week. And, eventually, I could hold my head above water long enough to introduce myself. And then to tell them Bea's name. And then to say what happened. And, within a year, I was strong enough, afloat enough, to become the leader of the group, which led onto others.'

'Which is why the hall is so important to you,' says Conn, nodding slowly.

'That hall saved my life. It has saved hundreds of lives. And even the ones it didn't save, it has made better. It's a draughty, old, energy-sucking, terribly-designed building, but it has done more good than I have in my whole career. And I was a damn fine social worker.'

'I have no doubt.'

'It cannot be allowed to be turned into a hotel. I will not let them do that. I will not let profit be put before people yet again. So today, Paul Murtagh is small fry.'

'Well he better hope he doesn't run into me,' says Conn, as the building appears in the distance.

'Or Malachy.'

'He was that hurt by the piece?'

We drive past a line of people. I look back and realise they're queueing to get into the grounds.

'Let's just say,' I reply, slowing down as we approach the entrance, 'that he's already been on to Dano.'

# CHLOE

● ● ● ● ● ● ● ● ● ● ●

**I** **'ve been** called up to man the coffee van while the current volunteer runs into the hall for his one scene in *Angela's Ashes: An Alternative Ending*. I help him fold his wings inward and lower the halo so he can make it out through the hatch door. (He's part of the alternative ending.)

'You should be grand,' he says. 'There were a lot of people queueing at first, but I guess word got around that we have nothing except decaf tea. And beef jerky.' He nods towards a jar of what looks like bark on the counter. 'Meals on Wheels got it in a donation, but it doesn't fit with their aesthetic. Too much chewing required.'

'Is there any coffee?' I ask, giving the water boiler and scattered paraphernalia a quick once-over. My phone is buzzing in my front pocket.

He shakes his head, making his halo wobble from side to side.

'Decaf coffee?'

'There's decaf tea,' he offers.

'But it says "coffee" over the van.'

'It's a euphemism.'

'For what?'

'Decaf tea.'

'Right,' I say. 'Got it.' I reach over the counter and straighten the wire hanger so his halo is centred. 'Break a leg.'

He disappears into the crowd and I marvel at just how many

people are here. The place is jammed. The only demonstration I can make out from my spot in the van is the first-aid one and that's because Malachy has gotten over his disappointment at not being needed as a life model by committing fully to the part of road accident victim who must be put back together by bandages, antibacterial wipes and safety pins. His arms flail over the spectators' heads and his groans transcend the hubbub.

It's the one tiny positive about Paul's article – that at least it did its job and got people here. I really cannot understand why he wrote what he did. Conn is right; Tessa's personal tragedy doesn't have anything to do with the campaign. Doesn't Paul realise how annoyed the article will make Tessa and Malachy and everyone else and that these people are my friends? How is he going to get on with them after this?

When I take out my phone, there are two more missed calls from Mam. I haven't heard from her in weeks, but she started phoning again when I was on my way here. She's obviously seen the article too.

I consider phoning her back. But what could I say? That I've been thinking about my life with her and realising how weird it is that we lived on a tiny cul-de-sac and I only ever knew one neighbour's name? Or that I was never allowed to invite a friend home from school? Or that she lied to me for two years straight about *having cancer*?

She won't have liked my name appearing in the newspaper. My whole name. That makes it about her. Nothing gets to my mother like the idea that people are talking about her.

'There you are!'

A pram, followed by a harried young woman with walnut-hued skin, breaks through the crowd.

'Yemi!' I shriek, shoving my phone back in my pocket. I pull the hatch door open and hop down so I can engulf her with my whole body. 'Yemi, Yemi!' It suddenly hits me how much I've missed her.

'All right, careful now. My stitches are still delicate.'

'Oh, sorry,' I say, pulling myself off, but she's grinning too. 'And Akin!' I peer into the pram and realise he is asleep. 'Sorry,' I say again, voice lower. 'Look at him. He's gorgeous!'

'He looks like Peter's uncle Patsy after a feed of pints, but somehow he manages to pull it off,' says Yemi. I can hear the adoration in her voice.

'Gosh, it's so good to see you,' I say, squeezing her shoulders. 'I assume the baby didn't come out up here.'

'You're safe enough,' she says as she squeezes mine back. 'Right, so, where is he? I've heard enough, I want to see him in the flesh.'

'Paul?' I ask, confused. 'You've seen Paul.'

'No, not Paul,' she scoffs. 'Conn. You've been talking about him incessantly since you moved into that house. I've tried to find him online, but he appears to have less of a presence there than you.'

'Easier for him to hide what he's up to that way.'

'And what exactly is he up to? Have you solved that great mystery?'

'Not yet,' I admit. 'I did trail him last night. I heard him leaving and I ran out after him, but then I lost him. Though I don't know how. He doesn't drive, has no bike or scooter, and the house is at the end of a cul-de-sac. There's only one road, and footpath, away from the place, and I can say with near certainty that he wasn't on it. Unless he decided to take his life into his hands and do the cliff walk at midnight, he has to have taken that road. But he just vanished.' I really haven't a clue how. It's a straight road the whole way down. He only had a couple of minutes of a head start and I must have walked up and down the thing five times before giving up and heading back to bed.

'Wait. This was at midnight? You got out of bed and tailed this guy in the middle of the night?'

'I didn't tail him though. I lost him. That's the problem.'

'Yes, *that's* the problem.'

I throw my best friend a look. 'I'm just concerned for Tessa. She's a lovely woman. I don't want her living with some criminal or whatever he is. I don't want him taking advantage of her. He's living in her house rent-free and he doesn't need to be.'

'Not to state the obvious for the hundredth time, but aren't you doing the same?'

'Yes, but I had nowhere else to live, and I'm from the area. Howth is nowhere near where Conn's from or where he was living. And why Tessa's house, in particular? He told me it was the perfect house for him, and then he denied saying it. Why would he do that?'

'I don't know,' says Yemi in a tone that lets me know she's sorry she reopened this can of worms.

Well, it's too late. We're here now and I have thoughts.

'I have a new theory.'

'Oh goodie.'

'Drugs. He's a drug smuggler.'

'You've moved on from toy boy honey trap, at least.'

That was last week's theory. 'He's too irritating to be carrying out a romance scam, and Tessa's too smart. But drug dealer makes sense,' I say. 'Howth's a port town. And where do drugs come in? Ports. And when do they land? The middle of the night.' I am mainly basing this on *Famous Five* books, but it adds up. 'I know a girlfriend makes the most sense. But if he was sneaking off to see a girlfriend—'

'Why wouldn't he just say it. I know, I know. Please, let's not go over it again.' Yemi puts the brake on the buggy and turns to survey the crowd. 'Is that him?'

I follow Yemi's gaze to a young handsome biracial man with perfectly coiffed hair and a tight denim shirt. He's watching the meditation group who, last time I passed, were in the exact same poses. I scoff. 'He wishes.'

'I thought you said he was good-looking.'

'I said he *thinks* he's good-looking. Two very different things.'

'Ah ha.'

I gasp. 'Unless it's got something to do with her missing daughter!' I ponder this, but no, nothing is coming to me to link Conn to the disappearance. 'Never mind.'

'I read about that this morning.'

I groan. 'Even the mothers of tiny children have found the time to read it... Poor Tessa.'

'Did she not know Paul was going to write about it?'

'No. She never told him anything about her daughter. I did.' I throw my head into my hands. 'I thought it was only between us. We were in the back of the van, just talking, it wasn't like an interview or anything. I should have said it was off the record. I'm such an idiot.'

'Sounds like typical Paul Murtagh behaviour to me,' says Yemi. 'Do you remember in college he'd always want to pair up with you for projects?'

'Yeah, because he was my boyfriend.'

'And because he knew you'd do all the work and he could just come in at the end, read it out to the tutorial group and get half the marks and all the praise? He was always about himself; he was always about the glory. He knew you idolised him and he took advantage of that.'

'That's not true.'

Yemi shrugs, grabbing a piece of jerky. 'At least he didn't name her daughter.'

I cringe. 'That's only because I don't know what it is.'

'I don't get why you want him back so badly, Chloe.'

My face is burning, but it's more irritation than embarrassment. 'Because I love him.'

'Do you?'

'Yes. Why would I say I did if I didn't?'

She shrugs. 'I just don't remember you ever really being in love with him. I know you were sad when you broke up, he was your ticket out of your mam's house, and suddenly it was gone. But I don't remember you being sad about *him*.'

I don't know why she's distorting things. Of course I was sad about him. Of course I loved him.

'Tell me one thing you missed about him.'

'Everything!'

'Name one.'

I think. It's not that I can't come up with something; it's just that there's too much, all jumbled together. It's more of a feeling. A feeling of... freedom? But I don't say that. She'd wilfully take it up wrong. 'The sex,' I say instead, my defiant face dropping when she bursts into laughter.

'The sex was terrible!'

'What? No it wasn't!' I'm trying to conjure up a specific memory of our diagonal bodies, but my brain appears to have been wiped.

'I'm sorry, Chloe, but it was. Peter and Paul lived together, remember? We shared a wall with you. And you used to tell me that he made you suck his fingers even though they always tasted of... what was it? Something awful...'

It comes back to me before she says it. From somewhere deep in my subconscious, buried down with a lot of elements of my relationship with my mother. It's so vivid I can almost taste it.

She finds the word. 'Earwax.'

How had I forgotten that?

Yemi shakes her head sadly. 'If you're only going to sleep with one man, you really should be getting something better than earwax fingers in your mouth.'

'Shhh!' I hiss, mortified.

She pops the end of the jerky in her own gob. I don't know how she's eating after that. Especially something so... finger-shaped.

'If Paul is the one, then fair enough, but I have to say something. If I didn't, I'd be a shit friend.'

I don't give her verbal permission, but I don't stop her either.

'I always thought you settled,' she says. 'Your upbringing

didn't instil you with the sort of confidence that you should have. You're always apologising for who you are, but you just keep on being that person. You're so yourself. You're an exceptional person, Chloe. And you're stunning. But you were taught to hide; not to make a scene or be different or do anything that might attract attention. So when non-threatening, out-for-himself Paul came along, you were all in. Here was someone you could hide behind. Here was someone you could submit to, just as you had submitted to your mother. He was a port in a storm, which was fine. But now you're figuring out how to steer your own boat and the waters aren't so choppy any more. So why are you going back? You need to keep sailing forward. Who knows what undiscovered lands await.'

She purses her lips, then grimaces. 'Sorry. I've been watching a lot of sailing videos since I've been on maternity leave. I find the lapping waters and all the complex terminology soothing.'

Riotous applause explodes to our left and I look over to see the Irish dancers taking bows on the main stage.

'Are we still friends?' She grimaces more, so her eyes are practically closed.

'There he is.'

She whizzes around so we're looking in the same direction. 'Who? Paul? Conn? Oh, Paul.'

He's sauntering in our general direction, doing his best to keep the swaying press lanyard from dipping into the aluminium tray that he's eating from. He's obviously been by the Meals on Wheels buffet.

Yemi wrinkles her nose. 'Is he eating boiled vegetables?'

'Paul!' I call out, but then I notice the deranged figure tracking him. A man head-to-toe in bandages. I'd be sure he'd just been in a terrible accident if it wasn't for the speed at which he was moving and the familiar bulbous cranium throbbing through the dressings.

'I need your help,' I say to Yemi, cutting her off before she can protest: 'You just shat all over the only man I've ever loved, so you owe me. I need to talk to Paul. And you see that mummified creature heading straight for him?'

'Jesus, is that lad all right?'

'I need you to stop him,' I say.

'How? He looks like he should be in hospital.'

'Just think of something,' I say, hauling her after me as she unlocks the pram. 'His name's Malachy. And I need to get to Paul before he does.'

# TESSA

**• • • • • • • • • • •**

The Irish dancers are just leaving the main stage and Saviour Hall is ascending the steps to similar enthusiasm. She introduces her backing dancers – a consortium of other civically-minded drag queens – as 'Powder to the People'. As she says this, they each pop open a large make-up compact, do a high kick and thrust the gold cases forward like these are the security passes that will get them into the halls of power. Needless to say, the crowd completely loses it.

I may have spent far too much of my morning smiling gratefully at strangers as they mumbled their condolences at me, but I cannot fault the turnout. Maura has appointed herself bouncer and taken up position at the entrance gates where she's operating a one-in one-out policy to maintain some control. All official raffle tickets have already been sold and the volunteers on the stall are now just writing out numbers as people approach them. Cynthia, who looks after Meals on Wheels, says she's two vats of spuds away from having to crack open the emergency industrial-sized cans of Ambrosia rice pudding. The officials cannot ignore this sort of public support.

I'm currently at the edge of the Rumba for Retirees dance marathon. They're four hours in and have already lost all but three couples. Trevor is among those still standing, although I can't be sure that his partner still is. There is an air of Norman Bates waltzing his mother's skeleton about the place.

A group of men in suits appear at the edge of the circle, and Trevor risks releasing his dance partner's left arm for the briefest of moments as he waves and then proceeds to drag the poor, flailing woman across the circle to them.

Maura and Susan have confirmed that Paul is here, somewhere, interviewing the masses. He should also be glad he's helped to attract such a crowd. It's probably the only reason Malachy hasn't spotted him yet.

The familiar opening chords of Bob Marley and the Wailers' 'Get Up, Stand Up' blast from the stage as Saviour Hall moves into the centre.

I raise my hands and clap in unison with everyone else. My leg isn't so bad now. Once I keep moving, it's fine.

Saviour starts to sing the familiar opening lines.

Oh, this takes me back. Bernard and I used to get stoned to this song.

I'm laughing and cheering with such abandon that I don't notice Trevor dancing towards me until he is box-stepping a mere foot away. It's a relief to see his partner is alive, just about.

'Tessa,' he says, breathlessly. 'These are some of the councillors who've come to show their support.'

The gaggle of suits are standing to the right. Trevor sways for a second before remembering that he has to keep moving.

'How do you do?' I say to the men, who are nodding at me now.

'Sorry for your troubles,' says one.

'Deepest condolences.' Another.

'A terrible thing to happen.'

I manage a tight smile.

'And this is Paudie Connaughton, the minister of state with responsibility for offshore fishing and marine wildlife.' He nods towards the man with the awful combover and half-drops his partner in the effort. That last sentence nearly finished him off completely.

'I'll just...' says Trevor, pressing his right shoulder against the woman's so that they're two lifeless rods propping each other up.

'Thank you for coming,' I say to the minister as Trevor and the other half of his inverted V stumble back towards the remaining dancers. Offshore fishing and marine life isn't exactly the area of influence we're after, but I'll take what I can get. 'It's great to have your support.'

'Not a bother,' he says. 'I'm looking at a move into this constituency in the next election, so...'

'Good to show your face,' I supply.

'And I'm very into community,' he adds.

'Of course.'

'Sure, isn't it communities that elect me.'

I nod politely, wondering if this man inherited his seat from his father or his uncle.

'I've been hearing good things coming out of An Bord Pleanála. Very good things,' he says.

'Really?'

'Oh yeah. We'd have a fair bit of dealings with those lads. I'd know a few of them personally.'

'What are they saying?'

'There's a lot of sympathy in there for your position,' he says, giving me a look that implies that what he's saying is of utmost importance. He has that political trait down, anyway. 'They know what way the wind is blowing, and all the media coverage certainly hasn't hurt your cause. I'm hearing there's going to be an early decision on it.'

'Like how early?'

'You didn't hear it from me now, but...' He tilts his head briefly to the left. 'Could be as soon as Monday.'

'Hardly.'

The minister winks and gives another head tilt. 'You didn't hear it from me now,' he says, 'until you do hear it, and then remember the name. Paudie Connaughton. Next election, I'll be on the ballot paper.'

I nod vaguely. A positive decision – and within as little as two days!

He's a couple of steps away when he turns back. 'Oh yeah, and sorry to read about your troubles. Shocking stuff,' he says.

I search the crowd for Maura or Conn or Chloe; anyone to share the good news with. And then I spot him. Paul Murtagh. Walking past the water dispenser, polishing off a Meals on Wheels tray.

I make a beeline for him and am at the Tai Chi demonstration when I notice I'm not the only one in pursuit. Malachy is about twenty paces ahead. And I'll tell you this: you've never seen a man with a head bandage, arm sling, and splints tied to both knees move so fast.

# CHLOE

· · · · · · · · · · ·

'**P**aul!' I shout, making a grab for the lanyard and pulling him out of sight behind the raffle stand.

'Hey! Chloe. Careful! That's my press accreditation you're messing with,' he says, producing a napkin from under his tinfoil tray and wiping the thing down.

'What was with the article today? You said it was going to be an embedded piece, going door-to-door with the campaigners. You never said anything about including Tessa's family history.'

'The embedded piece was the plan,' he says, tossing the napkin into a nearby bin. 'But it was too dull. Maybe if your donation woman had agreed to go on the record... My editor was going to pull it. There was good filler there, but nothing to make a headline, nothing to make people click. The last article I did on this was our most successful story online for the whole week. I was under pressure to match that and a piece about going canvassing with you just wasn't cutting it.'

'I did go back and ask if she'd talk to you about the donation,' I mumble.

'It's okay. You gave me a new, better angle. A journalist can't go in with a fixed idea of what a story is going to be. I have to be open to what happens – to finding the truth. Tessa's story was the best truth.'

'But I told you about her daughter in confidence.'

He frowns, licking some sauce from his index finger. *Earwax, earwax.* All I can think of is earwax.

'I don't recall you saying it was off the record. I can check my notes, but—'

'I didn't say it was off the record.' I try to shake the defensiveness from my voice. 'I just assumed. Since we're... since we're friends, I didn't think it needed saying.'

He looks at me sympathetically. 'Journalism 101: it always needs saying.'

I didn't take Journalism 101, or any other journalism modules. Is this one of those things that everyone else knows, but I am clueless about?

'I asked if you were happy to be named in the article.'

'Yeah...'

'So that means you're on the record. Anyway, I didn't actually attribute that information to you, so I don't know why you're worrying.'

'Tessa was upset. Not a lot of people know about her daughter and she wanted to keep it private.'

The queue for raffle tickets winds along the side of the stand, and we inch further to avoid colliding with it. All the prizes are on display; a Waterford Crystal vase, two vouchers for Misunderstood Mutts, a dart board with Charles Bentley's photograph at its centre, a jumbo-sized box of decaffeinated tea.

'I thought she'd be thrilled, to be honest,' says Paul, as the queue shuffles forward. 'She comes across as stoic and admirable; like a modern-day martyr, putting her own pain to one side for a cause that serves the greater good.'

'Well she doesn't see it like that. And I feel like I've betrayed her.'

'That's because you're such a good person, Clo,' he says, as he readjusts his glasses. 'You always were.' He finishes off the dinner tray. 'Boiled chicken,' he says, chewing. 'Not half as bad as you'd think.'

I laugh, despite myself, and his own smile widens.

Yemi doesn't know what she's talking about. Paul isn't just about himself. He sees me, and he cares about me.

I'm not like her or Conn or even Tessa. They take love for granted. They grew up with it. I don't have multiple family members and friends to flit between, being adored. I have no idea what that feels like. I'm not easy to love, but Paul cared about me. I'm lucky someone ever did.

'What really mattered to Tessa,' I say, starting to feel less annoyed, 'was saving the hall – raising awareness and getting as many people as possible involved.'

'Well job done,' he says, lifting his two hands in the air and pivoting around so he's taking in the line-dancing, the main stage, the rumba marathon (only two couples left now) and the massive crowds watching them all. 'People are here *because* of Tessa's story. Pain sells. I'm not saying it's right, I'm just telling you how it is. And it's not the big, bad media's fault. If people didn't want to read about those kinds of things, we wouldn't write about them.'

I can see his point. I'm often drawn to the most miserable articles even though they leave me feeling terrible for the rest of the day. Half the news I read, I don't actually think should be considered news.

'If I'd written a straight piece about how the hall helps lots of faceless, unnamed people, and this event was happening today to help save it, nobody would have read it. Nobody would have turned up. If the hall is saved, it'll be because she told her story.'

'Except she didn't actually tell –

'Tessa is the reason they're all here,' he says, assuredly. 'She should be proud of herself.'

One of the things that first drew me to Paul was his certainty. I rarely feel certain about anything. I envy the sort of conviction Paul has. If I can't have it, at least I can be close to it.

'You're probably right...'

'This story has been a huge success. I've got a source in the planning office who tells me things are looking very good.'

'Really?' I say, feeling a quiver of excitement.

'Really,' he repeats. 'This is my job, Clo. I know what I'm doing. Trust me.' He peers down at me and, in his pupils, I watch the reflection of my head nodding. I have never relished being looked at. I mean, there isn't much *to* look at, but it's different with Paul because it's just Paul. His attention is as much as I need.

I'm not hiding behind him. Paul is standing in front, protecting me.

'You should come for a drink to celebrate,' he says, pulling his phone from his pocket.

I freeze. 'Seriously?'

'Yeah, tonight.'

'With you?'

He laughs. 'Yes, Chloe, with me.'

I've been waiting weeks for him to ask me out and now the

moment is finally here. This is what I've been preparing for, daydreaming about. Only I don't feel how I expected. I feel bad. I feel sort of guilty.

Why do I *always* feel guilty?

He scrolls through something, gives a half-smile and returns the phone to the back pocket of his loose jeans. He pushes his glasses over the bump on his nose and waits for my response.

This is what I wanted. This man is all I wanted and now he's here, right in front of me, asking me on a date. Yes, he shouldn't have written the article, and yes, I'd like him to be different in some ways, but we can't change people, can we? We have to accept them for who they are. That's what love is. This man loved me. Literally nobody else has ever loved me. The least I can do is to make a few small allowances. Otherwise I deserve to be on my own.

'Okay, yes, great,' I say, pulling my shoulders in and smiling brightly.

'Excellent,' he replies. 'Aimee has organised a little gathering – to mark my success. Not many journalists create such a zeitgeist this early in their career.'

'No, absolutely,' I say, nodding, 'Aimee?'

'Aimee.' He looks at me like I should really know who he's talking about. Then I remember. I met her in the *Dublin Press* reception.

'From work, right, right.'

'Couple of other journos said they'd stop by. And it'd be cool for you guys to meet properly. The story wouldn't exist without you.'

Okay, so drinks with co-workers isn't exactly what I'd envisaged, but it's good that he wants me to meet his friends, integrate me into his new life.

I ignore the unease sloshing about in my gut.

'Sounds good,' I trill, just as something hits me softly from behind. 'I'll be there.'

'I think I lost him,' says Yemi, reversing the pram out of my back and pulling it up beside her. 'I told him someone was looking for him urgently in the hall. He didn't look convinced, but then I said it was Tessa who needed help and he ran off. Hello, Paul.'

'Oh, hello.'

'Yemi,' she supplies. 'Chloe's best friend? The girlfriend, now wife, of the man you shared a flat with throughout college?'

'I knew that. Of course. How's Peter?'

'Fine,' she says flatly. 'Anyway, I've saved your skin for a little while, so you're welcome. That lad was pretty angry.'

'Which lad?' asks Paul.

'Malachy,' I say. 'He wasn't happy with how you wrote about him in the paper, either.'

'Oh,' he says, surprised and possibly a little concerned. 'Didn't have him down as the reading type.'

Yemi rolls her eyes, which I ignore.

'I should probably make tracks anyway,' says Paul. 'I've gotten everything I need for a follow-up. And I'll see you tonight.'

I go to hug him goodbye, but Yemi holds an arm out between us. 'Too late,' she says with what can only be described as glee.

About twenty feet away is Malachy. One of the leg splints is gone, the other is snapped in half and the bandages that were holding them both in place are now flapping in the wind after him like an experimental, ostentatious wedding train.

Not far behind is Maura. Then comes Reggie and Susan. I've never seen Susan scowl, but I think that's what's happening on her face. Trevor, who looks like he could do with Malachy's bandages and then some, is dragging himself along at the rear.

'It's the battered and the bloodthirsty,' remarks Yemi, as I notice a sixth figure heading for us. Conn Horgan.

I spread my feet slightly, steeling myself for the onslaught, while Yemi throws an arm around my shoulders, her body teeming with anticipation. 'This should be fun.'

# TESSA

. . . . . . . . . .

'Tessa.'

I'm about fifty metres from Paul when my daughter-in-law steps in front of me.

'Audrey,' I say, peering around her. 'I can't stop now, I have to—'

'I really think we should talk,' she says, with a deep inhale. 'You've been avoiding me and it's not healthy, for either of us, and I would like to talk to you, no judgement, no embarrassment, just a mingling of words.' She is holding her arms straight by her sides, hands in fists. She's nervous. I feel culpable, and also generous. The news about the expected planning permission decision has me buoyed.

Anyway, Paul has disappeared. And Malachy is being accosted by a woman with a pram.

'All right,' I say. 'Let's talk.'

'Okay,' she says, as if I'm the one who's just sprung this tête-à-tête on her. 'Well, right. I want to clear the air between us. Things have been off since your fall and—'

'You discovering me half-naked on my landing?'

'Yes, that. But the body is a beautiful thing, Tessa. Your body is beautiful.'

'Thank you, Audrey. I'm pretty fond of it too. I've never been prudish about nudity. It wasn't that. I was more ashamed of the mental state you found me in, rather than the physical one.'

'You were talking to Bea when I found you.'

'Yes,' I say, trying not to flinch. I'm too long in the tooth to be embarrassed. 'I know you probably think I'm mad—'

'Not at all.'

'And I don't need it explained to me that she wasn't really there. I'm not losing my marbles. I was just enjoying one little moment of lunacy and I really, really don't need to be set straight. I know she wasn't there. I know it. I do. Okay?'

'Or maybe she was.'

'Excuse me?'

Audrey blinks. 'Maybe Bea was there. Maybe her aura continues to fly close to yours. Maybe she sensed you were in need of comfort, a special, specific type of comfort that only a child can give a mother. Her aura may have felt such a magnetic calling that it was compelled by the universe to take on a physical form and deliver the most basic, understandable form of care.'

On the main stage, Saviour Hall and Powder to the People are reaching a crescendo. The singing blares through as myself and Audrey stand there, looking at each other.

She's smiling at me with her mouth, her eyes, even her nose crinkles. She's practically humming with goodwill.

Oh god, she thinks she's found a kindred spirit.

I am overcome by the desire to laugh, but I swallow it down, for the good of my relationship with what remains of my family. Not that I'd be laughing at her. It's relieved laughter.

How could I possibly have thought that Audrey, of all people, would judge me for communing with the shadow of someone? Audrey, who owns a ouija board and gets her cards read with the commitment that other women visit the nail salon. The incident on the stairs wasn't an awkward occurrence for Audrey; it was run of the mill.

'And you don't have the stick,' she affirms, glancing down. 'Maybe Bea helped to heal you.'

'Maybe,' I say as sceptically as I can manage. I need to be careful or she'll be inviting me along to her next crystals session.

I'm shuffling, but she's not taking the hint.

She's still smiling with every feature her face possesses.

'It's a special day today.'

I grimace and wait for her to bring up the article.

'When I offered up my intentions this morning, I dedicated them to Bea.'

I nod politely. 'That's nice.'

'And I felt like I got something back.'

'You did?' I say, despite myself.

'An energy... like something might happen.'

I hold my tongue this time, but the truth is I've been feeling that way too. It could be because it's a big anniversary, but it feels like there's more than that. I even thought I saw her earlier, in the crowd. That hasn't happened in years.

'I wouldn't be able to give up hope either,' Audrey says.

Can the woman actually read minds?

She puts her hand out and touches mine. 'I mean it, Tessa. If it was Otis, and the universe wasn't telling me to give up, I never would.'

There's heat in her fingers, in her words.

Maybe it's the airy-fairy way she speaks, or maybe it's wishful thinking, but for the briefest of moments, I feel lifted.

# CHLOE

· · · · · · · · · · ·

'**C**olour writing? I'll give you colour writing! I'll have the colour purple written all over your eyes in a minute!'

'Careful, Malachy,' murmurs Susan, who really is giving Paul an exemplary scowl.

'And the stuff about my ex! That was between us, man to man.'

'Now, I didn't name her,' tries Paul, who has been on the defensive since Malachy started his tirade and is now so backed into the raffle stand that I'm mildly anxious.

'Which ex is this?' whispers Susan.

'Didn't you read the piece?' replies Maura, not so quietly. 'There only is one ex.'

'You see?' wails Malachy. 'She was as good as named. I saw Jimbo on the way in this morning and the look of pity he gave me... I'll never be able to show my face here again.'

'I'm sorry if your feelings were hurt,' says Paul. 'It wasn't my intention.' He's going for sincerity, I know he is, but it's coming off as condescension. I take a half-step closer and place a hand on his arm, just as Susan is doing with Malachy. But Paul mustn't be as good at reading body language because then he says: 'To be honest, I never thought you'd read it. I thought you'd be more of a tabloid man.'

Malachy's nostrils flair.

'Paul...' I try.

'It's okay,' he says, shaking me off. 'I've got this.'

'Do you think I'm too thick to read your shite paper, is that it?'

'No, no. That's not what I'm saying.'

'Well it sounds like that's what you're saying.'

'Sounds like it to me too,' says Reggie.

'And me,' chimes in Maura, as Susan murmurs her agreement. Even Trevor, who is currently being propped up by Reggie and Maura, finds the energy to deliver a few nods.

This isn't going well. I wish Paul would let me step in and clear it all up. If they knew him like I did, they wouldn't be so mad. Although, honestly, he's not helping himself.

Conn is the only one who doesn't say anything. I'm surprised he's not taking the opportunity to get the boot in too.

'Conn,' says Paul, also noticing his silence. 'You know what I'm saying?'

'I can't say I do,' replies my housemate, flatly. 'But I do know you have something to tell Chloe.'

'Hmm? No.'

'Have you done that yet?'

'Oh, so *this* is Conn,' enthuses Yemi. 'Nice to meet you, finally,' she says, beaming, as she takes a hand off the pram and stretches it out. 'I'm Yemi. Chloe's friend.' Eyes still on Paul, Conn shakes it.

'What's he talking about?' I ask Paul, voice low.

'He thinks...' Paul turns his head in towards me. 'I'll tell you later.' Then to the group, with some regained composure: 'I'm sorry if everyone wasn't happy. But sometimes journalism means publishing things people don't want printed. Everything else is PR.'

'That's a George Orwell quote,' states an irritated Yemi. 'Are you ever not taking credit for other people's work?'

'I, for one, never liked the tosser,' says Reggie.

'Nor me,' says Maura. 'What is it about him, do you think?'

'Is that... are you talking about me?'

'Height, maybe?' wagers Reggie, ignoring Paul entirely.

'What's wrong with my height?'

'The weird long limbs,' Maura concurs. 'Like you never know where they might end up.'

'You couldn't trust them,' surmises Reggie.

'Untrustworthy limbs,' nods Maura.

'All right, I appreciate some of you are upset but there's no need for insults...'

'That's not an insult,' says Reggie. 'Arrogant arse – that's an insult.'

'Or pompous prat.' Maura.

'Spineless letch?' chimes in Susan. 'Oh, sorry, does it have to have alliteration?'

'How about lanky string of piss?'

'Yes, Malo, my palo,' squeals Reggie, slapping Malachy on the back, which replaces the man's rage with pride, if only momentarily.

'Is that a good one?'

'Best so far.'

'Look at us now, using our words,' says Malachy, casting about. 'Where has Mrs Doherty gotten to? She'd be proud.'

'If you're all done calling me names, I am going to leave,' says Paul, straightening his lanyard. 'But let me say this before I go: I went above and beyond on this series of articles, trying to make it as impactful as it could be, for you. You see all these people here today? They're here because of what I wrote.'

'No,' corrects Maura. 'They're here because of the hall. Maybe your article attracted some of them, but so did all our canvassing and campaigning.'

'And my mural,' pipes up Reggie.

'Oh yeah!' declares Malachy. 'On the side of Dano's house. He sent me photos. It's bloody brilliant, Reggie. You did all that with water?'

'It's reverse graffiti. Instead of spraying paint, you use water, so you sort of clean the image onto the dirty surface. It's totally legal and all, so the cops can't touch you.'

'I saw that too,' says Susan. 'I'd say lots of people are here because of that.'

'Marvellous,' wheezes Trevor who is leaning against Maura.

'Yes, okay, everyone's here because of some water on a wall,' says Paul, zipping up his sweatshirt. 'That's fine, you all carry on. I'm off.'

And then he's gone, without another word to me or anyone else.

I consider going after him. But then I don't. I tell myself it's because I'm going to see him. I catch Conn's gaze and my face is ablaze with shame.

I'm feeling everything all at once and I don't understand any of it.

Susan squeals. 'Oh look!' she says, pointing towards the main stage. 'Saviour Hall is about to call the raffle!'

# TESSA

· · · · · · · · · ·

I t's 4 p.m. The open day was supposed to end an hour ago, but there's still a queue at the gate. Nobody who's made it in is willing to leave, and Saviour Hall and Powder to the People have just returned to the stage to fill the lull. Aside from my personal pain being laid bare for the whole nation to read about, the day couldn't have gone better.

I even have a warm, fuzzy feeling towards my daughter-in-law. I doubt it will last long, but I'm enjoying it while it does.

'We're fully out of food,' says Conn, approaching from the hall wearing a 'Stand by Your Nan' apron. He's been doling out Meals on Wheels fare for the last while. I haven't actually been inside to check out the buffet – as technically I am still boycotting the hall – but Cynthia says he's a dab hand with a ladle.

'Even the Ambrosia?'

'Served our last bowl half an hour ago. Someone just left the buffet with a plate of salt sachets and a half-used mayonnaise portion, so we've shut up shop. That okay?'

'We should probably wind down the whole thing. It's more than done its job. The politicians got a good show and there were a few media outlets here, not just the *Dublin Press.*'

'I saw some photographers,' says Conn, scratching his beard.

'It suits you,' I say, 'the enlarged facial hair.'

His hand pauses. 'Thanks.' He smiles through the coarse strands. 'Fergal was a fan. But my job didn't allow proper beards. Too scruffy.'

'It suits your lumberjack phase.'

'I'm thinking of fixing your kitchen chairs next. You know one of them has a wobble?'

'I do, but don't fix it. I like that wobble. You could look at the front door instead, see if you could get it to stop sounding like it's opening into the halls of hell.'

'I'll put it on my list,' he says, glancing around. 'Have you seen Chloe?'

'I was just looking for her myself. I heard about the standoff with Paul.'

'I don't understand what she sees in him. I see what he's after, obviously, but Chloe could do miles better.' Then after another search of the crowd: 'I really don't like the guy.'

'I know. You've said.'

'I don't like the way he treats her.'

I put a hand on his shoulder. 'Come on,' I say. 'Let's go find her.'

We wander past the raffle stall, which is now barren save for the Misunderstood Mutts vouchers, which winner after winner refused to take. There's an angel manning the coffee truck and the line dancers and Tai Chi group have merged into some sort of experimental dance troupe. It doesn't work at all and they can't seem to agree on a pace, but the crowd is sticking around.

The meditation group are *still* holding the poses they've been in since 9 a.m. (I hope they took a lunch break) and an exhausted Trevor is sitting beside a bandaged Malachy on a prop stretcher.

Over by the water barrel, I spot Chloe.

'If you're here for a drink, I'm afraid there's none left. Some woman just ate six sachets of salt and took the end of our reserves.'

'We're wrapping up anyway,' I say, as Chloe busies herself clearing away reusable cups. 'How are you doing? I hear there were some cross words with Paul.'

She continues stacking them into three even towers. 'It's all fine. He's fine.' She pauses. 'I'm meeting him for a drink tonight.'

'Like a date?' I ask, although what I'm really thinking is: *Why would you go out with that man?*

Chloe peeks up at Conn, eyes lingering on his apron, which is both ridiculous and surprisingly sexy. It works with the beard. It says: Here's a man who could build you a table, then cook the food to put on it, then knock it all to the ground and ravage you over the centrepiece.

'Yes. Like a date.'

'Right,' I say, doing my best to be happy for her, if not with the situation. I was never sure her interest in Paul was returned. I just don't see that man as a sexual being with primal urges. And there's no apron that could convince me otherwise.

'You sure it's a date?' asks Conn, and I suck in my cheeks in anticipation of the response.

'Yes, I'm sure,' she shoots back with predictable, and justifiable, indignation. What is Conn doing, sticking his oar in? 'Not that it's any of your business.'

'You're too good for him.'

I shut my eyes. *Stay out of it.*

But Conn's not finished: 'He's not telling you everything.'

'That makes two of you so,' retorts Chloe. 'You disappear into thin air at night and refuse to tell anyone what you're up to.'

'I don't disappear. And you weren't forthcoming either about—'

'Mam.'

'Well, yes, but—'

'What are you doing here?'

It is clear now that Chloe is no longer speaking to Conn, or to me.

We turn to see that the woman who appeared on my doorstep a couple of weeks ago is now standing behind us. She's still wearing the headscarf though she looks a lot less pale and feeble.

Chloe's right hand has moved to grab the edge of the table.

Laura Darvin looks at myself and Conn before directing her words at Chloe, as quietly as is feasible. 'I was phoning you all morning. I was worried about you.'

Her daughter takes this in. She's still taking in the woman's presence. 'You haven't called me for weeks. Were you not worried then?'

Laura glances at Conn. He told me about his time inside her house. How he asked Laura a few innocuous questions and she became incensed and shut down completely.

'Can we have some privacy, please?' she says primly.

Neither of us budge. I have no intention of going anywhere unless Chloe tells me to. Conn looks even more committed to his spot on the grass. He's widened his gait, as if this tiny woman might try to bulldoze him out of the way.

'This is a family matter,' adds Laura when nobody answers her question.

'These are my friends,' replies Chloe, steadily if not quite confidently. 'Anything you have to say, you can say in front of them.'

I'm watching Laura carefully. Otherwise I'd have missed the flash of rage. Chloe sees it too. Her fingers grip the table a little tighter, but her face doesn't falter.

'We don't wash our laundry in public, Chloe. You know that. You must have taken leave of your senses contributing to that pity party in today's newspaper.'

I bristle.

*Pity party!* As if I wanted the damn thing written.

'That's how you knew I'd be here,' says Chloe. Then something else dawns on her. 'That's why you're here. You're embarrassed.' She tries to scoff, but it's too weighed down by sadness and comes out more like a moan. 'I didn't even say anything significant in the piece.'

'It says you're living with another woman, and a man,' her mother splutters. 'What will people think?'

'What people, Mam? We don't know any people. You think everyone is sitting around talking about you, but they don't even know who you are because you don't talk to them. There's nobody *to* think about you! There's nobody to talk about you!'

'Though of course I saw who wrote it,' says Laura. A slightly raised chin the only sign that she's heard any of what her daughter just said.

'Yes, Mam. Paul wrote it. Paul, my ex-boyfriend. Paul, who you were so determined to keep me from you lied about having cancer!'

A couple I recognise from Pottery slow down as they pass.

I throw them a look that quickens their pace.

'Have you anything to say about that?'

Laura shakes her head curtly, eyes travelling from me to Conn like a sword slashing through silk.

'I'm going on a date with him. Tonight,' adds Chloe, bolstered. 'I'm very excited about it. He is too.'

Her head whips forward again. 'You're not getting back together.'

'We might be.'

There it is. Less fleeting this time. Eyes aflame. The rage isn't even directed my way, but I feel it.

'You're making a show of yourself, Chloe,' she says, words barely audible.

'You lied about having cancer! Who does that? Seriously, I'd love to know. Why would you do that to me? You're supposed to love me.'

Now it's a woman from Am-dram lingering. She's pretending to inspect the water barrel.

'It's empty,' I hiss.

'I am sick, Chloe,' says Laura, who is wrapping her coat tighter with every passer-by and is now practically a chrysalis.

'No you're not,' her daughter replies.

'Not cancer, okay, but something worse. Munchausen's disorder. I've been reading about it. I've even been to Doctor Conlon. It's psychological and it's very serious.'

After talking to my own doctor, I did a bit of further research – mainly finding out about Laura from Chloe, rather than about the disorder, which is pretty straightforward – and I feel confident Munchausen's is not what's going on here. Look at the woman. Now that Chloe doesn't believe her cancer pretence, she's not even trying to keep it up. It's not about being sick, it's about maintaining control.

Chloe may not think there's anything sinister about a grown woman not being 'allowed' to have social media accounts, or boyfriends, or really even friends, but I saw enough in my forty-three years on the job to disagree.

Chloe regards her mother warily. 'I've heard of Munch-ausen's...'

'It's rare, very rare,' Laura jumps in immediately. 'But recovery is possible, with a lot of support.'

It's Chloe's ingenuous expression that breaks me. She wants this to be the case. She wants there to be something definable wrong rather than having to accept that her mother is just someone who puts herself first.

Laura Darvin has deep-seated issues, but selfishness is still the result.

'Does your doctor agree?' I ask.

'Excuse me?' Laura all but spits.

'Does your doctor agree with the Munchausen's diagnosis?' I clarify. 'I understand it's notoriously difficult to ascertain.'

Her eyes bore into me. How awful it must have felt to be regarded like this as a child.

'Yes,' she says without blinking, and I already know it was futile to ask. I wouldn't trust a thing this woman says.

She's rattled now though. Literally, her right leg is jigging and she's shaking a finger at me. 'I knew what you were up to the first time I met you, and that article confirmed it. Luring Chloe up to your big, fancy house. Trying to take her from me. Can you not see what's happening?' she says, turning back to Chloe. 'This woman is trying to replace her daughter.'

I feel like I've been slapped.

'Mam!' admonishes Chloe.

I could do with the stick now.

'I think you should leave,' says Conn. It's the first thing he's said since she appeared and his voice is like gravel. I feel calmer because of it. Even Laura is still. Conn doesn't move from where he stands beside Chloe, but his jaw sets and he's breathing deeper. He is suddenly impossible to ignore.

'You can't say things like that, Mam,' pleads Chloe.

Laura isn't done. Conn has unnerved her but, with her shaking finger, she turns to me again. 'You couldn't keep your own daughter alive so you're trying to steal mine.'

I barely draw breath before Conn is between us. 'That's it. Leave. Now!' he says, facing the woman.

'This has nothing to do with you,' she replies, putting a hand on his arm in a futile bid to get around him. She'd have as much hope of moving the hall.

'Fine,' she says, curtly, straightening the modest brown scarf that hangs around her neck. 'I'm ready to be driven home. Chloe.'

The girl lets go of the table and slowly, clumsily, takes up her bag. 'We're done here anyway, right, Tessa? I can wash the cups if you bring the box home,' she says apologetically.

'Home,' derides Laura under her breath.

I go to tell Chloe that she does not need to drive this woman anywhere, but once again Conn gets there before me.

Chloe takes a step towards her mother, and he twists his torso, bending his head towards her.

'I can drive her,' he says, voice low.

'It's okay,' she mumbles, shaking hands going to her pockets as she thrashes about for keys.

He sinks his head further again, his body blocking Laura and shielding Chloe. He says something that I can't make out.

'She's my mother,' replies Chloe in a severed whisper.

This time his words are clearer: 'But she doesn't have to be your family.'

Chloe looks up at him and something passes between them. I'm not known for minding my own business, but I feel like I'm intruding.

Connor murmurs something, head and voice still low.

Slowly, purposefully, Chloe nods.

She is trusting in him. She's taking a leap of faith.

'I'm going to drive you,' he says, louder now as he turns back to Laura. 'Okay if I take your car, Tessa, and Chloe gives you a lift back to Hope House?'

'I think that's an excellent idea,' I say.

When Laura doesn't take the initiative and leave, I usher Chloe away. She has all her stuff in hand.

'Let's go pack up the tables,' I say.

She takes my arm but doesn't move. So I wait. She has to be the one to leave.

'Thank you,' she says to Conn, who looks at her like she's all he can see.

And as we walk away, I feel a surge of regret. Not for myself or for Chloe and her mother, but for my lodgers. I rub the girl's back gently and wish with all my might that it was Conn she was meeting tonight, not Paul.

# CHLOE

**·········**

The last bus stop before I turn onto Nevin Way tells me I'm even later than I thought.

11.42 p.m.

I pick up the pace, doing my best to avoid the cracks in the pavement.

I forgot my phone. Which would be fine except that I removed my watch earlier because the yellow strap didn't go with my green dress.

What a ridiculous sacrifice to make. As if, what? Paul – madly, deeply in love with me – would have taken one look at my wrist and decided that, actually no, he could never be with someone who doesn't respect complementary colours. I laugh at the absurdity. Except it doesn't come out like a laugh, due to all the tears. It just adds a gasping-for-air quality to my sobbing. Good thing the houses on Nevin Way are set so far back from the road, or they'd all be twitching at their curtains, wondering who is drowning a hyena in the middle of the night.

Half an hour I spent on the phone to Yemi, trying to decide what to wear before settling on this dress, which she bought me years ago but I was never allowed to wear; too short and showy. We'd seen it in town and Yemi obviously went back and bought it because she presented it to me just before a Monday morning lecture and I was so shook by the gesture that she gave me the receipt. 'See?' she whispered, as the basics of assignment marking were explained to us. 'Twenty quid. I didn't sell a kidney for it.' I can't explain why it meant so much. I didn't have many friends, not least ones who would spend their money on me for no reason (one thing about Paul, the man is tight) but it was more than that. It was like someone was going the extra mile for me when I couldn't go there for myself. Is that silly? Of course it is. It's only a dress.

I nearly go tumbling outside Hallow House, catching myself on their iron gates just in time. This gives an extra surge to my upset, rage and general sense of besiegement. I cover my mouth as a frustrated shriek escapes. More bag of cats than single hyena. This accelerated walking speed seems to be giving the upset new momentum. I slow down.

My legs grew heavy somewhere around Kilbarrack. I would not recommend walking and crying. Both are gruelling feats of endurance that require a surprising amount of brain power and are best undertaken on their own. The multitasking is exhausting.

I didn't intend to walk the whole way. I kept thinking I'd jump on a bus when I was ready (aka: when my tear ducts dried up), but I was never ready (they never dried up) and then the idea of getting home to Tessa and Conn still up and pottering around the house was even less appealing than having to tap my Leap card while I whimpered in front of a Dublin Bus driver. So here I am, three hours later, still hobbling home, still doing my crying in the dark.

Mam would be happy with that at least.

*Mam.*

I've just had the door closed on a relationship with the man I was, until very recently, convinced I was going to spend the rest of my life with and yet these tears have not been shed over Paul Murtagh. Everything keeps coming back to Mam.

I was in North Strand when I had a flashback to my first period. Crying, hyperventilating at the brown sludge leaving my body in alarming quantities. Convinced I was dying. Mam saying I was too young for this and that I must have been thinking about boys. Terrified for the next two years that thinking about boys would lead to internal bleeding. She refused to acknowledge it again until I was fourteen. For two years, five out of every twenty-eight days were spent racked with guilt. Toilet paper stuffed in my underwear.

Around Clontarf, I thought of the last time I saw my aunt. She had left our house and was looking in at me through the front window. She wouldn't be coming back. I was sad about it, because I loved her and she was the only one who ever told me anything about my dad. But I was also angry, because Mam told me she was trying to take me from her and I believed it. You would think living with a compulsive liar would make you more discerning, but actually it makes you gullible – you're just so desperate for something to be true.

Mam hated this dress. She hated when I wore make-up. She hated when I fought against my God-given plainness. Making a show of yourself was the worst thing you could do, second only to making a show of her. I imagine her seeing me now and the self-loathing is an electric shock.

More recent memories then. Yemi insisting I keep this dress. Making me go to the bathroom after class to try it on. The look on her face when I came back. The word 'beautiful' several times. Being a good friend, yes, but maybe a grain of truth too?

Paul in his old college bedroom, telling me my chest was the perfect size. Said matter-of-factly, like he was a carpenter measuring an alcove for a wardrobe, but still said and meant. Blushing now as I recall how much it was meant.

Penny at the depot. First job I did, she said I was too vibrant to sit in a car alone all day. Later said I was too naïve to be real, but first impressions must be worth something too. Trevor describing my idea to source a villainous photo of Charles Bentley for the *Dublin Press* article as 'exceptionally clever'. Maura observing that my enthusiasm was infectious. Tessa telling me I was prettier, cleverer, more worthwhile that I realised.

Conn saying I'm too good for Paul. Conn laughing at my jokes, finding me interesting, calling me a woman of taste. Conn volunteering to drive Mam home today. Conn looking at me just before they left. Conn looking at me again this evening. Pausing on his way into the kitchen as I descended the stairs. Eyes fixed on me in this same green dress.

The whole way home it has been like this. My brain zipping between memories of Mam, scenes from the pub tonight, and these flickering flashes of hope.

It's embarrassing how I cling to these snatches of approval from people I barely know. I'm not good at knowing people. I'm not good at making friends, at keeping friends, at being loved. But there must be something to me. If I add them all up, they must equal something close to acceptance. Surely. Maybe. Possibly.

But then Mam *was* right. Today, when I told her (told Tessa and Conn too. Oh *god*.) about my 'date' with Paul and she said I was making a show of myself. I did make a show of myself – though it's possible I'm the only one who registered it. And, in the end, I didn't really care.

I think about her, standing in front of Conn and Tessa and essentially telling them how little I matter to her. She wasn't at the hall because she cares about me, she was there because she cares about herself. She doesn't want to be alone. Doesn't want me to leave her. She doesn't actually want *me* – she just wants someone, and I'm all there is.

I nearly did the same thing tonight. I didn't want to meet Paul but I convinced myself the dread was actually nerves and forced myself out of the house. I was so scared of not having anyone that I was willing to ignore the fact that I don't want Paul. Not any more. He isn't the person he used to be. Or, actually, that's not true. He's probably the exact same. It's me who has changed.

I'm recalling how things were, and I'm seeing it all differently.

And then, one house away from Hope House, I stop in my tracks. For the umpteenth time, I'm thinking about the Emmas. Every time I get angry at my mother, I remember how she stood up for me that day. And here it is again, the memory, only it's different now. The facts are the same, but they don't scan how they used to.

Mam didn't confront them because I was upset. She did it because she didn't want anyone talking about her – and my lack of a father was more about her than me. That is so apparent now.

And worse than children talking about her was adults talking about her. That's why she didn't go to their parents. It had nothing to do with respecting my wishes. She was cutting the gossip off at the source. If she was to go to the parents she would have had to tell them what their daughters were saying about me, which was of course really what they were saying about her.

It's all suddenly so apparent.

As mean as the Emmas were to me, they were still children. What grown woman threatens children? I don't know what she threatened them with, but it must have been something truly scary for them to completely avoid me for the rest of primary school.

How dare Mam make me feel sorry for my bullies fifteen years on.

I'm angry at her for always putting herself first. I'm angry at her for leaving me so alone and so unprepared to be alone.

I need to keep moving. After walking nearly twenty kilometres, I am a mere fifty metres from home and I am spent.

I lean against the railings, just for a minute.

What must it be like to grow up with home as a place to relax? Imagine stability being a given. Imagine not spending your life waiting for the next erratic, seismic shift. Imagine being able to let your guard down in your own house. What must it be like for your house to feel like a home? How glorious it is for those children who get to be children safe in the knowledge that their parents will be parents.

*Pity party.*

My mother's phrase rings in my ears.

I drag myself onwards. Tessa is always in bed by 11 p.m., and little ill is likely to befall her in the first forty-five minutes of sleep. Not that a single ill has befallen her since we moved in; if anything, she's been taking care of us.

Metres from the front gates, I hear harsh crunching. Footsteps on the gravel. I pull myself in so that my back is against the railings again. I regret this almost as soon as I've done it, because if it is Conn leaving Hope House, he's going to have to walk past me to get anywhere, and there's zero chance of him not seeing me.

I'm suddenly wishing I'd worn that awful polyester cardigan. At least it's black.

It's too late to move now, so I hold my position and my breath, steeling myself for a continuation of this night of humiliation.

Six seconds later and a shadow appears from the driveway.

I was right. It is Conn.

But I was also wrong. He's not walking this way.

He has turned left, instead of the obvious right. Where is he going? Hope House is the end of the road, literally. There's nothing that way except the former marsh, the makeshift gap in the bushes and the small incline that leads to the less popular end of the cliff walk.

As he continues to walk away, I pull out from the wall and watch.

He is heading for the gap.

Surely not. Nobody does the cliff walk at night. There's nothing to see. And it would be freezing. Not to mention lethal.

But yes, that's exactly where he's going, in through the gap and down the incline.

He disappears from view.

I don't need to think about it, never mind decide. I am already running after him, as quickly and quietly as my exhausted limbs will carry me.

# CONN

· · · · · · · · · ·

I t takes the average person sixty-six days to form a habit.

Sven, my old boss, told every new employee this. It was his way of saying we had sixty-six days to get into the habit of making the company buckets of cash. Which is why the probation period was two months and three days exactly. Which, depending on the months, is actually sixty-four or sixty-five days. That's because it takes the *average* person sixty-six days, but his hires had to be better than average.

One week before probation was up, a large clock would appear on your desk – a reminder that you had seven days left to prove yourself. Any questions you asked Sven in that week were met with one response, and one response only: 'Tick tock'.

Sometimes I don't feel so bad for sleeping with the man's wife. She thought he was an arse as well.

When I looked up Sven's habit 'fact' I found that, actually, the length of time varies greatly. Depending on the person, and the habit, it can take anywhere from eighteen to 254 days to form.

I have been coming here for 114 days – or, more accurately, nights – and I would say I am now in the habit.

If I doze off before coming out, I always wake by midnight. No need to set an alarm; my internal clock has been conditioned. On autopilot, I'll pull on my largest coat and the gloves Fergal made me last Christmas and I'll take up the backpack of emergency supplies. I will make my way out of Hope House, along the driveway, across the former marsh (where my feet instinctively know the most solid path to take), through the hedges, and down onto the cliff walk. The first couple of months I used the torch function on my phone. If the moon isn't playing ball, it's pitch-black up here. But I no longer need that light. I remember where the potholes are, and the tuft of grass that doubles as a trip hazard, and the large, long crack that always seems to contain water no matter the weather.

If I turned left, I'd soon meet the main cliff walk path, but I always go right. I make my way through the overgrown brambles and thick flowering gorse. My first visit here was during daylight and the scent of the yellow petals was overwhelming, sweet and coconutty. At night, they smell of nothing. I keep to the path until I reach the clearing. This is easy to do; even if you can't fully see, there's a marked change in the terrain. Anyone going over this cliff isn't doing so by accident.

Then I go through the routine.

I stand as close to the edge as I dare, rocking gently on the balls of my feet, imagining how it must feel to be so tortured by living up here that you'd rather be dying down there, in the crashing, unknowable, but definitely painful, abyss.

I breathe deeply, often bracing myself against violent winds, and try to defy the space–time continuum by offering solace in retrospect. I tell Fergal not to be afraid. I tell him I'm sorry. In my mind, I hug him. He was always the one embracing me. I like hugs. I wish I'd given him more.

I walk back to the weather-beaten bench with the peeling green paint and various initials etched into the back panels. The bench is on the far side of the pebble track. There are just eleven steps between the edge and it (or five giant ones, if I'm bored and trying to beat my record). I take a seat and pull out my phone. I open my voicemail and listen to the last message Fergal ever left. I block out the gales vying for my attention and I take in every one of its 180 seconds. I listen so intently that my ear hurts.

And then, coat zipped the whole way up and mitten section of gloves firmly buttoned over, I sit there on the edge of existence and I wait.

Sometimes it only takes a few minutes, other times it takes hours, and most of the time my waiting is in vain. I stay there until 4 a.m., regardless. Then I get up and I leave.

I don't have to check my phone any more. My body knows when it's time.

The habit has been formed.

Tonight, though, we appear to have a new record. I've barely pressed Play on the voicemail when I hear shuffling from the way I just came.

It has never happened this quickly.

I'm not known for my complex emotions but they always come thick and fast at this point; trepidation, exhilaration, worry, resolve.

The footsteps draw closer and the moon escapes from behind a cloud.

It's a few more seconds before a body emerges from the shadows and I see that it's not who I was expecting.

It's possibly the last person I was expecting – and she's moving at a rapid speed.

She comes marching along the path, colliding with both the tuft of grass and the constant puddle. 'Can a girl not catch a break?' she yelps. She keeps moving, half-jogging, half-dragging her body along the cliff edge.

'Chloe.'

'Jesus flipping Christ!' Her feet actually leave the ground.

She looks like she did the first time I saw her, through the window of her jam-packed car. Both hands to her chest, expression somewhere between apology and outrage, and make-up almost certainly not where it was first positioned. Only this time she's wearing a dress. The same one she had on this evening. The same one I've been thinking about ever since.

'What are *you* doing here?'

'What are you doing here, more like,' she retorts. 'Sitting back there in the shadows in the middle of the night, like some sort of psychopath. You nearly gave me a heart attack.' A few deep breaths. 'Christ,' she says again, half under her breath.

'Don't let me stop you.'

'What?' She brushes hair from her face. It was neater when she left the house, pulled back in a tight ponytail. I prefer it this way though; erratic and nonsensical. Sort of like her.

'Wherever you were off to in such a hurry,' I say, stuffing both hands into my coat pockets as I angle my head in the direction she was marching. 'Don't let me stop you.'

'Oh, right.' She straightens her dress and wraps her hands around her arms. She squints in the same direction. There's nothing to see but darkness.

'Cold?' I ask. The exposure of the cliffs means it about ten degrees cooler out here.

'No.'

'Okay.'

She catches the end of her dress as a gust threatens to drag it skyward.

Then another squall comes for her hair.

'It's sheltered back here,' I say, moving over on the bench.

She regards me for a moment, still holding the pose of a woman playing vertical Twister. She trudges over.

'You were following me,' I say, as she sits down at a considered distance and continues to hug herself.

'No I wasn't.'

'Okay.'

I undo the right mitten flap, zip open my backpack and hand over my favourite, and warmest, jumper. Dark-grey Aran wool with a slight stretch at the neck.

Wordlessly, she takes it and pulls it on.

'How did the date go?'

'Fine,' she replies, the word escaping like a squeak.

I glance over. Then face forward again. 'So fine that you're up on the edge of a cliff right after it?'

'He has work tomorrow.'

'O—'

'Do not say okay!' she fumes, turning on me. '*Okay, okay.* Stop saying that. You always say "okay" and it always means that the thing is *not* okay. It's incredibly annoying, do you know that? I can only assume you don't know that or you do know it and you don't care because nothing ever bothers you ever. Ever ever ever!'

I think defensive indignation is my favourite of her many over-the-top states.

'Okay.'

Her face crumbles as her hands fly up to catch it.

'Hey, Chloe, I was only slagging...'

'Could this night get any worse?' comes the muffled voice from beyond the mess of hair, pale fingers and coarse charcoal wool. 'Seriously, could it?'

*That depends*, I think to myself, *on whether someone else shows up.*

'It wasn't a date, all right?' she declares, bringing her head up with force. 'Of course it wasn't. That was just one of the many delusions that I was suffering under. Paul's not interested in me; he doesn't want us to get back together. In fact, he's so over me that... Oh god. Oh god!' she wails, head back in hands.

'He has a girlfriend?' I supply.

Her head shoots up. 'How did you know that?'

I shrug, focus back on the dark nothingness before us. 'Just a guess.'

I gave Paul until this weekend to tell Chloe. I sensed from the start that he was messing her around so I asked him straight out when we were canvassing: Are you getting back together? He laughed and told me I had the wrong end of the stick and that they were just friends. He had a girlfriend, he couldn't help but add, and she was an editor at the paper. The way he said it, he's lucky I didn't punch him right on his stupid, scrawny nose. I might have if Chloe hadn't interrupted us. I know how status-obsessed arseholes operate. I used to be one.

'Well you're nearly right,' she says, slumping back on the bench. 'Only it's more than a girlfriend. He has a fiancée. Aimee Wenders: the *Dublin Press*'s features editor and Paul Murtagh's future wife. They haven't even known each other a year.' She sinks down further so that her chin disappears into the jumper. 'Is spontaneous combustion really a thing? Because I feel like I might be on the verge of it.'

'I'm sorry,' I say without any conviction.

'It's not even about him. I don't want him back. I knew that before I went out. I knew it at the open day. I probably knew it before that. I have all these memories of our relationship and how he used to be, but they were slightly off. He wasn't so great.'

Now here's a topic I could spend a long time discussing: Ways in which Paul Murtagh is not so great.

'Go on,' I say.

'I thought it was nice how Paul was the only person who didn't make fun of me for being a Luddite. But now I realise he liked me without technology because it meant I was in the dark; he could be the one in charge of things, explaining things.'

'Mmm.'

'What?' she says, turning to me, chin reappearing from the confines of my jumper. 'Was that obvious?'

I shrug.

'Well, there's loads of stuff like that. And the whole business with Tessa and that article... I was so ashamed. I don't want to feel that way. I want to be proud of the people in my life.' She sighs loudly, stretching the sleeves of my jumper down over her hands and into her fists. 'Paul never wanted to get back together; it was all about the story. I don't even care about the fiancée. Honestly. Good luck to them. I just felt stupid. Again. Stupid and alone and unlovable.'

Out of nowhere, she does a full-body flinch.

'I thought he was going to kiss me. We were sitting on the stinking, damp ground of Dano's mutt mobile and I seriously thought we were going to kiss.' She gives a low, manic laugh through the wool. I wince. I know it's not the most important thing right now, but I really would like the neckline to retain some shape. 'What is wrong with me?'

I saw that encounter, sitting up front with Malachy, and I feared the same outcome.

'How could I have thought *that* was a near-kiss? Do I have no radar for this stuff any more? Am I so out of practice?'

'You still have a radar,' I reassure her. Then: 'A real near-kiss is hard to miss.' I say it as neutrally as I can, but she grows still.

Is she thinking about that moment in the apartment block too?

'Kill me now,' she says because she always has to say something. 'Seriously, take me over to the edge there and give me a good shove. What? I'm joking, obviously, although also kind of not. I would welcome the crushed bones at this stage. Why are you— What did I say?'

I avert my attention back towards the indiscernible sea.

She stops. Pieces slotting into place.

'Is this where you go every night?' She's staring at me. I can feel it. 'Conn? Is this where your brother killed himself?'

If you tune into it, the wind sounds like a hundred voices shouting at once. Sometimes I think that with enough focus, I'll be able to make out what they're saying.

'Conn?'

'Is it odd that I feel closest to him here when this was the place where he was least himself?' I ask. 'Tessa said something this morning about how a person is defined by the last thing they do and I keep thinking about that.'

Chloe shifts beside me, but she doesn't say anything. So I keep going.

'Her daughter will always be the girl who went missing. The most notable thing about Fergal now is that he killed himself – even though that is also the least Fergal-like thing he ever did. It's like life is one big game of musical chairs and the song just happened to stop when he was in a dark hole and, even though he spent less than point one per cent of his life down there, now he's stuck in it for ever.' The cold air stings my nostrils. 'Ninety-nine-point-nine per cent of the time he was *so fucking alive.*'

The last three words knock the air from me. I barely get them out. This is why I don't talk about it. I'm not able. Chloe shares this trait with my brother, being fully alive, operating at full capacity, heart, soul and nerve-endings wide open. It's the best way to be. But I don't know how to make her see that. I don't know how else to put it.

'This must have been the last thing he saw,' I say.

She gazes out into the blackness too.

'They found his phone here.' I point to the spot between us on the bench. 'And that jumper.'

She sits up straighter. 'This was his?'

'It was mine, but he wore it mostly. No call for that in Dubai.'

'Well he had good taste,' she says, peering down at the pattern. 'I've always liked it.'

'The neck is a weird shape because it's hand-knit so it has quirks. Although Fergal said it was because my fat head had stretched it.'

I laugh, or I mean to, but it emerges like a shout.

One desperate cry.

Was that what he was like in the water? Gasping, shouting, regretting, scared. Or was he paralysed before he hit the bottom? When I stand at the edge and look down, I have no way of telling where the cliff ends and oblivion begins.

'Do you really want to hear this?' I ask, removing my right glove entirely and scratching my beard.

'An eye for an eye. Not that your brother dying is the same as a disappointing ex-boyfriend,' she adds hastily. 'I just mean... Yes, I do want to hear.'

'His call history showed three calls right before he jumped, all to me. On the last one, he didn't hang up. He left me a voicemail. He didn't say anything and I don't know if he meant to leave it or not. I don't think he did. I've listened to it hundreds of times and I think I've pinpointed the moment when he goes over. There's a scraping sound, at around the one-minute mark. I believe that's his feet literally dragging their heels. That's how I think he went; walking off rather than jumping.'

'Conn.'

I get in before she can object. This sequence of events has been living in my head for months. I need to see if it makes sense anywhere else.

'If he made the call from this bench, then got up and walked to the edge, he'd have stood there for forty seconds, fifty, maybe. That's a fair amount of time to spend having second thoughts when your soul is on fire. He was racking his brain for a reason to stay. I'm convinced of it. That's why I don't think he meant to leave the voicemail. He was waiting to see if I'd call him back.'

'You can't possibly know that.'

'He wouldn't have jumped if I'd answered.'

'You can't know that either.'

'I should have just answered,' I say, breathless, helpless, like it's the most obvious solution to anything ever in the history of the world. 'I could have given him a million reasons.'

'Conn.'

I bring a frozen hand to my frozen nose and push it in, hard.

'Are you hungry?' I ask, pulling up my backpack as I right myself. 'I keep an emergency stash in here... I'd say it's still good.'

Chloe looks like she wants to say something else, but the sight of food distracts her. I undo the vacuum seal on the trail mix. 'Here.'

'Thank you,' she says, mouth already full. 'Last thing I had today was some beef jerky.' She goes back for more. 'I had this dread in my stomach that stopped me eating before – Jesus! Your fingers! They're like icicles.'

'Terrible circulation,' I say, fully handing her the bag and pulling back on my glove. 'I got chilblains as a teenager and had to wear gloves all winter, indoors and outdoors.'

'Even in school?'

'I was lucky I was tall.'

She grins, chewing rapidly. 'Like Bob Cratchit.'

'Or Scrooge, if you're a bunch of teenage lads who'd never let accuracy get in the way of a good slagging.'

'That's why you were called Scrooge?'

'"Bob" doesn't carry enough insult.'

She regards me, still chewing. 'I thought it was because...'

'Because of all the money I hoard instead of shelling out for things like rent?' I raise my eyebrows. 'I know.'

She looks contrite. 'I'm sorry. I'm insufferable.'

'Ah,' I say, shoving my hands back into my pockets. 'You've got other attributes.'

*Attributes*, I can practically hear Fergal, *is that what you're calling them now?*

But Chloe obviously has a cleaner mind than the Horgans. She's still focused on being insufferable. 'I just decide something about someone – that they're loaded or they love me or they're sick – and then I refuse to budge from that opinion.'

I de-mitten again and reach over and take some trail mix. Half of Chloe's face is in my jumper, but now I think it's for warmth rather than refuge from embarrassment.

'Did you believe your mam today, the stuff about Munchausen's?'

'It makes sense that she'd want that kind of diagnosis,' she says, forming the words carefully. 'Its rarity fits well with her general sense of being better than everyone else – but no. It doesn't add up. Tessa doesn't think so either.'

'Tessa is very wise, I find.'

'That she is,' Chloe agrees.

She hands me back the near-empty bag of trail mix. 'Have you ever fallen asleep up here?' she asks. 'I mean, I know it's fairly uncomfortable, but you must get tired…'

'Once.'

'Really?'

I nod, chewing the dregs. 'I was travelling out from Dun Laoghaire back then so I was exhausted. When I woke up, I was in a serious panic. My phone was dead, but the sun was up so I knew I was late. I needed to get home before my parents woke. They didn't know I was leaving the house in the middle of the night. And the thing about being the only remaining child is that you absolutely cannot give them any reason to worry. I ran all the way to the train station, but it was a Sunday and the next train wasn't for twenty-three minutes so I needed a taxi. Only, like I said, my phone was dead. I think I forgot to turn off the torch function.'

'Disaster.'

'It was, at first. But in the end, it was the best thing that could have happened. I needed to find a local taxi and an elderly man at the station told me to try the old parish hall, which turned out to be the Project hall, which...'

'Was where you saw Tessa's sign about the room.'

'Exactly.'

'And this is the perfect house for you because it's so close to the cliffs.'

I nod. 'Before this I was crossing the city twice every night. Now I'm right here, and I can see this same view from my bedroom window. I don't know why that comforts me, but it does; to be the last place he was and see the last thing he saw and hear the same sounds.'

'So you come up here every night because you want to be close to him?'

'No.'

Her face is out of the jumper now, the moon lighting the nearer side, her freckles visible, the black smudges around her eyes giving her a – what do women call it? A smoky eye? No, that can't be right. Whatever it is, it's sexy. It's beautiful. She's beautiful.

'This is a black spot,' I say. 'The Samaritans have signs up further down the path with helpline numbers. There was talk once about putting an emergency phone up here with a direct line to a suicide support network.'

'Is this where Tessa's daughter jumped from too?'

'Probably. Although Tessa doesn't believe she jumped.'

'What does she think happened?' asks Chloe. 'That she ran away? I didn't think there was any suggestion of that.'

'I guess it's just a feeling,' I say, not wanting to betray Tessa's confidence. Besides, I know she doesn't take a feverish apparition as proof that Bea is still alive.

'I don't understand. You don't come up here to be close to Fergal? So why do you come?'

'I came back to Ireland because I needed to feel close to my brother. But I also needed to make up for his death. Fergal should be the one still here. And I have to make amends for that; for him being gone, and for me being the one to remain.'

She frowns.

Still beautiful.

Damn.

'If there'd even been a random stranger on this hill, I know he wouldn't have jumped. He just needed human interaction to snap out of it. Things would have seemed better in the morning.' I've developed this disconcerting habit of humming when I want to calm myself. Luckily the wind mostly drowns it out. 'I wasn't here for Fergal. But maybe I can be here for someone else.'

'So you come here...'

'In case anyone else comes here,' I say, turning back to the sea.

'How long do you stay?'

'Four hours. Suicide is more common after midnight and the rate peaks between two and three a.m. So I stay until four.'

'When did you start doing this?'

'The day after I got back from Dubai. Nearly four months ago now.'

'Every night?'

'I haven't missed one yet.'

I don't tell her that it's a compulsion, that sometimes I am struck by such self-loathing during the day that the only thing that sees me through is the thought of coming here that night. I have built my days, my life around sitting on this cliff. It's the thing that justifies me living. It's the time when it matters that I am alive.

'Has anyone ever come? Anyone who planned to jump?'

'I can't say for sure if they were going to jump or not.'

'But you think so?'

'In one case. Maybe, two.'

'And you saved their lives?'

'It's not like I charge at them, wailing "Nooo, don't jump". I just said hello. I talked to them. If someone actually went ahead and jumped there's nothing I could do to stop them. I guess I'm just hoping they don't want to do it, not really, not when there's someone there to remind them that they exist.'

'So tell me about the one case, or maybe two.'

'One guy was young, maybe twenty, and on drugs, I think. He was pretty rattled. He came here from a club. He was out with his girlfriend and she told him it was over. I talked him down. We walked back into the village together.'

'And the other?'

'The other guy, I don't know. He was older. Seventy, maybe. He was nice, seemed pretty normal. At first, I thought he was just out for a walk – that has happened too – but he kept talking and I could tell he didn't want to be on his own. His wife was in a hospice and he had a grown daughter at home. She's disabled. He and his wife thought she would die before them. That's what they were told to expect. He couldn't face caring for her alone. He couldn't say that to me because of how it would sound, but I got it. He had a shake and the more he talked, the worse it got.'

'What happened to him?'

'He's alive,' I say.

'How can you be sure? Not to make you feel bad or anything, but how do you know he didn't come back at 5 a.m., or you know, do it some other way?'

'Because I saw him, when we were canvassing. I talked to him. He brought me in to meet his daughter, Ruth. Maybe he was contemplating it. But I don't know if he would have jumped. It was hard to believe in the light of day.'

She slumps back again and pulls her knees up under the jumper. We listen to the wind yelling at the sea and the waves roaring back.

'You're getting better at silences,' I say when a good minute has passed.

'It's easier when I'm stunned.' Another half a minute of wailing weather passes, then: 'How long are you going to keep it up for?'

'Forever.'

'No, seriously.'

'I am serious. I mean I don't know, but forever is as likely as anything else. If I stop then what's the point?'

'What do you mean? The point of what?'

I glance down at the gloves on my lap, at the beautiful zig-zag pattern that Fergal created with his nimble hands and innate talents. 'I don't know.'

'The point of what?' she repeats.

I look at her and I half-shrug. 'The point of me.'

'Conn.'

'I'm not suicidal,' I say, meaning every syllable of it. 'I could never do what Fergal did. I'm just... I'm plagued. And this is the thing that makes me feel better. I was his big brother. I knew he was in pain. He needed and deserved my help. And I, I did not answer the phone.'

'It's not your fault.'

'Yeah, it is.'

She doesn't try to argue with me. Instead she takes her hand and places it on my face. Her thumb on my cheek, her little finger hooking my jaw gently. It's warm still, somehow. How did she manage that?

I turn fully so that I'm facing her. The hand slips down. She pulls it back onto her lap.

'Don't do that,' I say.

'Sorry, I just, I wasn't thinking –'

'Don't take your touch away.'

'Oh.'

She looks down at her hand, turning it over with the other one.

'You shouldn't feel so bad,' she says. 'Obviously you're allowed to feel bad, your brother died, but, I mean, you shouldn't feel so responsible.' She swallows. She frowns at her fingers. 'I'd no idea you felt so bad.'

'I don't around you.'

She looks up, eyes big and round. They're so exposed that I feel voyeuristic just looking at them.

'It's all the insults you throw my way and the deep-rooted prejudices,' I say, slowly. 'How could I feel bad around that?'

She frowns. 'Don't make fun of me.'

'Sorry.' I swallow, hard. 'I never talk that much,' I keep my breathing even but also focus on getting words out. A trickier feat than it sounds. 'An eye for an eye, you said. Only that was more like an eye for the whole face.'

I square my jaw to stop it betraying me and her face grows serious too.

'I gave you everything, Prairie.'

She holds my gaze. Her breathing is deeper now. It has slackened to match mine.

'I know,' she says.

She moves her hand forward and I take it. She flinches at the coldness of my touch.

'Sorry,' I whisper again, but she shakes her head, so I bring her fingers back to my face, to my cheek. I hold them there and I inhale. I breathe the moment in.

I'm reaching for her other hand now and I'm standing. I'm pulling her up with me. I'm pulling her to me.

'Is this okay?' I ask, each syllable catching in my throat, my body rigid.

'Yes,' she replies, the word instantly whipped away by the wind.

I move my hands up her arms, then down to her sides. It's my jumper, which feels weird, so I slip my hands under and find her shape. I allow the air to stagger out of me without trying to mask it and I pull her into me. Not too hard. I want this to be the first kiss, not the zenith. I want her to feel desired and beautiful and understood. I want her to know how much I want this.

Mostly, I don't want her to feel alone.

Our waists press together, torsos still that bit apart. The moon highlights her cheeks and forehead and the tip of her exceptionally cute nose. Her eyes look to me to decide what's next and her lips demand to be kissed.

Or maybe I'm projecting. Maybe it's just my mouth pushing for action.

Behind her the sky is electric blue, shards of black and navy and large patches of dark. The gale rages, roaring and cheering us on. Does she hear that too?

She reaches up to brush my beard, her fingers rising further to trace below my eyes.

She smiles, and the wind goes wild.

I bring my mouth down to hers and our lips instantly meet. She responds with the same longing and I pull her closer again.

I think she moans, but I can't be sure. The cacophony drowns it out. My entire body hums. Nobody can hear that either.

I want her. I want her very badly.

I open my eyes, just for a second, to check she's real. Then I slam them shut, wrap my arms even tighter, and feel the glory of being the only two people, standing as one, right here on the edge of the world.

# TESSA

· · · · · · · · · · ·

It's **Chloe** at the door. I can tell by how faintly the key rattles. Conn favours a clunky insertion and brisk, abrasive rotation. Whereas Senan always turns the key the wrong way initially (his own front door has it backwards). But with Chloe, you're not sure you've heard anything. Then you worry it's mice, rattling around at a forgotten crisp packet downstairs. But it goes on so long that you have time to figure it out. And ultimately, though she's trying to be as quiet as possible, it's so protracted and niggly that it's just as intrusive as how anyone else does it.

I have to strain my ears to hear the faintest thud as the heavy door closes. She must really inch the thing into place.

Poor Chloe. I do wish she wouldn't worry so much.

I'm glad she came home. There was a while there where I feared the date went too well and she had decided to spend the night at Paul's. She wouldn't text me to let me know something like that, would she? I'm not her mother. Although I am her roomie. Is that the sort of thing housemates tell each other? A quick text. Have pulled. Don't wait up. More likely than telling their mothers, maybe. Though still not very likely.

She's in now, anyway. Home safe and sound. She won't be long coming up. She likes to get to bed early and rise early. Although it's not early any more. It must be approaching 1 a.m.

I go to turn onto my side before thinking the better of it. I'm comfortable like this, on my back. No need to chance it.

Footsteps on the stairs.

Didn't I call it? She's really not much of a potterer.

But wait now. That's more than one pair of feet, surely.

Yes, definitely.

Four steps forward, two steps back. The squeaking stair getting a few goes.

That's simultaneous shuffling. That's feet tripping over each other.

I gasp.

That's *smooching* shuffling!

A giggle. Chloe.

Then a man's voice. The words (not that there are many) too low to distinguish. Whatever he's saying, it makes Chloe shriek. Then muffled giggles.

Oh lord. The date *did* go too well.

The day Paul came to interview me, he left with two biscuits wrapped in a tissue that he had produced *from his sleeve*. They were to have later. To save him buying dinner.

And now he's canoodling on my stairs.

Despite everything else, *this* is when I actually feel ill.

How, in the name of God, could that man make anyone shriek, with pleasure?

*Squeak.*

They're clearly struggling to make it past the return.

I go to roll over again, then remember, and stop.

They're on the second flight, gaining a bit of momentum as they approach the bedrooms. I did say they could have guests over. I'm just sorry this is who Chloe has invited.

They're just beyond the archway that leads onto the landing

now and I brace myself for the light being flicked on. I can't say I'm sorry that I'm about to put a spanner in the works, but I do wish I could have gone about it differently.

'Tessa!' Chloe yells as I shut my eyes against the harsh fluorescent bulb.

'Hello, Chloe,' I say, eyes squeezed shut as I raise my hand slightly. 'Hello, Paul.'

'Is she hallucinating again?'

'When did she hallucinate before?'

'Are you okay, Tessa? She can't have been here that long.'

Am I hallucinating? I might be. Because that sounded an awful lot like Conn.

I inch my eyes open so they can adapt to the light.

He's down by my side, helpfully blocking out the worst of the overhead glare. 'Conn!'

'She's good.'

'Conn!' I pronounce again. 'And Chloe! Conn and Chloe!' Joy surges through me. No sign of that knobbly cheapskate. 'Conn and Chloe on my stairs!'

He turns back to Chloe. 'Or maybe she's not good. It's hard to tell.'

'Tessa, are you okay?' asks Chloe, dropping to the ground just beyond Conn.

Look at them there together. They look so good together!

Chloe takes my hand. 'What happened? What are you doing on the floor?'

'I'm fine, I'm fine,' I say, batting away her concern, and my own. 'I just... I heard the pipes going hell for leather in the bathroom again and I knew nobody was in there so I was on my way to check it out. I should have ignored it and gone back to sleep. But I ran into the plumber at the end of the open day and he told me to brace myself for the quote he'd be sending my way this week and I suppose I was thinking about that and I feared the worst and' – I look down the far side of me – 'I don't even know what I tripped over. I'm not sure there was anything. Do you see anything?'

They both glance around before shaking their heads.

I feared as much. 'I think I was just tired. Long day, you know, and I was doing a lot of running around and then I didn't have a great sleep last night either—'

'And no nap,' adds Chloe, anxiously. 'There wasn't any time today. We should have thought of that.'

'I don't always have a nap,' I say with more indignation than a mature woman sprawled on the floor in an oversized Backstreet Boys t-shirt is arguably entitled to. (It was Bea's. I wear it sparingly.) 'But yes, I concede, this probably would have been a day for one. Now could you both stop looking at me like that, please? I'm having a rather unpleasant premonition of what it would be like to have an open casket funeral.'

'Sorry,' says Chloe, and they look at each other.

They smile instinctively, then drop that expression too. Presumably out of respect for me. But honestly, it almost makes my predicament worthwhile.

They really do make a beautiful couple, even if Chloe's make-up could do with some work.

'I'm so sorry, Tessa, this is all my fault. I meant to be home at 11 p.m.'

'Chloe, please, I've told you before, you do not have a curfew. You're in this house plenty. It was never the agreement that you be chained to it for twelve hours out of every twenty-four.'

'I know, but I really meant to be home at 11 p.m., or at least before midnight, but I was late getting back and then I... I met Conn and I... got distracted and...'

She's the colour of a beetroot, the poor girl.

'Can you move?'

'I think so,' I tell Conn. 'I feel a twinge in my right hip when I shift it, but otherwise things are okay. I think. I didn't want to chance it.'

'What should we do? Should we help her up? Should we help you up?' Chloe leans past him now. 'Shoot! Sorry. Did that hurt?' she says, grabbing her left hand off my right arm. 'Didn't mean to... What should we do?'

'I could try and stand...'

'I think you're right. It's not worth chancing,' says Conn.

'No,' I agree. 'Probably not.'

I had hoped whoever found me would insist I stop being a drama queen and get up off the ground. No such luck when you've recently had hip surgery, I suppose.

'Phone Senan?'

'God, no!' He'll be furious. I promised I'd start turning on the light when I got up at night. I don't think his nerves could handle another fall. 'Let's not wake him,' I clarify.

'Or your doctor?'

If Doctor O'Shea finds out about me going rogue with the ditched stick, she'll tell Senan. Give me the whole duty of care spiel. The landing light will be small fry then. He'll have me bombarded with retirement village leaflets. 'Definitely no need to wake her.'

'Ambulance?' suggests Chloe.

'That sounds very dramatic...'

'What else then? We can't just all stay here on the floor forever.'

'I suppose not.'

'We could try getting you up ourselves?'

'You could,' I agree, though there's a creeping terror in my gut. Everything feels okay but I haven't properly tried to move any of it.

When I fell, my first reaction was annoyance, at myself. But before that I was mainly just scared. I really don't want to lose the use of my legs. I should have kept the bloody stick.

'Let's go with the ambulance. But tell them there's no rush,' I say as Conn pulls his phone from his pocket and stands.

He looms large over me, concern smeared across his face.

'Do things look that bad?'

I do not like the expression I get in response.

'It could be worse,' I say, as cheerfully as I can manage. 'At least I'm wearing clothes this time.'

# CHLOE

· · · · · · · · · · ·

**W**e **were** waiting two hours for the ambulance. When Conn described her condition, she was deemed non-critical, an assessment Tessa readily agreed with. We were instructed to place a blanket over her, alter her position every half hour, and keep conversing with her. Although after a while she asked me to do a little less of the conversing; she said she'd let me know if she was about to lose consciousness.

The paramedics took Tessa in the ambulance and said we would have to travel separately, but that only one of us could wait with her in A&E. Conn said I should go. Maybe he could tell how responsible I felt for her fall. He knows what lingering guilt can do.

By the time she was triaged and then properly examined it was 7 a.m.

The ER doctor said it didn't look as though she'd done any damage but she wanted to be sure. Tessa was reporting a mild twinge in her side, but it was hard to know how accurate that description was. It turned out Tessa's GP had not approved her retiring the walking stick. The doctor described this as reckless. It was surprising to see a woman not much older than me admonish Tessa (albeit in a neutral, professional tone), and more surprising again to see my landlady take it. Tessa couldn't recall whether or not she'd hit her head when she fell. So they're keeping her in for twenty-four hours. It's Sunday now and the consultant who oversaw her surgery will be in tomorrow morning. He can examine and hopefully discharge her then.

If Tessa had fought it, they'd probably have let her go home. But she didn't. She must have given herself a real fright.

I phoned Conn to give him the update. We didn't talk about what happened on the cliff or what nearly happened in the house. There was a silent agreement that that section of the evening was on hold while we dealt with the more pressing matter. He said he'd be by when visiting hours started and to text him with anything we wanted brought in. I said I'd check with Tessa, but that I was fine. I was still wearing his knitted jumper over my dress and I didn't relish the idea of him rooting through my drawers to find clothes. Plus I'd already bought wet wipes in the tiny shop to deal with last night's make-up. I was amazed when I went to the bathroom to see the true extent of its migration. I was like a panda, only significantly less cute. A raccoon, maybe. I'll say this: Conn must really like me.

Conn offered to phone Senan, but I wanted to do it. He was the one who established the division of the day agreement when we first moved in and I was ready to take any blame he might wish to place. Only Senan wasn't interested in that. He just wanted to get off the phone and up to the hospital to see his mother as quickly as possible.

I let Maura know too. Tessa was supposed to meet her for coffee in the village this morning. Tessa pointed out that she could make phone calls herself, but she was so exhausted that she was asleep by the time I rooted out her phone. I didn't feel the slightest bit tired myself, despite being awake for a full twenty-four hours. I was running on adrenaline and this ethereal feeling that I was in the middle of something new and exciting.

Those initial phone calls led to further phone calls, which led to the arrival of several carloads of Tessa's supporters in the hospital car park, which led to one very stressed ward nurse.

'How did you get back in here?' she demands, appearing in the doorway of Tessa's room yet again. I've tried to read her name badge a couple of times, but she always clocks me.

'*Moi?*' asks Malachy, doing a pantomime-worthy rendition of looking behind him. Every time the matron comes in to chuck people out, Malachy volunteers to leave. Then he pops downstairs for a toilet break or a cigarette, and comes right back up again.

'I told you – and you,' she says, eyes falling on Susan now, 'to leave twenty minutes ago.'

Her heart's not in the admonishment. We've worn her down. She's just going through the motions.

'I did leave,' says Susan, 'but then I came back again. I forgot my brolly,' she adds brightly, lifting the polka dot umbrella from under her chair.

The nurse sighs. 'You know the rules. Two visitors at a time, not...' She counts us. 'Not eleven.'

'We're ten actually, matron. I think you might be including Tessa there,' says Trevor.

'Why don't you leave this time.'

'Oh I can't leave. I'm family,' he says, moving a little closer to the bed. 'I'm the husband.'

Tessa gives a tiny screech as Trevor grabs her hand.

The nurse delivers a withering stare. Malachy claimed to be Tessa's husband about two hours ago. Though I think him continuing to call her 'Mrs Doherty' gave that game away.

'You've ten more minutes, then visiting hours are officially over for everybody,' she says. 'Tessa should be discharged before they start up again in the morning, which is about the only thing stopping me from phoning in sick tomorrow...'

'Sorry, Margaret,' calls Tessa from the bed.

Margaret. Yes. I thought I distinguished an 'M'.

'You're fine. It's your friends,' she says, throwing a death stare around the room. 'They might be good for your health, but they are not helping my adrenal glands.'

'Am I imagining it or was there a bit of chemistry there?' asks Trevor when the nurse has left. 'I definitely got the impression she was looking at me. No? Nobody else?'

'Not unless she has a thing for bigamists,' says Tessa, shaking her hand free of his.

'Polygamy is traditionally seen as anti-feminist but some research suggests there could be advantages for women,' says Audrey, who is sitting between Senan and Otis on two pushed-together chairs.

'What's polygamy?' whispers Reggie, who hasn't said anything out loud since Senan and Otis arrived and he realised that Tessa was the principal's mam.

'Having lots of wives, or husbands, but usually wives,' I whisper back.

'What sort of advantages?' asks Maura, who has her head out the window now the nurse is gone and is giving her vape a quick suck.

'In traditional societies, where the bulk of childrearing falls to women, it can be more beneficial to have several women, even if they are mothers as well, to help with the rearing and household chores, rather than a single man.'

'Makes sense to me,' remarks Susan.

'Like how many wives are we talking?' Reggie whispers again.

I shrug. 'How many wives would it usually be?' I ask Audrey.

I catch Conn's eye from across the room and his eyebrows shoot up. I bite back a laugh.

'It can be any amount,' replies Audrey. 'There were also findings to suggest multiple wives led to higher income and greater companionship for everyone, as well as continued sexual variety, obviously. Of course the subjects for the study were all in Mormon breakaway sects but...'

'All right, sweetheart,' says Senan. 'I think you're going to give Reggie a heart attack if you keep going.'

'Oh, sorry, Reggie,' she calls across the room. 'Did I offend you?'

The teenager sucks in his lips and shakes his head.

'You'd think having the principal for your dad would take care of the most embarrassing parent title,' says Otis, 'but not necessarily...'

Reggie laughs at this. Then instantly puts his hand over his mouth.

'It's okay, Reggie, you can laugh. What happens outside school stays outside school,' says Senan.

The teenager lowers his hand. 'Really?'

Senan nods. 'Really. Which is why as your principal I couldn't possibly condone the graffiti you did on the side of that house up by the new estate—'

369

'You told him!' Reggie accuses Tessa.

'*But* as we're not in school now, and I am not your principal at this very moment, I can say that it is one of the most accomplished murals I've seen anywhere in the city.'

Reggie is a different shade of red now.

'We've been looking to do something with the back wall at the school. This would require all the correct planning permissions and authority approvals, so it might be a while, but I was thinking you could do something in a similar vein for us. I love the use of water; very clever, very eco-friendly. There wouldn't be a massive budget, but we'd pay you fairly.'

Reggie is staring agog at the man. His eyes darting momentarily to Tessa. Then back. 'You mean like a *commission*?'

'Remember us when you're rich and famous,' says Malachy, slapping the teenager on the back so hard that he staggers forward on his chair. 'Maybe I'll be able to sell that We Want Bins poster you drew for me.'

'Did you not impale that on the waste management guy's birch tree when you took the dogs for a walk?'

'Ah, feck it anyway. I did, yeah.'

It's lovely to be here, like this, with all of them. I'm a little tired now and my dress is starting to feel grubby (although I'd happily wear Conn's jumper until the end of days) but I've had the best afternoon, just sitting in this room, getting to be part of their gang. They all came so quickly when they heard about Tessa. They tease each other, but they care. It's more a family than a group. And she built this for herself. How lucky I am to be a part of it.

'This English artist sold her bed for two and a half million pounds a few years ago,' says Malachy.

'Her actual bed?' Otis.

'Was it made out of gold?' Reggie.

Malachy shakes his head. 'She didn't even bother making the thing.'

'Two and a half million pounds for an unmade bed?' scoffs Susan. 'I've got four of those at home.'

'You could cut them a deal,' honks Malachy. 'Buy three, get one free!'

The door opens and the nurse reappears. This time she's got two orderlies behind her. 'Out, all of you.' She narrows her eyes at Malachy. 'No exceptions.'

We all file out, calling our goodbyes to Tessa.

'I'll be back to collect you in the morning,' says Senan. 'No buts. I have the deputy stepping in for the first half of the day.'

Trevor slips the nurse his card on the way out. In the corridor, he turns to me. 'The laptop! I nearly forgot.'

'It's okay, I don't really need it.'

'No, no. I've got it. It's all done. I had a lad who owed me a favour give it a once-over, put spyware and the basic programmes on it, you know. It's good to go. I'll drop it up during the week.'

I'm so disarmed by his casual kindness that it takes me too long to respond and he's already heading off down the corridor when I manage to shout, 'Thank you!' He waves back at me without turning or slowing his pace.

Conn is at my side. His arm brushes mine. This is the first time I've been close to him since last night.

'Give me a lift home?' he murmurs.

'Delighted to,' I say, as that ethereal feeling descends again and propels me along the corridor.

We don't talk much in the car. I go to say something, anything, as we drive out of the hospital car park but he puts his hand on my knee and I stop. I don't need to fill this silence. It is entirely comfortable.

In the house, Conn puts on a frozen pizza and makes up some salad while I run upstairs to have the quickest shower. The pipes really do sound bad. I towel dry my hair and whack on moisturiser. I pull on my nicest underwear and then leggings and a thin white jumper. I give my room a quick tidy – mainly shoving what is on the bed under it and throwing some extra books on my beautiful bookcase – then I grab Conn's jumper and run downstairs.

'Thank you,' I say, placing the thick, folded garment on the table.

He turns from the counter where he is grinding pepper over the salad. He glances at the jumper, then up at me.

He takes in a longer breath and I do the same.

I open my mouth to make fun of his salad (there's far too much pepper) but he shakes his head and I close my mouth. Then I grin. He grins too.

He crosses the floor in no more than four steps and lifts me up by the hips. I wrap my legs around him and he kisses me, hard.

Then he deposits me onto the table.

'I've wanted to do that since I got to the hospital.'

'Well they are very sexy places,' I reason.

'Though I preferred you in my jumper.'

'I preferred me in it too.'

He moves his nose into my still-damp hair, and when he emerges I wipe at it with my sleeve.

'How hungry are you?' he asks.

'Well, I mean, not *that* hungry... What—'

He's back at the counter, pizza out of the Aga. Then over by the door, shoving it open with his foot. Now back in front of me.

'All right, I suppose we – woah!'

I'm off the table, roaring with laughing, and we're out the door, moving across the hall towards the stairs.

'I can walk, you know.'

'I know,' he mumbles, awkwardly climbing the first couple of stairs. 'But that's not very romantic... Sorry! Got you.'

'How about I take the steps unaided and then you can carry me over the bedroom threshold.'

He looks at me. Still holding me up, legs wrapped around him, faces centimetres apart.

'Oh god. We are going to a bedroom, aren't we? Please tell me we're going to a bedroom. If I've called this one wrong too, I am going to stitch my own mouth shut.'

'Yes, Prairie, we are very much going to a bedroom.'

'Okay.'

He raises his eyebrows.

'What?'

'I didn't know saying "Okay" was still allowed.'

I slide down from him and take his hand. 'Come on,' I say, pulling him up the stairs. 'Let's see if we can do better than okay.'

This elicits his best goofy laugh and I am delighted with myself.

'Too cheesy for you?' I say. I love the weight of his fingers in mine. I love knowing that pizza could never compete with me.

'I was going to make a comment downstairs about having my dessert before my dinner. I'm sorry I stopped myself now,' he says.

'A real missed opportunity.'

We stop outside his bedroom and he takes my other hand, linking the fingers, bringing his head down to mine. I swear there's a magnet in my lips, pulling them straight to his.

'Just to check,' he murmurs. 'This isn't some rebound thing from Journalist What's His Face, right?'

'Definitely not,' I say, stepping closer, bringing my forehead up to meet his. 'I told you: that was over for me before it really was.' I haven't thought about Paul once since last night. I never felt anything like this for him. I've never felt anything like this full stop. The want is pouring from me, every pore, every fibre. My hairs are standing on end just to get that bit nearer. There's no part of me that isn't yearning to be closer, closer, closer still. I want to jump up and down with impatience. Gimme, gimme! Gimme Conn now! This is desire. And it has clouded all my senses.

'Can we go in now, please?'

'Okay,' he says, and I open my mouth, then snap it shut.

I actually love the way he says 'Okay'. I wish I could say as much with so little.

'Just one more question,' he says.

God help me but I actually whine. I don't feel nervous or embarrassed or anything like that. I just want his body against mine and no stupid clothes in the way.

'Out with it!'

His cheeks strain against the force of his smile. 'Your place or mine?'

The sex is lovely. I don't know if it's what I expected or not because I never imagined it. I thought about Conn a lot over the past few weeks. I enjoyed watching him working out the back more than I could admit to myself, but I never entered the realm of daydreams.

There's an urgency from Conn but also a sense of focus, of being only in this moment – that intense stare really comes into its own between the covers – and nothing feels rushed. It's an experience and we enjoy figuring it out; where limbs should go, how our bodies fit together, who should move when and where and how fast. I think that's what I like most about it; that it feels like we're in it together. Well, that and the orgasm.

After, Conn goes downstairs to retrieve dinner, and we lie in his bed eating cold pizza and talking. I am very happy. Like, very happy. But also, content, I think. I can't remember ever feeling like this.

'My turn,' I say, sitting up against the headboard, admiring the soft muscles of his arm. 'What happened with Linda when you ran after her?'

'Nope,' he says, reaching over me for another slice.

'Oh come on, it's called Ask Me Anything for a reason. You have to answer.'

He takes a bite, chews, and sighs. 'She did not forgive me.'

'Fair enough.'

'Yeah, it is,' he says. 'But she did propose sex.'

'What? Seriously?' I say, swallowing quickly. 'Like there and then?'

'I caught up with her in the car park. She had a key to the bike shed.'

'Right,' I say, wondering now if what I just considered exhilarating was actually a pretty tame encounter for Conn. 'And?'

'Oh well yes, obviously. I ravaged her between a Raleigh and a Vespa. No, Chloe. I declined the offer and ran back around to the foyer to see the mutt mobile sailing away.'

'Sorry about that,' I say, taking another bite.

'No you're not,' he says. 'But it's fine. Okay. My turn. How did you really know about the room here? No way you saw that sign at the hall.'

'It was an accident,' I admit. 'Or actually maybe it was fate. I was here to make a delivery and then you mentioned the room for rent. I had left Mam's that morning and I had nowhere to go. I have absolutely no idea what I would have done otherwise.'

'Where was the delivery for? Here?'

'Yeah, but it was a wrong address. Tessa says it happens. I left the package on the hall table and I guess they sent it back because it was gone by the evening. I felt kind of bad because it came with this big tip, but I did deliver it to the address I was given and I really needed somewhere to stay.'

Conn finishes his slice. 'What was it?'

'I don't know. I don't open the packages. I just hand them over. It was small and it was for someone called Bee-ah. That's all I know.'

Conn pushes himself up in the bed, chewing awkwardly. 'Bee-ah,' he questions, hand to mouth and swallows. 'Do you mean Bea?'

'B-E-A,' I say.

'Yeah, that's pronounced Bee.'

'Okay,' I say, picking a crumb from the centre of one of the bedspread's roses and depositing it back onto the plate. His mother bought him the duvet cover; it was my first question.

'Bea, as in short for Beatrice.'

'Oh. Kay. Jeez, understood.'

'No, Chloe, do you not get it? Bea. Bea Pearson, right?'

'Yes...'

'Pearson. That was for here.'

I scrunch up my face. 'No it wasn't.'

'Tessa's surname is Doherty, but the rest of the family is Pearson. Senan Pearson, Otis Pearson, Bea Pearson. Bea Pearson.'

I did not know Senan and Otis's surnames were Pearson. 'Why do you keep repeating the name?'

'Because Bea is Tessa's daughter,' he says, eyes wide. 'Chloe. That package was for here. It was for Tessa's daughter.'

# TESSA

· · · · · · · · · · ·

**I**'m sitting on a bench along the set-down area outside the hospital. I'm dressed in my coat and the clothes Conn brought for me (he packed navy socks for black slacks, but otherwise he did well). On my knee, there's a plastic bag filled with Bea's old Backstreet Boys t-shirt, my glasses, a pamphlet on 'keeping mobile' and the few toiletries I needed. Resting against the bench to my left, is my stick. It's not actually my old stick but it might as well be. It's identical. I am right back to where I started four months ago.

The consultant officially discharged me fifteen minutes ago. I didn't phone Senan until I was already downstairs. I couldn't get out of the place fast enough. It was fine yesterday, when everyone was there, laughing and telling stories and generally keeping my morale up. But I felt a little down last night. Unusual for me, but it does happen. I was thinking about the future and for the first time I was worrying. It was the fall, but Bea kept niggling at me too. Ten years is an arbitrary length of time. She was no more missing yesterday than she was the day before. But there's something about that milestone, something about how time and I and the rest of the world have just sailed on past it that has left me dejected.

I didn't fight the stick and I agreed to have an occupational therapist assess my house and its suitability. I reserve the right to cancel that appointment when I get home. I just didn't have the fight in me this morning.

I cast around for a rainbow or a pregnant woman; anything I could construe as a sign of hope. But all I'm greeted by are grey clouds, a taxi driver emptying his sandwich crusts out his window and a white work van parked on double yellow lines.

I close my eyes as the winds whip around me and three bad nights' sleep start to catch up. Half-dozing off, I think I hear a woman call my name.

I must be desperate. I'm conjuring up my own sign.

I allow my head to fall back as I wait for my subconscious to whisper something more.

But instead, I am jolted to consciousness by the long blast of a horn. Then two shorter blasts.

I squint across the road at the double-parked van.

'Tessa!' I hear again.

I take my glasses from the plastic bag and push them on. Then I gather up the rest of my stuff and hurry across the road. I'm halfway there when I remember the stick and reluctantly go back for it.

'Maura,' I say, leaning into the passenger window of what turns out to be the Misunderstood Mutt van. The logo side was just facing the other way. 'Malachy. What are you two doing here? Senan is collecting me. And doesn't Dano ever need this van?'

'Business is a little slow at the moment,' says Malachy from the driver's seat. 'He's actually looking at getting into capricious cats instead.'

'Achoo!'

I peer into the back of the van.

'What are you *all* doing here?'

Trevor and Susan each raise a hand, although Trevor simultaneously wipes his along his nose.

'Doesn't anyone have jobs to go to?'

They all shake their heads. 'But thanks for rubbing it in,' adds Malachy.

'Reggie! Why aren't you at school?'

'I had intel that the principal was mitching this morning too,' says the teenager, emerging from behind Susan.

'Yes, and he's going to be here any minute!'

Reggie shrugs. 'What happens outside school stays outside school. Me and Mr P – I mean *Senan* – are tight now. And, you know, some things are more important than education.'

'Like what?' I demand sceptically.

'Like the goddamn fat cats being burnt to the goddamn ground!'

'Excuse me?'

'The planning permission,' Maura says. 'It's been rejected.'

'The – no! Seriously? *Seriously*?' The last one comes out like a shriek.

'As serious as a broken hip,' she replies, and I start yelping and jigging on the spot.

I pick up the stick and bang it against the side of the van. I forgot all about the impending decision!

'Hey, careful. Dano will still need transport for the cats.'

'I knew it would be worth telling you in person,' grins Maura.

'This is the best fecking news! Unbelievable. It's... I can't believe it. I mean I hoped, but I didn't want to hope too much. It's official? Paperwork and all?'

'Yep. They cannot turn the hall into a hotel.'

Susan moves up nearer to the cab part of the van. 'I talked to my brother and he said they could still appeal, but he doubts it,' she says, leaning over Trevor, who is scratching at his shoulder. 'In all his time in the planning office, he never saw observations like it. 648 submissions in total. Five supporting the development and 643 objecting.'

'Wow,' I say, body calming now. 'That's a lot of people.'

'And a lot of money,' adds Malachy. 'All those people paid twenty quid each, or forty even. I know people who submitted. Some of them have money, but a lot don't have it to spare. But this mattered to them. And they came out and showed their support.'

This is why I believe in protest, in the power of a collective. So many things seem unsurmountable on our own. It's easy to be daunted. But when you're standing before the gatekeepers of power with an army behind you, they have to let you in.

I throw my head back in relief. 'So, what do we do now?'

It's Trevor's turn to clamber forward. To be fair to the man, his nose is red. He should probably be sitting up front. 'We wait to see if they appeal and what they plan to do, but I can't see how they can change things. Presumably, hopefully, they'll just keep on renting it to the council and taking what they can get. Achoo!'

'But for now,' says Maura, wincing as she wipes at the shoulder nearest Trevor, 'we celebrate. So, get in. We're going to the hall.'

Susan and Reggie help me into the back, while Trevor pulls in my stick. I try phoning Senan, but there's no signal in the back of the mutt wagon, much to Reggie's relief.

'You're not going to dob me in, are you?' he says, staring down at Senan's name and the 'call failed' sign.

'That depends. Will you try out for the athletics team again?'

'I told you, effort isn't a good look on me.'

'Fine, I'll just have my son swing by and collect me from the hall...'

'All right, all right. No need to be a rat. I'll sign up.'

'When?'

He sighs loudly. 'This week. Happy?'

'Very,' I say, biting my cheeks to contain the smile. 'And remember, I'll be checking in.'

There are about a dozen other people at the hall when we arrive, all of them Project regulars. Cynthia, who organises the Meals on Wheels, pulls me into a wide embrace as soon as I'm out of the van and two of the crafters start applauding. A quick elbow and their dart-playing partners join in too.

'Thanks, thanks, Jimbo, thank you, everybody.'

I excuse myself from the celebrations and excited talk to phone Senan. He's at the hospital when I get through, but he's not too annoyed. He hasn't been there long. He's just run into Chloe and Conn in the ward foyer. They're looking for me too. I say there's no need to come and collect me, that Malachy will drop me home in the van. He wants to come anyway, but I insist. I have to keep my word to Reggie if I want him to keep his.

When I rejoin the crowd, a few more people have arrived. There's a woman who was in the grief support group the very first week I came here. She takes the life-drawing course now. She's the one who told me what a good model Malachy made. We wave to each other across the crowd, and I saddle up beside Kate Moss himself and listen as he gives a vastly exaggerated version of my calling to Charles Bentley's door.

'He had this massive statue in the hall that he stole from the Louvre and there was a housekeeper trembling behind it...'

Maura comes and stands beside me, arm slipping through mine. 'Well done, you,' she says, leaning her head against mine.

'It was a team effort,' I say. 'Genuinely. That's why it's so brilliant. On my own, I'd have made zero impact. But as a group, we saved this place.'

'Well, well done to all of us so,' she says.

'Exactly.'

Cynthia emerges from the hall again, carrying a large drum and one of the fat candles we keep at reception for power cuts. A little closer and I see it's an industrial-sized can of Ambrosia.

'We need some form of cake if we're going to call this a celebration, and this was the best of this morning's delivery. We're completely out of everything after Saturday so it'll have to do.'

'Tessa!' someone shouts. 'You do the honours.'

'No way,' I say through a smattering of applause. 'We'll all blow it out. Ready?' General nodding. 'Okay, to the North Dublin Community Project and all who sail in her.'

'To the Project!' they cheer and there's an awkward, glorious and ineffective collective blowing before we all break into more clapping.

I cheer along with everyone else, peering beyond the crowd to see two more arrivals. Chloe and Conn!

I push my way through the group and hop along to deliver the good news. 'Did you hear? We saved the hall!'

Chloe, grief-stricken, looks to Conn.

'We heard. That's great,' he says.

'You don't look like you think it's great.' Chloe appears to be on the verge of tears. 'What's wrong?' I ask. 'What is it?'

'Tessa, I'm so sorry. I—' The girl clamps her hand to her mouth. 'I'm so, so sorry.'

'What – what…' I grapple for my stick. 'What's wrong? Is it – is it Senan? Is it Otis?'

But the girl just shakes her head.

'It's Bea,' says Conn. 'Chloe had a parcel for your daughter, but now we don't know where it is.'

# CHLOE

●●●●●●●●●●●

Tessa has torn the house apart.

It never seemed like there was that much stuff here, but now that it is strewn all over the floor and furniture, I can't believe it was ever contained.

The foyer has taken the brunt of it because that's where I told her I left the package. This *is* where I left the package.

She has asked me so many times if I'm sure, if it was definitely here, if I definitely left it in this exact spot, that I'm starting to doubt myself. I do not naturally possess a lot of conviction, I have generally relied on my mother to tell me what I feel, and the store that I have built up over the past month is being depleted, rapidly.

'Could you have brought it up to your room with you? Chloe? Could you?'

'I don't know...'

'Well just think! You were moving in, you were bringing all your stuff up...'

'Maybe...'

And so my room was ransacked too. The bookcase took a battering during the process and there's now a scrape down the left-hand side of it. I don't have the right to feel sorry for myself, but I couldn't help it. I had to excuse myself to the bathroom until I pulled myself together.

It's upsetting to see Tessa like this. I've seen her passionate, worked up, plenty of times. But never like this. Never like a woman possessed. And it's all my doing. She hasn't done her usual thing of instructing me to stop apologising or of telling me it is not my fault. She's just kept on firing questions at me and tearing the house asunder.

'What did it look like? Do you know who sent it? Was it heavy? Where was it sent from? Was there a return to sender address? Did it have a postmark? Was it definitely recent? Do you know where it came from? Can you find out? Why would someone be posting Bea a parcel now? What does it mean? Are there records at the company? Is there any way to find out where it came from?'

I do my best to field the questions, but I can't provide answers as fast as she can pose them. Many are the same query in ten different forms, but she never asks the only one she really wants to. She never asks if this means her daughter is alive.

'I didn't know your daughter's name,' I say, standing to one side as Tessa lies down flat on the kitchen floor and peers in under the fridge. 'I didn't know her surname either, or Senan's. I just assumed you were all Doherty...'

She's back on her feet, wincing slightly, and I worry that she's going to do herself an injury. She's only a few hours out of hospital.

'I should have asked. It's not that I didn't care, I just didn't feel it was my place to pry. And it's been so long, ten years, it never crossed my mind that she might be getting post...'

Tessa starts yanking at the fridge and I rush forward to help. 'Conn!' He comes over from the dresser where he has been searching.

'It's okay, Tessa, I'll move that out for you.'

She stands back, hands on hips, irritated by this ten seconds delay. She taps her foot rapidly, eyes wild and scouring the floor, as Conn moves the fridge away from the wall.

She walks around to check the back, the sides. There's nothing there.

She doesn't ask him to put it back. She doesn't care. She just moves on to the washing machine, leaning over the top to check the back of it.

'I know it came from England and it was certainly sent that week. And I've asked Delivery Dash if they can tell me who sent it, but there are strict rules about that information, and I don't know if I'll be able to access it.'

'You've said that already,' she says without feeling, head and chest vanishing down the back of the machine. 'Come back to me when you have something new.'

I give Conn a desperate look, throwing my head in the direction of Tessa's latest acrobatics. I cannot be responsible for anything else!

'I'll move that for you too,' he says, coming over and tugging at the machine. It doesn't shift much. He tugs it again and it comes away fully, ripping a tube from the floor as it does so. 'Shit, sorry.'

But Tessa doesn't see the hole. She doesn't see any destruction any more. She just gives the back of the machine a once-over and disappears from the room.

We hear her thrashing about in the large dumping area by the bottom of the stairs. Something smashes. Then something else falls to the ground.

I cover my mouth and bite down on my fingers. It is not my place to cry.

I keep searching until midnight. Conn doesn't say anything, but I can tell he wants to go out and sit on the cliff. His innate obligation is no less strong than Tessa's, I suppose. But I can't stop looking until Tessa does and I guess he can't stop searching until I do.

At midnight though, I do give up. I am bone tired. It has been so long since I slept that I fear I might vomit. I have to go to bed. I wish him goodnight and I go to my own room. He understands this, and he goes out to the cliff anyway. Oh my. I like him so much. I never felt like this about Paul. This is how it's supposed to feel. I understand now why there are so many films and songs and books about falling for someone. It's been two days and I want to write a bloody symphony. Only I'm too tired and I have zero musical ability. So I drag my body into bed, and I squeeze my eyes shut as Tessa bangs and tosses and pulls. I feel the worst and the best I've ever felt. It's an indescribable blend and, when I finally doze off, I have the most messed-up dreams.

I get a fright in the morning. I thought Tessa had done as much damage as she could, but this is beyond. She has pulled the covers off all the upholstery and the drawers clean out of the old sideboard in the hall that has been through generations of her husband's family. I don't think she'll get those back in. There's a whole floorboard torn up from under the same sideboard, the spot where I told her I left the package. (Where I definitely left the package.) There's a crowbar lying beside the splintered wood. It's the one I accidentally carried in with me on the first day.

Conn appears shortly after me. It's 9 a.m. so he can't have gotten more than a few hours' sleep. He must have heard me coming downstairs. He smiles from across the foyer, cheekbones still sharp enough to be defined through the growing beard, and it's about all that pulls me back from the brink of tears.

Together we go into the kitchen. Tessa is sitting at the table. She appears smaller somehow, and frailer. Now she does look like someone who would fall and break their hip and need a stick. I don't think she's slept. She's exhausted. Depleted. That's probably the best word. But she is calm at least.

'Do you want tea?' I ask, hesitantly.

She shakes her head.

'I'll make some,' says Conn, and I watch as he puts on the kettle and gets himself a yoghurt from the fridge.

I don't know what to say to Tessa. I am racking my brain, but I cannot think of a single thing to say.

'Let's go over that day,' she says, the words coming from her like punctured tyres.

'Okay,' I say eagerly, pulling up a chair and beckoning for Conn to do the same. Anything to feel like I'm helping.

'You brought the package into the house,' she says, bringing her index finger down on the table as if there's a map laid out here, rather than the contents of her domestic filing cabinet, and she's going to chart a way out of this.

'Yes,' I say. 'I had it in the waistband of my shorts. And when you told me and Conn to wait in the hallway while you talked amongst yourselves, I took it out in the foyer and left it on the far right-hand side of the sideboard.'

'Definitely that sideboard? Definitely the right-hand side?'

'Definitely,' I manage with conviction.

'And then when was it gone?'

'That evening, maybe five or six hours later? I can't remember exactly. But it was definitely gone before I came down for lasagne with Conn.'

'And you never saw it?' she says to Conn.

He shakes his head. 'No.'

She pushes herself back, both hands going to her cropped grey hair. 'Is there anything else you can think of, Chloe, anything? Please, just think.'

I am thinking. I've been doing nothing but thinking. I've literally walked myself back through it a dozen times and I can't think of—

'Oh!'

Both Tessa's hands slam onto the table. 'Yes?'

'There was... there was *stuff* on the other side of the sideboard.'

'What stuff? What stuff?'

'I don't know, it was... like stationery, maybe? There were lots of colours, I remember that, and pens, or pencils? I don't remember exactly.'

'Pens... Pencils...'

'Maybe not, maybe I have it wrong. I'm sorry, Tessa, I'm trying...'

'Art supplies,' says Conn, suddenly. 'It was art supplies, Tessa. You told me to put them all in a box for you, do you remember? You had to bring them to the hall for something.'

'Yes. Yes, yes, yes! I do! I remember!' Both Tessa's hands are up, and they're shaking. Her whole body is suddenly vibrating. 'Art supplies for the life-drawing class. I brought them down to the hall. You put the stuff in the box. I didn't check it after, I just handed it over. Would you have put the package in?'

'Possibly. Yes. I mean I don't remember leaving anything behind...'

'Okay, okay,' says Tessa, out of her chair with alarming swiftness and forgetting her stick. 'I'm going to phone Carla, the life-drawing teacher. I left the box at the hall for her, she would have taken it, she would have...' Tessa trails off as she presses at her phone. 'Shit!' The thing slips from her hand onto the floor. I jump up to get it. She tries again. Phone to her ear. 'Hello!' She disappears from the kitchen.

Conn and I sit there, not daring to move, barely daring to breathe.

Two minutes later, Tessa comes flying back into the room.

'She says the box is still at the Project. She says it's in her classroom. It's... We have to go down there. We have to get it. I was supposed to teach Beginners' Gardening this morning, but I cancelled. But we have to go down to the hall now and get...' This time it's the keys that slide from her hand.

'Maybe I should go,' I suggest.

'No!'

The answer comes so swiftly and venomously that I immediately take a step back.

'I mean, no. It's fine.'

'You haven't slept much,' says Conn, who I know is trying to catch my eye but I'm not able.

'I can... I can ask Senan. He said he could step out today if I needed him...'

I nod and dig my nails into the palms of my hands. She doesn't trust me. She thinks I'll lose the thing again.

While she phones Senan and we wait for him to call to the

hall and check, I go upstairs and take a shower. I get all my sorry for myself tears out of my system, then I put on fresh clothes and come back down.

There's still no word. Conn is eating another yoghurt and offers me one, but I have no appetite. I can't imagine eating ever again.

'He knows it's urgent. I told him what it was. The hall is only ten minutes from the school. I don't understand...'

'He might still be looking,' suggests Conn, but this clearly isn't what Tessa wants to hear and her foot goes back to tapping frantically.

Then, two minutes later. 'What's that?' Tessa is out of the chair, grabbing her stick this time, and hopping over to the window.

'It's him! It's Senan! He's here.'

I look at Conn, eyes round. He lifts his two hands, like he's conducting an orchestra, and he instructs me, the brass, wind and percussion section, to mellow.

I take a deep breath. We follow Tessa out of the room.

The front door is open and Senan is running up the steps. There's something in his hand.

A brown, well-packaged something.

I inhale sharply.

I grab for Conn's hand and it's right there. Right where I need it to be.

'I got it,' he says, panting slightly as he thrusts it towards his mother.

'Oh,' whimpers Tessa, as she turns it over and reads the name on the front. 'Oh.' I literally see her knees quiver and even though she has the stick, I take a massive step away from Conn and catch her by the left side. He holds her up from behind.

Together, the four of us walk indoors, back to the kitchen.

Tessa places the package on the table. She draws her hand back as if the thing has suddenly caught fire.

'I should open it.'

Everyone is staring at the package. It's smaller than I remember; a C5 envelope rather than C4. I thought it was padded but it's not. It's just exceptionally well-wrapped, lots of tape wound around and around.

Tessa looks at her son, who nods.

He pulls out a chair and she does the same.

Conn takes a pair of scissors from the cutlery drawer. He hands them to Tessa, then walks away and stands with his back against the counter.

I do the same. This is a family matter. And no matter what Conn says, Tessa choosing us doesn't bestow the same status as her son.

Tessa takes the scissors in her hands. They're not shaking any more. Suddenly, they are still.

Expertly and without hesitation, she snips the envelope the whole way across the top. Then she pulls the thing open.

This time it's Conn who clutches for my hand. I squeeze hard.

Tessa reaches into the envelope, her eyes going to Senan.

I bring my other hand around so they're both gripping Conn's.

Then I see what Tessa pulls out and I freeze.

# MURIEL

· · · · · · · · · · ·

**M**uriel Fairway's phone beeps.

She picks it up from the worktop as her husband continues to move the packet of tortellini further away from him and then closer again as he tries in vain to read the cooking instructions on the back.

'What does he say?' asks Toby, eyes still on the pasta, feet still refusing to go upstairs and get his glasses.

Muriel has messaged their eldest son to see if he, his wife, and little Sadie would like to come to them for lunch in a couple of weeks' time.

'He says... He says he can't do the twelfth. He's working.'

'I thought you organised it for a Saturday.'

'I did.'

'Well, what's he doing working on a Saturday?'

'I don't know. I'll ask him,' she mutters, typing out the message.

Toby has the packet open and is emptying it into the saucepan of boiling water. It looks like a lot for two people. 'Are you sure you've read that right?' she asks, as her phone beeps again.

'That was quick,' Toby remarks. 'We must have caught him with a free minute for once.'

Muriel takes back up the phone.

'What does he say now,' Toby prompts, as if she wasn't going to tell him as soon as she had the thing read.

'He says October twelfth is not a Saturday. He says it's a Thursday.'

'Is it?'

'No, of course not,' replies Muriel, searching for the calendar app on her phone before giving up and walking over to the physical one their granddaughter gave them last Christmas – the one full of photos of her. They haven't actually used it since June. Muriel flicks through the pages.

'Oh,' she says.

'Is he right?'

'He is.' She frowns at the dates as she flicks back to the cover (a picture of Sadie in face paints) to check that they have the right year. They do. 'That's strange...'

'Why did you think it was a Saturday?'

'I don't know.' Muriel is trying to remember. She more than thought it; she knew it. How could she have been so certain, but so wrong?

Then it hits her. The thing that put that date in her head in the first place. Which was also the thing that made her make an effort to see more of her eldest son.

It was the invitation to Bea Parson's mother's surprise party. *The Party of the Century*, the invite declared. It had the venue: Hope House, Howth. The person being feted: Tessa Doherty. The RSVP details: a phone number and email address for Senan Pearson, Tessa's son. And the date and time: Saturday, October 12, 8 p.m.

The invitation, like everything else, was a little wet from having been dropped so close to the sea, but the writing was still intact. That was definitely what it said.

Saturday, October 12, 8 p.m.

'Oh,' says Muriel, as the pages of the calendar fall through her fingers. 'Oh no.'

'Not to worry. We'll just reschedule for the Saturday,' says Toby.

But Muriel doesn't immediately set about fixing the problem. Instead, she stands in the middle of the kitchen with horror on her face.

'Muriel? What is it?'

'Oh, no,' she says, the awful reality flooding her body. She brings her hands up and spreads her fingers flat across her cheeks. 'Oh, Toby.'

'What is it?' he asks impatiently.

But she just shakes her head slowly and fixes him with a ghostly stare. 'I've made a terrible, terrible mistake,' she says.

# TESSA

· · · · · · · · · ·

t's like being hit by a truck from the front and a bullet train from behind.

My organs are crushed, my lungs no longer have space to expand, but it turns out I didn't need those things anyway because my hands still move and my eyes still work and there's enough oxygen getting to my brain to enable me to comprehend what I'm seeing. Everyone and everything else in the room and all the rooms beyond this one evaporate.

Perhaps this is how it feels to be dead; to be one of Audrey's auras lingering on earth with a single purpose.

It's bubbly against my fingers. Blistered and worn, but patches of it are still the same vibrant pink as when Bea bought it years – maybe a full decade? – before she disappeared. First time Bernard saw it, in all its garish PVC glory, he said it looked like it could survive a nuclear disaster.

And here it is, in my very hand. Still standing.

If someone had asked me yesterday what Bea's purse looked like, I wouldn't have had a clue. But now that I see it, it's obvious. It's like I watched her stuff it into her parka pocket only yesterday.

'Is that...?' Senan is staring hard.

I turn it over in my hands.

Then frontwards again.

Then back.

'Do you want me to...?'

'I've got it,' I say, my voice calm and far away.

I was so hungry to find this thing. The need for it replaced the usual human requirements in keeping me alive. I don't think I've had a sip of water in twenty-four hours. And I certainly haven't had any sleep. Now that I've found it though, I can't bring myself to hurry. I wouldn't have to think long to come up with the reason for that, but those thoughts don't exist, not yet.

It is just me and the purse. This link to my girl.

I pull open the Velcro, and then the inside zip. If the outside has taken a few hits, the inside knows nothing about it. There's barely a scratch.

I unfold the whole thing so it's lying flat on the table. I trace my fingers across the plastic, the individual card pouches, the larger folds, the two smaller zip pockets, and the label that Bea had me stitch in for her when she first got it.

> *If lost, return to BEA PEARSON*
> *as a matter of urgency.*
>
> *Use whatever means necessary!*

That's my girl. Ever the drama queen.

I reach into the first pouch and pull out Bea's library card. Then her old student ID. Behind that is her driver's licence. She'd only just gotten this. I took her ability to sit and pass the test first time around as a sign of her improved mental state. I look at it now, imprinted with all her most basic details: name, date of birth, address, and a beautiful photo of my beautiful girl. Even the black and white can't hide the vivacity of her smile. When things were good, there was nobody happier.

I place the cards on the table and remove the only item from an internal pouch. I know what it is before it's out. Bernard's laminated Mass card. The same one I have in our bedroom.

Bea loved her father. And he loved her.

And I loved them both.

So bloody much.

'Did you see the date...' begins Senan, but I cut him off with a nod.

He's holding her licence. He has slid the cards across the table and is examining the driver's permit now. But I don't want to address that yet. I need to see what else remains.

I push open the main slit at the top, the one designed for bank notes, but there is no money inside, just a folded over piece of thick cardboard. It's white with black embossed text, like you'd see on a modern wedding invite.

## The Party of the Century!

Senan and Bea Pearson kindly invite you
to celebrate the 60th birthday of their mother

### Tessa Doherty

Where? Hope House, Nevin Way, Howth
When: Saturday, October 12, 8pm til late

RSVP: To Senan Pearson at SenanP21@gmail.com
or 087-2173641

*And SHHH! It's a surprise!*

The party that never happened. The party that was cancelled before I ever learned it was due to take place. Senan had organised the whole thing. He just stuck Bea's name on it so she wouldn't feel excluded. I remember nothing of my sixtieth birthday, falling as it did just weeks after Bea disappeared. I've never wanted to celebrate a birthday since. Senan thought the connection would fade over time, but the dates are too close. The events feel too linked.

'It expired several weeks ago,' says Senan, and I nod again.

I know what the dates means. I know what it all means. But I'm not ready. Just another minute or two more. There's not much left.

Two pockets. Made for coins. But there's no rattle to this purse. I don't think there's any money in it at all. Not even a bank card. Bea was forever losing those.

I unzip the smaller of the pockets and stick my finger in. Nothing.

Then I open the second. I know there's something in here. I can feel it straining against the zip. I push my fingers in and inch the items out.

A folded photo pops open.

It lands on its front so that I see the reverse first. 'Mammy, Senan, Me. Curracloe '92,' scrawled across the once glossy surface in her thin loopy writing. There's a small square of paper folded loosely around it, but I push this to one side and turn the image over.

Sand, clouds, smiling, happy faces. Senan dodging my hug. Bea with her arm thrown around me as she half-falls, the other hand brandishing a spade. I forgot about the spade. Senan and I are just as this photo exists in my mind's eye, but not Bea. How did I forget she was holding a spade?

The smile has barely formed on my face when it gives way to a low, long whine.

Senan extends his hand across the table, but I withdraw mine and suck the sound back in.

Nearly. We are nearly there.

There is just the scrap of paper.

> Mammy and Senan
> Please forgive me.
> I keep you with me always.

I turn it over again, but that's it. After years of clinging to the absence of this very thing, I find it, and that's all I get.

You get ten years from a driver's licence. Bea never renewed hers. Her student ID is older still and library cards no longer look like that. Nothing in this purse was added after September 2013. Nothing in this purse suggests she is still alive. And it contains the two pieces of evidence I kept saying I needed in order to believe in her death.

'There's water damage.'

'I know.'

Senan reaches across the table for the suicide note and I want to stop him because I am his mother but I don't because he is an adult and it is also addressed to him.

I watch his eyes flick across the lines. The slightest tremor as he places it down, still looking.

'It's not,' he tries when he's regained some poise. 'None of this is recent.'

'I know.'

I stare at the items all laid out across the table, moving my hand from one to another. But it's pointless. There's no hope to be absorbed here.

Conn and Chloe are still standing by the sink. Conn's face is as unreadable as usual. Chloe looks worried, but also hopeful, like just maybe things could still go two ways. They see what we see but they don't know what we know, and I'm afraid I don't have the fortitude to explain.

Senan reaches over for the brown envelope that the purse arrived in. Because, of course, the purse did not just appear. It was sent.

'There's a letter,' he says, fishing out a piece of pale-blue paper, folded in half. It is in much better condition than the purse.

He hands it over.

September, 2023

Dear Bea,

I found your purse on Blackpool Beach. Were you shell hunting? If so, that's where you dropped it. My dog sniffed it out from between two of the high rocks. She got an extra treat for that! I imagine you searched high and low for it, but don't beat yourself up. It was really wedged in there.

I followed your instructions to return it by whatever means necessary and used the money inside to pay the courier. So hopefully it gets to you in pristine condition.

All the best to you, and I hope you have a blast at your mother's sixtieth.

Muriel

PS. I Googled your address (just to be sure I had the correct country!) and found it on Streetview. You know you're just across the sea from us? Next time you're looking out, give us a quick wave!

# CHLOE

· · · · · · · · · · ·

**I**t's been three weeks since Bea's purse was found and, in that time, I have knitted seven scarves, four hats and one and a half pairs of mittens. During the great upending of Hope House, I found a pair of needles thrown to the back of a forgotten drawer and I started taking my anxiety out on them. The missing glove is because I forgot the thumb hole on one mitten and didn't realise until I had finished the whole thing. That's how far away my mind has been. That's how hard it's been to think about anything other than Tessa.

She has become a woman of few words. In the most basic sense, she continues to function. She gets up at a reasonable hour, eats some of every meal, and goes to bed every night. I'm not sure about going to sleep.

She didn't leave Hope House for the first week. Except for work, neither did I. I want to be as close to her as I can, although she wants to be on her own, so the same building, if not the same room, is where we find ourselves. Now she has returned to leaving the house for errands and she is back teaching Beginners' Gardening. I think because it doesn't require too much chat or passion. Radical Activism is on hold. (There was talk of Trevor stepping in for a while, but I think Trevor was the only one doing that talking.)

I am still confining myself to these walls as much as possible. I am giving her space, but at least she knows I am here, just in case. I want to be useful.

I'm afraid she might have another fall.

I'm afraid I might mess up again.

'No offence to the couturière, but I really don't need another scarf,' says Conn, standing in the kitchen as I wrap the near finished garment around him.

'This one is a cravat, actually.'

'Oh well then.'

I remove my hands from his neck.

'Come back, come back,' he implores, arms out but staying where he has been instructed to stand. 'Give me back those hands.'

'I don't know what else to do with myself. I don't have the focus to read. I don't want to watch a film without Tessa. I can only work so many hours... Besides, you look handsome in wool.'

He takes my hands and slides them back around his neck. 'Well then, get working on the balaclava, baby.'

I laugh. 'My wrists are actually a little sore...'

'Let's go for a walk.'

'Both of us? Are you insane?'

'Maura is in the library. It's not like she's on her own.'

'Who knows when Maura will leave? Tessa will be chucking her out any minute. No. Thank you, and sorry, but no. I can't.'

'Okay,' he says, planting a kiss on my crown as I close my eyes and breathe in his scent. The man always smells good. 'I was actually in the market for a new cravat anyway.'

'You were, were you?'

A glint of mischief as his hands slide down my sides. 'I was,' he says, hands still roaming. 'Lost my old one at the last polo tournament.'

I haven't slept with Conn since that first night. My body wants to. At every feasible moment, I am touching him, standing with my side pressed against his, even though we are invariably in an otherwise empty room the size of a tennis court. Every time I am this close, I want to throw the other leg over and straddle his thigh. It is the most alarming sensation and makes me feel far too literally like a lovesick puppy. He wants me too. He has said so, on many occasions. If I were to slip my hand into his right now and lead him upstairs, he wouldn't even be a step behind. And I would very much like to slip my hand into his.

Only I can't. It would feel like sneaking around behind Tessa's back. It doesn't feel right to be embarking on something so joyous while she is grieving all over again just down the corridor from us.

I don't want her to feel like we're crowding her out either, like she's the outsider in her own home. Maura warned us not to end up in this exact situation. There are just too many worries. I couldn't enjoy it.

But I do enjoy *this*. Touching, kissing, breathing him in. I have taken to knitting with my legs on his lap while he works his way through my Chelsea Mangan books. I have no problem with that silence. It doesn't feel like the calm before a storm. There's nothing lurking there. It is still rather than pregnant, and I bask in it.

Autumn arrived quickly and already carrying the promise of winter. As Senan predicted, we are now making multiple journeys to the fuel shed every day and still the place is never truly warm. At least my woollen creations are being put to use.

It goes without saying that the surprise party was called off. Nobody remembered to cancel the balloons though and a vanload turned up on the Saturday afternoon. Thankfully Tessa was at the shops, so Conn and I took them out back and burst them. All seventy of them. Pop, pop, pop. Senan and Otis stopped by after school with a cake on her actual birthday and Tessa dutifully sat there as we sang to her. But Otis blew out the candles in the end and she declined to try a slice.

After that the bad news just kept coming. The plumber, who originally hit Tessa with an astronomical quote, then got cold feet, said the job was too big for him, and organised for a company specialising in older houses to have a look. Their quote was double the original. Senan had to sit down to take in that news. I immediately started to panic. Tessa, however, didn't blink. She took the letter, read it, nodded, and gave it back to Senan. When, a couple of days later, he asked her what she was going to do, she replied, 'I don't know' and left the room like nothing could interest her less.

She had a similar reaction to the awful twist in the hall saga. The owners are selling. The planning authorities denied their request to build a six-storey hotel, but they believe another enterprise would prove more successful. They don't want the hassle of dealing with the council any more, or the paltry rent they get from them. So they are putting it on the market. When you consider the green area at the front and the small woodland at the back, they are confident they can get a decent sum for it.

Everyone at the hall is devastated and the Radical Activists are taking it especially hard. Trevor and Susan called here to deliver the news to Tessa, but she already knew. Charles Bentley had personally phoned to inform her. It just washed over her. One by one, the Radical Activists turned up at the house, waiting for her to be as outraged as them, waiting for her to tell them what to do. But Tessa just shrugged and said she didn't know.

Trevor was up again yesterday. He dropped in his old laptop a few weeks ago, but then he found the case for it, so decided to bring that over too. I'm fairly sure it was just an excuse. He seems lost without the weekly meetings. A lot of them do. Even Reggie has stopped by a couple of times. He invited Tessa to his first school race next week. She said she'd go if she could, but she was very busy. And he said that actually yeah, she was right, it was only a stupid friendly anyway and he probably wouldn't bother himself.

But nobody is as upset as Malachy. It's like he's going through his own bereavement. The meditation teacher asked him to picture a life without the hall in it and he nearly had a breakdown right there on the ex-school PE mat. He's started writing letters at a furious rate, but without Tessa's green light, he hasn't had the confidence to post them. Yemi, whose love of sailing videos is continuing at pace, stopped by with Akin one afternoon and ended up getting the ear talked off her by Malachy, who was on his way out of the house. She put it best. 'He's a dedicated oarsman who suddenly finds himself without a captain, and soon a ship,' she said.

It all seems rather hopeless: the hall, our futures at Hope House, Tessa. And unless the problems suddenly become linked to cold necks, I can't do a single thing to help.

'Chloe? Oh hello, Conn,' says Maura, her head appearing around the kitchen door. 'Just letting you know I'm off and that the stove in the library could do with a couple more blocks.'

408

'Do you want some tea?' I ask, dropping the wool onto the kitchen table. 'That was very quick.'

'Isn't it always,' says Maura, shaking her arm at the kettle as I go to fill it. 'I'm fine, thanks. I tried to coax Tessa out of the library for a cup, but she declined.'

'Should I bring her in one, do you think?'

'I don't think so,' she answers kindly.

Conn puts his arm around my shoulders. I like how he does that so casually in company. It shouldn't matter what other people think, I know, but it makes me feel wanted. I like that he's proud to be seen with me.

I admitted this to him once and he laughed like I was insane. 'Were there no mirrors in your house?' he asked incredulously. Then when it was clear I didn't understand: 'You're talking like you've never seen yourself. You're a knockout, Prairie.' 'Yeah, right,' I scoffed, until he placed a hand on each arm and said: 'Whatever restraint I'm showing in not throwing you over my shoulder and carrying you off to my cave, it's nothing compared to how much I have to hold myself back from stopping random strangers on the street, showing them a photo of you, and screaming "And she's mine!"'

I roared laughing at this, but I also knew it was half-true.

'Chloe feels responsible,' he says now, pulling me closer as Maura smiles at us. She wasn't so taken with me at the start, but I seem to have won her over.

'That's ridiculous. You didn't make Bea take her own life.'

'Yes but I held the key, didn't I? If I had just delivered the package like I was supposed to...'

'What? Tessa would have had the same evidence that her

daughter killed herself, but just a month earlier. What earthly difference would that make?'

'I don't know, I just... I feel like I benefited from her pain being postponed.'

Maura looks at me cluelessly.

'Because I got somewhere to live,' I elaborate.

Why can't people just see the truth? Why do I have to keep telling them how awful I am? Or maybe it's a good thing. Maybe this is part of the punishment.

'I got a roof over my head when I was beyond desperate. I got a way out of my mother's house that was on my own terms. I got... I mean I met Conn. I met all of you. And I got someone like Tessa to care about me, to talk to me and look out for me like my mother never did. In a way, I got Bea's mother. And if I'd delivered the parcel on day one that wouldn't have happened. So I benefited. Everyone else suffers, but I benefited.'

I look to the door, suddenly paranoid I've heard something. But no. Of course not. Tessa is still in the library, hiding away from me.

Conn heads out to the fuel shed and Maura leaves to meet Susan for coffee. Susan is worried about a future without the Project too. She's just started to re-establish herself as a whole person as opposed to an extension of her children, and she's afraid that without the meetings and events to escape the house for, she'll be chained to cooking for and cleaning up after men for the rest of her days. So Maura is buying her cake.

I drive out onto Nevin Way shortly after her. I'm heading for the depot. I got a last-minute shift for this afternoon. Conn has promised not to leave Hope House until I'm back.

It's a busy afternoon of deliveries – five hours' worth stuffed into a four-hour shift. There's been a lot of that recently. They're really trying to squeeze every second out of us, and there was no increase for petrol this year either. I was thinking about looking into teaching jobs, or maybe even librarian studies, but things feel too uncertain again so I'm putting it off a little longer. Although when my last drop of the day results in a couple – in the middle of a screaming match when I ring the doorbell and seeing no need to stop – demanding that I come inside and judge whether the mark on their brand-new floorboards is the result of a stiletto heel or a football boot stud, I really consider driving straight out to the university and requesting the forms.

Conn is in his room when I get back to Hope House. I can see the light from the driveway. There's no obvious light downstairs, but it's only 7 p.m. and Tessa never goes upstairs this early.

When I get inside, I find her sitting in the library. Has she been there since I left?

'Would you like a cup of tea?' I ask, stepping inside the door.

'No, thank you.' She's sitting in her usual armchair, but without a book on her lap.

'I'm going to make one myself. It's no trouble.'

'I'm fine.'

'How about some more fuel?'

'Conn already did that.'

'Okay,' I say and I go to leave, but stop on the turn. 'Any plans for the evening?' I cringe. What am I expecting here? *Why yes, Chloe, I'm off to paint the town red. Don't wait up!*

She shakes her head. 'I don't know what to do with myself,' she says vaguely.

I see my chance and I seize it. 'We could watch a movie. Not one of yours, if you don't want to, I mean.' I know now that the DVDs were all Bea's. And I'm not bringing that up. 'I have one, actually.' I don't mention that I bought it last week in case of this very situation. I stopped off at the library and did a big search of the internet for the ideal film for a seventy-year-old woman with a strong social conscience, no time for new-age stuff, and a reluctant love of a happy ending. 'If you'd like to watch my film? *Calendar Girls*. Have you heard of it? It's supposed to be very good.'

'*Calendar Girls*,' Tessa repeats.

'Yes. Yes, that's it. I have it upstairs. I can run up right now and get—'

'No thank you.'

'Oh. Okay.' I think for a moment. 'Well, maybe later.'

'No,' she says. Then nothing else.

'I—'

'Can you close the door after you?'

I shut my mouth. 'Yes, of course,' I reply, stepping out of the room and pulling the door as dejection returns to its familiar place in the pit of my stomach.

# TESSA

· · · · · · · · · ·

**M**alachy is standing before me like he's the father of a dying boy and I'm the only surgeon who can save him. He has the look of a man one gut-wrenching cough away from dropping to his knees and begging me to open the operating theatre.

Except we're not talking about a dying boy. We're talking about an inanimate object. A hall. A building with four walls, dodgy windows and not a whisper of a heartbeat.

'Did you hear what I said, Mrs Doherty?' he implores, as I turn to put away the cheese and relish that I was using to make lunch before he arrived unannounced.

'For sale sign went up this morning,' I say. 'A purchase is expected before the year is out. Price tag is €1.8m. Yes, I think I got it all.'

'€1.8m is the *asking price*,' he corrects me. 'We all know that's not the price tag for property, it's just the starting point for negotiations.'

'I can't see who'd want to pay nearly €2m for the place, but I guess we'll find out.'

'Trevor's source at the estate agency says there's already been interest.'

'So much of selling property is hot air.'

Malachy shakes his head frantically. 'No, no,' he insists. 'People have been dropping by already, to give it the once-over. You could spot them a mile away; they weren't there to use the services.' His eyes plead with me. 'And that was *before* the listing went up.'

'I'm not sure what you're expecting me to do, Malachy.'

'We need a plan of action. We have to do something before the hall is gone for ever and all we have is a supermarket or a warehouse or a bloody data centre. I don't know what's going to go in its place but I know that if it costs that much to buy it's going to have to make the owners a lot of money and a community hall just isn't going to cut it. We were thinking we could fundraise, you know? When we first heard it was going up for sale. But €1.8m is beyond our abilities. The Project users don't have that sort of cash.'

The man has always been intense, but I'm not sure the passion has ever come with such despair.

'Maybe the council will buy it.'

'Well see now, I suggested that,' he says quickly. 'I said that to the others, that we should go after the council, organise a campaign like we did to object to the planning objections and really put the pressure on them. But nobody else was enthusiastic. The council say they don't have that kind of money and the others believe them, but isn't that always what they say? That they can't afford stuff? And then if there's loads of pressure, from people and politicians and all that, then they suddenly find it somewhere. Doesn't that happen? I think it does. So why couldn't it happen here?'

'I suppose,' I say vaguely, checking the clock. Twenty minutes he's been here, and there's nothing new to say.

'But we need someone to organise it. I'm trying, but Trevor has decided he's in charge and he's pissing people off. Maura refuses to do anything he says and Reggie is only interested if he can spray stuff. Did you hear he quit the athletics team? Me and Susan tried to persuade him, but he said it was stupid and wasn't worth the time. He's even wilder now. And Susan gets quite stressed out by all the fighting. I often end up having to leave the room and take a few breaths myself. All Trevor wants to do is make bloody banners and explain stuff to us. We don't need explaining, we need action. Isn't that right, Mrs Doherty? Isn't that what protest is?'

'Maybe the council really doesn't have the money. €1.8m is a lot.' I glance towards the clock, more blatantly this time.

But we can't just accept that. With all due respect, I don't think you get how serious this is. Someone could buy it tomorrow.'

'Sales don't tend to move that quickly...'

'Mrs Doherty, please. This is our last chance!'

I am tired. Malachy's desperation is making me tired.

'I know you've had a tough couple of months and I'm really sorry about that, but we need you. We need you to come back, Mrs Doherty. We need you to organise something before it's too late.'

'I'm sorry, Malachy, but I can't.'

'But why not?'

I regard him. His despair making me angry now. A hall is not worthy of despair. 'Because,' I begin, searching for a polite way to put it. But there isn't one, so I opt for the truth. 'Because I don't care.'

I refrain from adding that it's not personal. I don't care about anything any more. But if I say that, he might see a chink of hope. I want him to get the message. And I want him gone.

Some of the others have taken the hint. Reggie stopped calling after I couldn't make his race and Maura has reduced her visits to every other week. Even Chloe has relented. But Malachy just keeps on coming. He thinks I'm some great saviour and it makes me furious. How is it my job to save anybody? I heard Chloe a few weeks ago telling Maura how she benefited from the parcel being mislaid and I half-thought of correcting her, but stopped myself because it's not my responsibility. Her guilt is not my concern. They are telling themselves that they are doing this for me, calling here in an attempt to pull me out of my grief, but they all want something. If they want me to be my old self it's for their benefit, not mine.

Anyway, this isn't grief. I didn't just lose my daughter. Bea has been dead for ten years. All I've lost is hope. After the purse turned up, Senan made some half-hearted attempts to find the sender, but looking for a Muriel in Blackpool is more pointless than looking for a needle in the proverbial. Audrey's cousin's friend is an oceanographer at the university in Galway and Senan contacted him for an assessment. He even drove across the country to show him the thing.

His prognosis was that the purse was too well preserved to have been in the water for years. He said it most likely washed up on the rocks in Blackpool shortly after the event (this is what he called it; or at least how Senan relayed it) and was preserved there, like a form of fossilisation. Senan came straight to my house from Galway to tell me this as if there was an iota of urgency about it. I knew from the moment I saw the purse that she was dead, and it only took me the length of going through its contents to accept that.

Sometimes I wake in the morning with a flurry in my chest and then I remember that there is absolutely zero possibility that today will be the day I see my girl again, and the flurry dies away, and I roll over and go back to sleep, or stare at the wall. It was hope that was driving me, I can see that now, and without it I have to dig deeper to think of why I'm bothering to get out of bed at all.

But I'm not in a hole of grief. I've Googled the stages and none of them fit. So either this is a bonus stage – like the secret tracks Bea used to listen for at the end of her CDs – or it's just reality now. I'm not depressed; I'm accepting. And I'm not in some sleepy stupor; I'm wide awake and I can see the world around me for what it is. This is, as the younger generation say, 'the new normal'.

From the look on Malachy's face though, it's going to take some people longer than others to get used to it.

'You don't care,' he clarifies, suddenly morphing from the father of the dying boy into the boy himself. 'You don't care about the Project?'

I feel bad for him, and then angry. Anger is easier, and also more warranted. 'No, Malachy,' I say, evenly, not blinking. 'I don't care about the hall. It's just a hall. You'll survive. It seems terrible now, but in a couple of months it'll be gone from our minds. You'll have forgotten all about it.'

He's wavering now, wringing his hands, glancing down at the scuffed floor. The house seems to have expanded in the past couple of months. It feels emptier and bigger and is suddenly impossible to keep clean.

He gets the message, but I don't want to be having this conversation again tomorrow, or the next day. I need him to take the new normal and make it clear to the rest of them.

'And, Malachy?' I add, as he glances up hopefully. I wait until he's looking at me, properly, eyes steady. Then, slowly, I say: 'There are far worse losses than a hall.'

His eyes bulge. 'You're right, of course, I know you're right. I'm sorry, I should have thought, I-I'm sorry. I'll go now, Mrs Doherty.'

'Okay, Malachy,' I say, ignoring the tug in my chest. 'Have a nice afternoon.'

Then I walk him to the front door, watch as he blunders down the steps towards his mother's ancient Nissan Micra and close the door to the sound of him cutting out once, twice, three times before finally getting his act together and leaving me in peace.

·········

'Oh.'

'Sorry,' says Conn, appearing in the kitchen dressed in a thick ski jacket and multicoloured gloves.

The clock above his head says midnight. How did that happen? It was barely ten when I sat down for a final cup of tea.

I bring my hand to the untouched mug. Stone cold.

Conn fills a glass with water and downs it.

He doesn't ask what I'm still doing up or make any reference to how he's about to head out into the night. Conn is one of the few people who has left me alone these past months. He hasn't sought to turn back the clock to how things were.

'Good night, so,' he says, heading for the door.

'Where do you go at night?' I ask when he's got one foot in the hallway.

He slowly comes back into the room.

I've heard him slipping out a lot this past while and I know Chloe knows what he's up to, because I've heard her leaving with him a few times too.

'Have you a warm jacket?' he asks.

'You don't spend a lifetime attending marches without acquiring a few quilted coats.'

'Come on so,' he says, zipping up his own. 'I'll show you.'

·········

'It's...'

'Yeah,' says Conn, whose gloves also have a mitten portion and still he has to sit on his hands to keep them warm. 'This is the coldest it's been. I guess it's winter now.'

I pull my hood tauter around my ears, lessening the wind's pushing and pulling. 'Will you still come in December? January?'

'No plans to stop,' he says. 'Not sure I'd know how to.'

I sit back and stare. I've been here plenty of times, but never at this hour. It's otherworldly. I can't see much except the muddy grass and the path and the pitch-blackness beyond, but the sky has never looked so immense. An expanse of navy blue with whisps of white strewn across it, as though a spell is being conjured just beyond. I feel gratifyingly irrelevant under it.

There is constant howling and crashing and shaking and yet this is as much peace as I've felt in a long time.

Conn points out the spot from which his brother jumped. Neither of us observe that it is likely where Bea jumped from too.

It should make this place eerie, but it doesn't.

'All those nights, you were out here,' I say, still marvelling at the revelation. 'Never once did this cross my mind.'

'Did you think I was a drug smuggler too?'

'Pardon?'

'Never mind.'

Would it have happened if we'd lived somewhere different? Might she have stuck around if a popular, dramatic suicide option wasn't right around the corner? A silly thought. I did copious modules and training days around suicide prevention, I know it doesn't work like this, but I let the possibility linger.

'Do you think I'm crazy?' Conn asks, breaking the raucous silence. 'To keep coming out here, I mean. Chloe does. She wouldn't say that, but I know she worries.'

'Why would she worry?'

'Well, it's not normal, is it? And I guess, from the outside, it doesn't look very healthy. Maybe she thinks it's making me dwell on Fergal's death for longer.'

'Is it?'

He shakes his head. 'It's how I manage to get something out of life in spite of it.'

I nestle down in the coat, feeling my shoulders relax. 'How are things with you and Chloe?'

He inhales fully and breaks into a smile. 'Good,' he says in an obvious understatement.

I smile too. 'Good,' I repeat. It really is good. I am delighted about this union. Though I hear very little movement at night, so I wonder if they are taking things slow or if one of them has strong religious views. My money would be on Chloe. Her mother is the type to have gone fundamentalist.

'And how is Chloe?' I ask, a slight twang of regret for how consistently I have brushed her off this past while. 'I know she feels somehow responsible for...' *What exactly*? 'For me,' I settle on. 'For how I am now. But it's not necessary. I'm glad she has got good things out of staying at the house.'

'I know that. And she probably does too, on some level.'

'And what's in favour of you coming here?' I ask, as a large wave smashes against the cliff below. 'Whether it's good for you or not depends on why you do it.' Most of the crashing is lost to the general deafening din, but this one rises above. I burrow down further. It's like being in a big, warm bed, but without it having to be my bed in my house with my thoughts. It's too loud for much in the way of thoughts here. A flurry of wind and I grab my stick just before it is blown clean over. 'Though I can see the appeal,' I add. 'I've never felt so inconsequential in the universe's grand plan, and I have to say it's very comforting.'

'I feel like I'm helping people,' he says. 'The dream outcome is that nobody shows up here, but if they do, at least they won't be alone.'

'And what if you saw someone jump?'

'I've pictured Fergal do it a thousand times. It can't be worse than that.'

I don't comment on this, though I tend to disagree.

'It feels good to be dedicating my time to trying to make things a little better. I'm taking this awful thing that happened to me, to my family, and I guess I'm trying to, I don't know...'

'Turn it into a force for good?'

'Yes, exactly,' he approves. 'I'm taking this awful thing and I'm turning it into a force for good.'

421

You live by words for long enough and you stop hearing them. They're still my words. I know what they mean. But they no longer have the same effect. Perhaps there's only so long you can generate energy from pain. Or maybe you need hope too, and mine has been depleted.

I shouldn't have said what I did to Malachy. It was cruel and untrue. He will not have forgotten about the hall in a few months. His life will be immeasurably worse for not having the Project in it. He is a vulnerable, beautiful human and yes, he still has somewhere to live, but he is being made homeless in another way.

There was a time when the thought of Malachy and Trevor and the rest of them being lost would have invigorated me. But now it feels like pressure and I can't seem to shift my thinking.

A hand in front of me.

I look down to see an open packet of crisps.

'You bring snacks?'

'I go through phases,' says Conn, munching. 'Chloe packed these.'

I free my hand from my pocket and take a handful.

It was the sense that something was coming that made it worse. I had such a strong feeling that this anniversary was going to be significant. And, in the end, it was. But I feel foolish for ever thinking, even on the lowest level, that my daughter was on her way back. I didn't realise how far I had gotten my hopes up, until they suddenly came plummeting down.

I feel more alone now. I haven't felt any sense of Bea since we found that purse. I have it, the last known thing she touched, in the drawer of my bedside locker but I don't feel anything. The house seems bigger, as if the possibility of her had been taking up space. Conn and Chloe are there – they are *always* there – but it feels unwieldy and vast. It feels empty.

If anything, I have a greater sense of Bea here than I do at home. It's as close as she has to a final resting place. And it's so bloody dramatic – which is very her. It's the noise, too, and the sense of peace that comes with that. The house is echoingly silent. There's nothing of Bea in that. If any of her was lingering there, it's gone from Hope House now.

'Being a force for good is great,' I say, knocking Conn from his reverie too. 'But it has to work for you. Is it sustainable? Is it compatible with your life? Is it costing you too much? Those are the questions you have to ask.'

'Maybe it only works for now,' he acknowledges. 'Eventually I'll have to pay rent or a mortgage and I'll need steady income. This couldn't work with a job.'

'And a relationship? I'm not prying but one day you will probably want to share a bed with Chloe. I'm not sure how well that will go if you're sneaking out every night.'

'I guess it's not sustainable,' he says. 'What were the other ones?'

'Costing you too much?'

'Not right now, but...'

'Compatible with your life?'

We leave that one hanging in the gale.

I consider the questions in relation to my own situation. Is it sustainable for me to be invested in the future of the hall?

Does it cost me too much to care about my friends? Is passion compatible with my life?

The answers are the opposite of Conn's, but just as impossible to ignore.

# CHLOE

• • • • • • • • • • •

'Is that the door again?' calls Conn.

'Yep,' I shout into him as I pass the kitchen, where he's sitting with a newly arrived Trevor and Susan. Senan, Audrey and Otis are also there. They let themselves in just before and are now warming their backs against the Aga.

The foyer floor is wet from all the coming and going and some of the jackets on the coat stand are still dripping.

I pull open the front door to Malachy, Maura, Reggie and the continuing storm. Malachy is over the threshold before I have the thing fully open.

'What's the emergency? What is it? Where is she? Did she fall again? Is she okay?'

'For the love of god, Malachy, will you stop it!'

That's Maura, she's through the door after him, shaking out her umbrella and shirking off her raincoat. 'Didn't she tell you she was fine on the phone?'

Malachy pulls down the well-worn hood on his well-worn North Face jacket.

'That's exactly the kind of thing Mrs Doherty would say. If she was bleeding out on the side of a motorway, that woman would still be thinking of other people.'

'Give me strength,' mutters Maura. 'If she was bleeding out at the side of a motorway, she'd hardly ask you to come and meet her at her house a day later, now would she?'

But it's no good. The dramatic image is in Malachy's head and he's becoming quite emotional.

'Are you coming in, Reggie?' I ask the teenager still standing on the porch, not wearing any coat.

'What's it about?' he replies, kicking at some imaginary affront on the porch slab in front of him.

'I haven't a clue. I don't know any more than anyone else.'

He looks up at me and sighs. 'My step-mam said I had to come. That's the only reason I'm here,' he clarifies, as he slowly drags himself over the threshold and into the house.

'Come on through,' I say, when they're all in and those with coats have deposited them. 'Everyone else is in the kitchen.'

'Everyone else?' echoes Maura as they follow after me.

'Hello!' The legs of Susan's chair squeal as she clambers out of it. 'So good to see you all!' She embraces Maura, rubs Malachy's arm and holds her hand up for some sort of fist bump with Reggie. 'My boys love that I know that,' she says to me.

'How have you been?' asks Maura. 'Is your youngest feeling better? What was it he had? Foot and mouth disease?'

'Hand, foot and mouth,' the other woman corrects. 'And yes, that passed, but he's had two more illnesses since. I haven't been more than arm's length from a sick bowl or a snot sucker in two long months.'

'No offence, Susan, but you are not a great advertisement for procreation.'

'Good,' she says, retaking her seat. 'More people should know the truth. I like your hair, Reggie!'

'Do you?' asks the teenager, sceptically. The high top is gone. He now has what I think is called a crew cut.

'Yes, I really do, it's very smart.'

'Isn't it?' says Senan, who has abandoned the Aga to make tea – one standard cup and another with a yellow-looking bag he has produced from a pouch in his pocket. That must be for Audrey. 'Smart is the very word.'

'And I like the little right angles shaved in at the front,' adds Susan. 'Fun!'

Reggie throws himself back against the worktop, and wails. 'My step-mam likes it, too!'

'Haven't you seen each other?' I ask, casting around for anything else we could use as a chair. No room in Hope House is small, but if you were to pick one to cram ten people into, the kitchen, with its chunky table and awkwardly shaped window recesses, wouldn't be it.

'We haven't had a meeting in a few weeks,' says Maura.

'I thought you guys were still holding Radical Activism sessions at the hall?'

'We did start them back up, but it didn't last.'

'There were some organisational conflicts,' says Susan diplomatically.

'Trevor was insisting we call him sir,' clarifies Malachy.

'I was only looking to put a bit of order on things! It had turned into a mad house.'

Malachy scoffs. 'This is how dictatorships happen. Some ordinary pleb is accidentally put in charge and then he gets a taste for the power and before you know it dissent is outlawed.'

'I resent that!'

But Malachy's still looking at him with displeasure. 'How quickly you forgot your proletariat roots.'

'So, Chloe, what is this about?' asks Susan, getting up from her seat and guiding Trevor over to take it before things escalate.

'I don't know. Conn and I got the same request as you all did. Emergency Radical Activists meeting. Today. Here. 5 p.m.'

'Do you know more, Senan?' asks Maura.

Senan shakes his head. 'Got a text saying the same thing.'

'I don't even know if she wants me here,' says Audrey. Whatever type of tea she's drinking, I can smell it from here.

'Of course she does,' replies Senan, placing a hand on her arm as he slips back in between his wife and son. 'She told me to bring the family.'

'You don't think she's dying, do you?' asks Malachy, suddenly worried.

'Dying? What? Dad?'

'No she's not dying,' rebukes Senan, extending his other hand to Otis's arm. 'In fact she's livelier these days than she's been for months.'

This is true. Tessa has been showing more signs of her previous self in the past few weeks. Conn brought her up to the cliff with him one night. I don't know what they talked about, but it shifted something for her. Or maybe it's a coincidence. But since then, she's been talking more. She doesn't leave the room if there's someone else in it and, two nights ago, we even sat down to watch a film. All three of us. It was beyond lovely.

'Where is Tessa, anyway?' asks Trevor. 'Isn't she here?'

'She went into the village at about three. She said she'd be back for five...' I glance up at the clock. 5.07 p.m. It is pretty blustery out...

428

She's been going more places, asking us to make dinner because she has to meet someone or go into town. She hasn't returned to teaching Radical Activism though, and she has shown no interest in Malachy's efforts to stop the sale of the hall. To be fair, Malachy hasn't directly asked her to be involved. He said she made her position clear last time he visited, which, come to think of it, was a long time ago now.

It's not looking good, anyway. Even Malachy is starting to give up hope. There have been bids. Trevor has a source at the estate agency. One offer is from a developer looking to turn it into a strip of shops – takeaway, bookies, that sort of thing. That was the highest one last we heard. The other bidders are all rumours: a warehouse, a retirement home, even a strip club. Somehow, I doubt they'd get the planning permission for that one either. Charles Bentley doesn't care what the buyer does with the place, he's just waiting on the highest offer. It's December now, so their aim to sell before the year is out may come to fruition.

Trevor and Malachy are arguing about whether Michael Collins was a dictator or a democrat when Tessa appears in the doorway. I glance out the window to see her car.

'What are you all doing squashed in there? Come into the library.' And then she's gone, stick in hand, banging her way quickly down the hall.

Everyone gets up and follows her. Senan, Audrey and Otis first, with the Radical Activists going after.

'Did you not think she looked a little green around the gills,' I hear Malachy whisper to Maura, who responds with an elbow to his ribs.

Conn and I follow at the rear, hand in hand. The only thing he did tell me about their summit on the summit was that Tessa was very happy that we were together. I still like to sleep in my own bed, if only because I don't want her thinking I'm taking the space for granted, but I have been sneaking in and out of Conn's room on occasion. Like I say, Tessa is out more now. Not that we've managed to keep it all to ourselves. When we were watching *Calendar Girls* the other night, she mentioned the possibility of Conn getting out his carpentry tools and taking a look at some squeaky floorboards. 'There's a particularly noisy one outside your bedroom,' she said pointedly, and gleefully, as she reached for another biscuit.

There are only three chairs in the library; two armchairs and a wooden one at the desk.

'Come in, sit,' says Tessa, placing a folder on the desk. 'Sit, sit.'

Eventually Maura takes the wooden chair. But everyone else is too on edge. We stand around in little clusters, waiting to hear what's coming.

'Is everything okay, Mrs Doherty? Is everything with *you* okay?'

'Yes, Malachy, everything's okay. Everything is peachy,' says Tessa, who is standing with her stick in front of one of the French windows. It's still lashing down outside and the rain blurs everything beyond the glass. It's hard to discern the sea from the murky sky.

'Thank you all for coming,' she says, eyes scanning over us. 'It really does mean a lot.'

'Oh god,' whispers Malachy in front of me. 'It's imminent. She's gathered us all to hear her last will and testament.'

430

'Shhh!' hisses Maura.

Tessa waits for everyone to quiet.

'I called you all here today...'

A sob escapes from Malachy. Then a clatter from Maura.

'...because I want to let you know that I am selling the house.'

'Which house?' asks Trevor when nobody responds immediately.

'This house,' says Tessa, raising her arms. 'Hope House.'

I look at Conn who looks at me. She's selling the house?

'Mam, since when? I thought you were, and I believe these were your exact words, "leaving this place in a box".'

'Yes well, to quote you, Senan, needs change. And my needs have changed. I've been in and out of estate agencies these past few weeks and finally it's all in motion. I have not gone with that vulture you brought to the house months ago. I am selling it through George Slope's business.'

'No Hope Slope?' queries Senan. 'The guy above the laundrette off Main Street? He gave most of his earnings to the dog shelter last year and didn't have enough left for his taxes. Why would you go with him?'

'That's exactly why I am going with him. He's a terrible businessman, but an excellent man and I want him to have my commission. It is, by all accounts, going to be an easy sell. And I'm not looking for someone to squeeze every penny from the buyer. I just want what's fair.'

'Why are you selling, Gran?'

'Oh, lots of reasons my darling. Firstly, I don't think I can afford not to. The pipes are a few showers away from giving up entirely and I haven't the funds to fix them. The place is costing me too much.'

'We could pay rent,' I interject. 'I'm making okay money and Conn can easily get a bit more work.'

'That's right, Tessa. We really should be paying you.'

'No, no, thank you but no. It's not just the cost. It's the upkeep, the cleaning, practicalities, this stick isn't going anywhere and it is awkward to get around. And then there are bigger things, harder to explain. There were cords binding me to this place, and they have been untied now. I no longer feel I have to be here. Anyway, Slope has found me a nice little cottage nearer the village and still with a sea view. Don't worry, Senan, I won't be in on top of you. It's the other side. Just a couple of roads over from you actually, Maura.'

Trevor's phone beeps loudly and he pulls it from the pocket of his brown blazer.

'Why are you telling me your plans to buy a smaller gaff,' grouses Reggie, who is pulling at a thread on the cuff of his hoodie, undoing the stitch work. 'I'm missing a Twitch livestream for this.'

Meanwhile Trevor has passed his phone to Susan who is now handing it back to Maura and Malachy.

'What is it?' I ask, leaning forward as each of their faces falls to dread like a slow game of human dominos.

'They've sold the hall,' says Maura.

'It's sold?' echoes Reggie, suddenly forgetting about the destruction of his clothing.

'It's gone, sale agreed,' confirms Maura, passing Trevor back his phone.

'The offer was accepted this afternoon, according to my source,' says the older man, staring anew at the screen.

'Who bought it?' asks Susan.

'Was it the strip club?' adds Reggie, hopefully.

'I don't know,' says Trevor. 'That's all the information I have.'

I can no longer see Malachy's face, but if I ever doubted that a back could look devastated, I was wrong. His shoulders are drooping so far that they're really just an extension of his arms and his head is practically on his chest.

'I'm so sorry,' says Senan, as Audrey and Otis murmur their condolences too.

'Oh yes, that's the other thing,' interjects Tessa, in a jovial tone that is entirely out of place in this room. 'I've bought the hall.'

Everyone's head turns. Malachy's nearly flies backwards with how quickly it comes off his chest.

'*What?!*'

Tessa nods. 'That's the bit I more thought you might be interested in, Reggie. And most of you really. I've made an offer on the hall and it has formally been accepted.'

I look at Conn again and then around at the others. Everyone is in shock. Nobody knows what to say.

'I got it for the asking price. Even with the cottage, I'll have a nice little sum left over. And I've been on to the council too – it's been a very busy few weeks, meeting after meeting after meeting – and I have agreed to gift it to them for the exclusive purposes of non-profit community use. They've agreed to continue paying the energy bills and for any upgrades that may arise in the future. Well of course they have, I'm giving them the place for nothing.'

'What does this mean?' asks Susan, the hope just about audible.

'It means the North Dublin Community Project stays. It means everything there continues as it is. It means the hall is saved. Oh, Malachy!' she exclaims, rushing over to the man and enveloping him into a hug even though he is about three times the breadth of her.

He blubbers on her shoulder.

'I'm sorry for what I said last time,' she murmurs to him. 'That was all about me and not about you. It was unkind and I'm sorry.'

'You never have to apologise to me, Mrs Doherty,' says Malachy, pulling his face from her, still sniffling. 'You saved my life.'

'No I didn't,' she smiles. 'Maybe the hall did, but—'

'No,' he insists, eyes red but face deadly serious. '*You* did.'

'This is savage,' exclaims Reggie, smiling for the first time since he arrived at the house. 'Not for me, but like, for this big cry baby and Sir Trevor over there.'

Trevor dutifully looks fit to burst.

'Those lads need somewhere to go.'

'It's still in the final stages, but that is the plan. I'm leaving the details to the lawyers now,' says Tessa, and I turn to Conn.

'Don't look at me,' he says. 'I knew nothing about any of this.'

'I went elsewhere for legal advice this time,' confirms Tessa. 'Decided if some looper is going to hand over three million for this place, I can probably afford to pay a solicitor, instead of leaning on poor Conn again.'

'I really wouldn't mind. I've never done conveyancing before, but—'

Tessa shakes her head. 'Slope thinks I can have a buyer agreed in the next week or two, so that the hall purchase doesn't fall through. But there will be a clause in the contract stating that we can stay on here for another six months after the deal is done. He's confident that won't be an issue. Whoever buys it will need to get contractors and builders lined up anyway. And that buys us all time. You and me, Conn, Chloe? Is that okay?'

I beam at her. I didn't realise how much I'd missed her energy until it was back. If it really is true that you can choose your family, and I sincerely hope it is because I haven't spoken to my mother since the open day, then I will always choose people like Tessa. I'll choose people whose souls just sing.

Conn is right. Alive is the best thing you can be.

'That's brilliant, Tessa. Thank you,' I say, as Conn takes my hand and squeezes it.

'We'll be fine,' he adds.

I squeeze his back. We will be more than fine.

'Right so, that's it. You're all free to go,' says Tessa, picking up her folder, which I can now see has George Slope Properties and Charitable Causes stamped across the front. She stops in front of the Radical Activists. 'I'll see you all next Friday.'

'Next Friday?'

'For the next class. There's a housing crisis march planned for the week before Christmas and if we get ourselves together, I reckon we can have some decent banners ready to go.'

Trevor rubs his hands together at this. Malachy throws his arms around Tessa again.

'Except for you, Reggie,' she says, freeing herself from the tree trunk arms.

'I'm not allowed to come? Is this 'cause I did a bit of mitching? We were only doing the Prussian War that afternoon and that place isn't even real. I checked the map and all.' He shoots Senan a wounded look. 'So much for the separation of home and school...'

'No, Reggie, I will see you on Friday, but I will see you before that too. I will see you on Thursday.'

'What? Why?'

'For the next race meet.'

'I quit the team, Mrs Doherty. It was just fast nerds running in circles.'

'Well you can rejoin. I believe there's space. Senan?'

'Plenty,' her son replies.

'There you are. I'll see you then. I'll be front and centre on the bleachers. Who knows, maybe I'll make a cool graffiti banner of my own.'

Reggie's lip curls up so far at the horror of this that it's practically in his nose.

'Now, have a nice afternoon all,' says Tessa, sweeping out of the room like she used to sweep everywhere, regardless of whether or not she had a stick. 'I've got furniture to measure and chandeliers to have valued.'

# TESSA

• • • • • • • • • •

'Any biscuits left?' I ask, leaning over Conn as Chloe produces the Tupperware box from the far side of her.

'One white chocolate chip and half a fruit one.'

'I'll take the half, thank you,' I say, and she hands it to Conn, who passes it along to me. You might have hygiene concerns if it wasn't for Conn's massive gloves. 'Do you really still need those?' I ask, tapping his multicoloured paws as I extract the biscuit from them.

The first signs of spring are all around us. Granted they're not as visible as in daylight, but they're there all the same. The gorse is in full bloom and the wind has subsided significantly since I was last up here. The path is dry and I'm almost sure I spotted a few daisies growing through the gravel. Although that might have been a trick of the moonlight.

'I could probably go without them,' accepts Conn. 'Do you need that scarf?'

I tug proudly at my favourite of my Chloe Darvin creations. 'This? This is a fashion statement.'

'Wasted on the pitch-black darkness, so.'

'I like that you like my scarf, Tessa,' says the young woman leaning over her boyfriend again. 'I think it brings out your eyes. That's why I chose that shade of maroon.'

'And there I was thinking you just had wool left over from my hat,' says Conn, tongue literally poking at his cheek.

'No,' replies Chloe primly. 'I chose that colour for your hat because it goes so well with your beard. There's thought in everything I make.'

I nibble the biscuit slowly in an effort to make it last. I will miss many things about Chloe, not least her occasional baking spurts.

'I like the shorter length on the beard,' I say, licking a crumb from my lip. 'Have I said that to you? It was getting a little out of hand there in December. You could have taken a stab at playing Santa.'

'Chloe likes it like this.'

'I do,' she grins.

'And, like you say, I don't really need the extra warmth. Spring is coming.'

'Yes it is,' I say with a satisfied sigh.

The sea may be calmer than the last time I sat on this bench, but the view is no less dramatic. All the swirls of the sky and the shades of navy I never knew existed – it's like being trapped in a marble.

I take a surreptitious glance at my phone. 1.55 a.m. Another two hours to go.

It's lovely with other people for company, but I'm not sure how well I'd get on up here on my own, night after night. I don't find it scary, the very opposite. It's so soothing – and, after a while, no doubt boring – that I'd probably fall asleep.

'Will you miss this?' I ask Conn, as he and Chloe share the last remaining biscuit.

'Yes,' he says. 'Definitely.' He chews, then swallows. 'But it's right to draw a line under it. We're not going to be so near the cliffs any more.'

Conn and Chloe have just this week secured a flat on the far side of the city. Chloe is applying to return to college in September and the flat is near the university. Conn has done plenty of job interviews and gotten almost as many offers, but he can't bring himself to commit, just yet.

My own cottage is ready to go. Senan and Otis have painted most of it and the bulk of the furniture I'm bringing is in place. The electricity and gas are being switched back on tomorrow. Hope House has been thoroughly decluttered and everything boxed up. Senan and I sorted Bea's room with a little help from Otis. It was nice to get to tell him snippets about his aunt as we went through her things. He remembers Bea, but not well, and everything we found seemed to lead to a funny or interesting story. And it was lovely to hear Senan speak about his sister with affection. He's not angry with her any more. I didn't realise what a gift that was until it happened. We speak about her more now and it's easy, it's nice.

'Thank you both for coming with me,' says Conn as Chloe takes his gloved hand in her lap.

'Not at all. I love it up here,' I say. 'But if you change your mind and you do want to be alone, or just with Chloe, you just say the word and I'll head on back.'

He shakes his head. 'This is good,' he says, leaning back and squinting slightly.

'I'm going to miss you both,' I declare, pulling my scarf a little looser. Despite my best efforts I seem incapable of delivering meaningful statements in anything but a highly matter-of-fact tone. Then, with a bit of determination: 'I have forgotten what it's like to live alone.'

'I doubt you'll be alone much. You're a magnet for people,' says Chloe. 'And you'll be busy at the hall.'

'Don't remind me,' I mutter, taking another slug from my tea flask. 'I thought handing over the place would reduce my involvement, not increase it. You know Malachy phoned again this morning?'

'He wants you to teach *another* class?'

'They've a Thursday morning slot to fill and they're desperate, apparently. Which is just what a woman likes to hear.'

'Oh, oh!' shouts Chloe, reaching an arm towards me and knocking over her and Conn's shared flask in the process.

'Hey!'

'Sorry,' she says, wiping at the tea in a manner that only manages to spread the stain on Conn's trousers. 'I could teach a class. Well maybe not *teach*, but I could lead a group. A knitting group! I know you have the crafters, but their focus is very much on paper and felt and those sorts of materials. A bit of sewing, tapestry at a push, but no knitting. They don't do any knitting. But I could!'

'Chloe, dear,' I say kindly, because I know this is still a tender point, 'you're going to be miles away.'

'Yes, but this way I'll have a reason to come back here and see everyone and oh please, Tessa, please please. College doesn't start until September and I can pick and choose my delivery schedules until then. Thursday morning would be perfect. I'd love to do it. Please.'

'Well okay, I don't see why not. I'll say it to Malachy.'

'Maybe mention it to Susan too?'

'Yes,' I agree. 'Good idea.'

Signing the hall over to the council was straightforward. However, once it was under their control, things got a little more complicated. Everything had to be official, above board and formalised. The downsides to this include a restriction on the number of people who can be in the building at one time, the need to spread the classes more evenly across the week, and the separation of Darts and Crafts. It was a health and safety risk apparently; too many stray arrows. The men were entirely at sea, although the women seemed happy enough.

There were also positives. Namely, that the council had to formally hire a full-time manager for the hall. They held interviews and plenty of people applied, but nobody could hold a candle to Malachy for experience. He's been running the place for years. They also needed a part-time administrator to coordinate the weekly class schedule. Step forward Susan. The money isn't much, but the hours are perfect and it gets her out of the house and away from her kids for a little bit every day. Plus Malachy is very good at almost every aspect of the hall, but timetabling is the greatest threat to his heart since the public bin was removed from outside his house.

'Do you feel proud, Tessa?'

I glance up at Conn. He may mock me but, as well as the gloves, he is currently wearing a Chloe Darvin scarf *and* hat.

'You should be,' he adds. 'It's a huge thing what you've done, giving all those people a place they can go without fear of the rug being pulled from under them.'

'It is, it's a real gift,' agrees Chloe, 'to allow someone else to feel secure.'

I hadn't really thought of it that way. 'I suppose,' I say.

'No, it is, Tessa,' insists Chloe, with unusual persistence. 'It's a real gift. You've given them stability, and I'm sure they're all very grateful.'

I frown at her saucer-wide eyes, trying to figure out what she means.

And then I do.

That is what I have done for Chloe.

I have given her stability, maybe for the first time in her life, and look how she has thrived.

So much has changed these past few months, for all of us, and nothing will ever be the same. Though sitting here facing the crashing waters and the infinite possibilities of our lives to come and all the lives we'll never know, I'm not sure I'd want to go back.

'I have benefited from having you here too,' I say, abruptly. 'So you know. I have benefited too. From both of you. Just.' I nod curtly and pull my jacket up to my chin, despite the lack of breeze.

Chloe gives me a teary-eyed smile as she grabs Conn's arm, and he inclines his head so the crown of it tips the crown of mine.

Then we all sit and face the sea as the waves below whisper their incantations and the clouds above brandish charms.

'I have benefited,' I say, half to myself.

The world is large and it continues to turn. The sun sets and the moon rises, no matter what befalls us. We do not matter to the existence of many and how liberating that is. But how much joy there is, too, in mattering to a few. The key, I think, is to find the right few.

And so there we sit, three strangers who have changed each other's lives.

Three friends who have bound ourselves to each other.

Three souls, lost then found, and now still.

Her and him and me, staring out from our place on the edge of everything.

# EPILOGUE

. . . . . . . . . . . . . . . .

## THREE YEARS LATER

Muriel opens her email in anticipation of the latest instalment from Sadie. Her granddaughter's correspondences have gotten substantially longer since she discovered boys. And Muriel knows there were two discos this weekend.

Muriel's daughter-in-law pounds her for information when they come to stay on the last weekend of every month. But Muriel keeps Sadie's counsel. She honours the teenager's trust and, truth be told, she relishes that the girl tells her more than anyone else. She always suspected she was cool for an old dear. She's glad she made all that effort to strengthen the relationship with her son a few years ago. She can't remember what the impetus was now but she's grateful for it all the same.

No Sadie missive. But there is one message. A Google Alert. What has Barry Gibb been up to now, she wonders, as she clicks the message open.

But the update is not about her favourite Bee Gee and lifelong crush. It's one of the two other Google Alerts she set up, three years ago: Bea Pearson and Tessa Doherty. The night she realised she had sent a wallet to a woman who had drowned ten years earlier, and that it had most likely been received by her poor mother, she trawled the internet for information on Bea and Tessa. There were a couple of articles about Tessa, including a very recent one about a campaign to save a local hall. Muriel toed and fro-ed on getting in contact to apologise for her thoughtless blunder. It wasn't until she clocked the date on the party invitation that the pieces started to slot into place. She thought the purse had been lost on the beach that week. She never considered it had crossed the Irish Sea.

In the end, she didn't get in contact. What good would it do? There was no more information or words of comfort that she could impart and she had imposed herself on this woman's life enough. So she left well enough alone. Well, almost. She set up a Google Alert. In case the body was ever found, she would like to know.

But then life got busy and Muriel forgot all about it. The searches never got a hit – until now.

While the alert does link to a news article, it doesn't look like a sombre affair about a maritime tragedy. It's from the property section of something called the *Dublin Press*, and the headline reads 'Iconic Makeover for an Iconic Home – With Priceless Sea Views!'

She clicks in.

## Iconic Makeover for an Iconic Home – With Priceless Sea Views!

by Margaret McDonnell

Hope House had been home to just two families when the last of these owners,

Tessa Doherty, wife of the deceased Bernard Pearson, decided to sell up. Her husband's family had lived there for four generations but the building – measuring 312msq and then without central heating – had become incompatible with modern life.

Three years on from the sale, Ms Doherty puts it simply. 'It was time to leave,' says the woman who is well known locally for her role in preserving the North Dublin Community Project, a social initiative.

Hope House, which has retained its name, was taken over by Philip and Farrah Costigan and their four children ranging in age from seven to twenty-three. The Costigans spent nearly three years lovingly restoring the property, upgrading the basic utilities, retrofitting where allowed, and adding outhouse accommodation and function buildings at the rear.

While the family will live in the house year-round, they will also operate it as a business, opening it to the public for architectural tours several days a month and hosting events at weekends.

Hope House will officially open for business in May and it is booked out with weddings, family get-togethers and big birthday parties for the entire Spring/Summer season. Next year is filling up quickly, according to Mr Costigan.

'It's a truly unique building and though it has been hard work at times – the pipes have probably been the biggest stress of my life – it has been a vocation. The previous owners clearly loved this place too, but it needed an injection of cash. Thankfully the signs are good that we can, in time, make that money back.'

The Costigans used the architectural services of Howth-based Rodgers Davitt Ltd and sourced all tradespeople and materials locally where possible. Interior design was largely led by Mrs Costigan, with help from Suzie Jones Homes in Donabate.

'We couldn't be happier with it,' says Mrs Costigan, who declined to say how much was spent on the fit-out, though the property register lists the house as having sold for €3.1m three years ago. 'It is our dream home and I hope it will be a dream venue for our guests.'

Ms Doherty had not returned to Hope House since selling the place but, as chance would have it, she found herself there just last month for an entirely different reason.

'I accompanied a friend who was finalising the details on an event she is hosting there in the summer,' Ms Doherty confirmed.

That event is a wedding. It is the first that will be held at Hope House and will involve the marriage of Chloe Darvin, a librarian who grew up twenty minutes from Hope House, and Conn Horgan, a south Dublin 'blow in' who is said to have a special attachment to the area.

Will Ms Doherty be attending the nuptials at her former home?

'Oh yes,' says the woman, with a twinkle in her eye. 'I will be giving the bride away.'

# ACKNOWLEDGEMENTS

Thank you to my editor Sarah Hodgson at Corvus, who was encouraging of this novel from the get-go and who gave me excellent feedback and notes. Thank you to everyone at Corvus and to all members of the wider Atlantic Books team who work on my novels. Further thanks to Helen McKean, Simon Hess and Declan Heeney at Gill Hess in Ireland. With every book, I become more and more aware that it takes a village. I am grateful to my copy editor, Nicky Lovick; to budding copy editor, Julia McLarnon; and to my pal and personal proofreader Carol Mulligan, for their help. Thanks also to the very talented and lovely Sarah Lutyens and all the team at Lutyens & Rubinstein.

Hope House is inspired by one of my favourite buildings: my grandmother's house. My granny lives in the depths of the Irish countryside as opposed to on the Dublin coast, but otherwise the buildings are almost identical – right down to the lack of central heating which, my granny once told me, 'makes you soft'. She is the toughest person I know, so she may be right. I have yet to write a book without her in there somewhere and here she is again, albeit as bricks and mortar rather than flesh and bone. It is because of her home that I understand what it is to love a building more than you rationally should.

I must offer my sincere apologies to the people of Howth for messing with the geography of your beautiful village. I have taken its essence rather than its reality for this book, which is probably just as well; no fictional version could ever rival the real thing. Solidarity, too, to the people of Drumcondra in Dublin who are fighting to save their local community hall.

My final thanks go to my family. Thank you, Mam and Dad, for the babysitting and for biting your tongues when I gave up the day job. Thank you, Colm, for the constant encouragement.

To Ruan and Nora: Neither of you can read yet but one day you will learn, and this will be as true then as it is now: You are the lights of my life.